THE KINGDOM BEYC

Stephen Hunt has worked as a writer, editor and publisher for a number of magazines and national newspaper groups in the UK, and is currently employed by the research arm of an investment bank. He is also the founder of www.SFcrowsnest.com, one of the oldest and most popular fan-run science fiction and fantasy websites, with over a quarter of a million readers each month. Born in Canada, the author presently lives in London, as well as spending a lot of time during the year with his family in Spain.

Also by Stephen Hunt

The Court of the Air

THE
KINGDOM
BEYOND THE
WAVES

Stephen Hunt

HARPER
Voyager

Harper*Voyager*
An imprint of HarperCollins*Publishers*
77–85 Fulham Palace Road,
Hammersmith, London W6 8JB

www.voyager-books.co.uk

This paperback edition 2008
1

First published in Great Britain by
HarperCollins*Publishers* 2008

A catalogue record for this book is
available from the British Library

ISBN-13: 978-0-00-723221-5

Typeset in Sabon by Palimpsest Book Production Limited,
Grangemouth, Stirlingshire

Printed and bound in Great Britain by
Clays Limited, St Ives plc

Mixed Sources
Product group from well-managed
forests and other controlled sources
www.fsc.org   Cert no. SW-COC-1806
© 1996 Forest Stewardship Council

FSC is a non-profit international organisation established to promote
the responsible management of the world's forests. Products carrying
the FSC label are independently certified to assure consumers that
they come from forests that are managed to meet the social, economic
and ecological needs of present and future generations.

Find out more about HarperCollins and the environment at
www.harpercollins.co.uk/green

CHAPTER ONE

Amelia Harsh wiped the sweat from her hands across her leather trousers, then thrust her fingers up into Mombiko's vice-tight grip. The ex-slave hauled her onto the ledge, the veins on his arms bulging as he lifted her up the final few feet to the summit. Bickering voices chased Amelia up the face of the blisteringly hot mountainside like the chattering of sand beetles.

'You climb better than them, even with your poisoned arm,' said Mombiko.

Amelia rubbed at the raw wound on her right shoulder – like her left, as large as that of a gorilla. Not due to the stinging scorpion that had crept into her tent two nights earlier, but the result of a worldsinger's sorcery. Large sculpted biceps muscles that could rip a door apart or cave in the skull of a camel; a physique that was rendered near useless by that bloody insect's barbed tail. The scorpion had to have stung her gun arm, too.

Mombiko passed the professor a blessedly cool canteen and she took a greedy swig of water before checking the progress of the Macanalie brothers. They were a minute away from

1

the ledge, cursing each other and squabbling over the best footholds and grips to reach the summit.

'The brothers got us through the Northern Desert,' said Amelia. 'There are not many uplanders who could have done that.'

'You know where those three scum developed their knowledge of the sands, mma,' said Mombiko, accusingly. 'The brothers guide traders over the border in both directions – avoiding the kingdom's revenue men to the north and the caliph's tax collectors to the south.'

Amelia pointed to the sea of wind-scoured dunes stretched out beneath them. 'It's not much of a border. Besides, I know about their side-trade as well as you do, capturing escaped slaves who make it to the uplands and dragging them back for the caliph's bounty on the slaves' heads.'

'They are not good men, professor.'

Amelia checked the sling of the rifle strapped to her back. 'They were as good as we were going to get without the university's help.'

Mombiko nodded and clipped the precious water canteen back onto his belt.

Damn the pedants on the High Table. A pocket airship could have crossed the desert in a day rather than the weeks of sun-scorched marching Amelia's expedition had endured. But the college at Saint Vines did not want the technology of an airship falling into the caliph's hands. And it was a fine excuse for the college authorities to drop another barrier in front of her studies, her obsession.

'You wait here,' Amelia said to Mombiko. 'Help them up.'

'If they try anything?'

She pointed to his pistol and the bandolier of crystal charges strapped over his white robes. 'Why do you think I made sure we were climbing at the front? I wouldn't trust a Macanalie to hold my guide rope.'

A sound like a crow screeched in the distance. Shielding her eyes, Amelia scanned the sky. Blue, cloudless. Clear of any telltale dots around the sun that would indicate the presence of the lizard-things that the caliph's scouts flew. No match for an airship's guns, but the unnatural creatures could fall upon the five of them easily enough; rip their spines out in a dive and carry their shredded remains back to one of Cassarabia's military garrisons. Again, the screech. She saw a dark shape shuffling higher up the mountainside – a sand hawk – and relaxed. It was eying up one of the small salamanders on the dunes beneath them, no doubt.

Professor Harsh returned her attention to the wall on the ledge, following the trail of stone sigils worn away to near-indecipherability by Cassarabia's sandstorms over the millennia. Mombiko's contact had been right after all; a miracle the deserter from the caliph's army had made it this far, had spotted the carving in the rocks below. Had possessed enough education to know what the carving might signify and the sand-craft to reach the uplands of Jackals and the safety of the clans. The path between the crags led to a wall of boulders with a circular stone slab embedded in it. A door! Shielded from the worst of the storm abrasions, the sigils on the portal had fared better than the worn iconography that had led her up here.

Amelia marvelled at the ancient calligraphy. So primitive, yet so beautiful. There were illustrations too, a swarm of brutal-looking vehicles ridden by fierce barbarians – horse-less carriages, but not powered by the high-tension clockwork milled by her own nation of Jackals. Engines from a darker time.

Her revelry at the discovery was interrupted by the snarling voices behind her.

'Is this it, then, lassie?'

Amelia looked at the three upland smugglers, practically drooling at the thought of the treasures they were imagining behind the door. 'Roll the door back, but *carefully*,' she ordered. Dipping into her backpack she pulled out five cotton masks with string ties. 'Put these on before you go in.'

'Are you daft, lassie?' spat the oldest of the brothers. 'There's no sandstorm coming.'

'These are not sand masks,' Amelia said, tapping a thumb on the door. 'You are standing outside the tomb of a powerful chieftain. He would have owned worldsingers as part of his slave-clan and would not have been above having them leave a sprinkling of curse-dust in his tomb to kill grave robbers, bandits and any of his rivals tempted to desecrate his grave.' She slipped the mask over her mouth, the chemicals in the fabric filling her nose with a honey-sweet smell. 'But you are free to go in without protection.'

The brothers each gave her a foul look, but pulled on the masks all the same, then got to work rolling the door back with all the vigour that only greed could generate. Mombiko drew out a gas spike and ignited the lantern. 'I shall go first, mma.'

Amelia signalled her agreement. Mombiko had been raised in the great forests of the far south and possessed an uncanny sixth sense. Curse-dust aside, there should only be a single trap in this ancient tomb – the mausoleum's creators were an unsubtle brutish people – but it was best to be sure.

The door rolled back. Mombiko held the gas spike in front of him, shadows dancing in the dark tunnel that lay revealed behind the stone slab. It was cool inside after the heat of the desert. Crude stone-hewn steps led downward, iron brackets in the wall where lanterns would once have hung.

'Did you hear something?' asked one of the brothers.

'Put your gun down, you fool,' said Amelia. 'It's just an echo. You fire your pistol in here and the ricochet of your ball will be what kills you.'

'If there's a treasure, there will be something to guard it,' insisted one of the brothers. 'A wee beastie.'

'Nothing that could survive over two thousand years trapped down here without any food,' said Amelia.

'Holster your pistol,' ordered the oldest brother, 'the lass is right. Besides, it's her laddie-boy that's going in first, right?'

Followed by the cold echoes of their own steps, the five interlopers walked down the carved passage; at the bottom of the sloping cut was a foreboding stone door, a copper panel in a wall-niche by its side, the space filled with levers, nobs and handles.

'I've got a casket of blow-barrel sap back with the camels,' said one of the Macanalie brothers.

Amelia wiped the cobwebs off the copper panel. 'You got enough to blow up *all* the treasure, clansman? Leave the archaeology to me.'

Amelia touched the levers, tracing the ancient script with her fingers. Like most of the Black-oil Horde's legacy to history, their language was stolen, looted from one of the many non-nomadic nations the barbarians had over-run during their age. The script was a riddle – filled with jokes and black humour.

'The wrong choice . . .' whispered Mombiko behind her.

'I know, I know,' said Amelia, eyeing the impressions along the wall where the tomb builders had buried their compressed oil explosives. Surely the passage of time would have spoiled their potency? 'Now, let's see. In their legends the sun rises when the petrol-gods sleep, but sleeping is a play on words, so—' she grabbed two levers, sliding one up while shoving another into a side channel and down, then clicked one of the nobs clockwise to face the symbol of the sun.

Ancient counter-weights shifted and the door drew upwards into the ceiling of the passage with a *rack-rack-rack*. Mombiko let out his breath.

The oldest of the smuggler brothers nodded in approval. 'Clever lass. I knew there was a reason we brought you along.'

The professor flicked back her mane of dark hair. 'I'm not paying you extra for your poor sense of humour, Macanalie. Let's see what's down here.'

They walked into the burial chamber. With its rough, jagged walls, it might almost have been mistaken for a natural cavern were it not for the statues holding up the vaulted roof – squat totem-poles of granite carved with smirking goblin faces. Mombiko's gas spike was barely powerful enough to reveal the eight-wheeled carriage that rose on a dais in the centre of the chamber, spiral lines of gold rivets studding its armoured sides and exhaust stacks. The nearest of the smugglers gasped, scurrying over to the boat-sized machine to run his hand over the lance points protruding from the vehicle's prow. They were silver-plated, but Amelia knew that reinforced steel would lie hidden beneath each deadly lance head.

'It's true, after all this time,' said Amelia, as if she did not really believe it herself. 'A war chief of the Black-oil Horde, perhaps even the great Diesela-Khan himself.'

'This is a horseless carriage?' asked one of the Macanalies. 'I can't see the clockwork. Where's the clockwork?'

He was elbowed aside by his excited elder. 'What matters that? It's a wee fortune, man! Look at the gems on the thing – her hood here, is this beaten out of solid gold?'

'Oil,' said Amelia, distracted. 'They burnt oil in their engines, they hadn't mastered high-tension clockwork.'

'Slipsharp oil?' queried the smuggler. Surely there were not enough of the great beasts of the ocean swimming the world's seas to bleed blubber to fuel such a beautiful, deadly vehicle?

'Do you not know anything?' said Mombiko, waving the gas spike over the massive engine at the carriage's rear. 'Black water from the ground. This beautiful thing would have drunk it like a horse.'

Amelia nodded. One of the many devices that stopped functioning many thousands of years ago if the ancient sagas were to be believed – overwhelmed by the power of the worldsong and the changing universe. Mombiko pointed to a silver sarcophagus in the middle of the wagon and Amelia climbed in, pulling out her knife to lever open the ancient wax-sealed coffin.

'They must have taken the wagon to pieces outside,' laughed the youngest brother. 'Put it back together down here.'

'Obviously,' said Amelia, grunting as she pressed her knife under the coffin lid. Her shoulder burned with the effort. Damn that scorpion.

'Oh, you're a sly one, Professor Harsh,' spat the eldest brother. 'All your talk of science and the nobility of ancient history and all of the past's lessons. All those fine-sounding lectures back in the desert. And here you are, scrabbling for jewels in some quality's coffin. You almost had me believing you, lassie.'

She shot a glare at the smuggler, ignoring his taunts. She deserved it. Perhaps she was no better than these three gutter-scrapings of the kingdom's border towns.

'Her wheels weren't built to run on sand,' mused one of the Macanalies. He ran his hand covetously along the shining spikes of gold on the vehicle's rim.

Amelia was nearly done, the last piece of wax seal giving way. It was a desecration really. No wonder the eight great universities had denied her tenure, kept her begging for expedition funds like a hound kept underneath the High Table. But there might be treasure inside. *Her* treasure.

'There wasn't a desert outside when our chieftain here was buried,' said Amelia. 'It was all steppes and grassland. This mountain once stretched all the way back to the uplands, before the glaciers came and crushed the range to dust.'

At last the lid shifted and Amelia pushed the sarcophagus open. There were weapons in there alongside the bones, bags of coins too – looted from towns the ancient nomads had sacked, no doubt, given that the Black-oil Horde either wore or drove their wealth around. But might there be something else hidden amongst their looted booty? Amelia's hands pushed aside the diamond-encrusted ignition keys and the black-powder guns of the barbarian chief – torn between scrabbling among the find like a looter and honouring her archaeologist's pledge. There! Among the burial spoils, the hexagonal crystal-books she had crossed a desert for.

Professor Amelia Harsh lifted them out and then she sobbed. Each crystal-book was veined with information sickness, black lines threading out as if a cancer had infected the hard purple glass. Had the barbarians of the Black-oil Horde unknowingly spoiled the ancient information blocks? Or had their final guardian cursed the books even as the nomads smashed their way into the library of the ancient civilization that had created them? They were useless. Good for nothing except bookends for a rich merchant with a taste for antiques.

The oldest of the brothers mistook her sobs for tears of joy. 'There's enough trinkets in that dead lord's chest to pay for a mansion in Middlesteel.'

Amelia looked up at the ugly faces of the nomad gods on the columns. They stared back at her. Chubba-Gearshift. Tartar of the Axles. Useless deities that had not been worshipped for millennia, leering granite faces that seemed to be mocking her flesh-locked desires.

'The crystal-books are broken,' said Mombiko, climbing

up on the wagon to spill his light down over the contents of the coffin. 'That is too bad, mma. But with these other things here, you can finance a second expedition – there will be more chances, later . . .'

'I fear you have been misinformed.'

Amelia turned to see a company of black-clad desert warriors standing by the entrance to the tomb, gauze sand masks pushed up under their hoods. The three Macanalie brothers had moved to stand next to them, out of the line of fire of the soldiers' long spindly rifles.

'Never trust a Macanalie,' Amelia swore.

'Finding this hoard was never a sure thing,' said the eldest brother. 'But the price on your head, lassie, now that's filed away in the drawer of every garrison commander from here to Bladetenbul.'

'The caliph remembers those who promise much and do not keep their word,' said the captain of the company of soldiers. 'But not, I fear for you, with much fondness.'

Amelia saw the small desert hawk sitting on his leather glove. Just the right size to carry a message. Damn. She had let her excitement at finding the tomb blind her to the Macanalie brothers' treachery; they had sent for the scout patrol. She and Mombiko were royally betrayed.

'The caliph is still cross about Zal-Rashid's vase?' Amelia eyed the soldiers. At least five of them. 'I told him it was nothing but a myth.'

'Far more equitable then, Professor Harsh, if you had given the vase to his excellency *after* you had dug it out of his dunes,' said the soldier. 'Just as you had agreed. Rather than stealing it and taking it back to Jackals with you.'

'Oh, that. I can explain that,' said Amelia. 'There's an explanation, really. What is it that your people say, the sand has many secrets?'

'You will have much time to debate the sayings of the hundred prophets with his exulted highness,' said the officer. 'Much time.'

Mombiko looked at Amelia with real fear in his eyes and she bit her lip. His fate as an escaped slave of a Cassarabian nobleman would be no kinder than her own. It would be little consolation for Mombiko that he did not have a womb as Amelia did, that could be twisted into a breeding tank for Cassarabia's dark sorcerers to nurture their pets and monstrosities inside. One of the Macanalie brothers sniggered at the thought of the fates awaiting the haughty Jackelian professor and her colleague, but when the smuggler tried to move towards the ancient vehicle, a desert warrior shoved him back with his bone-like rifle butt.

'What's this, laddie?' spat the eldest of the brothers. 'We had a deal. You get these two. We get the reward and all of this.'

'And so you shall receive your reward,' said the caliph's officer. He waved at the ancient wagon. 'But *this* was not part of our arrangement.'

'You have to be joking me, laddie. Listen to me, you swindling jiggers, there's enough down here to share out for all of us.'

The caliph's man pointed to the leering bodies on the totem-pole columns. 'There will be nothing left to share, effendi. These bloated infidel toads are not of the Hundred Ways, they are idols of darkness and shall be cast down.' He gestured to one of the sand warriors. 'Go back to the saddlebags and bring enough charges to bury this unholy place under rock for another thousand years.'

'Are you out of your skull, laddie? There's wealth enough here to make us all rich! We can live like kings, you could live like an emir.'

The officer laughed with contempt. 'The caliph has lived two-score of your miserable lifetimes and if the hundred prophets be blessed, he shall live two-score more. What need does he have for the unclean gold of infidel gods when he has countless servants in every province of Cassarabia labouring to offer him their tribute for eternity?'

Amelia looked at Mombiko and understanding flashed between them. Mombiko would never again be a slave, and Amelia was jiggered if she would be used as a breeder, or allow herself to be handed over to a Cassarabian torture-sculptor to twist and mutate her bones until she was left stretched out like a human oak tree in the caliph's scented punishment gardens.

'He may be hundreds of years old,' said Amelia, 'but let me tell you a few home truths about your ruler. One, the caliph is too boring for me to listen to for a single hour, let alone a lifetime of agonized captivity. Two, he's not even a man. He's a woman dressed up as a male, and a damned ugly one at that. How she continues to fool all of you desert lads is beyond me.'

There was an intake of breath at her blasphemy.

'And three – next time you try and sneak up on me, bring your *own* damn lamp!'

Mombiko killed the gas spike. With a hissing sputter the chamber was plunged into absolute darkness. Amelia kicked down the lever alongside the carriage's steering wheel and the hisses from the spring-mounted spears decorating the wagon's prow were followed by screams and shouts and sickening thuds as the steel heads found their mark. This was followed by a crack of snapping glass. One of the collapsing desert soldier's spindly rifles splintering its charge, providing a brief gun-fire illumination of the carnage in which all the professor noticed was Mombiko sprinting before her towards the exit.

11

Someone tried to grab Amelia and she heard the rustle of a dagger being slid from its hilt. She used her left arm to shove out towards where her assailant's throat should be, and was rewarded by a snap and a body falling limp against her own. Amelia vaulted the corpse and found the stairs out of the tomb, nearly tripping over a speared soldier.

One of their treacherous guides was screaming for his brothers, something about trying to scrape up the gems inside the sarcophagus. Groping inside the panel-niche Amelia reversed the levers and the door started to lower itself with its *rack-rack-rack* rasp. She had brought herself and Mombiko a couple of minutes as the caliph's survivors, left in the dark, tried to locate the door release wheel she had spotted back inside the burial chamber. Amelia panted, taking the stairs three treads at a time. Damn, the steps had not seemed so long nor so steep on the way down. And her rifle – a trusty Jackelian Brown Bess – was not going to be much good to her one-armed.

'Professor!'

'Keep going, Mombiko. Beware the ledge. The caliph's boys might have left sentries outside.'

She pulled out a glass charge from her bandolier, cracking it against the wall so the two chambers of blow-barrel sap nearly mixed, then, still sprinting, bent down to roll the shell along the stone floor behind her. A wall of searing heat greeted Amelia as she left the tomb, the sun raised to its midday zenith. Thank the Circle, the ledge was clear of desert warriors.

Mombiko peered over the cliff. 'There are their mounts. No soldiers that I can see.'

Amelia glanced down; sandpedes tethered together, long leathery hides and a hundred insect-like legs: the ingenuity of this heat-blasted land's womb mages unrestrained by ethics or her own nation's Circlist teachings. Amelia let her good arm take the strain of the downward climb, aided by gravity and the rush of blood thumping through her heart. Crumbling dust from the scramble down coated her hair, making her cough. Her gun arm was burning in agony. She had accidentally thumped it into one of the cliff's outcrops and the scorpion-poisoned flesh felt like the caliph's torturers were already extracting their revenge from her body. They were near the bottom of the cliff face when an explosion sounded. Someone had stepped on her half-shattered shell, mixed the explosive sap in the firing chamber.

Amelia dropped the remaining few feet onto the warm orange sands. 'I do hope that was one of the Macanalies.'

'Better it was one of the soldiers, professor.' Mombiko had his knife out and advanced to where the caliph's men had picketed their sandpedes. The creatures' legs fluttered nervously as he approached them and reached out to slice their tethers free. Mandibles chattered, the sandpedes exchanging nervous glances, only the green human eyes in their beetle-black faces betraying their origins in some slave's sorcery-twisted womb. Too well trained, they were failing to escape. Amelia picked up a rock with her left hand and lobbed it hard at the creatures, the mounts exploding in an eruption of bony feet as they fled the shadow of the mountains.

Cracks sounded from the top of the peak, spouts of sand spewing up where the lead balls struck close to Mombiko and Amelia. The caliph's bullyboys had found the chamber's door release faster than she had hoped. Sand spilled down Amelia's boots as the two of them scrambled for their camels, the creatures whining as the soldiers' bullets whistled past their ears. There was a grunt from Mombiko, and he clutched his side in pain with one hand, but he spurred his camel after the retreating sandpedes, waving at her to ride on. Amelia urged her camel into an uncustomarily fast pace for the heat of the day. Luckily, the ornery beasts were skittish after seeing the unnatural sandpedes and only too glad to gallop away from the mountainside's shade.

Once the pursuit was lost behind the boundless dunes, Amelia drew to a halt, Mombiko sagging in his saddle. She pulled him off his camel and laid him down in the sand, turning aside his robes to find the wound.

'It's not too deep, Mombiko.'

'Poisoned,' hissed Mombiko. 'The soldiers hollow out their balls and fill them with the potions of their garrison mages. Look at my camel.'

His steed was groaning, sinking to its stomach on the sands while Amelia's camel tried to nuzzle it back to its feet. The creature had been struck on its flanks by one of the soldier's parting shots. Mombiko pointed to a protruding wooden handle strapped under his saddlebags. 'For the sun.'

She took it down and passed it to Mombiko. The umbrella had been her gift to him when he had started working at their university. Such a small thing in return for his prodigious talents. He could learn a new language in a week, quote verbatim from books he had read a year before. He had told her once that his seemingly unnatural memory was a common trait among many of his caste.

'The forest way,' said Mombiko.

Amelia nodded, tears in her eyes, understanding his request. No burial. From nature you have emerged, to nature so you shall return. The desert would blow over his unburied bones.

Mombiko reached out for Amelia's hand and when she opened her palm there was a cut diamond pressed inside it, the image of one of the Black-oil Horde's gods etched across the jewel's glittering prism.

'Sell it,' rasped Mombiko. 'Use the money to find the city – for both of us.'

14

'Are you an archaeologist's assistant or a crypt-robber, man?'

'I am Mombiko Tibar-Wellking,' said the ex-slave, raising his voice. Sweat was flooding down his face now. He was so wet he looked as if he had been pulled from the sea rather than stretched out across a sand dune. 'I am a lance lord of the Red Forest and I shall take my leave of my enemies – a – free – man.'

Amelia held him as he shuddered, each jolt arriving a little further apart, until he had stopped moving. His spirit was blowing south, back to the vast ruby forests of his home. But her path lay north to Jackals, the republic with a king. Her green and blessed land. A home she would in all likelihood never see again now.

Amelia closed his eyes. 'I shall be with you in a little while, Mombiko Tibar-Wellking.' She took the water canteen from the dead camel and left her friend's body behind, his umbrella held to his still chest for a lance.

The stars of the night sky would guide her true north, but not past the water holes that the Macanalie brothers had known about, nor past the dozens of fractious tribes that feuded across the treacherous sands. Amelia Harsh kicked her camel forward and tried to fill her mind with the dream of the lost city.

The city in the air.

One foot in front of the other, the last of her empty canteens trailing behind her boot on its leash. Too much energy required to bend down and cut the drained canteen's strap. Dark dots wheeled in front of the furnace sun. Even the cur-birds knew she was dead, a few hours away from being a meal for the gardeners of the sands. Every time the worn leather of her boots touched the burning dunes they seemed to suck a little

bit more of her life away. Amelia had been whittled down to
a core of determination, a bag of dehydrated flesh lurching
across the Northern Desert – no, use its Jackelian name – the
Southern Desert. Towards a goal that might as well lie on the
other side of the world.

Through her dry, sand-encrusted eyes Amelia glimpsed a
shimmer in the distance, sheets of heat twisting and snaking
over the dunes, sands bleached white by the height of the sun
raised to its midday zenith. Another mirage of a waddi sent
to tantalize her? No, not waters this time. The mirage was a
girl of about fourteen walking out of a door, following her
father into a garden. There was something familiar about the
scene. The parched passages of her mind tried to recall why
she should recognize the girl.

'What did that man at the table mean, pappa, when he said
that the title on the house wouldn't be enough to secure the
debts?'

'It doesn't matter,' said the girl's father. 'Just commerce, a
matter of commerce and coins and the merely mundane.'

'But he was talking about the sponging-house?'

'That's not a word to use in polite company, my sweet. I've
visited a few of my friends in debtor's prison,' said the girl's
father. 'Good people. With some of the hard days those in
trade have seen this year, it's a wonder any of my social circle
have lodgings anywhere outside a debtor's jail. It doesn't
matter.'

'I'm scared, pappa, those men who came to the house
yesterday . . .'

'The bailiffs can't get what doesn't belong to you.' The
father glanced back towards the sounds of their dinner guests
still drifting out of the doorway and pulled out a battered old
mumbleweed pipe, lighting a pinch of leaf with the pipe's
built-in steel flint. 'That's why your aunt came to visit last

week and left with a fair few more cases on top of her carriage than she arrived with. The antiques I've collected over the years and the books, of course. You always have to save the books. Enough to pay for your education to be finished.'

'You're not going to be sent to the sponging-house, are you?'

'Perish the thought,' said the girl's father. 'Nobody should go to such a place. We tried to amass enough support in parliament to abolish the wretched places last year, but it was no good. Too many who still want the example set, and set harsh with it. The guardians have forgotten there was a time in history when the existence of such a place would have been unthinkable, when destitution was unheard of, when the rule of reason was the only monarch people bent their knee to.'

'You mean the lost city?'

The girl's father puffed out a circle of mumbleweed smoke. He appeared almost contented. 'A lost age, my sweet. An entire age of reason. Those elusive Camlanteans. Almost as tricky to find in our times as it is to locate their noble ideals among the benches of parliament today, I fear. Most people don't believe that age even existed, but we do, don't we, my sweet?'

'Yes, pappa.'

'We'll find the ruins of that place one day.' He pointed out to the sky. 'Up there, that's where we'll find it. And when we do, we'll bring a little piece of it down here to Jackals, you and I. A little piece of sanity to calm an insane world. You go back inside to the warmth, now. I want to spend some time by your mother's grave.'

'Don't let pappa go,' croaked Amelia at the mirage, her hands clawing at the sand. 'Can't you see the bulge in his jacket? Stop him from going into the garden. He's been upstairs to his desk, the bloody gun's in his pocket.'

17

The report of a pistol echoed out, the heat-thrown vision collapsing into an explosion of feathers as the cur-birds that had been inspecting her from the top of the dune fled to the sky on the back of Amelia's unexpected howl of fury.

Amelia rubbed the crust out of her dry, swollen eyes. Not even enough moisture left in her body for tears. According to parliament's law, debts couldn't be passed down from one generation to the next. But dreams could.

From the fortress-wall of heat shimmer another blurred shape emerged, solidifying into something – a figure.

'Go away,' rasped Amelia in the direction of the mirage. 'Leave me alone to die in peace, will you. I've had enough of the past.'

But the figure wasn't going away. It was getting more defined with every step. Oh, Circle! Not a vision this time. She reached for her rifle, but the Brown Bess was no longer there. Amelia couldn't even remember having discarded the weight of the cheap but reliable weapon. She had kept her knife though, for the stalking snakes that slid towards her at night, drawn by her body-heat. But the knife seemed so heavy now as well, a steel burden she could not pull free from her belt.

The part of Amelia's brain that had not yet shut down recognized what she saw coming out of the heat shimmer before her. The water-filled hump on the stranger's back was unremarkable for the desert tribes – most of whom possessed the same adaptation. Red robes flowed behind the small woman and a train of retainers followed her, each one turning and twisting in a private dance.

'Witch of the dunes,' grated Amelia's throat. 'Witch!'

'It takes one to know one,' cackled the figure. 'I'm not travelling with your past, my sweet. I'm travelling with your future.'

18

The professor pitched forward into the embrace of the desert.

When Amelia woke up she was no longer on sand, she lay on the soft bracken of the upland foothills. Damp ground, soggy from actual rain. Jackelian rain. So, the border of Cassarabia was a couple of days behind her. The witch waited at Amelia's side, the retainers behind her in a silent horizontal line, held in her glamour and little more than zombies if half the tales Amelia had heard were true. There were no camels nearby, no sandpedes to explain how they had possibly travelled so far. Nothing to indicate how long Amelia had been unconscious. Her journey south towards the tomb had taken nine weeks, for Circle's sake.

'Why?'

The witch stopped swaying, the mad mumbling of her internal dialogue briefly stilled. 'Because you are needed, my large-armed beauty.'

Needed? The witches of the Southern Desert were mad, fey and capricious; certainly not given to helping stranded travellers.

Amelia looked at the witch. 'Needed by whom?'

The squat, humpbacked creature dipped down and picked up a leaf with a trail of ants on its blade. 'For want of this leaf, the ant will die; for want of the ant, the stag-beetle will die; for want of the stag-beetle, the lizard will die; for want of the lizard, the sand hawk will die; for want of the sand hawk, the hunter is blinded – and who is to say what the hunter might achieve?'

'There are a lot of leaves blowing in Jackals,' said Amelia. She twisted her shoulder and was hardly surprised to note that the scorpion-stung flesh had been bathed and healed.

'Oh, my pretty,' cackled the witch. 'You think I have done

19

you some kindness?' The witch's voice turned ugly. 'The true kindness would have been to let the sands of Cassarabia suck the marrow from your bones. You have left the easy path behind you now.'

'Thank you anyway,' said Amelia. Like all her kind, the old woman was as mad as a coot and as deadly as a viper. Better not to antagonize her. 'For the hard path forced upon me.'

A mist rose behind the witch. The weather systems of Jackals and Cassarabia collided in the hinterlands and mists were common enough. Usually.

'Such fine manners. What a perfect daughter of Jackals you are. Thank me next time you see me, if you *can*.'

The witch turned her back and stalked away, her silent retainers falling into line behind her like a tail of ducklings following their mother.

Around Amelia the sounds of border grouse returned to the foothills as the humpbacked creature vanished into the mist. 'Well, damn. Lucky me.'

Brushing the dew off her tattered clothes – too light for a chilly Jackelian morning – Amelia headed north into the uplands. Deeper into Jackals. Home.

CHAPTER TWO

The street urchin his friends called Ducker bent down to scoop up a lump of horse dung with his improvised wooden paddle. Overhall Corner was one of the busiest junctions at the heart of Middlesteel, rich pickings in the greatest city of the greatest nation on the continent. Why, with a full sack of horseshit patties drying out before the fire, you would have fuel enough to cook for a week. Cheaper than coal. And the smell? Well, for the price you paid, you quickly got used to that. But never let it be said that the dung collectors of Overhall Corner did not enjoy their job. From the other side of the boulevard William made a rude gesture, a cry of victory following quickly after the lump of horse-dirt whistling past Ducker's cloth cap. Scooping up a handful of ammunition, Ducker dodged past the hansom cabs and cask-filled wagons, the whinnies of offended shire horses in his ears, then let his missile of revenge fly back towards his colleague in the dung trade. The dung skimmed the other urchin and narrowly missed a mumbleweed-smoke seller, the man's tank of narcotic gas battered and rusty from the wet Middlesteel smog.

'Bloody dung boys,' the old vendor waved a fist at the two urchins.

'Take a puff of your own mumbleweed and calm down,' Ducker shouted back.

Their altercation, the best sport they had come across this morning, was interrupted by a jumpy clatter of hooves along the cobbled street. The whine of a horseless carriage had unsettled the horses, the low hum of its clockwork engine almost beyond the range of the race of man's ears.

'By the Circle,' said William, 'would you look at that beauty?'

Ducker pushed his friend out of the way for a closer peek. Was Will talking about the lady in the steering hole, or the carriage itself? Shining gold-plated steel, two wheels at the front twice the lads' own height and four smaller wheels at the rear of the passenger box, an oval stadium-seat of soft red leather mounted on top.

'That's not from any Jackelian workshop,' said William.

'Catosia,' said Ducker. 'The city-states.' Everyone knew they made the best horseless carriages. Unlike the Jackelian ones, the high-tension clockwork mechanisms of the Catosian League's manufactories did not suffer from a tendency to explode, showering pieces of carriage across the road. The crusher directing traffic at the junction stopped the flow of cabs, carts and penny-farthings along Ollard Street, waving forward the traffic on the other side of Overhall Corner. Ducker suspected the black-coated policeman wanted to halt the vehicle and gawp at its opulence along with all the other pedestrians.

'Not much dung out of one of them,' said Will, enviously.

An idea occurred to Ducker. A way to turn a penny and get a closer look at the carriage at the same time. He advanced on the vehicle and tugged off his cloth cap. 'Excuse me, sir, wipe your gas lamps, sir? They are looking a little sooty.'

The driver made to get out of the steering hole and Ducker saw beyond the short blonde curls and blue eyes for the first time, noticed her body. She was not just a beauty; she had the physique of someone who worked in the muscle pits. She was a whipper, a fighter for hire.

The sole passenger of the vehicle seemed amused. Young, handsome and as blonde as his driver, he possessed the air of authority that only came to those born to quality. One of the Lords Commercial. 'You can sit down, Veryann. A little free trade is much to be encouraged. Clean away, young fellow.'

Whether the polishing from his cap was removing the dirt on the lamps or adding to it was unclear, but Ducker did his best and, ignoring the pained expression of the chauffeur-guard – who obviously had a different payment in mind for him – he grinned up hopefully at the commercial lord. The man flipped a coin down towards Ducker and the urchin caught it, then returned to the pavement while the wagons and hansom cabs began moving again.

'Bleeding Circle,' said William. 'You're a ballsy one.'

'Look, a crown,' said Ducker, turning the coin over in his fingers. 'Not bad for a minute's work, eh?'

'Ain't you seen that gent's mug in the news sheets, Ducker? Don't you know who you are hobnobbing with?'

Ducker looked annoyed. His friend knew he did not have his letters – the streets of Middlesteel were his education. He never even looked at the penny sheets. They only reminded him of a world that would never be his; of reading and meals and warm rooms and caring parents.

'That was Quest, that was Abraham Quest!'

Quest? Ducker was amazed. Circle's turn; the cleverest man in Middlesteel, it was said. Probably the richest too.

Ducker looked towards the humming carriage disappearing into the distance, a glitter of gold among the dark, sooty streets.

'You should have asked for two crowns, you bleeding turnip,' laughed William.

'I expect we'll need to fit a footman's plate to the rear now,' announced the driver. 'Because when word of what you just did spreads among his friends, we're going to be mobbed by guttersnipes at every crossing in the city.'

Abraham Quest stretched back in his seat, unconcerned. 'Those young children are the future of Jackals, Veryann.'

'It's not as if you don't already give generously enough to the Board of the Poor. And there are those children's academies you sponsor . . .'

'As to the need, so to the means.' A quotation from the Circlist *Book of Common Reflections*. 'Do you never ponder, Veryann, why one child eats off a silver platter and sleeps warm under a woollen blanket, while another goes hungry to a bed filled with twelve others equally desperate? Do you never wonder what discrepancy in fate, motivation or resolve leads to the terrible disparities in this land of ours?'

Veryann turned the carriage onto Drury Dials, steering the humming vehicle towards the House of Guardians. 'Of all people, you should know the answer to that, Abraham Quest – you a workhouse child risen so far. The strong and the cunning and the quick thrive, the weak fail. It is the way of all nature.'

'Ah, yes, the answer of a true soldier of the city-states.' Quest glanced back sadly. 'I was just like that urchin once. I truly was. It is like staring into a mirror thirty years ago. But things do not have to be this way.'

They were meeting in the Strandswitch Club, two streets down from parliament itself. The First Guardian had a delicious sense of irony. Before the Leveller party swept into power during the last election, Benjamin Carl would have been just about the last person in the kingdom to be voted into Middlesteel's most prestigious political club. Now the club's committee had no choice at all but to admit the man.

Guardians and civil servants from Greenhall watched Abraham Quest's progress across the lush carpet and leather armchairs with the startled glances of those who had just found a copper ha'penny abandoned between the cobbles of the pavement. Did they see him, or did they see his wealth? He already knew the answer. Money was power and notoriety, a lens through which his humanity was distorted by any and all who saw him. All save perhaps the politician he had come to see, who had always seemed curiously unmoved by any such consideration. It was one of the reasons they got on so well.

'First Guardian,' announced the club butler. 'Your guest has arrived.'

Benjamin Carl lay down his copy of the *Middlesteel Illustrated News* and pointed to an armchair opposite the small table that concealed the frame of his wheelchair.

'Neutral ground, Benjamin?'

'Tongues would wag if I received you at my offices in parliament,' said Carl.

'More speculation on the amount of my donations to the Leveller party, perhaps?'

'Yes, it is curious how one's respect for the cheeky tenacity of Dock Street's pensmen when in opposition adjusts after winning a majority.'

'Freedom of expression is one of the great marks of our civilization,' said Abraham, picking up the politician's newspaper. There was a black linework cartoon on the front cover. The First Guardian facing down a gaggle of Guardians from the opposition parties in a challenge of debating sticks, a cloud of insults rising from the deliberately doll-sized mob of politicians. Benjamin Carl's wheelchair had been transformed into a war chariot with iron spikes, his wheels crushing the more radical members of his own party. A speech bubble rose out of Carl's grinning countenance: *'This ride is too strong for you, m'compatriots.'*

'So it is,' said the First Guardian, checking to make sure the club's other patrons were out of earshot. 'And it is a little frank speaking which I thought we might engage in this morning, Abraham.'

'I would expect nothing less from the firebrand author of *Community and the Commons.*'

Carl ignored the jibe about his book – barely off the banned list for as long as his election as First Guardian. 'The plain speaking is regarding your commercial concerns.'

'Another donation, perhaps? I heard parliament was getting sticky again about your proposed labour reforms. I do try and set an example with the House of Quest.'

'It is not your mill conditions which interest me – the long lines of prospective workers that queue up every time you open up a new concern speak well enough for those. It is your output I wish to discuss – more specifically, that of your airship works at Ruxley Waters.'

'The Board of the Admiralty haven't been complaining about the quality of the aerostats my mills turn out, have they, First Guardian?'

'Hardly,' replied Carl. 'Your airwrights are the most proficient in Jackals, your airship designs the most advanced – as you well know from the size of your order-book with the navy.' The politician jerked a finger towards the lady retainer standing discreetly by the door of the club's dining room. 'She is a free company fighter? From the Catosian city-states?'

'Veryann? Yes, she is.'

'Our nation has a long, regretful tradition of tolerating the rich and powerful keeping private armies under the fiction that they are fencibles, reserves salted away for times of war. I do not intend to be the first leader of parliament who starts tolerating private aerial navies too.'

'It's somewhat difficult to test new aerostat designs without celgas to float the airships we build,' said Quest.

'Jackals' monopoly on celgas has kept our state safe for hundreds of years,' replied the First Guardian. 'Your test flights are a little too regular and the discrepancies between the gas barrels you are sent and what comes out of your airship hangars at the other end a little too wide of the mark.'

'I shall have words with the yard's overseers,' said Quest.

'Please do,' said Carl. 'We have our merchant marine to serve our trade and we have the Royal Aerostatical Navy to serve our defence. Your proving flights are one thing, but let me make this absolutely clear: there is no room for a third force in the air above Jackals.'

Quest chortled. 'I am not a science pirate, Ben. I understand there are subtler ways to ensure reform for our people than standing an airship off the House of Guardians and dropping fin-bombs on the heads of your parliamentarians until you legislate for harmony among the nations and prosperity for the deserving poor.'

'Then you understand well. Our nation is surrounded by envious tyrannies that covet our people's wealth and would crush the freedoms that we enjoy; parliament's backbenches are packed with Heartlanders, Purists, Roarers and Middle Circleans who would all love to see the first Leveller government for a century fail, and as for you . . .'

'Mercantilism has always been a competitive business, First Guardian. The number of enemies that are out there circling me is one of the few ways I still keep score.'

A solicitous member of the club's staff came over, offering the two men a glass of jinn. The Strandswitch Club was traditional that way: brandy still out of fashion after the attempted invasion of Jackals by its neighbour, Quatérshift, a few years earlier. Benjamin Carl took the glass and swirled the alcohol around the rim as if trying to read the future in its pink eddies.

'We all operate within limitations, Abraham. I thought I could achieve so much in this position – but between the bureaucrats of Greenhall, the other parties and the infighting among my own Levellers, it seems I am only ever allowed to achieve one tenth of what I set out to accomplish.'

'Now that I understand,' said Quest. 'After all, look what those jiggers did to me.'

'Yet, even so, you still seem to prosper. However much they trim your sails.'

Quest filled his nostrils with the scent of the jinn. 'Trim my sails, or confiscate them? I see things differently, Ben. To some that makes me a genius, to others a lunatic and a fool. Succeeding in my business concerns, now, that is merely a game.'

'One you play so well,' noted the politician. 'So well, indeed, they changed the rules of the game just to fit around you.'

'Time for a new game then, Ben?'

'Let me tell you something.' The First Guardian leant in close. 'The establishment dislikes us both intensely, but with me, they at least know what to expect. Anyone with the wit to read *Community and the Commons* knows what I stand for. But with you, they have no reference points. You make yourself the richest man in Middlesteel and then you give your fortune away every year to the poor. They try and destroy you at every turn, yet it is always *you* that seems to end up taking over *their* bankrupted commercial concerns. You treat the greatest nation in the world as if it is a mere hand of cards, its sole purpose to serve as the source of your amusement. You scare them.'

'A little mischief,' said Quest. 'I just need a little mischief to keep my mind fresh, to keep the black dog at bay. Everything is so flat and grey without my miserable few distractions.'

'I understand that,' said Ben Carl. 'Just make sure your airwrights know you intend to restrict your game to the free market.'

'Has someone been telling tales on me, First Guardian?'

Carl pointed up towards the ceiling. 'An unattributed source. A note dropped down to land on my windowsill in parliament. You need to be careful, Abraham.'

Abraham Quest tapped the side of his nose. 'I quite understand. Enough said.'

Carl watched his wealthy friend departing across the clubroom. For the industrial lord's sake, Carl hoped Abraham Quest would be true to his word. Because if he was not, the statuesque mercenary he had watching his expensive back would not be nearly enough to protect him. Not if the Court of the Air came calling on him in judgement.

The butler returned to refill his jinn glass. His black club livery was barely enough to disguise the fact that the servant was really an agent of the political police. A g-man. Ben Carl was still not used to the fact these dogs were his hounds now, rather than part of a pursuit baying behind his own heels.

'Do you think he will listen to you, sir?'

'The cleverest gentleman in Middlesteel?' sighed the First Guardian. 'How should I know?'

'We still do not know what he is up to at the Ruxley Waters airworks.'

'Airships are just toys to him, like everything else,' said Carl. 'Toys to be made to go further, faster, higher.'

'They are the Royal Aerostatical Navy's toys, sir. He only gets to build them.'

'He is a good man,' said Carl. 'A humane man. Half of our land's mill workers eat better and work fewer hours because of the standards set by the model factories of the House of Quest. He has done more for the people of Jackals than I have managed to achieve with my factory acts. He is a patriot.'

The police agent refilled the politician's glass and gave a short bow. 'As are we all, sir, as are we all.'

Chivery did not like having the new boy foisted upon him like this. It was dangerous enough making a living as a smuggler in Jackals, rolling the dice that Greenhall's revenue agents didn't have the smuggler's favourite bay outside Shiptown under observation at night, looking for u-boats like theirs cutting the line. Dangerous enough, without having some green young 'un like Tom Gashford given into his care to nursemaid. A boy who talked too much when he should have been quiet and said nothing at all when he should have been talking. But it was understandable that the skipper of the *Pip Sissy* wanted to pair young Tom with an experienced moonlighter like Chivery. The lad needed experience of the hidden paths the smugglers took through the forest, the clearings where casks of untaxed brandy and mumbleweed could be passed onto the moonrakers' secretive wholesalers.

Young Tom seemed convinced that their proximity to the cursewall would lead the redcoats down upon them. Since the attempted invasion, the Frontier Foot had been reinforced all along the Jackelian border, from Hundred Locks in the north to the Steamman Free State in the south. But the tremblers that the redcoat engineers had burrowed into the ground were for detecting sappers' tunnels deep enough to cut under the cursewall, not designed to catch a couple of smugglers out plying the coast's oldest trade. Having the lad with him was a risk, all the same. Of all the cargoes the canny submariners of the *Pip Sissy* smuggled out of Quatérshift to bring into Jackals, the contents of Tom's sack were going to prove the most lucrative this cold night. The lad kicked his heels against the frost and the darkness. He obviously wished he were bunking back in the warmth of their u-boat too.

'If there weren't revenue men abroad tonight, I'd burn this rubbish to warm my fingers and damn the risk of the fire-light,' said Tom, swinging the sack nervously between his hands.

The older moonraker laid his hand menacingly on his belt dagger. 'Then you'd be a right fool, Tom. It'd be a tuppence turn of a coin whether our customer would slit your throat before the skipper tied you to the *Pip Sissy's* conning tower and towed you back to Quatérshift for the crabs.'

'Why should someone pay us good money for this rubbish, Chivery?' The lad pulled out a handful of yellowed pamphlets from the sack and read out a few of the titles in the moon-light. '*Directives of the First Committee. The heroes of the Faidéaux carriage works – an exhortation to labour. Equality's Tongue: the thoughts and purity of the revolution.* There ain't anybody in Jackals that collects this revolutionary guff anymore, not since the war.'

Chivery lit the bull's-eye lamp he carried with him, making the signal that they were ready to trade. He took advantage of the tightly focused light to unroll the penny sheet he had brought with him. *The Northern Monitor*: respectable opin-ions, honestly and directly expressed. Its front cover bore an illustration of the First Guardian, Benjamin Carl, holding a four-poles bat with the words *Jackelian oak* carved on it. Bounding off the wood was the head of one of the First

Committee of Quatérshift, while various caricatures from parliament clapped politely on the sidelines. There was a speech bubble rising from the leader of the opposition, Hoggstone, which read '*Your game m'lord.*'

The great terror was still in full swing in Jackals' neighbouring nation. Every month the *Pip Sissy* made its smuggling run, and every month their friends, contacts and colleagues in Quatérshift seemed gaunter and more malnourished. Made prematurely old by the upheavals – purge after purge – famine after famine – entire families dragged from their villages to the quick, deadly mercy of a Gideon's Collar, the steam-driven killing machines that dominated every town square in Quatérshift. As Chivery's news sheet indicated, even a high position within the Commonshare elite was no protection against the twitchy paranoia of the shifties' secret police units or the whims of the street mob. Quatérshift was not a functioning republic any more – it was a dog gnawing on its own wounded, diseased flesh. The smuggler shook his head sadly. People got themselves into the strangest of pickles with their damn fool passions. If anyone in Jackals started carrying on like that, why, their neighbours would sneak them a visit one evening and give them a right good dewskitching – look on it as a favour done to them, too.

'What's that noise?' Tom looked around.

A whistling from the sky, then a dark monstrous shape dropped through the canopy of trees, leathery wings folding up like an angel of hell. Yelping, the lad stumbled back and fell over a branch.

Chivery picked up the boy's fallen bag from the grass. The lad looked on in astonishment. It was not one monster – it was *two*. The reptilian flying creature had dropped his passenger in the middle of the clearing and stepped back, wrapping his wings around his sides. It was a lashlite. A lashlite carrying a human-shaped figure. But was it a human? Dark high boots, black cape, a face concealed underneath a devil's mask. Now the tales came back to the boy. The scourge of Quatérshift, vengeance taken human form. *Furnace-breath Nick.*

Some said Furnace-breath Nick was the ghost of a Quatérshiftian nobleman come back from hell to haunt his executioners. Others claimed that he was a member of the Carlist revolution who had been betrayed and purged by the new rulers of the land – a spirit of death hunting his old compatriots. A few maintained that Furnace-breath Nick was a dark angel of the Quatérshiftian sun god, sent to punish the newly atheist republic that shared half of Jackals' border.

'Do you have it?' The devil's voice echoed around the clearing as if it was being sucked up from hell. Something inside the figure's mask was altering his voice, making his words hideous.

Chivery was not bothered. He had gone through this ritual many times before. 'For the money, I have it.'

A black-gloved hand lashed out, and a purse of coins spun across to be caught by the smuggler. Chivery bounced the coins in his palm, jangling them. 'A bargain well met.' He tossed the sack filled with Quatérshiftian propaganda over to Furnace-breath Nick.

'I trust there will be another delivery next month?'

'It's getting harder,' said Chivery. 'Not because of the Carlists, mind. They're still in a right old state. The First Committee wouldn't notice if we snuck into the Palace of Equality and painted their arses blue right now.'

'There will be no extra money,' Furnace-breath Nick told the smuggler.

Chivery went on, ignoring the comment. 'It's our own damn navy. They've stepped up airship patrols along the coast. It's getting so we can't break the surface off a Quatérshiftian cove without some RAN stat chasing us down.'

'When the drinking houses of Hundred Locks run dry of smuggled brandy, I shall believe it's too dangerous for you to break the blockade,' said Furnace-breath Nick. 'Until then . . . besides, like your boy says, this literature is just worthless junk.'

Terrified, the young smuggler tried to crawl back into the woods. Furnace-breath Nick had been secretly listening in to *his* conversation.

'Worthless to some,' said Chivery, clinking the bag of coins again. 'Yet you seem to place some value on it.'

'Oh yes,' laughed Furnace-breath Nick – not an encouraging sound. 'But sink me, don't people say I am quite insane?'

With that, Furnace-breath Nick was seized by the lashlite, the beating of the creature's wings sending the two smugglers' tricorn hats blowing off into the trees as the devil-masked figure and the winged beast that served him vanished into the sky.

'That was him,' said young Tom. 'The one in the sheets. Furnace-breath Nick.'

'It was,' agreed Chivery. 'And you thought moonraking was boring, eh?'

'But he's the devil of Quatérshift, ain't he, the scourge of the Commonshare? What does he want with a sack full of useless shiftie political pamphlets?'

'Something to warm his fire during a cold evening, boy? Damned if I know. In fact, if I did know, I probably would be damned. Just, I suspect, like he must be.'

CHAPTER THREE

Quirke opened his door, the sadness in the academic's normally sparkling eyes a fair indication of what was to follow. 'Amelia, do come in.'

Professor Harsh followed the head of the School of Archaeology at Saint Vine's College into his comfortable old office, the sense of foreboding in her gut mounting. The table by the window held a steaming pot of caffeel, rising vapour from the brew obscuring the quad below, where gaggles of brown-gowned students were being called to seminar by the steam-driven whistles running along the battlements of the ancient university. The brew's presence settled it. Quirke might as well have placed an executioner's cap on his desk.

'Do sit down, my dear.' The elderly fellow pulled a polished gem out of his tweed waistcoat's pocket and placed it on his desk. It was the same jewel Mombiko had removed from the tomb in Cassarabia's mountains.

'I thought the university would have that under museum glass by now – or sold off by one of the Cripplecross auction houses?' said Amelia.

'The High Table does not know of its existence yet, Amelia.'

She looked across at Quirke, puzzled.

'This arrived for you while you were gone.' He passed a cream vellum envelope across to her. Taking the copper letter opener from the academic's desk, Amelia sliced the envelope open. She unfolded the notepaper, going numb as she read the words.

'They can't do this to me!'

'You don't have tenure, Amelia. Of course they can.'

She angrily crumpled the paper into a ball with a gorilla-sized arm. 'Saint Vines is the last college that would take me. What am I meant to do now? Accept a job as a governess teaching the snotty sons of Sun Gate quality the difference between the great civil war and last winter's bread riots?'

'What was the Chancellor expected to do, Amelia? You were supposed to be working at a dig along the dyke wall. Instead some uplanders discover you wandering about half-dead along the desert border. Your obsession with the city is destroying your life.'

'The High Table are fools,' said Amelia. 'Fools with closed minds who are so brim-full of prejudice that they can't see that the city is not a myth. It *existed*. Out in the desert I found the tomb of the man who as like destroyed it!'

Quirke shook his head and spun the globe that sat on his desk, his finger brushing the vast expanse of the Fire Sea as it rotated. 'The academic council values orthodoxy, Amelia. A legend without solid evidence makes for very poor archae-ology. You should be thankful that the Cassarabian ambas-sador was expelled last year, or I don't doubt we would have Greenhall's civil servants and magistrates crawling all over the college looking for you with a bag stuffed full of embassy grievances.'

'Give the jewel to the Chancellor,' said Amelia. 'The money from it—'

'—Will not make a difference,' said Quirke. He pushed the gem across the table to the professor. 'Not this time. You could have come back with an original scroll of the Circlist tenets and he still would have dismissed you. Even if by some miracle you could find evidence that the city of Camlantis really existed, that it is still intact and locked as a floatquake in the heavens, how would you reach it? The aerostats we have access to are only pocket dirigibles – do you think the RAN can be enlisted on your goose chase?'

'Admiralty House has been known to favour requests by the High Table . . .'

The old academic picked up a neatly folded copy of the *Middlesteel Illustrated News*. 'This is what the navy are concerned with.' He tapped a report about an airship of the merchant marine that had been savaged by a skrayper, one of the massive balloon-like creatures of the upper atmosphere that sometimes sank down to wreak havoc on Jackelian shipping. 'You find a text in a crystal-book about how to drive skraypers off our airships and you'll find the First Skylord willing to grant you an audience at Admiralty House quick enough. But searching the skies for Camlantis? What do you think the RAN will make of that proposal?'

'The city is up there,' insisted Amelia.

'If the ruins of Camlantis were at an altitude we could reach, someone would have sighted them. Circle knows, the jack cloudies are as bad as their maritime counterparts with their superstitions and their rituals and their cant. It wouldn't take much to add a story of a ghostly land ripped out in a floatquake to their tall tales of angels gliding around their airships and dark round stats of unknown origin whistling past their ears. And if your mystical city is resting at an altitude beyond our sight and reach, well . . . I am sure you can see the problem.'

'The lashlites believe the city is up there,' said Amelia. 'I told you about my trip to their nests in the mountains. Their songs tell of a city that could have been Camlantis, rising past a flight of warriors out hunting a skrayper pod.'

'The lashlites are a colourful race,' said the academic. 'I dare say I could find something in their aural teachings to support most of the tales of celestial fiction printed in the penny dreadfuls, if I chose to interpret their sagas in such a way.'

'You are sounding like the dullards on the High Table.'

'Yes,' sighed the academic. 'I believe I am.' He stood up and pulled out a tome from his shelves. 'Uriah Harthouse. Two years' worth of lashlite shaman sagas transcribed during an expedition to the peaks around Hundred Locks fifty-five years ago. I particularly like the story where the god Stormlick engages twelve ice demons in a whistle-song contest in a wager to end the coldtime, triumphing by cunningly adding a mustard-like spice to their wine goblets when the demons weren't looking. Try selling the Department of Geographical Studies that gem as an explanation of the glaciers' retreat from the continent.'

'This isn't myth we are talking about, it is history.'

'History is out of fashion in these corridors,' said Quirke. 'We have too much of it, we are drowning in it.' He opened a drawer in his desk and lifted out a coin in a glass box, the face on the silver so faded that the impression of the woman's head was barely discernible. 'How old do the wild papers in those disreputable journals of yours propose Camlantis might be? Seven thousand years? Eight thousand years? I found this coin in one of the archives downstairs while I was writing a piece on the reign of King Hull. Out of idle curiosity I had Pumblechook in metallurgy use that new dating process he's been boasting about – do you know how old this coin is according to his new method?'

'Chimecan slave-nation period?'

Quirke lifted an eyebrow. 'Two hundred and seventy thousand years old. How's that for a heresy?'

Amelia nearly spilt the contents of her cup. 'That's impossible. Pumblechook must have made an error.'

'You plough the fields in Jackals and you trip over history, you cast a fishing net in the Sepia Sea and you dredge up history. We have too much of it, and the High Table have had too much of yours.'

'What are you going to do with the coin?'

'What am I going to do?' Quirke opened the drawer and placed the artefact back inside the felt-lined case. 'I shall keep it as a reminder that there are things in this world older than I am. You'll see no papers from me speculating on the origins of the coin. I'll leave it to you in my will – you can have it along with my office, when the High Table have forgotten your name and your impudence towards them.'

'I shall never be the sort of person they believe fit to sit in here,' said Amelia.

'You'll see,' said the academic. 'In time, you'll see.'

'Fools, they're blind, bloody fools.'

'Some advice, Amelia,' said Quirke, passing a cup of cafeel over to the professor. 'As one of your father's oldest friends. Don't publish any more papers about the city; keep your head down and let the procession of nature take its course. The membership of the High Table will change, and in time fresh faces will arrive who have never heard of you. There is a dig along the foothills of Mechancia, some Chimecan-age ruins overrun by glaciers during the coldtime. I can get you on the expedition – you'll just be another anonymous face helping out, a few years beyond the reach of the official journals and your enemies.'

'Academic exile.' Amelia set aside her cup without drinking from it.

'I taught you better than that, my dear. A tactical withdrawal. Entropy can be an astonishingly powerful ally in these sleepy halls of ours. The long game, my dear, the long game.'

Amelia stood up. They both knew she was not going to follow his advice, and the old man had damaged his own prospects enough already by making Saint Vines her last bolt-hole within the eight universities.

'You stood by my father after he lost everything,' said Amelia, 'and you have done the same for me. You are a rare old bird, Sherlock Quirke.'

He shrugged. It had never even occurred to the old academic that there was an alternative way of doing things. He was a singular touch of humanity among all the bones and dust of forgotten things.

She made to open the door and leave.

'Amelia, did it ever occur to you that some things that are lost are meant to be that way for a reason?'

Now that was a queer thing to say. Was that the master of archaeology, or her dead father's friend talking?

Amelia shut the door on Quirke and her old life.

Amelia could see there was something wrong with the woman in the quad the moment she left the college building – something out of place. She was the right age to be a student but her poise was wrong; like a panther waiting patiently on the lawn, carefully watching the bustle of the undergraduates. Could she be a topper sent after her by the caliph? The Circle knows, there was always a surfeit of professional assassins in Middlesteel, ready to do the capital city's dirty work when enough coins were spilled over the bench tops of the more disreputable drinking houses.

She noticed Amelia and started to walk towards the professor, the shadows falling behind her. The visitor was approaching with the sun in her eyes. Amelia relaxed. The woman was not planning to try to sink a blade between her ribs after all.

'Damson Harsh?' enquired the young lady with a slight accent. Where was that accent from? It had been softened by years in Jackals.

'Professor Harsh,' said Amelia.

The woman pulled a folded sheet of notepaper from her jacket. 'You are, I believe, currently in need of employment. I represent an individual who may be interested in offering you a suitable position.'

Amelia arched an eyebrow. 'You are suspiciously well informed, damson.'

The visitor handed Amelia the piece of paper. 'The offer is contingent on you being able to translate the text you see here.'

Amelia unfolded the sheet. It was not possible! The script on the paper was nothing this young woman should have in her possession.

'Is this a joke?'

'I can assure you that the offer is quite genuine, *professor*.'

'Kid, where did you get this from?'

'The translation, if you would be so kind.'

'The last – book – of – Pairdan. Reader-Administrator of . . . Camlantis.' Amelia haltingly traced her finger across the ancient script. She had nearly died in the desert wastes of the caliph to get her hands on such a treasure, yet this young pup had breezed onto the college grounds blithely oblivious to the fact that she held in her possession the title inscription of a crystal-book that had been lost to humanity some six and a half thousand years ago.

'The crystal-book that this was taken from, does it have information blight?'

41

'Turn the paper over, professor.'

Amelia looked at the other side of the sheet. An address: Snowgrave Avenue – the richest district of Sun Gate, the beating heart of commerce that kept the currents of continental trade circulating for Jackals.

'Go there now, professor. You may see for yourself if the book is functioning or not.'

It was all Amelia could do to stop herself running.

Snowgrave Avenue lay five minutes' walk away from Guardian Wren station on the atmospheric, the underground transportation system that served the capital and was now spilling workers out onto the avenue's wide boulevards. This season, it seemed that the women had taken to wearing the severe uniform of the clerks – dark suits cut long to cover their dresses, and stovepipe hats. Last season it had been bonnets bearing the badges of the parliamentary parties sewn in lace. Amelia still kept an idle eye on the milliners' window displays in Middlesteel, even if she usually set aside her attentions and the increasingly slim pickings of her salary for following her vocation. Along the avenue, the richer denizens of the counting houses and commercial concerns were stepping out of hansom cabs clattering over Snowgrave's cobbles, while the truly wealthy – the capital's finest quality – brushed down their waistcoats and checked their gold pocket watches from the snug comfort of private coaches. To be poor of course, meant coming in by foot, trudging from the rookeries in the shadow of the vast new pneumatic towers, water-reinforced rubber gurgling over the vendors' cries of eels and fresh milk for sale.

Amelia gazed up at the tower that matched the address on her sheet. Seventy storeys high, but unlike its neighbours, the pneumatic building had no granite plinth outside, no brass plate announcing the names of the concerns inside. Perhaps they had yet to get around to erecting one? A lot of new towers had gone up after Quatérshift's invasion of Jackals a few years back; half the city had been left burning after Jackals' aerial navy had been turned against her own capital in an unspeakable act of treachery.

Inside, the atrium was polished marble, tall men in ornate frock coats waiting as if they were the sentries outside parliament. Each doorman held a bulldog on a leash, the creatures' black noses swollen to the size of a tomato. The canines had been twisted – either by worldsinger sorcery or by the even more disrerutable hands of womb mages.

'Damson Harsh,' said one of the doormen. 'Please do come in. We have been expecting you.'

Amelia looked down at the bulldog sniffing suspiciously around her ankles.

'You have discharged a firearm recently, damson?'

'That's Professor Harsh, and I may have been smoked by a little blow-barrel sap last month. Who owns this tower?'

'A man of wealth, professor,' said the doorman, 'and taste.' He took out a gutta-percha punch card on a chain, walked over to the other end of the atrium, and pushed the card into a transaction engine mounted on the wall. Drums clicked and rotated on the steam-powered calculating machine. A shiny copper door drew back, revealing a lifting room larger than the lounge of Amelia's lodgings back in Crisparkle Street.

The large doorman indicated the lifting room. 'Please, professor.'

Amelia stepped into the room and pointed down at the bulldog. 'Can your pup smell out the edge on a dagger too?'

'Of course not, professor.' He winked and indicated one of the other bulldogs. 'That's his job.'

Amelia looked at herself in the lifting room's mirror. The yellow gaslight made her face look pale; she had still not recovered from the dehydration she had endured fleeing Cassarabia. There was no way around it, she looked like a mess and she could not imagine who in Jackals would possibly want to offer her a job now – Circle's teeth, she would not offer herself a job if she had walked into her old study back at the college.

After the lifting room had silently pulled itself as high as it was going to rise, its doors slid open. Amelia found herself facing three women who could have been sisters of the lady she had met in the college grounds. Hard, beautiful faces inspecting her, weighing her up. Calculating how difficult it would be to bring her down.

'Good morning, ladies,' said Amelia. 'Would you care to sniff my legs, too?'

'There are few academics who stroll the streets of Middlesteel carrying weapons,' said one of the guards, a scar across her cheek creasing as she talked. That strange accent again. All these whippers had lived in Jackals long enough for it to dwindle to a faint burr.

Amelia noted how one of the women opened the door for her, while the other two not-so-subtly positioned themselves behind her, just outside her field of vision. 'Weapons? Just a sharp mind, today. Is all this really necessary?'

'I believe so,' said scar-face. 'You have, after all, threatened to kill our employer.'

Amelia's eyes narrowed when she saw who was waiting for her inside the room. *Him.*

'So I have.'

'You made the threat at your father's funeral,' said Abraham Quest, 'as I recall.'

'Just a fourteen-year-old girl speaking. I imagine you must have been reading the obituaries very closely back then,' said Amelia. 'How many suicides did you cause that year?'

'None at all, professor. Suicide is caused when you place a gun to your temple and pull the trigger in a misguided attempt to cleanse the stain on your family's honour. The pistol is not the cause, and the course of your life is not an excuse for it. If you take a walk in Goldhair Park you must expect that sometimes it will rain and sometimes it will be sunny. It is no good whining when you get wet. You cannot control the weather; all you can control is how you feel about getting soaked. If you do not wish to get wet, you should avoid taking the walk in the first place.'

'It wasn't a shower that bloody bankrupted my father,' said Amelia, thrusting a finger towards Quest. 'It was you.'

'Everyone who places money on the Sun Gate Commercial Exchange knows their capital is at risk. That is what speculation is all about. The possibility of gains, or losses. I did nothing illegal. I merely leveraged my own wit to play the game significantly better than everyone else at the table.'

'I understand the exchange feels rather differently,' said Amelia. 'Which is why you and any factor who works for you has been banned for life from setting foot in the building again.'

'Mere petulance on their part,' said Quest. He turned to gaze out over a commanding view of the towers and spires of Middlesteel. 'It was not that I was a better player than the other members of the exchange that saw me disbarred, it was their *cupidity* – that I would not explain to them the predictive models I had set running on my transaction engines. They had not even realized it was possible to use a transaction engine in such a way and it does not matter how many engine men and cardsharps they buy in – they will never be able to reengineer my achievements. I showed them how unbearably dull they all are, and they will never forgive me for parading their ignorance in front of the nation.'

Amelia could not believe the sheer arrogance of the man. Abraham Quest, the only man in the history of Jackals to have a financial crash named after him. He had walked away from the table with all the chips and damn near shut down the whole financial gaming house in the process.

She screwed up the piece of paper that had led her here and threw it down on his expensive Cassarabian rug. 'That's what I think of your job offer, Quest. I'm off to join a dig along the Mechancian Spine.'

'Don't walk out of the door,' said Quest. 'At least, not until you see what I have uncovered. It appears we may disagree as to where responsibility for our personal choices rests, but believe me when I say I am truly sorry that your father lost his seat in parliament after he was declared bankrupt. I feel even sadder that he felt he had so little to live for that he took the so-called path of honour. When he was alive, I know he supported the Camlantean heresy – perhaps it is only fitting that it should be the House of Quest that helps you take a few steps closer to the lost city.'

Camlantis. 'What do you know about the city, Quest?'

'A few things that you won't find in the musty journals circulating around the College of Saint Vine's,' said Quest. 'Such as where the city is – or should I say, where the city was.'

'I don't believe—'

'Please,' said Quest, opening a door at the side of his office. 'See for yourself.'

Whoever had installed the reader knew what they were about. The hexagonal crystal-book sat in a snare of cables and wires, bubbling chemical batteries supplying the power electric – the wild energy. Quest must have hired colleagues Amelia had worked with to set up his apparatus. It was a rare skill, handling crystal-books; his mechomancers could not have worked this out for themselves.

'You have one,' whispered Amelia. 'You really do have a working crystal-book.'

'Not just any book,' said Quest. 'This is no ledger of raw trade data or random collection of personal poetry. This book belonged to one of the greatest Camlantean philosophers, one of the ruling librarians – Pairdan. He knew the Black-oil Horde was over-running their empire's provinces one by one. His story was inscribed on the crystal towards the end of their civilization.'

'This is *priceless*,' gasped Amelia. 'This could change everything we know about the Camlanteans.'

'Oh, the book had a price, professor,' said Quest. 'Believe me. One that made even myself think twice before paying it.'

'Why do you care about Camlantis?' demanded Amelia. 'This is my life's work – but for you? What is this? A minor distraction, in between raking in more money than the Greenhall treasury takes from the nation in a year's taxes?'

'It is ideas that truly interest me, professor. Concepts that fascinate me. Sadly, it must be admitted, more than people ever have. The legends say the Camlanteans had the perfect civilization. That they lived together in peace for centuries – lived in a society that had abolished hunger, poverty and violence. What lessons could we learn from their lives, what lessons?'

'That pacifists should build bigger walls to keep their enemies out,' said Amelia. 'Where did you get this crystal-book, Quest?'

'An antique dealer spotted it being used as a doorstop in a bakery in Lace Lane, sewn into a leather bag. The baker had taken it from his grandmother's cottage when she died and had no idea of its true worth. Unfortunately for myself, the dealer had all his wits about him when it came to placing an accurate value on the crystal-book.'

Amelia ran her fingers along the crystal-book's cold surface. 'You can't keep this here, Quest. Not even you. It has to be studied.'

'And so it shall be, but not by those dullards at the High Table for whom the existence of a functioning Camlantean society is tantamount to archaeological heresy. You know what they would do with this artefact as well as I do. They would bury the book in the vaults of Middlesteel Museum and take it out once a year for a good polish.'

'You want me to study it?'

'More than that . . . watch.' Quest walked over to the chemical drums and threw an activation lever, tiny sparks leaping from the wires coiled around the base of the book. With a green nimbus enveloping the crystal, a finger of light crept from the jewel's surface, fanning out in front of them like mist. The light resolved into an image of a man. He was speaking, but could not be heard – script scrolling up the air to the right of him.

'This is Pairdan you see here, professor, the last Reader-Administrator of Camlantis.'

Amelia barely heard Quest. She was following the ancient characters crawling up the air while simultaneously trying to watch Pairdan. How old was he? Thirty, perhaps? Young for such an elevated position of power. Pairdan's head moved to one side, his crown with a single jewel at its centre glinting from the fury of the fires outside, and Amelia saw what he was looking at. Pairdan's city was ablaze in the distance, fire-balls of burning petrol-soaked straw and tar arcing across from the catapults mounted on the Black-oil Horde's besieging war wagons. The juxtaposition between the communication crystals turning sedately in the high towers of Camlantis's ethereal spires and the pure animal carnage of the horde was almost too much for Amelia to bear, even with the passage of so many thousands of years. It was as if it was happening now, to one of Jackals' own cities.

'Poor Pairdan,' said Quest. 'Watch the sadness in the Reader-Administrator's eyes. He is gazing upon the end of his world, and you can tell that he knows it. The start of a dark age that lasted until the rise of the Chimecan Imperium.'

'Quiet.' Amelia was trying to keep up with the scrolling words. 'I need to concentrate. He is saying something about a plan.'

Quest moved the reader's control lever up a notch and the image froze in front of them, the bubbling of the vat filling the room with its rotten-egg stench. Amelia started to protest but Quest waved her to silence. 'The translator I hired lacked your proficiency, professor, but I already have the gist of the story.' Quest pointed to a high mountain in the image's distance and the stars glittering above, frozen in aspic and lost in time. 'This mountain is the key, Amelia. The glaciers passed it by during the coldtime. It hasn't changed that much over the ages.'

'You really do know where Camlantis is!' cried Amelia.

'Where its foundations were. As best as we can tell, Pairdan's plan was to deny the city to the Black-oil Horde. It was no random floatquake that destroyed Camlantis, professor.'

Amelia was dumbstruck by the implications. Among the few scholars who treated the Camlantean legends with any respect, Amelia knew the speculation had always been that after the city had been sacked, and the librarian-sorcerers murdered, there had been no one left alive to drain the flows of the world's energy and it was struck by a floatquake. The worldsingers' first duty was to tame the leylines that could rip miles of land from the ground and send it spinning up into the cold night. The order of worldsingers mastered the power of the Earth and used it to fuel their sorcery and rituals.

When civilizations fell, when order broke down, the incidence of floatquakes, volcanic eruptions and earthquakes striking the land also proliferated; that was an undeniable fact.

'Then the Camlanteans destroyed their own city.' Amelia could hardly believe her own conclusions.

'The barbarians weren't fools,' said Quest. 'The horde did not want to burn Camlantis to the ground out of pique or envy. They wanted control of the city of marvels for their own ends. They would have strapped the librarians to their wagons as slaves. With Camlantean power at their disposal, the Wheel Lords would have swept effortlessly across every kingdom of their age. I can imagine no worse fate for a society of pacifists, can you? Turned into grovelling court wizards for a pack of murderous warlords. Watching while the horde tied the children of their conquered subjects behind their wagons, dragging them to bloody ribbons over gravel in their honour races. Abetting in the sack of cities other than their own.'

Amelia looked at the noble frozen image of the Reader-Administrator. 'Poor man. Poor Pairdan.'

'Think of it, professor.' Quest walked towards a porthole-like window cut into his pneumatic tower's rubber walls. 'Somewhere in the heavens Camlantis is still spinning around the world. Not a sacked ruin of marble and stone, but intact, its empty streets a home for nesting eagles and the dust of Pairdan's hopes. That is your dream too, is it not?'

Damn his eyes. Quest knew it was. 'You said you know where the city was located, before the floatquake?'

'And the reason why its ruined foundations have never been discovered.' Quest led her back to a table in his office where one of his Catosian soldiers had unfurled a map. His finger hovered over a large swathe of territory, most of it coloured black for the unknown and the unexplored. 'Liongeli.'

Amelia looked askance at the featureless, uncharted expanse. A jungle hell without end. An environment so forbidding that only distant cousins of the race of man such as the shell-armoured craynarbians could make their home there. 'Your geographers must have made a mistake, Quest. All the ancient texts suggest that the location of Camlantis should lie far further north. My best guess is somewhere north of the Catosian League, or perhaps buried beneath the pampas of Kikkosico. It may even be underneath the wastes controlled by the polar barbarians.'

Quest shook his head. 'Trust me, Amelia. I have established my place in the world by following my contrarian instincts. Would it surprise you to learn that yours is not the only academic heresy I have been following? In matters of continental geography, there is a hypothesis currently proscribed by the High Table that posits our entire world may have shifted its position many times in the past, with north exchanging its position with south and the whole skin of the world sliding in upheaval. Earthquakes, floatquakes, fire and brimstone. You are correct, professor, in a manner of speaking. The foundations of Camlantis *are* further north – it is just that further north is now further south by seven hundred miles.'

How could that be true? Was their world so flimsy? But if it was, if it was . . .

'All those years scrabbling about the pampas,' said Amelia, the enormity of Quest's words sinking in, 'petitioning the God-Emperor of Kikkosico for just one more set of travel papers for just one more province. We weren't even searching for the city in the right country!'

Quest rolled out a second, more detailed map of Liongeli. A private trader's map, no doubt very expensive to obtain. Depressingly large areas of the jungle vastness were still left unmarked on it. 'But your instincts were correct, Amelia. The city is no myth. It is – was – here!' He tapped the source of the River Shedarkshe, a vast lake-like crater that fed the mightiest watercourse known to Jackelian cartographers. 'When the city was uprooted and blown into the sky by the Camlantean sorcerers it left a basin, one that was filled by rain and sink water. It's an inland sea now, called Lake Ataa Naa Nyongmo.'

Amelia shook her head in amazement. It was as if the Midwinter gift-giving by Mother White Horse had arrived early; a whole track of lost history opening up for her. It all made sense now. Why her digs had been so damned fruitless. The world had changed and changed again. What had once been a paradise with gentle weather systems now lay buried under a jungle.

'You can see for yourself in some of the other crystal-book recordings. Pairdan talks to a council of his people about building up the currents of earthflow, ready to crack the land and lift their city away from the horde.'

'Are there any clues to where the remains of Camlantis are floating now?'

Quest shook his head. 'Sadly, no, but there are hints that the location of the city might be inscribed on other crystal-books, buried as a time-capsule for their descendents, along with blueprints of their greatest marvels. I am hopeful the ruined foundations may contain clues to Camlantis's current location.'

'No airship crew has ever reported sighting Camlantis,' said Amelia. 'It has always been my belief that our aerostats cannot yet travel high enough to spot it.'

'That is a failing I am planning to remedy. I have my airwrights constructing a fleet of high-lifters, airships that will be capable of travelling into the thinnest atmosphere – so high we might touch the moons themselves.'

'You've been reading too much celestial fiction,' said Amelia.

'Imagination, professor. With imagination anything is possible. You imagined a lost city where everyone else saw only myth and an absence of evidence. The first step to achieving any task is imagining that it may be possible. Without such belief you would never begin your journey and would only follow your doubts to failure.'

'The RAN won't authorize a goose chase of this magnitude,' said Amelia. 'Not even for the great Abraham Quest.'

'What the Board of the Admiralty does not know, will not hurt them. Your task is to travel into Liongeli and find me the location of the city in the heavens. I shall provide us with the means to journey up to its airless temples and streets.'

She looked at the featureless anonymity of Liongeli on the map. The heart of darkness. Her expedition would need to travel further into the interior of the jungle than anyone had ever ventured to date.

'Have you squirrelled away enough celgas from the navy to make an airship flight to Liongeli?'

Quest shook his head. 'I might be able to land you at the foot of the Shedarkshe by aerostat, but not any further. The source of the river is in the heart of Daggish territory. The greenmesh. They would burn any trespassing Jackelian airship out of the sky with their flame cannons.'

Amelia sucked in her breath. She had enough craynarbian friends to have heard their tales of the terror of Liongeli. The greenmesh. A territory of animals and vegetation merged into a deadly living symbiosis of evil. The Daggish might be called an empire, considered a polity, but it was really an ancient hive, evolved out of the fierce fight for resources at the jungle's deep interior into something alien and brooding. At best, outsiders were just rogue cells to be absorbed into its co-operative. At worst they were enemies to be slain on sight.

Quest must be insane. Her expedition would need to do their work on the bed of Lake Ataa Naa Nyongmo, carry out sensitive underwater archaeology while trying to remain undetected by creatures that would rip them apart merely for the crime of violating their realm.

'If the city's foundations are on Daggish territory I don't think it can be done,' said Amelia. 'There must be another way to uncover the location of Camlantis in the heavens?'

'Whatever remains of their civilization on earth is under the waters of this lake.' Quest paced up and down, his arms waving as he became animated. 'The legends speak of a million people in Camlantis, close to a million citizens who sacrificed their lives so their legacy could not be perverted by the barbarian hordes of their age. Think of the absolute courage of such an act, blowing your own home into the heavens, a slow death of cold and airlessness for yourself and your friends and your family, rather than turning away from your ideals of pacifism. You could spend a lifetime futilely attending digs in Mechancia, Kikkosico, Cassarabia, hoping to find some clue in a trader's journal or a refugee's crystal-book as to where they sent their city.' His finger stabbed down on Liongeli. 'This is the mother lode. That it is now underwater close to the shores of a Daggish city in the jungle's heart is an accident of geography we must overcome.'

'Underwater,' mused Amelia. Then she grinned. 'How much money do you really want to spend on this expedition, Quest?'

'To unlock the secrets of the ancients, to give Jackals a chance of living in the prosperity and peace of the Camlantean age? How much money do you require?'

Amelia explained her plan.

Veryann watched the professor of archaeology leave the tower. 'She is almost as mad as you are, Abraham Quest.'

'Mad? No. Inspired,' said Quest. 'Her plan is quite inspired. Did you know she studied under Hull? The very fellow who translated the Camlantean language and worked out how the crystal-books could be activated.'

'If he were alive, I suppose you would also hire him for your expedition.'

'Yes, I suppose I would,' said Quest.

'Still, for all her cleverness, her *inspiration*, you did not show the professor the images from the second crystal-book of the pair you purchased.'

'The contents of the second crystal-book would disturb her,' said Quest. 'I prefer to keep Amelia's faith pure, unwavering.'

'Yes, I imagine the images would disturb her,' said Veryann. 'Your ideals have too high a risk attached to them. Paradise is not to be made on Earth.'

'It was made here once.' Quest stood in front of one of the large portholes, listening to the gurgle of water moving through his pneumatic tower. He pointed towards the sky. 'And the secret to unlocking it all again is hidden up there.'

Smike did not know what to make of the old fellow. It was not often a blind man would venture into the rookeries of Rottonbow. What would someone wearing heavy grey robes in the manner of a Circlist monk be doing wandering one of Middlesteel's most dangerous districts this late at night? Smike listened to the patter of the gnarled old cane, tapping along the cobbles of the lane between the ancient, tumbledown towers.

For a moment Smike considered letting the old twit keep on wandering deeper into Rottonbow, but even with his limited conscience, he could not do that. Smike skipped to catch up. The sightless visitor looked like an old man, but he was spry for his years.

'Grandfather,' called Smike, 'wait. Do you know where you're going?'

'Why yes, I do,' said the blind man, his face concealed by his hood and the night. 'I am heading for Furnival's Wark.'

Smike sucked on his mumbleweed pipe. 'Old fellow, there's nothing down there but the paupers' graveyard.'

'Yes, I believe an old friend of mine is resting there.'

'Hang on, grandfather, do you know what hour it is?'

'For me it is always night,' chortled the man in the robes.

'It'll be the long night for you, grandfather.' Smike tugged at the visitor's robes. 'You'll get yourself in the soup so you will, tap-tapping with your cane along these avenues. There's some right old bludgers lurking around Rottonbow. They'd think nothing of sinking a blade in your ribs and emptying your pockets.'

'But I have so little to steal,' said the visitor, 'now that you have taken my money.' The visitor's cane darted out and spun his lifted purse back out of the folds of Smike's tattered jacket. Like the tongue of a toad, a gnarled cold hand snaked out, catching the leather bag and concealing it under his robes again.

Smike stepped back, coughing on his mumbleweed pipe in shock. 'You can't blame a lad for trying, now, can you? Are you *really* blind, governor?'

'Oh yes,' the robed figure chortled. 'The eyes are the first thing to go. The treatment preserves everything else, but not the eyes.'

Smike glanced around nervously. He had thought this blind old fool was prey. But he was mad, or something very close to it.

'Down in the paupers' graveyard, have they held the funeral for Sixrivets yet?'

'The steamman?' said Smike. 'There's not much of his body

left in the graveyard, grandfather. After Sixrivets died, the state coroner sent his soul-board back to King Steam's mountains like the law requires. The rest of the old steamer was so old, the king didn't even want Sixrivets' iron bones back to recycle.'

'But the funeral, it has been held?'

'Yesterday. His friends from Steamside came over and sung in their strange voices – the machine tongue. Even though Sixrivets wanted to be buried down here, rather than over in Steamside, they still came.'

'They would come,' said the old man. 'Steammen never forget their own. Now, be off with you.'

Smike darted into an alley, then stopped. A thought had occurred to him. The strange old goat's interest in Sixrivets' corpse. He was a grave robber! Middlesteel's mechomancers often raided the graves and corpses of the race of steammen, prying the secrets of their architecture from their rusting crystals and decaying cogs. Sixrivets had been so ancient and obsolete that the denizens of Dwerrihouse Street had thought it safe to honour the steamman's last wish and inter him with the rest of their people down the road. But this sightless old man must be desperate, on his downers. No wonder he was wandering around at night in one of the least salubrious parts of the capital. He was about his filthy trade.

Smike stuck his head around the corner and watched the figure shuffling towards the graveyard. Smog was drifting across the cobbled streets – the miasma of industry, the currents of the capital's factories, workshops and manufactories. The blind devil had a bleeding cheek, so he did. Sixrivets was one of their own. They said the steamman had been old enough to see the clatter of steel and puff of gun smoke as the royalist guardsmen and the new pattern army clashed on the streets of Middlesteel during the civil war, six hundred years back.

Generations of Dwerrihouse Street's children had come and gone while Sixrivets pottered about Rottonbow's lanes. Who was this sightless goat to come and dig him out of their dirt and strip pieces off his body for souvenirs? Smike considered shouting for some of the others, but the canny old prowler might hear him and be off into the night, to return when no one was abroad. Best to watch and wait, catch him in the act, then raise the alarm.

Smike crept past the shadows of the old rookeries, his bare feet numb against the chill of the smog-cold cobbles. At the iron gates of the graveyard – two Circlist eels cast as wheels consuming their own tails – Smike heard voices whispering. He rubbed his eyes and searched for the corner plot where Sixrivets had been buried. Two shadows were there, digging. Neither of them were the old man, though. They were too big for a start. Their voices sounded familiar, too.

Smike slipped into the graveyard and used the cover of the tombs to get closer to the men. He heard the crunch of hard dirt being tossed back and a low cursing growl.

'Can you see the body yet?'

'It's in here somewhere.'

'I can see the head. The rest of it is coming. Keep at it, carefully now, don't break anything.'

'Break anything? Just me back, mate, just me back. This ain't clay we're digging through here, you know?'

Smike's eyes widened. No wonder the voices sounded familiar. It was two of the Catgibbon's bludgers – thugs that worked for the flash mob, and not just any gang either. The Catgibbon was the queen of the underworld in Middlesteel. They said she held the guardians and half the police of the capital in one pocket, while she kept a good share of the magistrates, doomsmen and other court functionaries in the other. Smike did not know this pair's names, but they were a familiar sight in the daytime, knocking up pennies with not-so-subtle insinuations of what happened to shop owners who didn't pay their 'fire and accident' money.

Smike was wondering where the sightless old prowler had got to, when a figure emerged from the mist behind the bludgers.

'Good evening, gentlemen. A cold night for it.'

Startled, they whirled around, one holding his spade ready like an axe, the other dropping his sack and pulling a pistol out from his coat pocket.

'He's not the police.'

'Course he isn't a crusher; he can't even see. Look at his cane.'

'Away with you, blind eyes,' said the one pointing the pistol. 'This body is ours.'

'That body belongs to Sixrivets, surely,' said the old prowler. 'And what use do you have for one of the people of the metal, now his ancient soul has passed into the great pattern?'

The spade man pulled out an evil-looking dagger. 'Let's do him silent, before he has half of Rottonbow up out of their beds and onto us.'

Spade man jumped across the open grave, but the old prowler had moved, moved faster than anything alive had a right to. The leaping bludger continued his motion; the top half of his body hitting a tombstone while his severed legs tumbled down across the opened grave. His colleague tried to trigger his pistol, but then it dawned on him he was holding a handle only, the other half of the weapon with the chambered crystal charge severed and falling down towards the dirt.

The old man had his legs in a fighter's position with a silver sword turning in the air, tracing a pattern like calligraphy in the smog, before returning it gracefully to his cane sheath.

Smike was about to run – this had all become a little too rich for his simple tastes – when he stepped on a branch, its snap sounding like a cannon shot even to his ears. The blind man moved his head slightly, evaluating the potential threat and choosing to ignore it, then pushed the tip of his cane in front of the frozen bludger's face. 'What does the Catgibbon want with ancient steamman body parts?'

Rather than answer, the terrified thug turned and sprinted across the graveyard.

'Ah well,' said the old man, staying put. 'I doubt you knew much, anyway. Breaking the fingers of anyone sticking their nose into one of your rackets, that's what your kind knows best.' He announced to the air: 'And why don't you come out from behind there, now? I want to thank you for all your help.'

'I was just keeping myself in reserve, grandfather,' said Smike. 'Always good to have someone watching your back. You seemed to be doing well enough against the two of them.'

'For an old blind man, you mean?'

'That's a good one,' said Smike. 'You're not really blind, are you? That's just a bit of grift to get people to underestimate you. You're good though, all that tapping you do with your cane. I couldn't tell from watching you.'

'I believe I gave you the answer to that question a minute ago, but I can see there's no fooling you, young fellow.'

'Did you know Sixrivets, grandfather? Were you protecting an old friend?'

'Something like that.'

Smike pointed to the opened grave, the steamman's remains keeping company with the two halves of the dead thug's body. 'What did the flash mob's lads want with Sixrivets' corpse, then?'

'I was hoping you might know the answer to that question.'

Smike shook his head. 'Not me, mate.'

'Pity. Well, I have my suspicions. But they are not for sharing.' The old man picked up the criminal's fallen sack, climbed into the grave and began to fill it with the rusted parts of the entombed steamman. When he had finished he pulled himself out and passed the sack to Smike.

Smike looked at the sack in disgust. 'What do you want me to do with this?'

'I'm sure you're not completely unacquainted with the means of concealing ill-gotten gains.' He produced two silver sovereigns. 'One of these is for hiding Sixrivets' body parts some place the flash mob will not be able to lay their hands on the old steamer. Please don't just toss the sack in the river, Sixrivets deserves better than that, and if that is what I desired, I could throw him in the Gambleflowers myself and save the cost of a sovereign.'

'And the other coin?'

'For carrying a message to someone who can help clear up this mess. You must tell them what you saw this night, and you must memorize what I am about to tell you.'

Smike listened intently to what the old man had to say. Those two shining coins were more than he usually managed to steal in a couple of months.

When the old man had finished relaying the message and answered most of Smike's queries to his satisfaction, the lad concluded by asking the obvious question. 'How do you know I won't just pocket your two coins and do a runner?'

'Firstly, because I will find you and remind you of a bargain badly made. Secondly, because when I return from my business I shall pass you another coin to befriend the two now warming your pocket.'

'But you don't even know where I live . . .' said Smike.

The old goat tapped the side of his nose. 'The musk of cheap mumbleweed? I shall find your lodgings. Even if you *move*. You will have to be patient for your third coin, though. I may be away some time, as my business will be taking me out of the capital for a little while.'

Smike waited until the blind old man had disappeared into the smog, the tapping of his cane against the gravestones fading to nothing, before he gathered the courage to bite into the silver sovereigns. The coins were real enough. Smike looked at the two halves of the Catgibbon's enforcer spilled across the grave that had been opened. Time to be off, in case the crimelord's blades came back in force.

The coins vanished back into the pickpocket's jacket and he slung the sack over his shoulder. '*Carry a message for me, boy. Hide Sixrivets for me, boy.* What does he think I am, a bleeding postman or a bleeding undertaker?'

But conceal the body and carry the message he would. Out of fear . . . and for the promise of another silver sovereign.

Professor Amelia Harsh nodded politely to the steamman pushing a flattening-roller across the lawn, a little iron goblin with a single telescope-like eye. It nodded back at her. The drone was not intelligent enough to enter directly into conversation with Amelia, but it would no doubt pass on word of her arrival back to the central consciousness that controlled it.

Amelia walked along the gravel path and looked up at the tower, a large clockface dominating the upper storey of the building. Tock House showed little sign of the ravages of war now, but it had been left in quite a state after the invasion of Middlesteel. Attacked, burnt, then finally occupied and looted by the shifties. Amelia knew she was lucky that she had been out in the counties in Stainfolk when Quatérshift's vicious Third Brigade had seized Jackals' capital; but she had counted as friends those who had lived here – and one of them, sadly, had not been as fortunate as she had. Amelia had helped the current tenants of Tock House search for Silas Nickleby's body in the undercity, but they had not even found enough of his corpse to bury out in the orchard.

Before Amelia got to the pair of stone lions flanking the stairs to the tower, the house's door pulled back, revealing a flame-haired young woman waiting to greet her. Amelia stuck out her over-sized hand to meet the pale, slim palm extended towards her.

'Professor Harsh, it has been too long. I heard about you losing your position at the college, but you weren't at your lodgings when I called on you.'

'I've been out and about, kid, you know me. So where did you hear that piece of scurrilous gossip?'

'A mutual friend,' said Molly Templar. 'One who works in the engine rooms at Greenhall.'

'That weasel Binchy? I'm surprised he's still talking to you after what happened to him during the invasion.'

Molly shrugged and led Amelia into the comfortable hallway of Tock House. 'Once a cardsharp, always a cardsharp. He's got nothing better to do than set his punch cards to work on the drums of Greenhall's engines. He's probably keeping tabs on all of us. Do you need money, professor, to finance your work?'

'My work always needs money, kid, but not from the likes of you.'

'You saved my life, professor, and whatever problems I have now, thankfully money is not one of them.'

'Yes, that much I figured,' said Amelia. 'I read your last novel, Molly, along with most of the rest of Jackals.'

'Just so that you know,' said Molly, 'the offer is always there if you need it.'

'Borrow money from your enemies. Never from your friends or family. That's an old Chimecan proverb. No, I've come to call on the old sea dog, if he's around?'

Molly took her along a sweeping staircase. 'The commodore is up with Aliquot Coppertracks. He has been helping the old steamer all week on his latest obsession.'

Amelia nodded. The enthusiasms of the steamman genius that shared Tock House's rooms with Molly and the commodore were never anything other than wholly committed. Coppertracks' laboratory resided alongside the clock mechanism of the tower's top floor. Sometimes it was hard to see where the cogs and parts of the clock house began and the rotating, twisting, chemical-misting mess of the steamman's research ended. Aliquot Coppertracks rolled across the floorboards, his transparent skull ablaze with the fizz of mental energies, drones – the mu-bodies of his expanded consciousness – scurrying about their steamman master, closely followed by Commodore Black. An oil-stained leather apron had replaced the submariner's usual waistcoat and jacket, and the bear-sized man was staggering under the weight of a crate of machinery.

'Ah, Aliquot. This is no work for a poor old fellow like me. Another box for hulking down to the woods.'

'Dear mammal,' said Coppertracks, 'the quicker we move this material to the woods the quicker we can begin work on the next stage of our project.'

The commodore saw Amelia standing with Molly and he stumbled across to them. 'Professor Harsh. Have you come to offer us the strength of your blessed muscled arms today? Coppertracks has us all building a mad temple to his genius out in our orchard. Most of Middlesteel would be pleased to grow apples and pears in their gardens, but we must labour on some damn fool tower for him.'

'Amelia softbody,' implored the steamman. 'As a fellow creature of learning you must talk some gumption into our recalcitrant friend. We are setting up a mechanism to detect vibrations across the aether. It is my contention that there are intelligences on the celestial spheres neighbouring our own world, and that they may wish to communicate with us should a suitable mechanism to commune with them be constructed.'

Amelia stepped aside as a couple of Coppertracks' iron goblins left the clock chamber with a heft of cable. 'Vibrations across the aether? I don't know, Aliquot, it sounds like you have been taking Molly's new fashion in novels a little too seriously.'

'Good for you, lass,' said the commodore, resting down his crate. 'The blessed voice of reason at last. I said this scheme was fit for nothing but the plot of a celestial fiction yarn when Aliquot started spending our precious few remaining coins on it.'

Amelia picked up the crate. 'I'll take this down to your orchard for you, Jared. You can listen to what I have to say, then tell me if I still sound like the voice of reason to you . . .'

'Liongeli,' spluttered the commodore in the shadow of a lashed-together tower of steel and crystals. 'Amelia, lass, it cannot be done. Nobody has ever navigated that far up the Shedarkshe before.'

'But the river is deep enough,' said Amelia. 'It's more like an inland sea along many stretches of the jungle.'

'Deep enough your river may be.' Black scratched nervously at his dark bushy beard. 'But there is a mighty fine reason why no u-boat or surface ship travels further east than the trading post at Rapalaw Junction. There's things biding in the jungle – in the river too – creatures that make the terrible beasts of the ocean I have faced look like so many pilchards on a plate.'

'There would be money, commodore, for mounting that kind of expedition.'

The commodore tapped the makeshift tower rising in Tock House's orchard. 'You can pile those guineas on my grave, lass. I will be staying here and helping Coppertracks build his mad tower to send messages out to the angels. The last time I listened to you, we both ended up being chased across the pampas of Kikkosico by those devils from the god-emperor's legions while trying to avoid the rebel army. I just need a few years to rest my mortal bones now. Good hearty food and a bottle of warm wine before I turn in for the night, that's enough excitement for me.'

'Just give me a day to change your mind, you old dog,' said Amelia. 'You owe me that much.'

'I'll give you your day,' said Commodore Black. 'But you might as well take a year, lass. Blacky's mind is not for changing anymore, not when it comes to putting my neck on the block for more fool adventures.'

Amelia smiled and produced two elegant-looking punch cards from her jacket.

'And what would those two be now, professor?'

'Boarding passes for an airship running out of Maydon Statodrome,' said Amelia. 'We're going for a day trip to Spumehead.'

Spumehead harbour lay crowded with the craft of commerce resting on the waters, as befitted the largest port on the west coast of Jackals. There was a familiar comfort to the sight. Commodore Black watched the clipper sails billowing as they turned to avoid cumbersome paddle steamers heading out for the colonies. Some of the larger vessels sailed in convoy, the shadow of RAN aerostats dark on the waves as the aerial navy escorted their merchants out through the pirate runs of the Adelphi Straits. Black's keen eye spotted the white trails of underwater boats tracing past the stone Martello towers guarding the harbour fortifications. He sighed as a submarine broke the surface next to a line of tramp freighters, ugly triple-hulled affairs designed to bypass the Garurian Boils and the dangerous tracts of the Fire Sea.

The commodore looked across at Amelia, her pocket book unusually flush with banknotes to spend on two expensive airship berths to the coast. His suspicious hackles had been prickled. 'I know a fine jinn house nearby, lass, if you have brought us here to feed and water poor old Blacky in an attempt to sign him up for your perilous enterprise. But I will warn you again, it'll take more than a sniff of salt down by the water of the harbour to make me find my sea legs.'

'Lunch later, Jared,' said Amelia. 'Whether you agree to skipper for me or not.'

'You seem blessed confident, professor.'

She led him down through the town, along quays covered with drying fishing nets, past traders wheeling barrows of food and victuals to vend off the skiffs plying the harbour. A large building had been built into the cliff at the opposite end of the harbour and a figure in a crimson-lined velvet cloak was standing by the iron gates of its entrance, waiting for them.

'Amelia,' the man greeted them, 'Commodore Black. I do not believe I have had the privilege before.'

With a start the old sea dog realized who he was looking at, that striking profile familiar from so many line-drawn cartoons in the capital's news sheets. 'Abraham Quest! Now

I know why the professor's pockets are suddenly fat with jingling pennies. What is this place, man, and what is your part in this fool enterprise of Amelia's to sail into uncharted Liongeli?'

'These are the Spumehead submarine pens,' said Quest. 'The House of Quest's submarine pens, to be precise. Amelia has led me to believe that you might be familiar with them.'

'Pah,' said the commodore. 'An independent skipper ties up on the surface and pays day-labour to scrape the barnacles off his hull, not your expensive grease monkeys. Are you here to offer me vast sums of money, Abraham Quest, to pay me to sail up the Shedarkshe? It's a one-way trip, I can tell you that.'

'Yes,' said Quest. 'I did rather assume that you still had enough of the treasure of the *Peacock Herne* left in the ledgers of the capital's counting houses to make any financial inducements I might offer you seem of limited appeal.'

The commodore and Amelia followed Quest through the mountain-carved passages of the submarine pens, into a gas-lit chamber, the flicker of large triple-headed lamps illuminating dry docks and water pens. Rows of underwater craft were being hammered and repaired by sturdy-looking jacks in leather aprons.

'You've been reading up on me,' said the commodore. 'But then, it must take a mortal clever mind to keep all this industry of yours ticking over.'

Quest seemed pleased at being flattered, although with his wealth, the mill owner should have been well-used to it. 'Clever enough to notice the discrepancies on your citizenship record, commodore. But the professor here believes you are the best skipper for our expedition, and I have come to trust her judgement in such things.'

Quest took them into a side-chamber sealed off from the

other pens, and pulled on a chain, lamps hissing into life along a rock-hewn wall.

'Sweet mercy!' Commodore Black nearly choked. 'You have found her!'

Quest's hand swept along the black hull of the submarine that filled the chamber, a double-turreted conning tower built low towards the rear of the long u-boat. 'Handsome isn't she? *Now*. She was not quite so pretty when I found her, though, beached and broken on the shore of the Isla Needless in the heart of the Fire Sea. I doubt there has ever been a recovery operation more difficult or more dangerous, but Amelia did so insist. I still don't know why. She could have had her pick of the u-boats built by my own yards . . . modern craft.'

'The *Sprite of the Lake*,' said the commodore, wiping the tears from his cheeks. 'Oh my beauty, my gorgeous girl. I thought you had died on the other side of the world.'

'According to the laws of salvage, I think you will find she is currently *my* beauty,' said Quest. 'And believe me, she had died. With the money I spent on repairing and refitting this damn craft, I could have paid for new boats for half of the free traders running from Spumehead to Hundred Locks.'

'Refitting!' Commodore Black was outraged. 'The *Sprite of the Lake* is a classic. If you have ripped her soul out, you'll need more than Amelia's strong arms to drag me off your wicked corpse.'

Quest waved the submariner's protests away. 'I only hire the best, sir. My engineer for this project was Robert Fulton – I trust you are familiar with his work?'

'Fulton? Yes, I can see it in the lines of her hull, where the breach has been repaired. Those are Fulton lines. Old Bob himself; so, if there was ever a man to do justice to my girl . . .'

'Fulton seemed to feel the same way about the vessel as

yourself, commodore,' said Quest. 'He dated her as nearly six hundred years old. The last of the royalist war boats was his estimation, a Queen Belinda-class seadrinker. Rated for thirty knots and sixty torpedoes. Personally speaking, I would be tempted to make her next berth the maritime wing of Middlesteel Museum.'

Commodore Black pointed to a spherical bulb forward of the two conning towers. 'What in Lord Tridentscale's name is that carbuncle?'

'A bathysphere. We added it along with a new docking ring.' Quest looked over at Amelia. 'You haven't told him what we need the u-boat for?'

'I just told Jared about the expedition into Liongeli,' said Amelia. 'It seemed a little superfluous to mention the underwater archaeology at the end of the journey.'

'Mortal me,' wheezed Black. 'Amelia, you are not taking my beauty up that river of hell? Say it is not true. Has the *Sprite* not already gone through enough? Boiled under the waters of the Fire Sea, fired upon by the rogues of Porto Principe, hunted by the warships of the Holy Kikkosico Empire. You cannot take her into such peril again.'

'I am afraid we can, commodore,' said Amelia. 'That's why I need you to skipper her for the expedition.'

'You can go with the *Sprite of the Lake* as her master; her owner after you return safely from Lake Ataa Naa Nyongmo,' said Quest. 'Or I can get one of my own seadrinker skippers to take her up the Shedarkshe.'

'Oh, you rogues,' cried the commodore. 'Oh, you pair of pirates. Is that to be my choice? Damned to lose my own boat, or damned to pilot her into the mouth of hell itself?'

'You'll understand when you see what we are trying to find,' said Amelia. 'The difference it could make to the people of Jackals.'

'Jackals be damned, lass. What has Jackals done for me? Except to line up her greedy Greenhall bureaucrats with their claim on the treasure of the *Peacock Herne* and their hands grasping for every honest coin my intrepid ventures ever gained.'

Quest walked up to the nose of the *Sprite of the Lake* and tapped the dark hull under the shadow of her bowsprit, a female warrior thrusting a lance forward towards the cavern wall. 'I think Fulton did an exceptional job, all things considered.'

Black seemed to crumple in front of them. 'Damn your wicked cunning eyes, Quest. I'll do it. But on one condition: I will pick my own crew.'

'I would expect nothing less,' said Quest. 'Just as Amelia has free choice for her members of the expedition. There will be a complement of marines on board too, well-armed to fend off any difficulties you may encounter.'

Black nodded in acquiescence, turning his gaze to the beautiful craft. *His* craft. The wily mill owner did not have to say that the marines would also be there to ensure he did not just turn the *Sprite* around and head for the ocean.

Heads turned in the jinn house as the well-dressed lady walked in. She did not look like any of the usual drinkers in the Bernal's Bacon, where 'drunk for a ha'penny, dead drunk for two' was the usual maxim.

She adjusted her bonnet and set a path towards the bar through the rowdy crowd of navvies that had been renovating the capital's canal navigations. She looked down with distaste at the sawdust streaking her fashionable leather thigh-boots, then met the neutral gaze of the jinn-house owner.

'Small, medium or large?' He pulled out three sizes of glass from under the counter.

The unlikely-looking customer sniffed and opened her palm, placing a small purple flower on the counter. It was a purpletwist, the rare plant whose pollen was favoured by sorcerers. Snuff to enhance the power of the worldsong that burned through their bodies.

'Oh, ho, I see.' The man opened his bar counter and led her through a back room stacked with jinn barrels. He unlocked a door and indicated she should step through. 'This way, damson.'

'There's nothing here, fellow,' she protested. 'This is your back courtyard?'

'I don't need to know what occurs out here, damson,' said the jinn keeper. 'You just wait a minute now.'

He shut the door and the woman looked around in disapproval. The clatter of a mill doing night work drifted over the yard's tall walls, the shadows of the shambling towers of the Middlesteel rookeries hiding the broken bottles and rubbish strewn over the mud.

A fluttering noise made her turn. There was a lashlite standing on the wall like a statue, the lizard creature's wings folded in. Behind her stood Furnace-breath Nick, his devilish mask staring accusingly at her.

'You have been asking a lot of questions,' he said, 'among the refugees. Trying to find me.'

She noticed the mask was changing his voice, making it sound inhuman. 'Many of those refugees owe their life to you. You saved them from the revolution, you brought them to Jackals from Quatérshift.'

'There are two types of people that come to stand in this yard,' said Furnace-breath Nick. 'There are the Quatérshift agents with gas guns in their pockets and daggers in their boots. And then there are those who need my help.'

'I don't have a dagger,' sobbed the woman. 'You are my

only remaining hope. I have spent my every last coin trying to get my father out of Quatérshift, but my resources have been stolen by traitors and squandered by tricksters.'

'Tell me of your family.'

'My father is Jules Robur, he was a member of the Sun King's court.'

'I have heard the name. He is a mechomancer?'

'An artificer,' said the woman. 'The greatest in Quatérshift, perhaps the greatest in the world. When the Sun King inspected the royal guard he rode a mechanical horse – a silver steed of my father's devising. When our armies clashed with the knights steammen on the border of the Free State it was always my father the king turned to first, to devise ways of fighting the people of the metal.'

'Yes,' said Furnace-breath Nick, 'I recall now. Robur made automen of such complexity that it was said King Steam himself was curious to see his methods of manufacture.'

'His finest creations had only one flaw,' said the woman. 'They were so life-like that when they realized they were created to be slaves, they went mad or shut themselves down. He had to create in the second-rate, below his talents, if he wanted his automen to last. You sound as if you are well acquainted with my land, sir?'

Furnace-breath Nick's cloak caught in the cold wind blowing across the yard, shifting as if it were part of his body. 'I have travelled there, damson. I have seen what has been done to it in the name of progress and the revolution.'

'Then you know,' cried the woman. 'You know they have my father in an organized community. In a *camp*. You know what happens in those places.'

'I know.' Furnace-breath Nick's altered voice hissed as if he was in pain. 'The First Committee has thrown every aristocrat they have yet to push into a Gideon's Collar into

73

such places. But of all the thousands who now labour and die in the camps, why should I single out your father for rescue?'

The woman seemed surprised by the question. 'Because he is a good man. Because I'm begging you. Because the First Committee have him there working on plans for revenge weapons to use against Jackals, and they will never release him, however many years he survives. His escape will hurt the revolution deeply.'

Furnace-breath Nick danced from foot to foot, his body twitching. The woman looked uneasily at the mad figure. How in the name of everything that was holy could she trust this creature with the task of saving the precious life of Jules Robur? He looked like one of the inmates in an asylum. Yet it was this madman who seemed able to cross the cursewall that sealed off Quatérshift from Jackals. This lunatic who moved across the revolution-wracked land like a will-o'-the-wisp, murdering Carlists and committeemen with impunity.

She opened her purse and proffered a white card, elegant copperplate script embossed on a stiff square of paper. 'This is my residence in Westcheap. You will accept my commission?'

Furnace-breath Nick took the card and sniffed it in a slightly obscene way. 'The property of a lady. If your father is alive, I shall find him.'

He walked along the wall, standing next to the silent, still lashlite.

'The Carlists,' called the woman. 'They've killed the Sun King, they've murdered most of my family and friends, stolen my lands and property, banned the worship of my god. All this they have done to me. But why do *you* hate them?'

'I don't hate them,' said Furnace-breath Nick. 'But I *shall* destroy them.'

The lashlite seized Furnace-breath Nick under the arms and lifted him corkscrewing into the night, leaving the lady alone with her fears. Her fears and the smell of stale jinn.

CHAPTER FOUR

'When you said you were going to pick your own crew,' said Amelia, 'I had imagined you would take the usual route and pin up a hiring notice outside the drinking houses of Spumehead.'

Commodore Black tapped his cane on the roof of the hansom cab, and there was a clatter of hooves outside as the horse drew to a stop. 'I want officers I have worked with, lass, and seadrinkers who have some knowledge of the rivers of Liongeli. Not the tavern sweepings of Jackals' ports; nor Quest's cautious house-men, for that matter.'

The cabbie jumped off his step behind the carriage and opened the door for them. Outside, the boulevards of Goldhair Park were still crowded with revellers despite – or perhaps, because of – the late hour. Women wore their finest shawls to warm themselves against the cold evening air, their escorts a sea of bobbing dark stovepipe hats.

'I was under the impression that you had buried most of your last crew on the Isla Needless after your boat was wrecked.'

'Don't speak of those terrible times, Amelia,' implored the

commodore. 'It was not the Fire Sea or the rocks around the island that did for my fine lads, it was the things on the island, along with the fever that near carried me away along the Circle's turn.'

Amelia looked about. They were at the west end of Goldhair Park's manicured gardens, near the gambling pits along the Tulkinghorn Road. 'What are you up to, Jared? The days when I needed to finance an expedition by betting on cock fights are behind me now.'

'Yes, there is you, flush with the jingle of that clever boy's coins in your pockets,' said the commodore. 'But it's a different sort of fight we have come to see tonight.'

A slight drizzle started to fall and promenading couples scattered for the trees and pavilions, parasols opening like flowers. Commodore Black took Amelia through a gate in the railing, towards the entrance of one of the brightly lit gambling pits. A grasper with a ruff of red fur poking out of his doorman's uniform admitted them with a nod towards the commodore. Inside, a narrow corridor led them to a large chamber where three separate seat-lined pits stood crowded with guests and gamblers. Lit by cheap-burning slipsharp oil, the top of the circular hall was lined with bars and food-serving hatches.

Amelia had to shout over the rumble of the crowds. 'I said I would help you find a crew, not a book-maker.'

One of the pits lay temporarily empty; while in the second a pair of snarling upland mountain cats circled each other, ignoring the roar of the crowd and the jabbing lances of their handlers. In the third pit a pair of men squatted, each trying to lift a heavier weight than his rival, dumbbells lined up in front of them in increasing size. Each of the muscle men was muttering a chant, trying to channel the capital's leylines and tap into the worldsong. It was a petty use of sorcery, for if either of the competitors had any real talent, they would have been admitted to the order of worldsingers and taken the purple robes.

Amelia followed the submariner down the steps to the empty pit, squeezing past the expectant Jackelians waiting there. At the end of the row, a female craynarbian sat next to a short old man with pale, staring eyes. The craynarbian appeared to recognize Jared Black, the clan patterns on her shell armour glimmering orange in the artificial light.

'A fine evening for it, is it not?' said the commodore.

'What ill tide has carried you in here?' asked the craynarbian woman, not bothering to hide the suspicion in her voice.

'Cannot a poor fellow go out for an evening's entertainment without his motives being impugned?' said the commodore. 'Although now you mention, I did recall hearing that the pair of you had blown in here with Gabriel.'

As the craynarbian glowered at the commodore, Amelia realized the short man next to her was blind.

'It's a mortal terrible thing,' Black told Amelia, 'the superstitious nature of submariners. You're on a boat that gets sunk by a pod of calfing slipsharps and you're one of the lucky ones that gets to a breather helmet and reaches the surface. Why, you'd think you'd thank your stars for your good fortune. But not a u-boat crew, no. Seadrinkers fear such people. Call them Jonahs. Shun them in case they put a hex on their screws or a curse on their air recyclers.'

'You should know all about keeping an unlucky boat, Jared Black,' said the blind man.

'Not so unlucky,' said the commodore. 'My beautiful *Sprite* might have taken a few bumps, but she saw me return safe to Jackals with the treasure of the *Peacock Herne* in my sea chest. But I can forgive you your waspish tongue. You see, professor, Billy Snow here is one of the finest phone-men this side of the west coast. With his old ears pressed up against a sonar trumpet he can tell you if it's a school of tuna or barracuda swimming a league beneath you, or listen to a slip-sharp's song and tell you if it be a cow or a bull.'

'Much good did it do when the pod attacked us,' said the craynarbian woman.

'Ah, but then if your last u-boat's skipper had decided to make a break for it rather than foolishly fighting it out, you would have been running away on the best-kept pair of expansion engines under the water, what with T'ricola's four sturdy arms to keep the boat humming and her pistons turning . . .'

Two figures stepped out onto the sawdust of the pit and the crowd around them hollered, the commodore's remaining words lost in the frenzy.

'Damsons and gentlemen—' announced the barker '—make your wagers now, before these two titans of pugilism engage in their noble art for your satisfaction, your delight, and, if the stars of fortune smile upon you, your profit!'

'And there is the third member of my trio of seadrinker artists,' said Black to Amelia.

'It is my privilege,' shouted the barker, 'nay, it is my *honour*, to give you Gabriel McCabe, the strongest man in Jackals.'

The light of the gambling pit glimmered off the giant's dark skin as he took an iron bar from the barker, bent it and tossed it with a clang onto the sawdust.

'He fits inside a submarine?' said Amelia.

'Lass, a first mate has to be able to crack a few heads together. Keeping order is a serious matter on a boat.'

'And facing this colossus from a legendary age, we have the most vicious fellow ever to step onto this floor . . . Club-handed Cratchit.'

Amelia did not fancy the chances of the commodore's friend.

The second pugilist had had his right arm twisted by the same back-street sorcerers that had given the professor her own over-sized arms. The bones of his right hand had been swollen and flowed into a massive anvil, an instrument of blunt force, muscles twisted into a corded engine of flesh. Stepping up to his reputation, Club-handed Cratchit did not wait for the barker to announce the start of the bout; he attacked Gabriel McCabe from behind as the submariner was taking the applause of the crowd. Cratchit's bony mace rebounded off McCabe's back, sending him sprawling into the pit's boundary rope, then he tried to kick the legs out from under the commodore's friend.

McCabe slipped to the floor, scissoring his legs around his opponent's on the way down and flipping the club-handed brute into the sawdust, then he twisted around to land a kick on Cratchit's face. They both stood up and warily circled each other. McCabe might be the strongest man in Jackals, but with his bulk, he was certainly not the fastest. Club-handed Cratchit got another strike in, his mace hand slapping McCabe's chest as if it was ringing off the hull of the commodore's u-boat. Cratchit went in to beat McCabe's ribs again, but the giant caught him with both arms and lifted the ferocious fighter off the ground. Club-handed Cratchit was spun around, flailing helplessly in the air.

Then the giant saw Commodore Black seated next to his two old comrades and a strange look crossed his face. Moving his right leg back for leverage, McCabe flung his opponent towards the commodore, the crowd momentarily falling silent as Professor Harsh caught the fighter a second before he crashed into Black.

'That's nice work,' said Cratchit, gazing down admiringly at Amelia's gorilla-sized arms.

The professor flung Club-handed Cratchit back into the

ring where McCabe caught the fighter and turned him over in the air, slamming him into the floor and unconsciousness.

'Strength trumps guile and viciousness,' called the barker, recovering from astonishment a second before the crowd, 'with a little help from his, umm, lady friend in the audience.'

'Oh, isn't that dandy?' said Amelia. 'Now I'm the strumpet for some pit-floor blade.'

The commodore turned to Billy Snow and T'ricola. 'Now then, mates, let's you and I talk about hearing the hiss of an honest gas scrubber in your ears and once more feeling the bob of a deck below your feet.'

'Have you taken leave of your senses?' Gabriel McCabe's eyes darted between Billy Snow and T'ricola. 'I always knew this old goat would end up impaled on a reef, but are you so intent to join him?'

'It is a boat,' said Billy Snow, 'and a berth. Those two have not been in over-supply for the three of us of late.'

'You cannot keep on taking punishment out there,' said T'ricola. 'Sooner or later someone like Cratchit is going to leave a fatal dent in your skull.'

'Better we take pit money than *this*,' said McCabe, looking at Amelia and the commodore. 'There's a reason no sane sea-drinker vessel ventures east of Rapalaw Junction, and that is it is suicide to do so.'

'There's never been a good enough reason to try before,' said Amelia. 'We're not slave traders or big-game hunters, and we're following the river Shedarkshe, not trying to explore the interior of Liongeli.'

'You are sailing into the heart of Daggish territory, damson,' said McCabe. 'Even the RAN's Fleet of the East does not overfly Daggish territory for fear of being brought down by their flame guns. The hive's heart beats with the reason of sap and bark, and they have all the care for our kind that you would show towards an oak tree that needs to be felled for lumber.'

'Our luck can be turned,' insisted Billy Snow. 'We can lift the sinker's curse that's been put on us. Black and his friends are sailing for treasure.'

Gabriel McCabe ran a hand through the stubble of his midnight scalp, still sweating after his bout with Club-handed Cratchit. 'Jared Black came back to Jackals with the treasure of the *Peacock Herne*. What he did not come back with was his last crew.'

'Ah, lad, that is low. I cared for those boys and girls like my own children,' said the commodore. 'It was a mortal cruel quirk of fate that led me to survive while their brave hearts perished on that terrible island.'

'And yet it is you that sits in a fine mansion in Middlesteel,' said McCabe, 'while the *Sprite of the Lake* rots on the rocks of your last folly along with your crew's bones.'

'This is no whim of the commodore's,' said Amelia. 'The *Sprite of the Lake* is in a dry dock in Spumehead and our expedition is backed by the House of Quest. We are going into Liongeli provisioned with the best equipment and fighting force his money can buy.'

That news seemed to take McCabe aback. Following the commodore was one thing. Following the cleverest money in Jackals was quite another.

'All right,' said McCabe. 'Let us say the three of us agree to officer for you, I as your first mate, Billy piloting on the phones and T'ricola in the engine room. Where exactly do you propose to find the rest of a crew so foolish as to follow you? With all the settlements opening up in the colonies now, there is hardly an unemployed seadrinker left between here and New Alban. River work is dangerous at the best of times, and you are talking about navigating the perils of the Shedarkshe . . .'

'I thought I would ask Bull,' said the commodore.

'Bull?' McCabe roared with laughter. 'If you convince Bull Kammerlan to ship with you, I shall follow you, Black. I shall follow you to Lord Tridentscale's bedroom and back and play you to sleep in your cabin each night with a tune on his seahorse's harp.'

Amelia followed the commodore as he left the gambling pit, the first mate's laughter still thundering after them. 'I thought we agreed to pick the rest of the hands from Quest's merchant fleet?'

Commodore Black shook his head. 'McCabe is right. We need deep-river experience, lass, and a crew with fighting spirit who are Liongeli-wise. Not some soft cargo-shifters for whom danger is an undercooked pie in a Shiptown jinn house.'

'You know where you can lay your hands on that kind of training, Jared?' asked Amelia. 'Because if you do, Quest's recruiters must have missed them.'

'That is because they were trawling Spumehead's drinking houses and the free traders' haunts, lass, and not the cells of Bonegate Prison!'

Bonegate was quite unlike Jackals' debtors' prisons. In the sponging-houses, at least, desperate relatives could purchase a few basic comforts for the inmates. At Bonegate, the only comfort was the hope of transportation instead of the quick drop of the noose on one of the scaffolds outside. It was said that the guards made so much money out of selling prime viewing spots in the square on hanging days, that they even bribed juries to ensure a ready supply of victims to dance the Bonegate jig.

Quest's money, it seemed, was good in the prison also. His

powder-wigged lawyer stood by the door while Amelia and the commodore listened to the clank of prisoners' chains in the corridor outside, the stench of urine and unwashed bodies strong even in the visitors' chamber.

'How much longer are they going to keep us waiting?' asked Amelia.

'The fellow we're due to see is serving a water sentence,' said the commodore. 'He's got to be fished out of the tanks and cracked out of his immersion helmet. They keep thousands down in the tanks, and even though each suit carries a number, it's mortal hard to tell those crabs apart down in the basement levels.'

'You sound like you've sailed close to being tanked yourself.'

'Not these poor old bones,' said the commodore. 'They have never seen the inside of this cursed place, nor will they.'

Amelia held her tongue. She was one of the few people in Jackals to know the commodore's true identity. The House of Guardians and its political police considered the once notorious rebel duke long dead, but if they ever found out he had been resurrected as Jared Black, the flotation tanks of Bonegate would be the least of the commodore's travails.

'This Bull Kammerlan has an entire crew in here?' asked Amelia.

'Such is the fate of slavers,' said the commodore, 'since the abolitionists had their way and the RAN has been enforcing the suppression act.'

'Slaving's a vile trade. You can't trust the type of pond scum that deals in human cargoes.'

'The caliph has it legal enough,' said the commodore. 'It's only when you are caught on the wrong side of the Saltless Sea that Jackelian law applies, and although I have no love for that foul trade myself, it's to the likes of Bull that we must turn for knowledge of your dark river, because there is no one else who sails the Shedarkshe for a profit.'

A clinking at the door signalled the arrival of Bonegate's 'guest'. Thanks to the chains connecting his ankles, Bull Kammerlan took small waddling steps. His rubber immersion suit still dripped, soaking the flagstones, and a bone-white nose piece dangled from his face where the breather helmet had been removed.

Two guards in black crushers' uniforms shoved Kammerlan to sit on a stool opposite Amelia and Black, departing quickly and leaving them with only Quest's silent lawyer for a witness.

'Not like diving off a boat on Porto Principe?' said the commodore.

Bull's eyes had difficulty focusing on them after so long in the darkness of the immersion tank, but he recognized the voice. 'Still alive, you miserable old goat? I thought the gout would have taken you by now, the rate of knots you must have been gorging yourself using the trinkets and jewels of the *Peacock Herne* to pay the bailiff.'

The commodore patted the paunch under his waistcoat. 'And I'm looking blessed good on it, too, Bull.'

'You've a cheek, old man, coming in here to see me. I only have to shout and tell the crushers who you really are, and they'd have you tossed in the tank alongside me and the boys, tossed in as soon as spit on you.'

'Nothing hasty now,' warned the commodore. 'Or you'll see both our necks stretched for royalists. Let us use our fine new names in this dark place.'

'You weren't in the royalist cause, Black,' said Bull in a low voice, 'you were just seated at its breakfast table, that's all. You were too soft and the fleet-in-exile was burned in its pens by the RAN because of you and your kind's weakness.'

'Ah, Bull, let's forget the old politics and our grievances

with the House of Guardians, for parliament still has you and your lads in its cells, even if it is for slavery rather than piracy and sedition. And I have an offer for you and yours that might let you all see the light of day again.'

'How are you going to do that?' said Bull. 'You been elected First Guardian, fat man? Is dimples here the new Chief Justice?'

Amelia leant forward. 'Dimples is all for tossing you back in the tank for the dirty slaver scum you are, sailor-boy.'

Bull laughed. 'Oh, I like this one. You always did have a taste for them spicy, Black. My little slavery jaunts up the Shedarkshe was just to pay the bills, girl, and I was doing them a favour. Why do you think the craynarbians carry that crab armour of theirs around on their backs? Compared with life in the jungle hell-hole of Liongeli, standing on a Cassarabian auction block has a lot to recommend it.'

The commodore pulled Amelia back before she could knock the prisoner off his stool. He looked Bull dead in the eyes. 'Isn't it a mortal shame the Jackelian airship that caught you on the surface with your holds packed full of pitiable craynarbian flesh did not feel the same way.'

'Jigger Jackals,' swore Bull, 'and jigger you too, fat man. We did what we needed to, to survive. You've gone native, Black, you've forgotten the cause; bought off with soft bedsheets and honeyed hams, paying your taxes to parliament each year like a good fat little shopkeeper.'

Amelia turned to their clerk by the door. 'Get his helmet and toss him back in the water, we've finished with him.'

'Damn your eyes,' shouted Bull, 'I haven't said I won't help you.'

'That's it,' said the commodore. 'You remember all your crew floating alongside you in your tank, you start thinking like the skipper you once were, rather than the man you've become. Here's the offer: you and your people crew for me, lad, a little jaunt up-river into Liongeli. I'll see your water sentences are converted into nominal transportation – not to the colonies, but to the plantations up at Rapalaw Junction. I'll hold your papers, and anyone who makes it back alive with me to Jackals will be sailing as a free citizen by the end of our trip.'

'You have that kind of influence, now?'

'Not I,' said the commodore. 'But old Blacky knows a certain shopkeeper who does.'

The fight seemed to go out of the convict. 'So, you're in the House of Guardians' pocket now, then?'

'And you are sitting in mine,' said the commodore, patting the side of his jacket. 'And we'll have lots of well-armed soldiers on board, with sharp steel and shells a-plenty to keep your compass true to my course.'

'Just in case you get any ideas about taking off with our u-boat,' added Amelia.

Black winked at the convict. 'You'll like them when you see them, Bull, that you will.'

Being a good soldier of the People's Revolutionary Second Brigade, the blue-coated trooper cracked his bayonet-tipped rifle on the floor as he recognized Compatriot Colonel Tarry. Like all trusted Carlists, the compatriot wore a red feather in his tricorn hat, not that Tarry's loyalty to the revolution could ever be called into question. Not safely, anyway.

Tarry ran a finger along the soldier's bayonet, testing the edge. 'I see there is at least one guard in this camp who knows how to use a whetstone on his cutlery.'

The trooper stood to attention even straighter. 'You do not forget what you learn in the field, compatriot colonel. A sharp bayonet is an effective bayonet.'

'A man of action, good.' The colonel leant in closer to the

soldier; not that there was anyone else in the corridor to over-hear them, but a little paranoia was a healthy reaction to the mores of Quatérshift's current society. In fact, a *lot* of para-noia was the healthiest reaction. 'Prisoner seventy-six is not being productive. The camp committee have been making excuses for him for months now, but I am frankly . . . disap-pointed. Have you heard any of the camp committee here speak against the community?'

'The prisoner is an aristocrat, compatriot colonel,' said the trooper. 'We mollycoddle him with coal for his fire and feed him two meals a day. To make a leech such as him product-ive, a more direct approach is required . . .'

'Direct, yes, I like that,' said the colonel. 'Yes, into the Gideon's Collar, a bolt through the neck and let his remains fertilize the people's fields. Well, we shall see. Open up. I have much to discuss with Compatriot Robur. Let us see how well this pampered aristocrat begs for his miserable life. If you hear any screams . . .'

'My hearing is much diminished by the damp of this miser-able corridor, compatriot colonel.'

Inside the cell, a hand lay poised above an ink well, a steel quill quivering in the cold, hovering above a sheet of drawing-paper pinned to a draughtsman's board that had seen better days.

'You are Robur?'

The prisoner pulled the soiled blankets that lay wrapped around him a little tighter, as if they might protect him from the violence of the colonel. 'I am Robur, compatriot.'

The officer picked up the cheap sheet of paper on which the prisoner had been sketching his designs. 'And what, pray tell, do you call this?'

'What the First Committee has instructed me to create for them, compatriot. A cannon with a firing mechanism controlled by a transaction engine. The improved accuracy will . . .'

'Such toys will not assist the revolution,' shouted the colonel. 'The people are starving in every province! Will your damn cannon feed our cities, will it put bread on our tables?'

'You seem well fed enough,' said Robur, regretting the words the moment they came out of his mouth.

Colonel Tarry backhanded the prisoner, knocking him to the ground. 'Maggot! You aristocratic, anti-revolutionary scum. You have been sabotaging our war efforts, dragging your heels, just to be fed while your compatriots starve in the world beyond your cell's comfortable four walls. Starve because your aristocrat friends have sabotaged all our farms. Now you shall pay the price for your treachery.'

The trooper, who had been eavesdropping, opened the door, smiling, sensing an end to his cold vigil outside the cell.

'Take him,' ordered the colonel, leading the way. 'I will not sully my hands by touching this uncommunityist criminal.'

The steel door at the other end of the corridor opened and a chilly gust blew down from Darksun Peak. Of all the organized communities in Quatérshift to be assigned to as a guard, Darksun Fortress was undoubtedly the most miserable. Before the Sun King's overthrow it had held only the most dangerous Carlist revolutionaries. Now that the men and women it had once held as prisoners sat on the land's ruling committees, the mountain-dug dungeons had been refilled with the dwindling number of recalcitrants from the old regime.

Colonel Tarry pointed down to the Gideon's Collar in the centre of the courtyard. The steam-driven killing machine was slowly rocking on its wooden stilts as its boiler hummed a lament. 'A quick and painless death for you, Robur. Although if I had my way, you would not receive such mercy from the Commonshare. I would pass you to the king's old torturers and let them quarter you alive after they had dragged the names of all your treacherous friends from your lips.'

Humming happily, the Second Brigade trooper slung his rifle over his shoulder so he didn't lose his balance; the steps down to the courtyard of this bleak fortress were treacherous enough at the best of times. Usually by now, an aristocrat would be begging for his life. Promising to offer up hidden caches of gold and gems they had buried as the revolution began. But not Robur. The miserable scarecrow had no real wealth, as the trooper well knew, given the number of times his watch had tried to shake him down for a centime or two.

On the battlements below, a gaggle of soldiers quick-stepped, one of them shouting something up that was lost in the cold of the perpetual mist that shrouded the fortress.

'Damn fools,' swore Colonel Tarry. 'Ignore them and bring the traitor over here.'

'But—'

Something was wrong. The trooper peered over the battlements at the group, looking down towards the crimson, angry face of – it could not be possible – Colonel Tarry!

The closer of the two Colonel Tarrys lifted the trooper's boots and flipped him over the battlements, his blue uniform flapping as he fell towards the courtyard below.

The gaunt figure of Robur stumbled back as Colonel Tarry's face melted and reformed into . . . a mirror image of Robur's own, right down to his sunken eyes and sallow, starved cheeks!

'Who are you?' Robur demanded.

'I have many faces, many names,' Robur's double hissed back at him, pushing him away from the steps and the sprinting soldiers. 'You may inquire after them later, should you live.'

'They'll shoot us both now, you fool.'

'They've had their pound of flesh from me,' laughed Robur's reflection, a finger on his left hand uncurling to reveal an iron barrel that began juddering as a stream of blue marble-sized spheres fired towards the guards, shattering and layering the steps with a veil of gas.

As the real Robur was shoved towards a nearby turret, he had to admire the design of the mechanical arm. You could barely tell it was artificial, even when you knew where to look for the signs of mechomancy. Balls from the guards' rifles began to hit the wall behind them, showering them both with shards of granite. The troopers were shooting blind through the gas. Robur turned. His insane rescuer was pulling up a pack that had been roped on the outside of the citadel's walls, left dangling from the crenellations. Once unfastened, the pack unfurled into a bone-like structure, bundles of silk hanging underneath, waiting to fold open. Robur had seen such a thing in journals, before the revolution: but only one nation in the world had a use for them.

'An airship's kite-chute. You're from Jackals! They said you would come, but I did not believe—'

'They said I would come!' Robur's reflection grabbed him and slung a leather harness over his shoulders, clipping Robur to a similar yoke concealed under the fake colonel's uniform. His face twisted in fury. 'Who said I would come?'

'One of the guards was bribed.' Robur was terrified now, lest his strange rescuer abandon him here on the peaks of Darksun Fortress. 'They said someone would come from Jackals for me. I thought it was just another of their games to break me.'

His doppelgänger lifted him up and flung them both off the battlements, the silk rustling out into a triangular sail that crackled above their heads – falling – falling – then picking up into the freezing mist that whistled past the mountain.

Robur was screaming, but his voice was drowned out by the wind and his liberator's animal-like howl of victory.

'If I drop you, Robur, you'll bloody *break*. I don't know why your fool family didn't just hand out personalized invites to the Committee of Public Security to come and view your break-out.'

Their hair-raising flight terminated ten minutes later in a soggy meadow at the foot of one of the alpine crags, a hard landing which sent Robur rolling into a goatherd's fence. A sixer lay tethered nearby, the horse scratching at the mud in its eagerness to be off, all six of its hooves shod in expensive, shining steel.

Stumbling to his feet, Robur turned to face his dangerous reflection. 'Who are you?'

The figure pulled something out of the horse's saddlebag and swivelled around, a demonic mask staring straight back at him. *Furnace-breath Nick*. The very devil himself.

'Here is my true face.'

Robur liked it little better than when the demon had stolen his own. He was backed into the fence now, without even realizing he was trying to flee. 'The Second Brigade will have their mountain trackers out of barracks and riding across the entire province by the end of the day. Every pass from here to the ocean will have a checkpoint. Unless you have an aerostat to get us over the cursewall . . .'

Furnace-breath Nick advanced on the emaciated figure. 'I do not.'

'Then how in the sun child's name are you going to get us out of Quatérshift?'

Furnace-breath Nick's arm twisted up. Robur heard the grinding from a clockwork mechanism beneath a torn fold of false skin on the arm. So, a trooper's rifle ball had shattered one of the cogs during their escape. Robur knew he could fix the demon's arm, but before he could make the offer – and see this marvel close up – there was a burst of air from an artery in Furnace-breath Nick's artificial wrist. Robur just had time to pluck the tiny feathered dart from his chest before he plunged to the grass, his limbs tightening as if he was crafted from clockwork himself. Paralysis became unconsciousness.

'That would be my problem,' said Furnace-breath Nick, scooping the aristocrat's body up from the grass.

Amelia Harsh grunted as she unclipped the refuelling pipe from the *Sprite of the Lake's* hull, the smell of expansion-engine gas lingering in the air as the gutta-percha cable dangled down from Quest's airship. This would be their final refuelling, now the moors and valleys of Jackals had given way to the endless Eastern Forest, a precursor to Liongeli's fierce, dense jungle.

Quest's female soldiers stepped back as the gas line was winched up inside the airship's chequerboard hull.

'Clear?' Gabriel McCabe called down from one of the u-boat's conning turrets.

Amelia flashed the first mate a thumb, then looked over at Veryann, Abraham Quest's personal angel of death on this expedition. There was something disconcerting about the woman, and not just the fact that she and her free company of fighters insisted on wearing their Catosian war jackets at all times. Their quilted armour was cut to accommodate the unnaturally swelled muscles that came from chewing the drug shine, and twin pistol holsters stretched over each breast. Veryann was a walking knife. Calm, courteous, but with an edge that could be turned against your throat quicker than your next breath.

'Do you have a family name, Veryann?' Amelia asked.

'Quest,' said the fighter.

'You are married—?'

She shook her head and pointed at her bare-armed soldiers as they closed the hatches to the fuel tank. 'We are all Quest, now. It is our way. You have never travelled to the Catosian League?'

Amelia demurred. The city-states were one of the few lands as advanced in industry and modern philosophy as Jackals, their horseless carriages and mechanical servants ferried across by traders to northern ports like Shiptown. Their insular nature and pure form of democracy – or anarchy, depending on your tastes – serving up endless amusements for the satirical cartoonists of Jackals' news sheets.

'Our city was Sathens, a significant trading partner for the House of Quest, but its council fell in a dispute with the city of Unarta. No other city would harbour a disgraced free company, only Abraham Quest stood by us. He was hardly involved in our war at all, yet still he took us in.'

Now Amelia understood why Veryann's people were so loyal to Quest. After losing one of the ritual wars the cities fought on the plains outside their walls, Veryann's soldiers would have been ghosts in their own land, turned away from the gates of every civilized state in the League.

A sailor turned the handle on the dive claxon, those still on the decks turning towards the open doors on the conning turrets.

'Living without a government sounds like a fine thing, doesn't it?'

Amelia looked behind her. It was Billy Snow, the blind sonar man taking the last opportunity for days to catch a breath in the open air. 'I'm sorry?'

'The Catosian anarchy,' said Billy, 'the system that led her mercenaries to Jackals and sanctuary with Quest. Having no authority to boss you around, to give you orders. Voting on every little thing that comes up. It sounds just dandy. Until you realize there is someone to call master – the passions of the mob, or the next person you meet who is stronger or cleverer or bigger than you – or five of their friends. Then it gets ugly real fast.'

Amelia shrugged. 'It doesn't sound so different from Jackals to me.'

'It's plenty different,' said Billy. 'Jackals has the law. Parliament's law.'

'My father was a Guardian,' said Amelia. 'At least, he was until he was disqualified from holding the post as a bankrupt – and he used to have to vote on every little thing that came around too.'

'He was voting on passing laws, not whether Damson Dawkins next door should be exiled for rumourmongery. Laws can be bigger than people; they can be better than us. I'll take a good law over a good man's benevolence every time. In fact, as a rule, I'll take a bad law over a good man's intentions.'

'You've been listening to the flow of the water on your phones for too long, old man,' said Amelia. 'You're in danger of becoming a philosopher. Do you need a hand back to the hatch?'

'Perish the thought that I should start thinking.' Billy Snow pointed down to the river. 'I can find my way back inside easily enough, professor; that's my compass down there, the waters of the Shedarkshe.'

A pod of green-scaled things pushed past the *Sprite*, heading towards the overgrown bank.

'You can get about just by the sounds of the jungle?' said Amelia.

'No,' said Billy. 'We've yet to hear the jungle, I think. Wait a week, then you'll see.'

* * *

Even in the *Sprite's* ready room, it was hard to escape from the scent of too many bodies squeezed together in their underwater tin can. Seven days under the surface of the river and the warm air had become a melange of smells. Duty on the conning turrets, when the *Sprite* briefly surfaced at night, had now officially become a tradable commodity among the expedition members. A brief intake of fresh air to the sound of chirruping from the night feeders in the jungle, the crew's clothes soaked in sweat from the febrile temperature – even hotter topside than within the *Sprite* – then the dark hull of the u-boat would slip beneath the water again, the portholes in the conning turret blanketed with bubbling water.

'We could make better time on the surface,' said T'ricola. The craynarbian engineer's sword arm was resting on the table, its serrated bone edge drumming nervously. Only the din of the engine room seemed to bring her comfort. 'There's less drag up there, given we're moving against the current.'

Commodore Black looked across at Bull Kammerlan, and Bull shook his head. 'It's safer down here.'

'We're not raiding villages for slaves, now,' said Amelia, 'and we're only a day out of Rapalaw Junction. There are still trading boats on the surface.'

'There's no greenmesh this far west, I'll grant you,' said Bull, 'but civilized it isn't. If you'd been topside in a raft with just a couple of bearers for company, you'd have seen how *friendly* some of them trading folk are. If I had my way, we'd sail on past Rapalaw Junction nice and silent.'

Bull seemed horrified by the very idea of the greenmesh. Jungle that cooperated, plants and animals bound together in an unholy symbiosis to form a single sentient killing machine.

Veryann spoke up, illuminated by the thin green light behind the stained glass dome of the *Sprite's* nose. 'That is not an option. There is someone waiting for us at Rapalaw Junction.'

'Ah lass, you and your blessed secrets.' Commodore Black watched as the flash of the u-boat's lamps briefly exposed several river predators darting out of the way of this strange metal intruder. 'But we must make land at Rapalaw Junction anyway for our last chance to load fresh water and victuals.'

'East of Rapalaw belongs to the tribes. Not nice civilized shells, either.' Bull pointed at T'ricola. 'You know what I'm talking about, don't you, girl? They would peel off the *Sprite's* hull and spear us for their younglings' supper as soon as look at us. And they have spies inside the trading post, keeping an eye on who is coming and going, counting how many guns we're sailing with. You want victuals and a full belly, commodore? I'll settle for one that's not turning on a craynarbian spit.'

Amelia wagged a finger at the submariner. 'Maybe if you hadn't been dirt-gassing their villages and taking their children for slaves—'

The chamber's hatch was thrown open, one of Bull's seadrinkers pitching in. 'Fire, fire in the engine room!'

Shouts echoed through the boat's corridors, crewmen sliding down ladders and securing compartments. After taking a flooding breach, a blaze in the confines of the underwater vessel was a seadrinker's worst fear. Commodore Black was at the speaking trumpet, barking orders to the pilot room and the *Sprite* bucked as she made a crash surface. Claxons began to sound. Amelia ran with the others for the rear of the boat, pushing past coughing sailors falling out of the engine-room hatch. Seadrinkers with leather fire hoods that made them resemble insects came rushing in behind the professor, lugging fire hoses and water pumps.

The angle of the floor pulled straight with a wrench, a sure sign they were on the surface of the Shedarkshe now.

'Close the room,' shouted T'ricola. 'Everyone out? Then drop the seals port and aft, vent the air and give the bitch nothing to breathe.'

Bull was sliding down a ladder behind them. He grabbed one of his men. 'Is the fire in the gas tanks?'

'No, the scrubber room.'

Amelia looked at the craynarbian officer. 'We're not going to blow?'

'Not if the fire's in our scrubbers, professor. But the scrubbers are a dry area; you hardly ever get a fire down there. I don't understand how—'

'The how of it doesn't matter,' said Bull. 'Let the fire burn down without air, then we go in and douse everything. Damn our luck. It seems we'll be running on the surface to Rapalaw Junction after all.'

'I thought you'd want to see this,' T'ricola said to the commodore, pointing to the burnt-out wreck of the *Sprite's* expansion-gas scrubbers. She ran the fingers of one of her manipulator arms through the brown liquid bubbling out of a metal grille.

Amelia looked at the sticky residue over the commodore's shoulder. 'What is it?'

'Hull-tile fixative, professor.' The commodore tapped the cork-like substance that had been exposed under the half-melted wall. 'But what in Tridentscale's name was this gunk doing blocking up the tubes on my gas scrubbers?'

'Some of it might have leaked into the machine when the *Sprite* was back in the pens,' said Amelia.

T'ricola indicated a hole in the copper tube feeding the scrubbers. 'This was holed through with a metal punch, and then the glue was deliberately poured in. I checked our stores. There's a can of fixative missing.'

Commodore Black tapped the burnt machinery in frustration. 'That's a mortal clever way to sabotage a boat. Not quite enough to sink us and move us all along the Circle, but sufficient to keep us on the surface like a dead fish waiting to be spotted by the gulls.'

Amelia looked at the commodore. 'We can't stay submerged under the river now?'

'We're not one of your pocket aerostats, Amelia. We have no chimneys on the *Sprite* and we can't vent our engines through the periscope. If the scrubbers have packed up, then we have to dump the exhaust manually, rather than converting it into dust bricks, and that means running with open vents up on the surface.'

T'ricola angrily kicked the puddled water left by the fire crew. 'It's one of Bull's people that did this. They think if we scratch the expedition before we get to Rapalaw Junction then they all get to sail free back to Jackals with full pardons in their pockets.'

'Then they'll be thinking wrong,' said Black. 'T'ricola, tell Billy and Gabriel to be keeping an eye on the crew. Then find Veryann and send her down here.'

Amelia almost felt sorry for whoever had done the damage when the situation was explained to Veryann. The Catosian turned pale with anger as the implications of the sabotage settled in.

'Can this be repaired?' Veryann asked.

'Ah, my poor boat. We may be able to jury-rig her at one of the larger workshops in Rapalaw Junction,' said the commodore. 'We shall see. If anyone can repair a gas scrubber in this state, it is T'ricola. She can coax melted iron and twisted steel back to life. I have seen her do it before.'

'I shall post armed sentries,' said Veryann. 'Have Gabriel McCabe indicate all your vital systems to us – the things a traitor would go for next: the main pistons, our water supply, fuel, our air. We must guard them all.'

'I'll do that, lass,' said the commodore. 'But be warned, there is not much on my beautiful *Sprite* that is not vital to our survival.'

Veryann stood looking crossly at the ruined machinery in the scrubber chamber as the commodore and Amelia turned to leave for the main engine room.

'My poor stars,' she heard Black groan. 'Is it not enough that to get my own boat back I have to plunge her into the heart of treacherous Liongeli? Now I find I have a wicked cuckoo making a home in my nest.'

A cuckoo? One of Bull Kammerlan's convicts trying to shorten their sentence? Veryann pulled out her boot knife – almost a short sword – and rammed it into the exposed tiles. If the commodore had been shown the second crystal-book back in Middlesteel, he might think differently. Someone on board was playing a very dangerous game in trying to stop Abraham Quest's expedition. Someone who obviously knew things they had no right to know. But a u-boat sailing up the Shedarkshe was a dangerous place to keep a secret. She would make sure that whoever held it would be leaving it in the jungle . . . along with their decaying bones.

CHAPTER FIVE

Damson Beeton clutched the cream card of the invitation, her cotton mittens barely keeping the chill out as the cold lifted off the Gambleflowers' waters and washed across the island. The Islands of the Skerries sat in the middle of Middlesteel's great river, their isolation making them an ideal home for the Jackelian quality; those rich enough not to want to bother with tall walls for their mansions, or private guards to keep the fingers of the capital's cracksmen, anglers, rampers and myriad other trades of the criminal flash mob out of their silver.

Rich enough to pay for isolation, although, much to the damson's disgust in this particular instance, not rich enough to want to pay for a full staff to clean Dolorous Hall. A single housekeeper and butler, and not much of a butler at that, to keep a gentleman of the master's station in the state he deserved to be kept in. It was not proper. No it wasn't. Not that anyone even knew where the master's wealth came from. Family money, so the gossip ran. Twenty thousand gold guineas a year. Almost as rich as a real gentleman like Abraham Quest, or one of the bankers from the counting houses of Sun Gate.

Jackals was a nation of shopkeepers and merchants, but as well as he paid her, the master of the house would not stretch to any staff larger than a few day-men and maids boated across every morning to help her dust, cook and keep the gardens. It simply was not *proper*.

'Every afternoon, he is always here,' she said to Septimoth, the silent butler waiting beside her. 'It is not right.'

Septimoth stood there, a statue in the cold – a bony lizard-like statue with wings folded like those of a stone angel. That was another thing. Who ever heard of having a lashlite as a retainer? Graspers made fine servants. Steammen would toil for you all day long and bear life's travails with stoic resolve. But a lashlite? They preferred their village nests in the mountains and hunts high in the airless atmosphere, tracking the balloon-like skraypers that preyed on airships. Now there was a valuable service to the nation. Hunting skraypers. As a butler, Septimoth – surly, enigmatic lashlite that he was – was frankly abominable.

'It is his habit,' said Septimoth. 'We must respect his wishes, Damson Beeton.'

'Tish and tosh,' said the housekeeper. 'He needs to be out and about, embracing society, not drinking alone in the cold halls of this old place.' She waved her invitation at the lashlite. 'Every day I feed the fireplace with a dozen such as this, all unanswered by him. The height of rudeness. Society wishes to clutch us to its bosom, Septimoth, and we should not turn our back on society.'

'I believe the master has finished his meditation now,' said Septimoth.

'Meditation is it, you say?' said Damson Beeton. 'That's a fancy name for moping about, in my book.'

Septimoth kept his own counsel, and Damson Beeton tutted. How many more nights would she have to stand and ogle the other islands of the Skerries – the river awash with taxi-boat lanterns rowing the great and the good to parties and dinners, the laughter in the gardens, the blaze of chandeliers? It was obvious that the grim corridors of Dolorous Hall would be better filled with the product of her social organizing. But then, would anyone come if she got her way? Dolorous Isle was said to be unlucky. Cursed by its proximity to the old heart of Middlesteel, the part of the city drowned by the great flood of 1570, and then drowned again by design when the river was widened to stop a reoccurrence of the disaster. River boats piloted by those new to the trade still often struck the spire of Lumphill Cathedral protruding from the water, despite parliament's red buoys bobbing in the currents nearby.

In the garden, the master stood up, leaving his apple tree behind as he shut the gate on the little enclosure. Cornelius Fortune looked tired, even to Damson Beeton's eyes. The lash-lite and the old woman followed their employer back to the steps of the mansion.

Cornelius noticed the invitation Damson Beeton was clutching. 'Is it tonight, damson? I had forgotten, to tell you the truth. I should sleep now, I am so tired, but if you have said yes . . .'

'Sleep? Why you are a slack-a-bed, sir, you have been sleeping all through the morning and the afternoon. The least you can do now is take the air of the evening in polite company.'

Cornelius rubbed his red eyes. 'Forgive me, Damson Beeton. It seems as if I have been up for hours.'

'This is an event to raise finances for the poor,' chided the housekeeper. 'Presided over by the House of Quest. There is a function every evening for the rest of the week, so if you can't make this night, you have no excuse for not attending the other evenings! There will be members of the House of

Guardians there, perhaps even the First himself, that old rascal Benjamin Carl. There will be many great ladies looking for suitable matches and—'

Cornelius took the invitation and ran his eyes over it before handing it back. 'I am glad to see the "poor" will be so well catered for, damson. Light a lantern to call a boat. I shall go.'

Oblivious to his sarcasm the housekeeper bustled off; mollified that she had got her way at last. As she left, she chuckled at herself. She was really very good as a housekeeper. Sometimes she could go for a couple of weeks without remembering once what she *really* was. But that was as it should be. 'Damson Beeton' had been very carefully crafted and put together. Every little quirk. Every little nuance. Now, where in the garden had she stored that damned lantern oil?

'Your arm is still hurting you; I can see it in the way you walk,' noted Septimoth. 'You are taking a boat to visit the old man in the shop?'

'You know me too well,' said Cornelius, watching their housekeeper waddle away. He flexed his right arm, the joints hardly moving. 'I think there's a rifle ball still lodged in it.'

'You take too many risks,' said Septimoth.

Cornelius reached out and touched his friend's leathery shoulder. 'No, old friend, most weeks I take far too few.'

'Do you wish me to come with you?'

'No. I shall travel to his house like a gentleman,' said Cornelius. 'His neighbours will certainly talk if they see you dropping me out of the sky on his roof.'

Septimoth nodded and pulled out his most precious possession, a bone-pipe: all that was left of his mother. 'Then I shall play for a while.'

Cornelius smiled. Damson Beeton *would* be pleased. He left Septimoth walking up the stairs to the hatch in the loft, the eyrie between the mansion's smoke stacks, where he would crouch like a leathery gargoyle and fill the island grounds with his inhuman tunes. It was no wonder the river's pilots believed this stretch of the water was haunted.

The alien melody had begun as Cornelius reached the quay, the glass door of Damson Beeton's lantern rattling in the breeze, spilling drops of slipsharp oil down onto the wooden planks.

A long dark shape pulled out of the river, the pilot at the back lifting his oars. 'Evening, squire.' The pilot pointed at the other figure sitting in the front of the skiff. 'Don't mind if you double up, do you, squire? The islands are fair humming tonight, as busy as I've ever seen them. Parties all over the place.'

Cornelius nodded and stepped down into the boat, the other passenger shifting uneasily. Cornelius's nondescript greatcoat was drawn tight and it gave little clue to its owner's station. The coat would have suited a private on leave from the regiments as well as it would have covered the finery of a dandy visiting a wealthy relative on the Skerries.

The fact that its social ambivalence allowed its wearer to play either part was not lost on the other passenger, who erred on the side of caution and gave a greeting. 'A cold night, sir, for such frivolity. It seems there is a ball on almost every piece of land along the river this night.'

Cornelius decided it would be easiest if he put his fellow passenger at ease. 'I shall have to take my cousin to task, sir, for it seems he never entertains at Dolorous Hall.'

'I did note the dark windows on your isle, but there is no shame in that. There is entirely too much frivolity in Middlesteel these days.' He lifted a surgeon's bag that had been hidden behind his seat. 'And as a man of medicine, I have often noted the effects that intemperate spirits may have on the body. Jinn, I would say, is the curse of our nation.'

'Ah, a doctor.' And a temperance man to boot.

'Not of the two-legged kind,' said the passenger. 'Although I did start out in that noble profession. No, I practise on animals now. A vet. I have noted those who are in a position to do so often care more for their pets than for members of their own family. Indeed, I have just come from the house of Hermia Durrington – perhaps you know the good lady?'

Cornelius shook his head.

'Her raven is sick and she is quite distraught. But I have prescribed a restorative and I have every confidence that the bird will soon be returned to its . . .'

Cornelius listened politely for the rest of the journey as the doctor of animals went on to describe every sick canine, feline, bird and mammal owned by the capital's quality. Even as Cornelius was about to depart, leaving him in the boat, the vet seemed barely aware that he had discovered nothing about his fellow passenger, or that the groans coming from the oarsman were not entirely the result of rowing against the current of the Gambleflowers.

'I should give you a discount on that ride, squire,' whispered the pilot as he stopped to let Cornelius alight along a row of dark steps cut into the river embankment.

Cornelius passed him twice the fare. 'And I shall give you a tip for bearing the rest of the journey.'

As Cornelius watched the boat slip back into the darkness of the river, his face began to melt, his skin turning to streams of liquid flesh, folding and refashioning itself into an exact duplicate of the vet's features.

'Her raven is sick and she is quite distraught,' Cornelius cackled. He pitched the voice again, lower, until it was an exact duplicate of the vet's own tones.

Anybody who had been watching would have seen a surgeon of animals stroll away into Middlesteel, while the river taxi bore away its remaining passenger – presumably one Cornelius Fortune – into the stream of the Gambleflowers.

As was his habit, Cornelius Fortune assumed the face of the man he had come to visit. Unlike most of those who were on the receiving end of Cornelius's visitations, Dred Lands – proprietor of the Old Mechomancery Shop along Knocking Yard – would not be shocked to meet someone wearing his own face. After all, Dred Lands hardly had much use for it himself these days.

The outside door of the shop was a cheap wooden affair with a latch that was easily lifted by a cracksman's jimmy, but it was the hall inside where the real security began.

Two iron doors that would have honoured the front of a bank vault barred Cornelius's way, an old but efficient blood-code machine jutting out from the wall. Cornelius pressed his thumb on the needle, a tear of his blood trickling into its nib as the transaction engine's drums clicked and clacked in their rotary chamber. Even Cornelius could not imitate another's essence to the level of detail required to fool one of these machines, but deception would not be needed here. Not when it was mainly his financial resources that funded the life and occupation of one of the few individuals in Middlesteel more reclusive than himself.

On the other side of the doors a steamman waited. Not one of the incredible beings of the life metal from the Steamman Free State, but a dull automaton – little more than an iron zombie – its parts scavenged from the unreliable Catosian servant machines that were available in the more exclusive markets of the capital. Lacking a voicebox as well as the wit to use it, the juddering creature limped down the corridor, through what passed for a showroom for the Old Mechomancery Shop, little more than a warehouse of pawned items awaiting repair.

The steamman's four arms turned in a slow windmill fashion, keeping balance and urging Cornelius down a spiral staircase. You really had to know where to look to spot the duke's hole inside the cellar; the fact that the shop was still standing was a testament to that. Six hundred years ago if Isambard Kirkhill and the parliamentarians' new pattern army had discovered the hidden door, they would have burned the shop down to its foundation stones, along with a few of its neighbours, as a lesson. The metal servant triggered a hidden hatch and a section of the cellar floor opened up, revealing a square of orange light. They went down a line of narrow iron treads like a ship's stairs. Below, more metal servants tended massive night orchids behind a glass wall, feeding the plants rats – no doubt cornered and trapped in the cold shop above. The rest of the chamber was fitted out like something from a Cassarabian harem or a Middlesteel bawdy house. When the royalists in the capital had hidden down here, they had hidden in style.

Lying on a scatter of large crimson velvet cushions holding a hookah filled with mumbleweed smoke was a figure that might have been mistaken for a steamman himself, but who – as he lifted himself up – revealed a largely human body, albeit one with a metal leg and a silvered face-mask riveted with gold pins that glowed in the orange gas light.

Burned, blackened lips just visible behind the mouth slash in the mask puckered in exasperation. 'Must you always visit me looking like that?'

'You with your mask,' said Cornelius, 'why should you mind?'

'You have a cheek, talking to me about wearing masks.'

Dred Lands got up from the cushions, a hiss of compressed steam from the artificial leg leaking out as it took his weight. 'I *need* to wear a mask so that people can bear to look at me.'

'While I need to wear one so they cannot.' Cornelius let his features re-form, his nose shortening to lose its hook while his brow reshaped and flattened out. 'There, I am myself again.'

'Now how can I be sure of that?' grumbled Dred Lands. 'For all I know, the real Cornelius Fortune could be a corpse you came across on a battlefield, or the face of your favourite teacher from your youth, now passed away.'

Cornelius tapped his arm. 'You are familiar enough with this, I think.'

Dred sighed. 'Enhancements? Or repairs, again?'

'The latter.' Cornelius picked up the book the mechomancer had been reading as his friend limped over to the side of the room, pulling back satin sheeting to reveal a luxuriously appointed workshop. Cornelius flicked through the first couple of pages. '*The Queen in the Leather Mask*, by M.W. Templar. You know this nearly made it onto parliament's sedition list, Dred, the similarities between our own Queen Charlotte and its sympathetic portrayal of a sitting monarch . . .'

'Pah,' said Dred, 'it is celestial fiction, nothing more. The queen escapes to the moon at the end of the novel. Besides, I thought you and your "friend" Furnace-breath Nick had a taste for sedition?'

'For if it prosper, it be not treason,' said Cornelius, quoting from the speech Isambard Kirkhill had made after the last true king had been captured, gagged, and had his arms surgically removed so that he might never again turn his hands against the people.

Cornelius sat down while Dred fixed a magnifying lens over

109

his mask and began to unlock the skin-coloured gutta-percha panels from Cornelius's artificial arm.

'Parliament really had to scrape the bottom of the barrel to find Queen Charlotte,' said the mechomancer. 'After they discovered the Commonshare had run the majority of the royal breeding house through a Gideon's Collar during the invasion.'

Cornelius winced, but not from the pain in his shoulder.

'Sorry, I forgot. But the point is, the *Middlesteel Illustrated* is still running editorials saying there's as much royal blood in the queen's veins as there is in your bath water. Rumour has it that she was found in the baggage train of the retreating Quatérshiftian army – that one of the shiftie officers had taken her from the breeding house and only kept her alive because she was a pretty little thing; well, that was when she still had her arms, of course.'

'The House of Guardians needs a symbol,' said Cornelius.

'Aha.' The mechomancer removed a lead ball with a pair of tweezers, and then pulled out another from Cornelius's arm. 'Talking of our compatriots in Quatérshift, I presume these two rascals are cast from Commonshare lead?'

'I may have made a flying visit there recently.'

Dred tutted. 'Your arm is rare, Cornelius – my skill combined with Catosian high-tension clockwork. I would rather you did not throw it away. One day the First Committee is going to get wise to those tricks of yours with your damn face. Their pamphleteers will stop flattering the egos of the leading Carlists with real-box pictures of the heroes of the revolution, leaving you to impersonate committee members from Gilroy's cartoons in the *Illustrated*. Their spies will stop trying to hunt down émigrés over here and start trying to steal the plans for a working blood-code machine.'

'Can you repair my arm?' asked Cornelius.

'Of course I can. You know, you never did tell me how you do your face thing – did you learn the sorcery from a worldsinger? Were you caught in a feymist as a child? Did you travel south to see a womb mage? There are back-street sorcerers who can change a face just the once, but they say you feel agony for the rest of your life . . .'

'I feel the pain,' said Cornelius. 'The difference is, I like to share it around.'

Dred pulled over a steam-powered winding machine and began to de-tension the clockwork inside the arm, still wary of another explosion, even after all these years. 'The Commonshare will fall one day, you know. Helped along by you, or more likely because they can't feed their own people. Or perhaps the God-Emperor in Kikkosico will tire of their insults and bypass the cursewall, land his legions on their shore and finish off Quatérshift for good. What will you do then, old friend?'

'Retire.'

Dred Lands teased out part of the arm mechanism, laying it down on the workbench. 'All right, don't tell me. I'll fix you up for your next attempt at suicide all the same.'

'You should be more appreciative of what I do,' said Cornelius. 'I even rescued one of your own from Quatérshift a couple of nights back. Jules Robur, the mechomancer. He would not have lasted another year in the Commonshare's "organized community" system.'

Dred's hand slipped on the wire cutter he was twisting. 'Sweet Circle, you got Jules Robur out of Quatérshift? I thought he was dead for sure. His designs, his technical architectures. He's the greatest of us, Cornelius, the greatest! Are you sure he's alive? Dear Circle!'

Cornelius had never seen Dred so animated. It was as if he had rescued the mechomancer's own father from the work camp. 'He is alive, have no worries on that account. When he woke up in Jackals, he could not stop expressing his gratitude, talking about the devices he could tinker into life now, with all of Jackelian industry and science at his disposal.'

'Tinker, indeed! You must bring him here to me; just convince him to visit me. I shall offer all my tools to his service. Do this one thing for me, Cornelius, and I shall work for you for the rest of the year for free.'

'You can go and see him yourself. He's here in the capital. I left him at his daughter's house in Westcheap.'

'His daughter? There must be some mistake.'

'No mistake,' said Cornelius. 'I saw him walk through the door of her house myself. It was his daughter who convinced me to rescue the man from Quatérshift.'

'But it was Robur's daughter who denounced him,' said Dred. 'She's a Carlist, married to a general in the revolutionary army. She was the bloody reason he was in the camps in the first place. She blew him out to their secret police, led the crushers to the home he was hiding in. Look—'

Dred went to a bookshelf and returned with an old volume of the *Journal of Philosophical Transactions*, then opened it to a page with a cartoon. A man in Sun Court finery, Robur down to his hook nose, was being dragged away by soldiers of the revolutionary army as a woman watched. A speech bubble from the struggling mechomancer proclaimed: 'Now this is a pretty penny in return for your mother's labours.' The woman was calling back, 'And now *your* labours shall belong to the commons, you royalist dog.' Pursed lips, staring eyes and wild hair – the daughter's caricature bore no relation to the elegant creature who had implored him for his help in the rear yard of a jinn house.

'It's not the same woman.' The anger leaked through Cornelius's steely demeanour.

'Keep your hair on, man,' said Dred. 'If she was an agent of the Commonshare, my fine arm and your strange bones would be lying dead in a ditch in Quatérshift by now. She was probably his young mistress. Would you have risked your neck so readily for a lover as a daughter? You rescued the genius of Jules Robur; believe me, that is all that matters.'

'Finish the arm,' ordered Cornelius. 'I'll take your invite to Robur's house personally tomorrow and see how well they like playing the fool with me when Furnace-breath Nick comes to call.'

Dred muttered, but he did as he was bid.

Cornelius's eyes narrowed. Something was wrong here, deeply wrong. Was Jackals in danger again from her ancient foe to the east? If so, the old enemy would count themselves lucky if they lived to regret it. That was the thing about invasions. In the end, it just meant the shifties were coming to *him*.

CHAPTER SIX

'What is going on here?' Gabriel McCabe pushed past the ring of sailors urging on the fight; one of the seadrinkers trading blows – badly – with a Catosian soldier in the confines of the *Sprite's* mid-deck. The first mate grabbed his sailor, Veryann moving in to pull off her fighter at the same time.

'She broke my jigging nose!' shouted the sailor, clutching a kerchief to stem the flow of blood as McCabe held him in the air.

'He gave challenge to me,' retorted the soldier, bridling and pushing her blonde hair back out of her face.

Commodore Black slid down a ladder and dropped to the deck, quickly followed by Amelia. 'A blessed challenge is it? *The Sprite of the Lake* is too small to be fighting duels.'

The sailor pointed at Veryann's soldier. 'It was no challenge. I only suggested to her that when we get to Rapalaw Junction we find a nice room and get down to the hey-jiggerty.'

Veryann stepped between the sailor and her mercenary. 'What manner of fool are you? No free company fighter will submit to mate with you until you have beaten her in combat.

114

You must prove yourself fit before you bed a Catosian, demonstrate the superiority of your blood lineage. You issued a challenge to my fighter, duel or not.'

'Ah,' said the commodore, 'I do not think any of us in Jackals do things in that way. There now, a simple misunderstanding of cultures. So let's be putting away our knives and cudgels before I have to bring out the keys for the *Sprite's* brig.'

Amelia did not like the gleam that had entered Black's eyes as he looked at the commander of their force of mercenary marines. That gleam meant mischief on its way.

Gabriel let go of his sailor and indicated the group of Catosians who, up until a few minutes before, had been wrestling on the deck, their taut bodies gleaming from the effects of the muscle-growth stimulant favoured by the Catosian regiments – the sacred drug shine. 'Must your people spar naked like that? Most of our crew were locked up in Bonegate before they came on board. Your soldiers are driving them crazy down here.'

'We need to maintain our edge,' insisted Veryann. 'It is the fighters' way. If your sailors have an issue with discipline, you should raise the matter with Bull Kammerlan, first mate.'

'No disrespect intended, lass,' said the commodore. 'It's a fine thing to see such a sight, indeed it is. But if you could see your way to modifying your fighters' code to include a few clothes when you spar, I may still have some sailors left alive when we reach Lake Ataa Naa Nyongmo.'

'Town ho,' called a sailor from the hatch above. 'It's Rapalaw Junction.'

'At last,' said Amelia. 'A chance for solid land and fresh air.'

The commodore climbed back up the ladder. 'Let us hope that they have the facilities to fix our gas scrubbers, professor, or this expedition may be limping back home next week with nothing but empty pockets to show your rich Mister Quest. Run up the cross and gate, lads.'

A sailor came past with the Jackelian flag, a red field bisected with a white cross, the portcullis of the House of Guardians on the upper right-hand corner, the lion rampant in the lower left. Now that was out of place. She knew how Commodore Black felt about that flag, what it would cost him inside to raise parliament's standard above his boat.

'He's not *my* Mister Quest,' said Amelia. She gazed up at the Jackelian flag, running up to flutter in the warm river breeze. 'Why the flag? I thought Rapalaw Junction was a free port.'

'Free it may be,' said Commodore Black, 'but the only law here belongs to the garrison of redcoats attached to our ambassador's residence, minding the trade and keeping the river open for Jackals this far out. Everything else at Rapalaw is far from free. Yes, the repairs'll be costing us a pretty farthing, unless their traders have changed their ways since I was last in these parts.'

A beaten-up collection of narrow-draught barges and river boats lay moored to a line of piers in front of the crumbling walls of the town; occasionally a listless figure propping up a rifle appeared above its baked adobe battlements. A few hired hands lethargically pushed carts filled with buckets of fruit away from a barge, as if they had all the time in the world to move them out of the range of the green buzzing insects circling the crop. Women dangled their feet off the wooden pier, mending fishing nets that looked as if they had seen better days. Plenty of craynarbians mingled with the junction traders, larger than their brethren in Middlesteel, shell armour glossy in the sunlight, not dulled by the smog and grime of a Jackelian city.

Drawn by the sight of the large u-boat coming towards port, a small crowd of children and onlookers began building by the gate, heads shielded from the sun by wide straw hats. As the *Sprite* lay mooring up, a more official-looking figure bypassed the ranks of children, followed by two soldiers in kilts, their bright but tattered uniforms at odds with the simple white cottons of the town folk.

Amelia was one of the first to cross the gantry that the *Sprite's* seadrinkers swung out to the pier, Commodore Black close on her heels, pulling on his blue officer's jacket, polished epaulettes gleaming in the bright jungle light.

'I'm with the residence,' said the official in the bored tones of Middlesteel's quality. He whipped at his face with a brush-like insect swatter. 'You would be Damson Veryann?'

Amelia pointed back to the *Sprite's* deck. The Catosian soldiers were taking position along the hull, holding short stocky carbines that would serve them as well in the confines of the jungle as along the passages of the u-boat. Their leader crossed the gantry; her pale skin and blonde hair serenely cool while the rest of them sweated like dogs in the febrile after-noon heat of Rapalaw's rainforest.

The official walked up to Veryann. 'The ambassador prom-ised we would extend every courtesy to Abraham Quest's expedition. Bit of a change of plans, then, what? I understood you were going to lay up north of here and we would resupply you on the quiet.'

'The situation has changed.'

'A little bad luck coming down here,' explained the commodore. 'We'll have need of your workshops before we can put out again.'

'Bad luck is one fruit you will always find growing on the vines of Liongeli.' The official gave a languid wave towards the other craft in port. 'Rapalaw Junction's shipwright business isn't much to look at, but such as it is, you're welcome to use what the town has. I'm sure the town's council will appreciate your money; just as I'm sure Abraham Quest's counting house has enough coinage to keep even the grasping rascals that run the free port happy. Will you still be requiring the services of your guide?'

'Guide?' said Amelia, bemused.

Veryann stepped in. 'We will.'

'Bit of bad luck there, too,' said the official. 'Ironflanks is in the garrison stockade at the moment. A couple of my up-landers dragged him in for disturbing the peace. Smashed up a place three nights ago. Nearly broke the neck of a drinking-house owner.'

Amelia could not believe her ears. 'That's a steamman name, surely? A steamman smashed up a jinn house?'

'He's not the normal sort of chap you find coming down from the Steamman Free State,' said the embassy man, 'that I will grant you. I suspect the town council will be only too glad to boot him out of here this time.'

Amelia raised an eyebrow at Veryann. 'Ironflanks . . . a steamman?'

'He came highly recommended,' said Veryann, a touch of defensiveness breaking through her icy demeanour.

'Oh, don't misunderstand me, there's much to recommend him,' said the embassy official. 'Whenever we get a party of hunters after thunder lizards, they always want to retain Ironflanks. Brings back more safari expeditions alive than any of the other trackers here, have no doubt on that score. But he does have his funny little ways . . .'

'Go on,' said Amelia.

'Well, not to put too fine a point on it, I am afraid the old steamer is as barmy as a barn full of badgers. He is under the impression that the jungle talks to him. Rumour has it that King Steam exiled him from the Free State when he wouldn't submit to some much needed mental adjustments.'

Amelia turned on Veryann. 'I told Quest at the start of this that I would only command this expedition if I had my pick of its team members.'

'Ironflanks will be a scout operating under my command,' said Veryann. 'We require his knowledge of the jungle. Besides, given what happened in the engine room at the hands of one of *your* people, I do not believe you are fit to sit in judgement on the House of Quest's choices of staff for this expedition.'

Commodore Black stepped between the two women when he saw Amelia starting to bridle. 'Professor, we'll be mortal glad to have someone with a knowledge of the lay of the land when we are further upriver. Bull's rascals know the rapids and flows of the Shedarkshe, but they never ventured further inland than the river villages they gassed for their slaves.'

'Take me to the stockade,' Amelia ordered. She glanced at the tartan on the two redcoats' kilts. 'Twelfth Kilkenny foot?'

'The Crimson Watch,' confirmed the official. 'Devils with that cutlery on the end of their rifles, but you'd better watch your pocketbook when you're in the garrison, damson, what? Now, I was never much of a one for books, but one thing has been puzzling me . . .' He waved his hand towards the tall dark jungle squatting ominously on the opposite side of the river 'Exactly what kind of science is your expedition proposing to conduct out *there*?'

Amelia remembered a cartoon in the *Illustrated* poking fun at Abraham Quest's Circleday pastime; pottering around the grounds of his mansion, personally helping the large army of gardeners he employed. A leering caricature of Quest knee deep in the mud of his pile's grounds, a sapling growing up before his legs in a phallic manner with the label 'money tree' hung around it, the speech bubble reading: 'Forsooth, my soil-fingered helpers, see here, I have grown another large one.'

'Orchids,' said Amelia, 'Abraham Quest is very fond of rare orchids.'

The official looked at the line of menacing Catosian mercenaries on the *Sprite's* deck, then at Bull Kammerlan's feral-looking sailors emerging to sniff the air – blinking at the novel freedom of being outdoors after serving years of a Bonegate water sentence, followed by long weeks cooped up inside their u-boat. 'Ah, yes, botanists. I'm surprised I did not see it before.'

A burly uplander leafed through the keys on his chain, searching for the one that would unlock Ironflanks' cell in the Rapalaw Junction garrison.

'He should have calmed down by now,' the guard explained to Amelia, Veryann and the commodore. 'Ironflanks is a bonny enough lad when he hasn't been snorting.'

'Snorting?' said Amelia.

'Chasing the silver-stack, my lady. He's a quicksilver user, but he's no' been putting any magnesium into his boiler while we've been holding him down here. Poor old Ironflanks is on a bit of a downer at the moment.' He pulled open the rusting door, revealing a steamman that bore little resemblance to the members of his race Amelia was used to back in Jackals. For a start, however battered and rusting the life metal became back home, they never, never, wore *clothes*.

The three visitors from the submarine stood there, lost for words. Ironflanks looked up at them, poking inside his filthy, bloodstained hunter's jacket with a stick, as if he was attempting to dislodge a leech.

'Ah, my friends from the House of Quest, I presume? You have, I trust, brought the filthily heavy chest full of Jackelian coins that I was promised?'

'Your fee is secure in our boat,' said Veryann.

'That's good, my little softbody beauty, because I have managed to mislay the agent's fee your people sent up. Damn careless of me, I know.' His two telescopic eyes increased their length, focusing on her in a way that could only be described as predatory. Ironflanks jangled the chains binding his four metal arms – his architecture looking like it had been modelled on a craynarbian. 'Then let's be about it, my good mammals. Tick tock. If we wait any longer it'll be night, and I doubt if you three can see in the dark, even if I can.'

'Same time next week, then, Ironflanks?' laughed the guard, unlocking the chains.

'I believe I shall forgo your hospitality for a while, McGregor softbody. Now be a good fighting unit and fetch me my cloak and the other property your ruffians removed from me last night.'

'It wasnae last night, man,' said the soldier, 'it was three bloody days ago.'

When the uplander returned to the cell he was struggling under the weight of a gun so large it should have been classed as an artillery piece.

'I was under the impression your people favoured pressure repeaters powered by your own bodies,' said Veryann.

Ironflanks shouldered the weapon and then tapped the twin stacks rising from his back. 'My boiler is not what it used to be, dear lady. Besides, a repeater might be adequate to shoot up the bluecoats of a Quatérshiftian brigade, but a thunder lizard is quite a different kettle of armoured-scale fish.'

Veryann led the steamman away, his clanking metal legs leaving impressions in the dried mud under his weight.

'You still think we need his help out in the jungle?' Amelia asked the commodore.

'Lass, this is a pretty pickle and no mistake.'

Amelia bit her lip. They were sailing an antique u-boat into one of the most dangerous, uncharted regions of the world; surrounded by a crew of convicts, a fighting force of hair-trigger mercenaries that even their own country didn't want, and carrying a saboteur determined to stop them. Now they could count among their group the maddest steamman outside of a Free State asylum. Her damn luck had to turn at some point.

Not for the first time, the undermaid wished the front door of their grand house in Westcheap had a speaking tube to filter out the callers. It was bad enough that every chimney sweep and hawker on the crescent called every morning trying to convince her or Cooky to purchase their wares, now she had to deal with simpletons too.

'This is not the house of any Damson Robur, sir. It belongs to Lord Leicester Effingham today, exactly as it has done every day for the last twenty years.'

'You are in error, damson,' insisted her lunatic visitor. 'I visited the lady just a few nights ago here and this house is the residence of Damson Robur.'

'You have the wrong address, fellow,' said the maid. 'All the crescents and lanes about these parts look alike if you do not live around here.'

'Then who was staying here three nights ago?' demanded the visitor.

'Exactly nobody was here, sir – the place was empty. Lord Effingham was at his country residence in Haslingshire. I have only just travelled down to Middlesteel with his cook to open up the house for the season.' She pointed to the dark rooms behind her, furniture in the hallway hung with white linen covers to protect them from the deposit left by the capital's smog. 'Does this look like an occupied house to you? There's dust all over the place; Circle knows, it's me that has to clean it all up. Try the crescent on the other side of the park, why don't you? The lanes all look alike, especially after a night of carousing.'

She shut the door on the unexpected caller and went back to sit with Cooky and their nice pot of warm caffeel down in the kitchen. Within five minutes she would have been hard-pressed to describe the visitor's nondescript face to anyone who might have asked. Which was precisely the point of that face.

Around the corner, her visitor entered a covered arcade of small shops selling pottery and walking sticks. Cornelius Fortune emerged from the exit at the other end, walking into the crowds of a teeming market. He feigned an interest in the long silver eels being slapped down on the wooden surface of one of the stalls, checking the reflection in a shop front to ensure there had been no watch set on the house. No tail emerged from the arcade, no confused expressions trying to locate the vanished visitor. So, what mischief was to be had out of the disappearance of Jules Robur, the continent's greatest mechomancer? Damson Robur did not exist, and now it seemed, neither did her father. There were always complex games of deception and guile being played between the paranoid members of the First Committee as they jockeyed for power and position across the border in Quatérshift. Had such a game been played with Furnace-breath Nick as one of their pawns? The thought of that ate at him like a cancer.

'Lovely, ain't they, squire?' said the fishmonger behind the stall. 'Special offer today, take away one of these lovelies and I'll throw in a free tub of sweet jelly.'

'The long one, there,' said Cornelius.

'I can throw in a nice piece of slipsharp heart for tuppence more. So oily you can cook it in its own juices.'

'Just the eel,' said Cornelius. 'I rather think I have other fish to fry now.'

Standing on the dock, Amelia moved out of the way of a chain of bearers carrying repaired components from the gas scrubbers deep into the interior of the u-boat for T'ricola to reassemble in her engine room. The sonar man Billy Snow was sitting on top of an upturned fishing boat, in a position where he could have seen everything going on in front of him – if he had only possessed the requisite sense.

Amelia went over to him. 'You get around Rapalaw Junction better than I do.'

'There's not much here, is there?' said Billy. 'But I can always follow my nose back to that soup that passes for air inside the *Sprite*.'

'Damn it, but I hope we can fix up our boat soon.'

'So eager for the greenmesh?' said Billy. 'I know why I'm here, professor – same as the rest of the seadrinkers. We only feel alive when you shove us in a can and push us beneath the waves. But you? Why do you care so much about some city that may or may not have been buried under Liongeli an eon ago, before a floatquake pushed it up towards the heavens?'

'You want the simple answer? It is knowledge. The Camlanteans had the perfect society,' said Amelia. 'They lived in peace without hunger or war or evil for a thousand times longer than Jackals has endured; but we know so little about them.'

'Your colleagues back at the universities doubt they even existed,' said Billy. 'I shall let you into a little secret. Before we left Jackals, I imposed on T'ricola to purchase the book that you wrote – *The Face of the Ancients*. She and Gabriel are kind enough to read me a chapter from it each evening.'

'Well then, I believe I might have trebled this year's sales of the damn thing,' said Amelia. 'I would have had more luck if the stationers in Middlesteel sold it as celestial fiction. That tome you are enjoying finished my career. The High Table made sure there was not an expedition or dig in Jackals that would take me with them after I had it published.'

'Admitting to what you don't know is even harder for the learned than the ignorant.' The sonar man waved out towards the jungle. 'They were not so perfect, I think. If they were, Middlesteel would be called Camlantis and their people would be here today, not dust and ruins under the weight of a half-sentient jungle.'

'But we don't know!' Amelia tried to communicate the depth of her passion for the subject. 'Circle knows, what we understand about the Chimecan Empire is sketchy enough, and they made their holds deep underground when the cold-time came – what preceded their time is shrouded in myth and legend. Where he could, my father collected every crystal-book, every piece of parchment with a legible script of Usglish, every paper and theory on the Camlanteans, and—'

'—And yet still what is lost, is lost,' said Billy Snow.

Amelia remembered when her father was still alive – sitting at his knee, the excitement with which he talked about how Jackals' ancient democracy was a hollow echo of the perfect utopia it could become. Somehow she could never pass on the vision as clearly as he could. 'My theory is that the Camlantean civilization was supported by the same techniques we see perverted today by Cassarabia's womb mages. They had found a way to live in harmony with their world, and most of their craft was lost to history for no other reason than it was living, alive. Apart from their crystal-books, most of it just rotted away after their realm fell.'

Billy shivered. 'Those who serve as slave wombs in

125

Cassarabia might debate your ideals of utopia, professor. I'm a u-boat hand, not a jack cloudie, but I know our aerostat crews have mapped most of the low-lying floatquake lands. No one has ever seen something the size of Camlantis drifting about up there in the heavens – not once. If your city is as lost as that, there is a reason for it.'

Superstition from a sailor? Well, Amelia was hardly surprised. Billy's trade were always genuflecting to some god of the sea or river down below decks, invoking spirits and chanting in the hidden corners of the *Sprite of the Lake*. No wonder the Circlist church refused entry to many of the men of the sea.

Amelia glanced curiously down the docks, towards a flurry of activity in the shadow of the trading town's walls. It looked like a newly arrived trader was finishing setting up shop, a crowd of people from the town gathering to see the merchant. The haste that was being shown by the audience was in stark contrast to the listless pace of business she had seen conducted everywhere else in Rapalaw Junction.

'That's odd,' noted Amelia. 'The market is in the centre of the town, but everyone is flocking out here to visit that stall?'

'Can't you hear the hawker's cries?' sighed Billy. 'Ah, of course, they're in bush tongue. It's not slyfish and game meat this one's selling. Come on, you might as well see the sight along with everyone else. Their kind aren't allowed within the trading post to conduct business.'

Now Amelia really was curious. As she and Billy got closer she saw a folding table had been set up in the shadow of a wooden platform, a line of figures standing aimlessly on the boards, the centre of attention of the gathering crowd.

'A slaver!' spat Amelia, reaching down for her pistol holster.

Billy's hand snaked out and gripped hers with an uncanny accuracy. 'No, quite the opposite in this instance. You might consider their vocation the liberation of slaves. It's called a comfort auction. Watch and keep quiet, whatever you see or hear. Rapalaw's citizens get very emotional when traders in this line of work visit the post. If you try and interfere we could both be ripped to pieces.'

The trader in charge of this miniature market was looking very pleased with himself, biding his time until the crowd grew large enough for his satisfaction. A plate of meat had been brought up to the trader's table, a flagon of beer by its side. The trader wiping his fingers on his sweat-soaked jacket looked like nothing so much as John Gloater, the cartoonists' favourite Jackelian everyman. Living up to the image of Dock Street's savage portly patriot, the trader gave out a belch and then waved at his craynarbian associates to push the goods forward on the platform. The figures Amelia had taken for slaves were a sickly-looking lot, gaunt, with vacant expressions frozen on their faces. Women, men, craynarbians, even a small grasper, all swaying slightly on the platform. There wasn't much fight left in them. The trader's assistants appeared to be there more to stop them stumbling off the edge of the platform than to prevent them from escaping. If this was an auction, it was one of zombies. But whatever their race, there was something the figures all had in common; it looked as if their skin had been scrubbed raw, the lines of their veins left exposed, an abnormal viridescent colour – a fretwork of green cables throbbing against their flesh.

Pushing to his feet, the trader waddled in front of the platform and raised his arms to still the crowd. 'Quiet now, my lovelies. My last voyage up river has, as you can see, been a fruitful one. But not without risks. It was a fierce expedition, our passage littered with the bodies of a dozen of our best porters. And in the dark heart of the jungle, on the edge of the greenmesh, we lay our ambush; luring two patrols into the pits we dug, dug with these hands . . .' He raised his soft white hands, palms out. Whoever had been doing the digging, it hadn't been the trader; those hands hadn't raised anything heavier than a fork for a long time.

Amelia looked at the platform with fresh eyes. *The green-mesh*. It began to dawn on her what this sale was about.

'Now do you see?' whispered Billy. 'His "goods" travelled too close to the greenmesh and were absorbed by the Daggish Empire, made slaves within the unity of the hive.'

Amelia felt sick. These trade goods had once been people with families and loved ones. Now what were they? Half-dead wasps waiting at the foot of Rapalaw Junction's walls for a bargain to be struck.

'He's chemically cleansed them of the hive's control,' said Billy. 'What you see up there is what the extrication process leaves. Although truth to tell, everything that made them who they were was scrubbed out of them a lot more assiduously by the Daggish when they were assimilated into the hive.'

'Do any of you lovelies who have come before me today recognize any of these splendid emancipated souls?' asked the trader.

'That one,' shouted one of the crowd, pointing to the man at the end of the line. 'He was on a safari that disappeared in the interior two years ago; come up from Middlesteel, I think.'

'Nobody here willing to pay for him, then?' The trader looked wistfully around the crowd, noted the silence, then scribbled a note of provenance against the names on his list. Perhaps there would be someone back in the civilized world of Jackals who would pay. Rich enough to hunt thunder lizards, there'd surely be someone with deep pockets at the other end of the river that would want their father or their husband back.

'What about this one, then?' said the trader, waving a chubby hand at a dark-haired man standing over six feet tall. 'One of my porters said they thought he was the pilot on a river-boat from Rapalaw that went missing a while back. An unlucky fellow who sailed too far east and ran into a Daggish seed ship.'

From further back in the crowd came a shriek of recognition, a woman pushing forward with a girl of about twelve hanging onto her coattails. 'Coll! Coll Ordie, don't you recognize me? Look —' she lifted up her girl so he could see '—it's your little Maddalena. She was only nine when you were taken.'

The ex-slave looked blankly down at the two of them from the platform, his face frozen in an emotionless rictus. Amelia saw the trader's subtle hand signal, and one of his craynar-bians gave the man a prod in the spine with a sharp stick.

'It's me,' coughed the man. 'I've come back.'

Amelia's eyes narrowed, and Billy gave her hand a warning squeeze. Whatever little was left of these unlucky wretches, the emancipated slaves of the Daggish had been well tutored to say one phrase since being freed. Amelia wagered that with a poke in the back, everyone standing on the platform could repeat that utterance.

'It warms my heart,' announced the trader. 'Oh, it truly does. This, damson, is what makes the dangers and perils of my endeavours worthwhile. This is what I live for. But a river pilot, someone who knows the flows and tricks of the great river Shedarkshe, I cannot let him return back to you as cheaply as I might a mere trapper of hides and furs, oh no. I have to pay for my porters and my soldiers and I have to pay for the families, like yours, left lonely where my brave crew have perished in our sallies against the fierce Daggish. So many mouths that must be fed. Shall we say sixteen guineas for your husband?'

'Sixteen guineas?' cried the woman. 'I should sell my house in the post and still be left five short!'

'Ah, damson, can there ever be a price put on the return of a father for your beautiful girl? Look at her standing there beside you, weeping. You haven't seen him for so long, have you, my little lovely? How you must have missed him. And you, damson, as much as you love your little one, you must have grown tired of being asked by her every night, "when will daddy return, when will I see him again?" Repeating the very same thing you must have been thinking yourself as you went to bed alone each evening.' The trader raised his arms in a magnanimous gesture. 'But your story has touched me. I shall let him go to you for only thirteen guineas. The price of your house and the good will and merciful coins of your husband's old friends will carry you that little extra way towards me, I am sure.'

'It's me,' repeated the river pilot after another poke. 'I've come back.'

Shaking and confused, the woman tried to withdraw back to the town through the press of the crowd, her daughter dragged against her will, fighting her mother every step of the way.

'Ah well,' laughed the merchant, winking at the men in the crowd after the woman and the girl had gone. 'Hopefully she'll come back with the guineas. Of course, sometimes they haven't been going to bed so alone every night, and then they slip me a guinea or two to apprentice their old man far down river from the trading post.'

Amelia's hand was shaking above her holster and Billy stopping it from dipping down with an iron grip. 'Whatever you think of this, these transactions are still legal. The comfort traders operate just the right side of the Suppression of Slavery Act. Murder, however, is punished the same here as back in Jackals. More swiftly, too.'

'I'll pay your damn leach's money,' shouted Amelia, shrugging off Billy's hand. 'Thirteen guineas.'

'It's not their husband or father you're buying back anymore,' whispered Billy. 'It won't be the same for them.'

An image of the half-empty rooms of her old home came to Amelia, waiting for her aunt to turn up while the bailiffs argued with each other over which of the bruisers would get to remove the choicest pieces of furniture, lifting her father's cheap old oil painting of an imagined Camlantis off the wall and almost coming to blows over it. 'No, it never is.'

'*Sixteen* guineas, my dear lady,' answered the trader. 'The special offer was only for the man's wife, because my heart is a big soft vessel easily touched by the cruel vagaries of our world.'

Amelia pointed down the river to where the *Sprite of the Lake* was tied up. 'And that's *my* vessel, my flabby friend. It's big, but as you can see from the lines of its torpedo tubes, not particularly soft. The *Sprite's* large enough that trading boats like yours are sometimes broken clean in two on our hull if we surface without first surveying the waters above us. You'll be surprised how easy it is to forget the periscope check.'

'You should have said so before, my dear lady,' said the trader. 'To honour a fellow swashbuckler braving the perils of the great river Shedarkshe is a pleasure, never a pain. For today only I shall extend the offer I made to the wife to you. A mere thirteen guineas, and as a token of my respect you may even keep the cotton breeches and shirt I have supplied this poor emancipated soul with.'

Amelia passed her coins across to one of the trader's craynarbian guards. 'Your respect is bought cheaply. Now take him into town and give him back to his family.'

'That trader respects the Daggish well enough, I think,' said Billy. 'As should we, if we are to return from our devil's errand alive. Getting close enough to the hive to tweak their nose – whether it is by stealing back those taken by the greenmesh, or by probing the ruins of Camlantis left on earth, that's not something to be taken lightly. If things go badly for us, I have nobody at home waiting to pay a comfort trader's price for me. I would be better off remaining part of the hive. At least the Daggish feed the slaves they absorb. There's not many who would be queuing up to hire an old blind man scrubbed clean of his schooling in sonar.'

Amelia looked at the people left standing on the platform, empty vessels trying to remember what it was to be human. The freed slave who had once been a river pilot was being led down the platform. How much comfort had she bought that little girl and her mother? Not nearly enough, Amelia suspected. 'If it comes to it, Billy, you shoot me rather than let me be taken alive as a slave by the Daggish.'

Suddenly Gabriel McCabe appeared, one of the *Sprite's* sailors frantically shouting for him across the press of the market.

Billy Snow recognized the first mate by the weight of his footsteps alone. 'Gabriel?'

'Trouble in the town – one of Bull's people.'

Amelia followed after McCabe as he pelted through Rapalaw's gates, heading for the main square. At the centre of the town a small brawl had broken out, sailors from the *Sprite* fighting with craynarbians, a small patrol of uplanders trying to pull them apart.

Gabriel McCabe waded in, lifting one of the crewmen off his feet and spinning him around in the air. The craynarbian the sailor had been fighting tried to slash at McCabe, perhaps thinking the giant was one of the brawler's friends. McCabe's leg had a longer reach than the craynarbian's sword arm and the first mate booted the craynarbian in his crotch shell, keeling him over. More uplanders arrived, the redcoats pushing the two sides apart with the butts of their rifles.

'Who started this?' boomed McCabe. 'You know the commodore's orders – you'll taste the cat-o'-nine-tails for this.'

'It was that thing.' One of the sailors pointed at an old craynarbian, hardly an inch of his shell not covered by rainbow-bright whirls of paint, hundreds of illustrations of eyes detailed on the creature's exo-armour. 'Bloody witch doctor! Said the potion he sold me would see me stay perky all night in the bawdy house . . . instead, I've been pissing out green water since yesterday.'

'It is not my fault,' said the craynarbian sorcerer, shaking his two manipulator arms while his sword and club arms remained vertical in anger. 'I warned this fool that the ways of magic and the worldsong work differently in our land. Leylines do not draw earthflow along predictable channels in Liongeli; the jungle drinks our power and radiates it. You use magic at your peril here.'

'Dear Circle,' Amelia swore in exasperation. 'Is that all you seadrinkers think about? Someone take this idiot away to a jinn house and buy him a *stiff* drink.'

The redcoats from the Crimson Watch hooted with laughter and a few flashed up their kilts in the traditional upland gesture at a joke well-appreciated. As the witch doctor noticed Amelia for the first time, his eyes widened in shock, then he slowly dropped down on his knees, human lips keening like a hound through his face's bone plate. As he did this the other craynarbians followed his lead and buried their knees in the dust of the square, bowing down before Amelia and half-howling, half-singing in nervous voices.

Bull Kammerlan appeared in the square with more sailors,

some carrying cudgels and obviously ready to aid their ship-mates. The convict leader took in the scene with bemusement. 'Everyone likes a lass with big arms, eh?'

'She is marked,' said the witch doctor, barely able to look up at Amelia. 'Do you not see it? She carries the mark of the south, the mark of the ancients. What can the presence of the mark mean for our people?'

'The south?' Amelia remembered the wild woman of the sands who had saved her from the burning desert. And the cryptic message she had given Amelia before she disappeared back home.

'On your knees, you river dogs,' the witch doctor shouted up at the sailors. 'Can you not see she has the mark of the ancients?'

Some of the submariners were backing away uneasily from Amelia, the murmur of 'Jonah' on their terrified lips.

Bull Kammerlan rounded on his men. 'Keep your heads, you damn fools. This old shell has been smoking some bad mumbleweed and you sorry lot start acting like the crew of a laundry house. Was it bad luck that saw us all freed from jail at Bonegate and put on the deck of a u-boat again?'

An old sailor scratched at his grizzled silver beard. 'This is bad, oh this is bad.'

'Hold your tongue, Roth,' ordered Gabriel McCabe.

'Do not show disrespect to the mark of the ancients,' warned the witch doctor, 'or you will invoke punishment.'

As soon as the craynarbian finished speaking a strange whining filled the air, coming from a small black dot in the cloudless sky that was gradually growing larger and larger. The whistle ended in a gurgle as an arrow as long as a spear thudded through the chest of the sailor Roth. He looked down at the projectile in disbelief, his fingers touching the carved bone arrowhead to see if it was real. His blood was flowing onto the ground from the arrowhead's fluted holes, pierced to sing a victory song to the jungle.

'Oh – jigger – that.'

Dark clouds of whining arrows filled the sky as the sailor fell face-first into the dirt, quite dead. On the town walls someone began ringing an alarm bell, the warning of a tribal assault echoing over the adobe and timber walls of Rapalaw Junction's buildings.

'Back to the *Sprite*,' Bull shouted, 'before they shut the town gates.'

'How safe will we be there?' said Amelia. 'We can't submerge yet, and the garrison may—'

'Roger that for a laugh, dimples,' said Bull, pulling out a pistol. 'I'm not camping down here. This place comes under siege by the feral shells at least once a year, and the attacks usually last until the RAN diverts one of the Fleet of the East's airships up here to rain fire-fins down on the craynarbians' armoured noggins. You want to be stuck inside Rapalaw Junction for the next two months, chewing on rat meat and hoping our well water lasts out until the relief force arrives?'

Amelia jolted left, a long arrow banging into the ground where she had been standing. 'I thought hunkering down here would suit you just fine, sailor boy.'

'Not me, girl,' said Bull. 'The richest man in Jackals didn't get to be that way by sending us up the Shedarkshe on a fool's errand. He knows that old sea dog Black has a nose for treasure, and he's paid a pretty farthing to make sure we get to it. Maybe there'll be enough left to fill me and my boys' pockets too, eh?'

By the docks, Quest's private army had taken up positions around the *Sprite of the Lake*. Her tanks had been partially flooded, leaving just her twin turrets visible and the deck an inch out of the river.

Veryann appeared, still serene in the face of the afternoon heat and the impending attack. She might as well have been carved from ice. 'Into the boat. We cast off within the half hour.'

Amelia unbuttoned the flap on her leather pistol holster, the heft of her old Tennyson and Bounder reassuring in her hand. 'We're days away from completing the repairs.'

From the jungle on the opposite side of the river, an armada of rafts was being pushed out into the Shedarkshe, each vessel filled by huge craynarbians, a blaze of war-painted shells.

'Chief T'ricola has the scrubbers running at ten per cent of their capacity,' said Veryann. 'Enough to get us out of the field of battle. The remaining repairs can be made during the voyage.'

Amelia looked across at the heavily armed tribesmen shaking their spears and spring-guns, thousands of them appearing on the opposite riverbank now. If they had half an hour before the *Sprite's* hull and Rapalaw Junction's walls were swarming with craynarbian warriors, siege ladders and hostile witch doctors, she could not see it.

Damson Beeton walked down the corridor of the mansion, her lantern's light flickering over the portraits that lined the gallery. Not that they were anything to do with the master's family – they had come along with the house, left by the previous owner. What had not come, however, was any decent clockwork-timed lighting or heating systems to enliven the draughty corridors and rooms. Where the other islands on the Skerries were palaces of light after night fell, Dolorous Isle stood alone as an oppressive dark mass, only a single pier lamp blowing in the wind to remind the river's pilots that there was life here.

Septimoth was approaching down the corridor from the opposite end, his wings tucked back so they did not knock over any of the table ornaments as he went. The housekeeper and the lashlite met in the middle of the corridor, outside the master's room.

'You heard it too?' asked the housekeeper.

Septimoth cocked an ear to the door. 'It is the dream, Damson Beeton. He is having the dream again.'

'It's not right,' said Damson Beeton, 'a man like him suffering like this. Can't you impose on him to see an alienist? With his money he could go to the best practice in Middlesteel.'

Septimoth shook his head. 'There are some things that are beyond even the powers of your surgeons of the mind and soul to heal.'

'He has the dream once a week now. It was bad enough when they came each month.'

'He is worried of late, I think,' said Septimoth.

The housekeeper waved an accusing finger at the lashlite. 'You two are as thick as thieves with your Circle-damned secrets. Don't think I don't see it. What is the dream, you wily old bird? Master Fortune won't tell me . . . but *you* know, I can see that much. It has something to do with your blind eye, doesn't it?'

Septimoth scratched the back of his neck, at the weal where his seeing eye should have been. The one that gave the aerial hunters their three-hundred-and-sixty-degree vision – along, it was rumoured, with other powers. Such as the ability to see into the future. 'Not directly, damson. I have told you before, this eye I lost because I lacked vision.'

'Teeth of the Circle,' the housekeeper growled in frustration. 'Damn your eyes then, Septimoth; the two you've kept, and the one you lost that makes you a useless manservant in this old heap. I'll be off to bed and hear no more of your double talk until I make the three of us breakfast.'

* * *

Hours later, on the other side of the door, Cornelius Fortune still tossed and turned, in the power of a dream as his two servants had suspected. A nightmare that had become habit.

Cornelius was walking across a recently ploughed field – tilled by hand, now all the horses had been slaughtered for food – in the company of the village simpleton the local committee had found to tend the orchard, leading him slowly across to the tree he was seeking.

'This is it,' said the newly recruited farmer, casting a sad eye over the barren stumps barely rising out of the ground – all apart from one. He raised a hand that had only three fingers on it towards the solitary budding tree. 'But look how this one grows. What a beauty. She's the only one to thrive here.'

'Look how she grows,' Cornelius moaned, his hands scrabbling through the dry mud around the tree. They didn't know how to grow anything in this land anymore. There were no irrigation channels. No water. They hadn't even buried the seedling orchard deep enough for its roots to take hold. One boy tending farm land meant to be worked by a hundred, while his compatriots debated furiously over which illustrious revolutionaries the fields should be named after, passing regulations to bid the crops to grow faster, enacting laws to make it rain more equitably across the regions.

'That's how I knew where to take you, she's the only tree to thrive out in the Glorious Orchard of the Revolution Seventy Six, Farming Community of Heroine Justine Taniayay,' said the boy, getting the mantra just right. 'They say I'm stupid, but I can remember them all, the names written on the sacks, the sacks that smelled so bad. That dead tree over there had a baron emptied over it. That tree next door got a woman who owned the manufactory that made rocking horses; I went on one of those once. Imagine that. I rode her wooden horses,

138

and then I got to empty her over a tree, a tree just for her. And this tree is the one you asked for. Look how she grows.'

Cornelius let his borrowed face slip. He could hold the image of the area inspector no more, his face warping back to his natural features, the tears streaming from his eyes. The simple peasant lad just looked on, as if a melting, changing face was something he saw every day. Cornelius dug out the young sapling with expert care, brushing away the dirt, removing the tree from the ground without killing it.

'You know about the growing and the planting and the old ways?' asked the boy.

'I was a farmer,' said Cornelius, cradling the plant. 'Once.'

'You should stay here, then,' said the boy, as if he was offering Cornelius the crown of the Sun King itself. 'This is a farm.'

Cornelius stood up and touched the boy's arm gently. 'Thank you, but I cannot – I am not a farmer any more.'

'There were more of us here last year,' said the boy. 'More of us helping with the trees and the turnips and the corn and the barley. At least ten people. I remember that – even though people keep on telling me I am wrong, there was never anyone else working with me. There was old farmer Adoulonge too, even though people say there was never a man of that name living here. What do you do now, compatriot sir?'

'Didn't you see my face, doesn't it scare you? I am a monster. But now I shall prey on other monsters. What do you call such a thing, boy? A monster that eats other monsters?'

'Furnace-breath Nick,' smiled the boy. 'The Sun Eater, Old Night-hand. The light priests will tell you stories about the Sun Eater, but I haven't seen any of them in the village for a long while.'

Poor young fool. He knew about the bags that smelled bad, but he hadn't made the connection between them and the diminishing population of his village. The human mind was such a complex instrument. Cornelius could feel his own slipping away even as he spoke, a dwindling dot of reason dimming to nothing along an impossibly long corridor.

'The priests have gone away,' said Cornelius, 'along with your other friends.' He lifted the precious sapling and shielded it inside his greatcoat. The boy stared out across the empty fields, not noticing that his visitor was stumbling west now, away from the farm. Away from Quatérshift.

'I like farming,' the boy said to himself. 'Better than dirty loom work, losing my fingers one by one.'

Howling like a dying fox, Cornelius glanced up at the sky as he lurched across the dead ground, the summer sun beating down. He should only look at the sky now, so clear and pure and unsullied. Filled with the sun. Waiting to be devoured. Don't look at the mud, don't see the ground bones lying between the furrows. White, angular bones. He lifted the sapling he had dug out high to the heavens, the young trunk left moist and supple by the fertilizer of his murdered wife's flesh. His tree, his darling tree. She would grow again, but not in the spoiled soil of Quatérshift.

He shook the young tree at the sky. 'This is my wife, this is the child that was in her belly.'

A shadow grew in the sky, dark, bloated, born in the sun and feeding on its warmth. '*She will live again. Your unborn child too. They will live in the torment of those that murdered them.*'

'I'll give you blood,' he screamed. 'Is this what you want? There's an ocean of it inside the bastards who did this – a whole jigging revolution's worth of blood.'

See the sky.

'*Yes.*'

See the sun.

140

'*I shall show you my face.*'

Sun.

'*My true face.*'

Sun Eater.

Master king of demons. With a smirking mouth concealing a furnace and the rotting heart of the devil. Licking at the splintered bones in the fields. Smacking his lips as the juice of mangled souls ran down his burning throat. Furnace-breath Nick.

The light grew brighter, blinding him, consuming the sun.

Cornelius sat bolt upright in bed, panting, the light fading away to become the shine of an oil lantern swinging in Septimoth's hand. In his other he held a squirming lad, dangling upside down with one of his boots clutched tightly by the lashlite's talons.

'I've told you before about going out fishing along the river late at night,' said Cornelius.

'This fish flopped onto our island all by itself,' said Septimoth. 'I heard him trying to force the lock to the east wing.'

'I wasn't trying to break into your house, mister,' said the boy. 'My name's Smike, I've been sent here with a message for you. What sort of bleeding nob are you anyway, employing the likes of some wild bloody lashlite to guard your place? There should be a law against it.'

'Knowing the House of Guardians, there probably is.' Cornelius looked at the lad; it was giving him a crink in his neck trying to talk to him upside down. He motioned to Septimoth and the lashlite flipped him around and put him back on his feet. Smike stood there shakily for a second, dripping water onto the floorboards. Cornelius waited until his silence had made the boy suitably nervous. 'You swam across?'

'You think there's a boat that would risk their river authority licence by dropping the likes of me onto your pier at this time of the night?'

'You mentioned a message,' said Cornelius. 'You must forgive my look of disbelief, because to the best of my knowledge, the only people who know that anyone other than a wealthy, reclusive hermit is living at this address are already inside this house's walls. And I'm afraid that doesn't include *you*.'

'Well now, how I got to be here is a right old tale for the telling,' explained Smike. 'I didn't catch a name, but the bloke who paid me was an old goat, robed like a Circlist monk. Going around pretending he was blind, but he wasn't, he could see well enough for me and him both.'

'A blind monk? That doesn't sound like anyone I know,' said Cornelius. 'Go on . . .'

'This old goat was worried about a run of Steamman grave robbing that's been going on in Middlesteel, organized by the flash mob. Not the new ones just down from the Free State, mind – but old models, the older the better. I saw a little of it going on myself, the Catgibbon's blades doing the dirty with the shovel work.'

'Is that all?' asked Cornelius. 'There's always some mechomancer trying to get hold of body parts from the Steamman Free Steam, trying to lift up their own craft by prying out the secrets of how King Steam puts his people together. Grave robbing's a crime for the crushers to solve, it gives the detectives from Ham Yard something to do.'

'Now if that isn't what advice I gave to this old bloke,' said Smike. 'He told me your reply would be along the lines of what you just said, too. But he paid me to tell you that one of the mechomancers who was after steammen parts was an old friend of yours from Quatérshift, one who, quote, "you would have been far better off leaving behind in a

Commonshare prison camp". Does that make any sense to you, mister?'

Cornelius pushed himself off the four-poster bed. 'When was this?'

'About a week ago. I would have come sooner, but the crushers took me in to discuss a small matter of some pocket-books going missing in the lanes of Rottonbow. They got the wrong'un, of course.'

'A week . . .'

That was hardly a day after he had gone over the curse-wall into Quatérshift to get Robur out. No one knew the timing of his incursions except himself and Septimoth. 'Did your friend say anything else?'

'Just that you would know what to do next,' said Smike.

'He was wrong about that,' said Cornelius, 'I'm damned if I know what to do next. How much did this man give you to memorize the message?'

'Five sovereigns,' lied Smike.

Cornelius's eyes twinkled in amusement. 'Sink me, but you're slightly more expensive than the penny post.' He walked to a drawer and slipped five coins out, passing them to the lad. 'That's to forget the message, and to forget the address of my house.'

'Address?' said Smike, pocketing the coins. 'We're in the upland glens, aren't we?'

'Just opposite the southern frontier, I'd say,' said Cornelius. He glanced at Septimoth. 'Ask the damson to take our young friend to the pier and hail him a boat. Do get her to check his pockets before he departs, though.'

'You're a right gent,' said Smike.

Cornelius looked out over the distant skyline resting beyond the river: the crumbling rookeries; the more modern pneu-matic towers swaying slightly in the fog; the dark silhouette

143

of an aerostat of the merchant fleet drifting across the half moon.

Septimoth returned, no doubt having been given a roasting for waking up their housekeeper at such an ungodly hour. 'You were wrong when you said that the only people who know that we are living at this address are inside our walls.' The lashlite pointed up towards the ceiling.

'I have an understanding with the Court of the Air,' said Cornelius. 'I don't bother them and they don't bother me. They think it's rather amusing, the jig we lead the First Committee over in Quatérshift. It suits their purposes. But their tolerance only stretches so far. If we start lifting the flash mob's bludgers from Middlesteel, it won't take the capital's pensmen long before ballads and penny dreadfuls begin to appear on the stationer's carts with Furnace-breath Nick's face painted on the cover. We need a safe base of operations on this side of the border to strike at the Commonshare. Life on the run will hamper our activities.'

Septimoth considered his friend's words. With their powerful wings, his race were the only people apart from the Court of the Air's own agents to have seen the connected aerospheres of the great aerial city, floating far beyond the reach of normal airships. The wisdom of lashlite sages' recalled a time when the watchers in the sky had not dwelled far above the land. For the people of Jackals below, the secret organization Isambard Kirkhill had built to safeguard parliament's victory in the civil war was a matter of conjecture, their agents, the wolftakers, a mere whisper in the jinn houses. Only by their wake could you know the Court of the Air. Missing rebels, the door left ajar on the oddly empty apartment of a crooked politician, science pirates who would simply disappear on the eve of a long-planned victory. Like the great sages of the people of the wind, the Court also attempted to peer ahead into the future. Not with any prophetic third eye, but with their mighty transaction engines, the steam from their endeavours forming a perpetual cloaking cloud around the city in the air. In that steam lay the future, it was said. Cornelius was quite right, of course. Neither of them could afford to become a rogue element in the Court's calculations of their perfect democracy, an element that would require *eliminating*.

'You already have a ballad on the stationer's carts,' said Septimoth. 'You must have heard it? They seek him here, they seek him there, the furnace-breath killer with the demon stare.'

'We hunt monsters.'

'Are we now to hunt them closer to home, Cornelius Fortune?'

'Take on the Catgibbon and the flash mob? Sweet bloody Circle,' said Cornelius.

'The monk appears dangerously well informed about our real purpose here and our activities,' said Septimoth. 'Even if his warning about rescuing Robur from the Commonshare finds us a little late.'

'Quite. But rotting steammen being turned out of their graves?' Cornelius scratched his unshaven cheeks. 'What do we know about the people of the metal? None of them stayed long in Quatérshift after the revolution, not after the Commonshare was declared. The Sun King used to treat the Steamman Free State as if it was just another of his dominions, and the Commonshare's First Committee act little differently now. The shifties have started more wars with the steammen than they've ever fought with Jackals, but why would their agents want to sponsor a spate of steammen grave-robbing?'

Cornelius sighed. He might have a scant understanding of the people of the metal, but he knew someone who did: at the Old Mechomancery Shop along Knocking Yard.

'I shall ponder the matter in my eyrie,' said Septimoth. 'You had your dream again, didn't you?'

Cornelius said nothing.

'You should try and dream less,' advised Septimoth, leaving and closing the door.

'Yes, I should.'

Cornelius got back into bed and tried to nod off to sleep again, a near impossible task. This was all wrong. Grave robbing, the game of mirrors that had been played on him across the border in Quatérshift to free Robur, a monk who knew all about his secret life as the scourge of the shifties. It was all wrong. Were the monsters coming to Middlesteel again?

Veryann's fighters had taken up positions on the dock, sheltering from the storm of darts being launched from the wild craynarbians' spring-guns. They returned fire in a smooth rattle; slipping crystal charges into their rifles, ejecting broken glass around the pier, burning blow-barrel hissing as it struck the planking. Above them, a short-nosed cannon had been pushed up to the fortifications of Rapalaw Junction, geysers of water erupting around the tribe's war rafts as the trading post's defenders tried to deny the tribesmen a firm foothold below the town's walls.

Amelia kept her spine pressed up against a low adobe wall, the thud of darts on the other side dissuading her from doing more than snapping off the occasional shot at the lead boats with her pistol. One of the sailors broke cover and tried to run across the boarding ramp to the *Sprite*, two darts spearing him in his chest and hammering him down into the water. There was a thrashing in the river as something small and hungry finished off the howling submariner in a froth of bubbles.

'Stay low,' shouted Bull Kammerlan. He pulled the ejector

rod on his carbine and a shower of broken crystal sprayed back as the clockwork mechanism forced the expended charge out. 'We need more covering fire from the walls before we can run for the boat.'

'Their rafts are going to be landing along the town's front within a couple of minutes,' said Amelia. 'Best we were gone from here before then.'

'Really? There's me thinking that the boys and me would be doing a bit of fishing along here later,' said Bull. 'You write a paper on it, dimples; leave the killing to the men.'

A ricocheting arrow interrupted Bull's stream of sarcasm – it glanced off Ironflanks, the steamman wandering out from the town's closing gates as carefree as if he were taking a stroll along Goldhair Park back in Jackals. Dart heads bounced off his iron body, one piercing his wide-rimmed hunter's hat. The steamman went up to the corpse of a fallen uplander in front of their adobe barricade and began tugging the soldier's long leather army boots off, a task made more difficult by the amount of blood soaking the pin-cushioned uniform.

He looked down at Amelia, crouching on the other side of the wall. 'Waste not, eh? Fine pair of boots, as fine a pair as I've ever seen.' He slid out a machete and began to hack the corpse's ankles away.

'Ironflanks!'

'Nothing to worry about,' said Ironflanks, mistaking the professor's disgust for concern about their predicament. He vaulted to their side of the wall. 'These mammal-shells attack every other season. They get their fever up listening to their gods' calls for sacrifices, get tired of eating their own braves out in the jungle. They're inconveniently early this year, I must say.'

Down the shoreline, the first rafts began to thump against the line of piers, craynarbian warriors that must have been twice the size of the largest of the defenders leaping out – some with grappling claws to scale the walls, others with heavy sacks connected to vine-woven ropes. These they whirled around their heads, releasing them up towards the battlements. As each vine snapped taut, it unplugged a valve in the attached bag – two chambers of blow-barrel sap mixing and exploding against Rapalaw's walls in a shower of clay fragments.

'To the u-boat,' shouted Ironflanks, tucking the bloody boots under his belt. 'I'm going to get my steam on.'

Amelia cracked a pistol shot off, ducking as a wave of darts answered back. 'It's suicide. There's too much fire coming across the *Sprite's* hull.'

Bull Kammerlan pointed up towards the battlements, where squat, toad-like mortars were being pushed forward. 'Dirt-gas, dimples. Once the feral shells hold this side of the shore, our garrison will soak the whole river in dirt-gas. Unless you've got a mask hidden underneath that blouse of yours, you're going to want to be breathing the wind from the commodore's arse inside the *Sprite*. It'll be a damn sight better than the air out here.'

On the exposed ground between the sailors and the Catosian fighters' position, Ironflanks danced a jig, his twin stacks glowing white-hot as he fed power to his ancient boiler. 'Now I'm sizzling, now I'm burning!'

Two craynarbians leapt from the prow of their canoe, Ironflanks meeting them in a fiery arc as he vaulted over the makeshift barricade protecting the expedition. Each of his four arms had produced a weapon, machetes and long knives blurring as he cut off the nearest of the warrior's heads, blocking a bony sword-arm and smashing down on the remaining fighter's knee joint with a cudgel. Both craynarbians were falling while the steamman sheathed two machetes, unslinging his thunder-lizard gun from his shoulder and jetting the canoe with its charge. Even in the steamman's manipulator hands the rifle bounced, the recoil sending Ironflanks back by a couple of steps. He had loaded a tree shredder – a jungle special – half a pound of shot humming down the length of the war crew like a nest of hornets. Screaming craynarbians fell into the water, their armour shells ruptured and torn by hundreds of lead balls.

Amelia had seen steammen knights fight before – awesome, powerful, a force of nature – but this was different. Even in their battle rage King Steam's knights retained a vestige of control; they fought like a focused storm of tonne-weight steel. But Ironflanks seemed to relish the danger as if he were a savage, bounding onto the raft with his rifle shouldered and his blades drawn, sadistically crushing falling braves under his metal feet, the craynarbians' blood splattering his safari suit as he laughed and danced and hacked his way through the ranks of struggling attackers.

'Now I'm burning,' called the steamman, his voicebox on full and a whistle on his back lifting in a victory scream, superheated air spearing upwards. 'I'm on fire.'

One of the surviving craynarbians, his breast-shell half-torn to pieces, tried to jump on top of Ironflanks' back, clutching onto the steamman's belt and the bloody boots he had looted. But Ironflanks twisted the craynarbian off, throwing him to the floor of the raft and burying the tip of his long knife in the creature's forehead. 'They're my boots, wild shell, mine! Patent leather is no good for your claws.'

War chants sounded from the armada of rafts in the river. One of the craynarbian witch doctors, identifiable by his fur-covered antlers, was calling on the worldsong, twisting the power of the rainforest-covered land to the tribe's own end. In front of their boats the fast-flowing waters began to froth and bubble. Shouts from up in the battlements of Rapalaw Junction urged the dispatch of more gas shells from the garrison's arsenal.

'That's not good,' said one of the Catosian fighters.

The storm of darts from the tribe's spring-guns had momentarily abated and Bull leapt up. '*The Sprite*, boys, to the *Sprite*.'

'Not with her!' A sailor pointed at Amelia. 'Not with the Jonah!'

'Oh, for Circle's sake.' Amelia took the initiative, pushed up and began to run towards the u-boat.

Out on the river Ironflanks twirled around in an obscene mockery of the craynarbian sorcerer's spell calling, almost perfect imitations of the jungle's animal-song echoing from his voicebox – tree monkeys, paradise wings, redcats, hunting spiders. Across the wide, deep river birds exploded into the sky and the creatures of the canopy howled and hooted back. Spooked into action by the flare-up of life in the jungle, the submariners broke for the *Sprite's* boarding gantry as a panicked mob. In contrast, the Catosian mercenaries fell back in two disciplined lines, one rank kneeling and firing, then stepping back through their comrades, smoothly reloading their carbines as the second rank poured fire back down the shoreline.

Out in the river the witch doctor's chants were finally answered by an eruption of winged fish, a cloud of purple scales and rainbow fins bursting out of the water, fluttering off the walls of Rapalaw like bats, others of their number bouncing across the river, skimming into the sailors still fleeing after their Jonah. Poison-barbed fish heads buried into the striped shirts of the *Sprite's* crewmen, tiny razored mouths gnawing at the flesh of their victims.

'Ironflanks,' Amelia cried, 'back to the boat!'

She tried to drag one of the fallen sailors towards the conning tower hatch, but his face was swelling like a balloon, the skin of his bloated fingers turning rigid as his throat muscles expanded and slowly strangled him.

Veryann appeared and rolled the dying man into the river with a kick. 'The toxin from the flying fish is fatal – there's no cure.'

Over the top of Rapalaw Junction's walls the thud of launching gas shells at last sounded, fingers of yellow gas trailing behind each projectile. Where they landed, clouds of noxious fumes mushroomed out, fountains of mustard tentacles curling up as far as the town's ramparts. The redcoats looking down on them had leather masks with locust-like goggles strapped under their shako hats now, a single tube swaying from the front of each soldier like the snout of an anteater. Amelia could smell the sickly-sweet gas already, the taste of cinders and the promise of burning lungs hanging in the air. Its presence in the wind made her skin itch and she had to fight to hold down her panic. Dirt-gas was meant to be humane – first unconsciousness for an oxygen-starved brain, then a quick smothering of the target's lungs – but she did not want to put their aerial navy's propaganda to the test.

Plunging into the safety of the conning tower Amelia turned to watch the scene of horror through a porthole; curtains of gas drifting across the river and masking the town's walls, sailors and Catosians running through the hail of devilbarb fish, spinning as their bodies were caught and pierced. The crackle of rifle fire echoed eerily through the mist, then out of that grim fog of death came Ironflanks, the steamman striding backwards with his four arms flickering in a dance of steel. His hunter's hat had been mounted with the antlers from the craynarbian witch doctor, still bloody where they had been removed – with some force, Amelia imagined – from their owner's skull. Three enraged craynarbian fighters followed from the fog, thrusting their spear-like spring-guns towards the steamman while he croaked at them in the voice of a rainforest moon-toad. Over their faces the feral shells had strapped on something that looked like a wet slug, a sack of pulsing black flesh. It was their answer to the redcoats' dirt-gas.

Bull Kammerlan ducked through the tower's hatch, the bloody body of one of his crewmen draped over his wide shoulders. 'Masks! Some of them have got gas masks. They've been gassed outside the junction for centuries and now the damn feral shells have finally found a way to even up the odds.'

Amelia had a sneaking suspicion that Bull's slave raids along the river might have educated the tribes in the use of gas as much as the defenders of the trading post, but she held her tongue. Pushing through the surviving sailors, Veryann appeared, replacing her carbine in its leg holster. 'The tribe's spring-gun darts are harmless against our hull, but if they should turn their improvised grenades against the boat . . .'

Amelia slid down a ladder into the pilot room. Commodore Black was hanging onto the periscope, watching war rafts emerge from the curtain of gas, heading straight towards the *Sprite*.

'Make ready for diving stations,' called the first mate. 'Everyone inside. Rapalaw will have to fend for itself.'

'The feral shells are mortal stirred up about something, lads.' Black reached over to the wall and pulled out a speaking trumpet from its bracket. 'T'ricola, I'm looking at you for some cheery news on our scrubber assembly now.'

Billy Snow flicked a switch on his console and the cray-narbian engineer's voice vibrated out of a voicebox above them. *'Two minutes more, skipper, maybe five.'*

'Gabriel?' The commodore looked across at his first mate.

'Diving stations aye, commodore. We're locked and sealed.'

'Time to show our teeth,' said the commodore.

Amelia borrowed the periscope. The war rafts were larger now, almost on top of the u-boat. 'They're too small to hit with torpedoes, Jared?'

'I would not be wasting my precious glass-tipped fishes on these beasts, professor,' said the commodore. He turned to Billy Snow, the blind sonar man's head heavy with an iron dome and cables hanging off his skull. 'Port lances?'

'Can you not hear them humming for you, skipper?'

'Those crabs up there are close enough to my lovely old lady now, Billy. Let them hear the hum too.'

Billy's fingers punched the console in front of him. Outside the hull there was a low hiss as pneumatic tubes opened, pushing out a series of serrated spikes from the u-boat's two conning towers, twin crowns of metal thorns emerging from the *Sprite*.

'Wild power,' said Amelia. 'Sweet Circle, you're carrying a capacitor on the *Sprite*.'

'The power electric,' said Billy, throwing down a switch.

She remembered the strange burned tiles she had seen exposed after their engine-room fire; it appeared they were insulation against more than just the cold of the open ocean. Amelia returned to the periscope. Beyond the u-boat, the river was lit by an undulating circle of lightning flickering from the *Sprite's* two towers, the waters burning, devilbarb fish fried in mid-flight, the blow-barrel grenades of the wild craynarbians detonating as the chambers of explosive sap were joined by the force electric. Pieces of wooden raft and smoking craynarbian exo-shell rained down around the u-boat, dead river creatures floating up to the surface of the Shedarkshe before being carried downstream, towards Jackals.

'It used to work better, the wild power,' said Billy. 'Something that people could control and direct. For peaceful uses too, not just war. But the world changed.'

Commodore Black took back the periscope from Amelia and gazed at the carnage across the water. Craynarbians on the far shore were already massing for a second attack, darts streaming over towards the *Sprite of the Lake*. 'You're a fine one for old legends, Billy Snow. The power electric works blessed well enough for my tastes.'

The voicebox sounded above their heads. *'Skipper, you have the scrubbers back again.'*

'Take us out, Gabriel,' ordered the commodore. 'Take us out slow and steady.'

Sailors bustled around their posts in the pilot room, but the only answer to their efforts was a hollow knocking running along the hull. It grew louder every second, the hull vibrating with a fury.

'First mate?'

'Something is wrong.' McCabe ran over to the double pilot seats.

'Kill the propellers,' ordered the commodore, 'shut down the screws before my girl burns out.' He turned his periscope towards the tail of the u-boat. 'Ah now, there's the wicked thing.'

One of the exploding war craft had been approaching the *Sprite's* stern and the force of it striking the u-boat had twisted one of their iron rudders into the path of a propeller. They were jammed and beached.

The first mate surveyed the damage through the periscope. 'The rudder's only slightly bent, but it's enough to foul the rotation of the screws.'

For the first time since the trip began, Amelia started to feel the claustrophobia the seadrinkers called the black tunnel.

'Can't we heat it up with welding torches, bang the rudder back into shape?'

'Do we have enough power left for a second tickle on the lances, Mister Snow?' asked the commodore.

'They're spent, skipper. Pistons need to be turning to recharge them.'

'Well then, there it is.' Black looked at Amelia sadly, as if he was disappointing a favourite granddaughter. 'A work crew will take too long. With our lances working we could hold the craynarbians back, give them a taste of the wild juice when they get too snappish. But without them . . .'

'There is another way.' Gabriel McCabe stood to his full height, his heavy frame nearly brushing the copper pipes along the pilot room's ceiling. 'If I go now, before the shells have a chance to reform their ranks, I might be able to bend the rudder back into shape.'

'That's suicide,' said Billy. 'The tribes' braves will be swarming over our hull and Rapalaw's walls like wasps smoked out of their nest.'

'You heard the applause of the crowds in the gambling pits, Billy Snow, when I bent steel bars for their wagers.'

'I had assumed that was a Circle-damned parlour trick, old friend.'

'Does the trick work as well for two?' Amelia's worldsinger-twisted arms lifted up to clutch onto the rungs of the conning-tower ladder.

'You do not have to do this,' said McCabe.

'To get away from this cursed corner of civilization and send us towards the foundation stones of Camlantis? Yes. Yes I do.'

'Let her go,' begged one of the sailors, 'she's a bloody Jonah. If we keep her on the boat we'll all—'

Commodore Black swung around, landing a pile driver on

the submariner's face and the ex-convict spun onto the deck, unconscious. 'No annoying the cargo, lads. If it weren't for the professor, *your* mortal luck would have left you all swimming back in the tanks at Bonegate. You ponder on that. If I hear any more fiendish talk of a Jonah on the *Sprite*, I'll walk the next of you rascals to speak such filth through the sea lock without a helmet.'

Gabriel showed Amelia how to suit up in the conning tower closest to the *Sprite's* screws; their rubber suits their only protection – not from the water, but from the waves of dirt-gas still being mortared out of Rapalaw Junction towards the attacking savages. Shaped like one of the seashells children in Jackals pushed against their ears to hear Lord Tridentscale's whispers, Amelia's copper helmet screwed down tight into her neck plate. Her crystal visor was barely wide enough to allow her to see her air tank, before the first mate slipped the tank's straps over her shoulders.

As Amelia finished suiting up, the handle on the sea lock spun and Ironflanks stepped into the small chamber. 'Excellent, Amelia softbody, I see that you have made a start without me.'

'This could be a one-way trip, old steamer,' said Amelia.

'I'll return from this trip in penury unless I get you to the source of the Shedarkshe,' said Ironflanks. 'If we stay behind here, the second half of my fee is going to stay locked up inside Abraham Quest's counting house.'

'You're quite the mercenary,' said Amelia. 'Most steammen of my acquaintance are happy enough with a pail of coke for their boiler and a single room to lay their head down at night.'

Ironflanks squawked a burst of what might have been laughter through his voicebox. 'For a short period, my boiler heart shall run as well on dirt-gas as it does on air. And as for your rich countryman's Jackelian guineas, don't you worry, I'll find something to squander his silver on.'

Gabriel McCabe moved his massive bulk – made even larger by the diving suit – towards the conning tower's outer lock. 'We will not be able to evade their spears in these suits.'

'You two see to this submersible's rudder,' said Ironflanks. 'I shall deal with your mammal-shell cousins when they come hunting for us.'

Choking green clouds muffled the sound of the water lapping against the *Sprite's* hull and the echo of rifle fire from the trading post. If the hell denied by the Circlist church's vicars existed, it might have looked something like this. Amelia's lead-lined boots clanked against the hull as blind shots from the garrison spouted in the river. She could hear Ironflanks' feet clanking behind her, the steamman sweeping the empty mist with the business end of his massive thunder-lizard gun.

Dead craynarbians bobbed in the water, shuddering as something still left alive in the river gnawed at their shells. She could just make out the war song of the savage craynarbians, a whistling fluting thing, followed by the crash of dart spears against their exo-armour. Amelia said a quick meditation to the Circle, imploring that the lunatic steamman escorting them did not join in the chorus; she and the first mate were exposed enough as it was in their clumsy diving suits.

Gabriel pointed ahead – there was a twinned assembly of propellers at the rear of their massive u-boat and the starboard side's screw blades were caught against a twisted fold in the rudder. Gabriel said something, then realized his words were too muted by their helmets to be audible. He pointed to the rudder and made a hand motion indicating they should both seize it. Amelia anchored her feet against the iron frame while the first mate took the opposite side, his glove-encased hands gripping the battered steering mechanism above hers. Together they applied their muscles to the metal, Amelia pushing it while Gabriel McCabe pulled from the opposite end. Behind his visor, the first mate's face was contorted in effort, condensation misting the crystal. Already stretched tight around her massive arms, the rubber of Amelia's diving suit dug deep as her muscles swelled taut. If the suit ripped, the best she could hope for would be burns along the skin where the dirt-gas worked its foul business . . . if the tear opened a path to her lungs, then bleeding, blistered skin would be the best of it. Gabriel roared with the exertion, the yell of anger audible to Amelia even inside her helmet. She could hardly see now, floods of sweat running down into her eyes. Somewhere above the gas clouds the Liongeli sun was pouring its fury down onto Rapalaw Junction, heedless of fools in rubber suits and their desperate efforts. The rudder just appeared to be moving when a dart jounced off the metal, blue drops of ichor splattering Amelia's visor as it broke. Poison. They filled their darts with venom milked from the flying fish!

Ironflanks stepped in to block the attack, darts glancing off the riveted metal under his hunter's jacket as he hefted up his thunder-lizard gun. The rifle bucked in his hands like an incensed dragon as he emptied a buckshot load towards the origin of the whistling darts.

Driven by the scare of nearly being injected with jungle venom, Amelia pushed at the rudder with all her might, screaming into the rubber-scented air of her helmet. Gabriel pulled, his grasp so tight he was leaving indentations in the metal. More darts punched down, a deadly rain, bouncing off the steel deck boards and into the river. Amelia felt rather than heard the bang of the craynarbian raft impacting the side of the *Sprite*. She tried to concentrate on moving the rudder, on clearing the bent metal from the propeller blades, ignoring the massive wild shells leaping onto the u-boat. Ironflanks ran towards the craynarbians, yelling abuse and rotating his machetes like an iron windmill enchanted to murderous sentience – but these savages were not for scaring.

At last, amazingly, the rudder suddenly began to move – bending easily, as if it had been heated in the afternoon sun and was now butter beneath their grasp. Down the deck Ironflanks fought the craynarbian savages with a precision only a steamman could muster, two arms trading blows with a wall of thrusting spears, while another two scissored out, severing the slug-like face mask of one of the warriors. Coughing in the dirt-gas, the craynarbian stumbled back, Ironflanks crushing the squirming living gas mask underfoot then swivelling to kick the warrior overboard.

More braves leapt off the raft, bypassing the craynarbian-steamman duel and running towards Amelia and the first mate. Their job on the rudder was done, but it looked like it was going to cost them dearly. Amelia swore, cursing her bulky gloves and the pistol she'd had to leave inside the *Sprite*. Gabriel gave a thumbs-up towards the periscope and drew a sea knife from his belt. Standing beside the giant submariner, Amelia slipped out her own blade. Craynarbians had a lifetime to learn how to fight inside their bulky exo-shells; Amelia was a newborn in her heavy, hot suit. One of the warriors jabbed at Amelia with his spear and she clumsily turned it aside with her knife arm, then grabbed the wooden shaft with her left arm, locking it into place. The craynarbian began a tug of war for the spear, trying to batter her with his shield, a round piece of bone armour from the corpse of one of the jungle beasts. Amelia rolled forward, unbalancing the brave and coming to her feet with possession of the spear. Her opponent came at her with his shield up, the perfect stance for deflecting a spear thrust. But Amelia Harsh was not a shell warrior – she was a Jackelian, the daughter of a disgraced politician. Ostracized perhaps, but her father had still been a master of debating sticks – trading blows on parliament's dais of democracy with the heavy staff of a Guardian. And how Amelia had studied at his feet! She swept the spear's shaft down into the warrior's knee, swivelling up, out, to whirl the brave's shield into the air. The brave thrust at her with his sword-arm, the serrated limb clearing her neck by an inch. With the spear-staff in her hands all her father's lessons were returning to her now, the sweet rhetoric of the debating stick, every dirty, nasty, street-fighting trick the political fighters of Middlesteel had developed on the capital's lanes and boulevards.

Tripping the craynarbian with a blow known as the 'chancellor's statement', Amelia ducked down and snapped a clout across the warrior's armoured forehead, giving him a 'second reading' with all the strength in her massive arms when he tried to stumble back to his feet. Behind her, Gabriel was using his gambling-pit pugilism, swinging the unconscious carcass of one of the craynarbians into the warrior's comrades, his body weaving left and right as they stabbed at him with their spears. More and more craynarbians were gathering behind, ready to wreak their revenge against these soft-skinned invaders of their realm. It was only going to take a minute more, with these odds. Gabriel and Amelia were surely both about to fall to a flurry of jabbing spear points.

Amelia glanced down at the water. With their wet suits she and Gabriel could leap into the river and cling onto the *Sprite* while the u-boat got underway – the risk of the river predators of the Shedarkshe surely better than certain death where they stood. It would mean leaving Ironflanks to fight his way back to the trading post, though. She was momentarily torn. Then she made her decision: better that the two of them survive – and there was always a chance for the steamman, however slim. Amelia was about to tackle the first mate from behind and cast them both into the river when a conning tower hatch opened. Bull Kammerlan strode out of the door, a couple of his sailors behind him, suited up with seashell-shaped air tanks – and something else, besides: they were bent under the weight of chemical batteries strapped to their backs, gutta-percha insulated cables dangling down to tridents almost twice as tall as the sailors stood.

Screaming war cries as loudly as they could with black gas-filter slugs strapped to their faces, the craynarbians charged at the submariners. Pulling up their heavy tridents, the crewmen swept arcs of crackling blue fire over the savages. Meant for driving off the tentacles of the leviathan-sized squids that were attracted to the superheated waters of the Fire Sea, the trident energy was devastating to the warriors. Expanding organs and veins blew out the thorax armour of the warriors in the front row of the charge, blood issuing out as hisses of red steam from inside their bodies. Behind them, the second wave contorted and danced in the wild cerulean flux of the power electric. Some of the boiling craynarbians near to Ironflanks flung themselves into the river, desperately trying to cool their bodies, with others who had escaped the combat following their lead, swimming out towards the veil of dirt-gas before they too were torched.

Amelia, Gabriel and Ironflanks made for the safety of the conning tower, trying not to slip on the smoking corpses that now littered their escape route. Bull Kammerlan played his trident around the river with a face as triumphant as a demon's, laughing inside his helmet as the fleeing savages jerked then sank beneath the waters. Despite owing him her life, Amelia wanted to smash in the visor of the dark-hearted slaver's helmet, but the instinct was suppressed as she winced at a sudden lance of pain in her arm. She stared down dumbly at the poisoned dart piercing her suit rubber, then collapsed as the air fled her lungs. Ironflanks and Gabriel caught her falling body, dragging it into the sea lock, red spots of pain swimming through Amelia's vision. Inside the *Sprite* someone began cutting the suit off Amelia's arm, her flesh expanding like a balloon. It was T'ricola, the craynarbian engineer peeling Amelia out of the diving suit with her bone-sword arm. Amelia gagged as she tried to say something, but her constricting throat smothered the words.

Bull was inside the tower, pointing the tip of his trident against her belly. 'Let me finish her now, it'll be a Circle-dammed kindness.'

As Amelia's oxygen-starved brain shut down, Veryann's words came back to her: '*The toxin from the flying fish is fatal – no cure.*'

The professor began her last convulsions.

CHAPTER SEVEN

Damson Beeton came into the servants' pantry with a beef and potato pie balanced on a pewter plate. Septimoth was accustomed enough to the race of man's eating conventions that he felt a pang of hunger at the sight of the steaming hot pie. Briefly he regretted how acclimatized he had become to Jackelian ways. No true flight brother would have been stimulated unless they had first seen their supper soaring in the currents of the sky, or scampering along the ground from a hundred foot-high glide. Lashlite brains were wired to detect movement and feed only after the chase. It was a measure of the depth of his fall from grace that his gut could now be urged into action by boiled roots and the motionless bovine carcass the housekeeper had squashed under her cooked pastry.

'Have you seen him, Septimoth, have you seen the master? It's well past time for supper.'

'He is about the house,' said Septimoth.

'Is that so, butler? About our corridors, is he? About our empty dusty rooms? How easy it seems to be for him to disappear into the vastness of this cold, dark place. This place which he seems unwilling to pay to adequately heat, staff, or adorn with the niceties of society.'

'He will return when he is ready, damson.'

'Of that I have no doubt.' The old lady carved off a quarter of the pie for Septimoth, pushing a chunk of warm bread onto his plate. Then she separated out a generous portion for Cornelius Fortune and tucked it into the warm oven, keeping the slimmest portion for her own supper. 'Point him in the direction of the oven when he appears, old bird. I have no doubt you will still be about when he chooses to show himself.'

'It shall be as you say,' noted Septimoth.

Before she turned in for the night, Damson Beeton produced a crimson feather. 'Have you been moulting. Septimoth?'

Septimoth stared intently at the semi-scaled feather. 'Where did you find that?'

'With a handful of others like it, you old pigeon. In the shrubbery in front of the house.'

Septimoth's tucked-back wings seemed to shiver with anticipation. 'In the garden?'

'Just so.' She placed the feather on the table. 'If the master will hire nothing but day labour to tend the garden, is it too much to ask you to drop your feathers in your own tower, or better yet, in the compost heap behind the lake?'

Septimoth watched the housekeeper waddle off to the warmth of her quarters at the far end of the house. He picked up the crimson feather from the table. This was something he had not seen for a long time, not since Quatérshift. Nor was it something he had expected to see in Jackals for the remainder of his lifetime. He was tempted to ignore the call. He was an outcast, so let him act like one. But it was too powerful a totem to resist.

Falling upon his slab of pie, he devoured it in a display of rapaciousness that would have turned Damson Beeton's stomach and earned him an admonishment had she still been in the room. Then he removed the portion that had been set aside for Cornelius Fortune and took it towards the lifting room in the corridor outside. There were only three storeys to Dolorous Hall, but the mansion's current owner had paid for an eyrie tower to be built for Septimoth, the round stone construction lancing out of the roof like a black finger. Septimoth corrected himself; at least, there were only three storeys that were *visible*. Once the lifting-room doors had closed, Septimoth pulled out an ivory handle from the copper wall panel, twisting a second handle counter-clockwise. Rather than rising up to his quarters, the room started to descend, falling through the bedrock of the island with the hiss of counterweights rising in the opposite direction and the clack of the turning clockwork cable feeder.

After three minutes the lifting-room doors opened onto a long corridor, rough-hewn rock walls dotted with flickering oil-fed lanterns mounted below the lead pipe that fed them. Before the capital's river had been artificially widened to prevent flooding, the islands of the Skerries had been hills, prosperous enclaves looking across the nearby Gambleflowers and the city below. Septimoth emerged in a large hall, briefly glancing up at the fish and the dark course of the river flowing over the atrium skylight of the old Middlesteel Museum. It had not taken much to seal the abandoned building underwater and pump it free of water. Even Jackals' most secret of police forces, the Court of the Air, were unable to peer beneath the Gambleflowers with their sorcerous watchers.

It was amazing how much of the old museum's stock the curators had abandoned in the basement chambers, before moving to their acreages of new marble over in the west of the capital. Unfashionable royalist statues and artefacts mostly – a cavalier on horseback, waving a carbine at a rearing goreback; the massive lion-headed iron expansion engine that had taken the royal airship *Scramblewolf* across the ocean to discover Concorzia and the other colonies. Now the abandoned museum had only one patron and a couple of regular visitors. Cornelius Fortune was in the museum's main hall at the centre of the building, sitting in the shadow of a large transaction engine that should by rights have been delivered to the endless engine rooms of Greenhall, but had instead been diverted to their island – piece by stolen piece. Septimoth placed the plate of supper next to the boxes of purloined punch cards that his friend had acquired from the civil service.

It never surprised Septimoth how easily such things came into Cornelius's possession. Before Quatérshift, before the mask, his friend had been Jackals' greatest thief. The thief with a thousand faces, with an identity so fluid he had flowed across the capital, taking what pleased him, making any mischief that entertained him. *The Nightshifter*. Many years ago. Before the curse of love.

'Your supper, sir.'

'You play the butler poorly, old friend. I'll take it in a little while.' Cornelius pointed at the pile of glossy gutta-percha punch cards, each one proudly embossed with Ham Yard's coat of arms in one corner. 'There's a pattern to the grave robbing. It's always steammen being turned out of their coffins and it's always the oldest corpses being taken. Where there's a young cadaver, the body is left untouched.'

'Young is a relative concept when applied to the people of the metal,' said Septimoth. 'Steammen outlive our flesh by many spans of both our races' lifetimes.'

Cornelius showed his friend the list he had compiled. 'None of the officers at Ham Yard know what to make of this.'

'Are you sure these crimes are linked to Robur?'

166

'Even if I hadn't been tipped off by that young urchin from Rottonbow . . . I can feel it, Septimoth. In my bones. He is behind it. You carried Robur's body over the cursewall, what do you think?'

'I have no talent for pre-vision now,' said Septimoth. He placed the crimson feather down on the table next to the plate. 'But there are others who have.'

Cornelius raised the feather between his fingers. 'Your people? I thought you carried the death mark, old friend? You've been exiled. They'll kill you if you fly into one of their nests, rip you to pieces.'

'I will not need to travel to one of our villages. They will come for me.'

'Let them bloody wait,' said Cornelius. 'Let them fly in circles around Middlesteel until their wings turn blue with cold and ache with tiredness. What do you owe them?'

Septimoth pulled out his bone pipe, turning the flute sadly in his long talon-like fingers – all that remained of his mother, the squadron-queen, his whole tribe. 'You know what debt I owe my people. Did we not escape from Quatérshift together, after you broke the door to my cage?'

'Sweet Circle,' Cornelius swore at his friend's stubbornness. 'You are dead to them, Septimoth. Your people's rulers can go jigger themselves, the way they have treated you.'

'The spirits of the wind still whisper to me,' said Septimoth, 'I can hear my gods again. Stormlick has not yet abandoned me. I must answer the mark of the crimson feather.'

'If you must,' said Cornelius. 'But if your people want you to go off on some mystical sky quest hunting for skraypers to bring down, you tell them you are otherwise engaged. We have work to do. I have compiled a list of locations where our grave-robbing friends are likely to strike next.'

'I shall be back in good time,' said Septimoth. 'There will

be hours enough for me to ride the fog above Middlesteel's graveyards for you.'

Cornelius underlined the name at the head of his list, a stolen census record selected from the pile of punch cards. 'Not a graveyard. Our opponents have already had their pick of the plots of the dead. The oldest steamman left in the city still has a beating boiler heart . . . and I have a suspicion our slippery refugee friend Robur is about to switch from troubling the deceased, to kidnapping and murdering the living.'

It had been an age since Septimoth had needed to follow the mark of his own kind. But even without his third eye, he could still smell the scent of a lashlite hunt on the breeze. It was strange that he now shared more in common with Cornelius Fortune than with his own people. The cold burning desire for revenge far stronger than any call he felt to hunt skraypers in the higher atmosphere. His once proudly held position as ambassador to the court of the Sun King had always marked him as an outsider, more fluent in monkey-tongue than the whistling true speech of his own people. How much stranger would he appear to his own kith and kin now he hobbled around Dolorous Hall with his wings bent small, living only to inflict terror and pain on those who had wrought his downfall?

Riding up the thermals from a line of mills along Bunsby Green, Septimoth turned towards the pneumatic towers of Sun Gate. How like those who sat in judgement upon him to pick the highest vantage point in Middlesteel for their meeting. Tucking his wings back, Septimoth plummeted like an arrow, spreading them in a fan configuration at the last second to hit the roof of the tower where their scent was emanating from. It was a showy entrance, the kind Furnace-breath Nick favoured to strike fear into the hearts of the enemy.

Standing on top of a line of smokeless chimneys were the four seers of the crimson feather, only the gurgle of the tower's water-filled wall support system for company this high up.

Septimoth nodded to them, denying them the customary full bow where he should expose his dead, scarred third eye to the seers. After all, what could they do – blind him a second time? 'I had not expected to receive the mark of your call again.'

'As we do not expect to be greeted in the tongue of the flightless monkeys.'

'You seem to understand it well enough.'

'You have become far too closely intertwined with their ways and memes.'

'The race of man call it "going native", I think you will find. A peril that comes with banishment.'

'And how have you atoned for your crimes, Septimoth? By random acts of violence against the tribe of flightless monkeys that stood—'

Septimoth pulled out his flute and waved the white instrument towards them in fury. 'By the bones of my mother! By the bones of my people and my family and my honour, I have sworn I will not rest until the Commonshare is pulled down around the First Committee's ears – death by death. You shall not speak of my vengeance, you are not fit to do so!'

'Fine words, Septimoth. It is a pity you did not caution your tribe with such prudence when the flightless monkeys in Quatérshift were undergoing their meme change. If you had done so, your squadron-queen, your mother, would still be alive in this realm, rather than floating in the song notes of her spine bone that you so angrily brandish towards us.'

It was as if the seers had twisted a knife in Septimoth's gut. All the pain and misery and bile of that wound overflowed. 'The court of the Sun King was corrupt, their people held in serfdom and bound by obsolete ritual. Those infected by the meme spoke noble words, of equality and fraternity and—'

'You were of the ambassador caste, Septimoth; you were not in the court of the Sun King to act as a participant. All new memes are accompanied by sound and fury as they establish their infection in the presence of the population. Did not Stormlick whisper vigilance to you as you studied these monkey communityists? How could you fail to notice the ferocity of their meme, its pure loathing for competing ideas, its *exclusivity*? For all its faults, the old regime was a multi-racial assembly. Whither now Quatérshift's graspers, its steammen, its craynarbians and lashlites? Those who have submitted are little better than slaves to the pink skins, and for those that fought . . . for your people, those fine flowery words you heard came at a terrible cost.'

Septimoth writhed on the roof in agony. 'I shall atone for my mistakes.'

'On your feet, ambassador,' said the tallest of the seers. 'We do not exile those of the true flight for poorly given advice. You know why you were banished.'

'There were so many bodies,' pleaded Septimoth, his figure briefly thrown into shadow by a passing aerostat, the airship's expansion engines a muted thrum above them. 'I was the only one left alive after the soldiers found the trail up into our mountains. My tribe was massacred, how could I eat so many?'

A long talon pointed accusingly at Septimoth. 'Do their souls speak to you with curses on their beaks, ambassador? The souls you left to be collected by Nightstorm and her devilish servants?'

'I tried,' said Septimoth, his voice falling into a fluting hack-whistle as he sobbed. He remembered his fallen family's flesh hanging from his mouth as he desperately tried to eat them all. So many hundreds of bodies strewn around his village, hanging out of eyrie slits, littering the streets with Quatérshiftian lances run through them. How could a single lashlite give so many of the dead their proper honours, even without the distraction of the laughing Commonshare soldiers? Calling him a filthy cannibal, cutting off limbs from the corpses and tossing them at him. Applauding him as he tried to save the souls of as many of his people as he could by feasting on them.

'The tribe consumes the tribe,' quoted the tallest of the seers.

'Nothing for the enemy, nothing left for Nightstorm to steal,' intoned the others.

'Nightstorm will release my tribe's souls,' cried Septimoth. 'She will release them when I nourish her with the feast I shall make of my flight's Quatérshiftian murderers.'

'Your feast of revenge shall wait,' commanded the seer. 'As miserable as you are, as pathetic a wretch of a hunter as I have ever seen, you carry the mark again now. The Seer of the Stalker Cave has foreseen you herself. Her will is law, even for an exiled monkey-talker like yourself.'

'I am in her visions?' The thought shocked Septimoth. He was unclean. Exiled and broken. How could he appear in the prophetic dreams of such as she? Supreme among the oracles.

'We are as appalled as you that it is so. After your time with the dirt dwellers, do you still recall the high hunt?'

Septimoth remembered the soaring joy of his youth; gliding so high he was only breathing through his sealed oxygen sacks. The rip of raw, savage elation as the hunt sighted a skrayper, diving on the zeppelin-sized creature, manoeuvring past its wavering tentacle stings to drive spears into its blue flesh. 'I do.'

'Then you must also remember the portion of the hunting territories that you were forbidden to enter?'

'You speak of the whispering sky.'

'This is what has been seen within the Stalker Cave. The whispering sky is evil and its song calls many to it. It has been foretold that the whispering sky shall awaken soon and that one of the flight will stand strong against it.'

'Me? How can this duty fall to me? I am broken wing, the walking dead uneaten.'

'You have a part to play, as do the flightless monkeys and the people of the metal. Our seer has foretold the violation of the cogs and crystals of the living metal. You must follow the steammen's path of pain.'

'The grave robberies in Middlesteel?' whispered Septimoth. 'Is that what the holy of holies means? Did she speak of a connection with a mechomancer from Quatérshift, or an old blind warrior?'

'She spoke of you, Septimoth, and that was enough to unsettle any who were bid to listen.'

'She said nothing else?'

'Only that you are to give us your bone flute to bear back to the Stalker Cave.'

'This is my mother's spine,' said Septimoth. 'I ate her corpse myself and I shall not relinquish it.'

'What we ask is as an act of faith, Septimoth, of devotion. Your bone flute shall be returned to you when you have flown along the currents that have been revealed by the Seer of the Stalker Cave. We ask this of you, but in return we must trust our people's fate to a dirt-grubbing exile. That is *our* act of faith.'

Septimoth hissed a curse and passed the instrument over to the outstretched talon awaiting it. 'Keep my mother's bone safe, seers of the crimson feather. That is not a request, you understand? Not a suggestion. Or you will discover how far I have fallen in my exile.'

With that, the lashlite stepped back off the hardened rubber roof and fell towards the ground before his wings spread out, and he glided up and out of the street below. On their chimneys the four seers stood, their heads nodding gently, lost in thought.

Then the tallest of the lashlites spoke. 'Can we trust him?'

'He is what we have. What the Stalker Cave has given us.'

'An ill-favoured wind blows,' complained the tallest. He sniffed at the polluted air of Middlesteel in disgust. 'And it is not the miasma of industry created by these eager little monkeys.'

'You forget, I have seen the future too.'

'It was empty in your vision?'

'As dead as a field of glaciers from the coldtime.'

One of the lashlites tutted. 'Septimoth will not be enough to save us.'

As one, the seers rose from their perches and broke for the sky, heading back to the mountains of the north.

Amelia did something she thought she would not do again – she blinked awake and tried to sit up. A hand pushed her down, human-like fingers backed by heavy shell armour. 'T'ricola.'

The craynarbian engineer was sitting on the edge of her bunk. 'Rest, professor. We had to bleed you in a dozen places or your body would have burst like a rotten fruit. You've lost nearly a quarter of your blood.'

As the craynarbian spoke, Amelia felt the sting of the wounds, the throb beneath bandages that had been expertly lashed around her arms and legs. 'I was reliably informed that devilbarb-fish poison is fatal.'

'To you soft skins,' said T'ricola, 'not to us; their sting is painful to craynarbians, like a Jackelian adder bite – but not lethal.' She raised her serrated sword arm. 'I opened you with this. My sweat contains an anti-toxin that allowed you to survive. I rubbed my tears over your wounds too, close to an incision I made above your heart.'

'Then I'm lucky to be alive,' said Amelia. 'And I'm sorry that I made you cry.'

'Even back in Middlesteel, in the streets of Shell Town, it is an important ritual,' said T'ricola. 'But you are lucky that part of your flesh has been turned by a worldsinger, yes? The muscles in your arms resisted the poison until I got to you. A normal body would have succumbed far faster.'

'Once a Shell Town girl, always a Shell Town girl, eh, T'ricola. I owe you my life.'

The engineer slapped the sides of the bulkhead. 'Shell Town is just where I bunk, professor. I'm a third generation sea-drinker, born on a u-boat beneath the Tharian Straits, swaddled alongside the pistons of an engine room. This is my home, not Jackals, and certainly not Liongeli.'

'An engineer of people as well as submarines – the commodore is lucky to have found you. I hope he's paying you well for this voyage.'

'People are not so different from machines – spleen and bone, rather than cogs and grease.' T'ricola pulled back the bunk niche's curtain – they were in a far more spacious accommodation than Amelia's cabin. At the other end of the room Commodore Black sat playing what looked like a game of chess with Veryann across a round oak table. For a moment Amelia was stunned by the size of the chamber. Then she remembered. The *Sprite* had once been a royalist u-boat, where the skipper was often lord of more than just the vessel.

'And this must be the first time I have shipped with the commodore and have actually been paid a salary commensurate with my skills.'

'You can thank the House of Quest for those guineas,' said Amelia, 'not that old sea dog.'

Seeing his guest was awake, Black left the mercenary commander pondering her next move and brought Amelia a cup of warm wine, T'ricola leaving to tend her engines. 'Professor, it's mortal good to see you back with us. I thought you might be pushing off along the Circle at one point.'

'Did everyone else make it back alive?' asked Amelia.

'That they did, lass. You and Gabriel cleared our screws and we are happily pushing our way up the Shedarkshe as we speak. Ironflanks took a dent or two from the wild shells, but he fights like a fury, and kept them off your backs long enough for Bull's boys to tickle them away from the *Sprite* with their tridents. We have gone further and deeper into Liongeli than any Jackelian before us. After we get back to the capital, the Dock Street pensmen will write a whole series of penny dreadfuls full of the wonders we have seen while you slept.'

'Just how long have I been out, Jared?'

'Two weeks, lass. Craynarbian tears are a powerful medicine. But you needed it. When I first brought you down here you were swelled up as round as an aerostat. It was a terrible thing to behold.'

Amelia gazed towards a large porthole on the other side of the chamber, small silver fish flashing past outside the armoured crystal. 'Two weeks! Sweet Circle. I don't remember a thing.'

'As well you do not, Amelia. The scrapes we've been in. Pursued upriver by the cunning wild shells for a week, intent on paying us back for the brave scrap we gave them. Set upon by a flock of petrodactyls as we came up for air one moonless night, nearly crushed amongst a pod of mating flipbacks. That the *Sprite* is here for you to wake up to at all is only due to my quick thinking and the guns of Veryann and her fair fighters.'

'Don't think I don't know what you are about, Jared Black,' whispered Amelia.

'Lass, what do you mean?'

'The gymnasia of the Catosian League is what I am talking about, you old dog. Trial by arms and flesh is only part of what free company fighters practise – they value trial by mind and wit equally well, don't they? Strength of arms being meaningless without strength of mind.'

The commodore looked red-faced. 'That may be so, lass.'

'You must prove yourself fit before you bed a Catosian, demonstrate the superiority of your blood lineage,' mimicked Amelia. 'How many games of chess have you lost already, Jared? You should be ashamed of yourself. You are old enough to be her grandfather.'

'Ah, but professor, she is a fine figure of a woman, is she not? You must admit that; she has the beauty of a Jackelian princess and the poise of a sleekclaw. As fine a prize as any skipper ever sailed for.'

'A sleekclaw has a glossy coat, Jared, but that doesn't disguise the heart of a killer beating within its chest.'

'You would not deny a bit of comfort to poor old Blacky, would you? I should be back in Tock House, resting my weary bones with a pot of beef gravy and a steaming loaf of bread by my side. Instead I am risking the precious hull of the *Sprite* for the sake of your career and the promise of the House of Quest's meagre pension, sailing into the heart of darkness, where no Jackelian has ever set foot and lived to speak of it.'

'Go back to your game, Jared. For your sake, I hope that Veryann is as quick with her wits as she is with that side-dagger strapped to her leg.'

'When I was younger, lass, I would not have needed to

prove myself on the chequered board of glory. Ah, I was a fast fellow back then, with a sabre arm that could see off twenty in a duel, a lucky twinkle in my eye that could melt the heart of even such as Veryann.'

'You'll need all your luck if you go biting the pillow with Abraham Quest's tame cobra,' said Amelia, her advice interrupted as the u-boat began to judder, the water outside the porthole flooding with light. 'We've surfaced?'

'So we have, professor. Ironflanks says there is a freshwater pool inland, half an hour away from our position. Our steamman guide has recovered from a little snit, after Veryann found a stash of quicksilver in his cabin and took it away from him. My darling girl's drinking system could do with a top-up now. This wicked river is as feverish as the Fire Sea in high summer. You should take a watch above, clear your head with a breath of the fresh stuff.'

Amelia got out of her bunk and nearly bashed her head on a copper ornament, a replica of the female lance warrior that swept out of the nose of the *Sprite*, except that this lady of the lake was surrounded by a school of dolphins leaping around her. She went to straighten the ornament where she had knocked it, but the commodore stayed her hand.

'Don't be bringing my lucky dolphins down on your head, Amelia. You've had enough of a convalescence already.'

Amelia steadied herself on the side of the bunk, vertical for the first time in weeks, the blood rushing to her head. On the other side of the captain's chamber, Veryann had stood up, checking the two pistols in her breast holsters. She gave Amelia an indecipherable look. Surely the mercenary did not regard her as competition for the vessel's commander?

Out on deck, Amelia saw that the river had grown broader during her recuperation, and was now at least the width of one of Jackals' great upland lochs. Ahead, the river forked and an obelisk rose out of the waters to the side of the junction. Amelia caught her breath and took a leather-lined telescope from one of the watch, focusing in on the figure on top of the granite carving. It was worn and dirty from the rainforest's wet seasons, but the lines of the statue were clear enough. It was a woman clutching a book to her breast.

Ironflanks came clunking over to her, his dirty human clothes lashed with an explorer's backpack dangling with machetes, iron cups and tent spikes. 'One of your Camlantean friends, Amelia softbody?'

'Not Camlantean, not even Chimecan,' said Amelia. The dress the statue was wearing could almost have been Jackelian – she would not have looked out of place buying fruit from a stall alongside the Gambleflowers or strolling through the gardens of Goldhair Park. 'With the amount of weathering on it, it could pre-date both those civilizations. Sweet Circle, how much history is there buried under this jungle?'

'There are such oddities all over Liongeli,' said the hulking steamman. 'The statue may not be as old as you think. The jungle rots and wears away at the craft of both our peoples faster than you might imagine. If you built a home out here and then abandoned it, it would look a thousand years old after only two rain seasons. As an archaeologist, you know well the story of Isambard Kirkhill?'

Amelia nodded. 'Of course.'

'What I am sure your colleges have omitted is that there was a side-history played out here. Forgotten, like everything else, under the weight and decay of the jungle. Following the civil war in Jackals there were schisms in his parliament's alliance – some of the more extreme factions attempted to set up colonies in Liongeli. Isolated communities where they could hold to their utopian ideals without interference. I often come across their bones and relics when I lead hunters out this way.'

'A lost colony of diggers, all the way out here? I have read of such finds in Concorzia, but never this far east. Well, old steamer, here's another heresy for the High Table to chalk up against me.' Amelia stared at the statue: no, the clothes were just wrong; they weren't of the civil war period. Not royalist fancy or parliamentarian plain. The carving had to be older than six hundred years. She felt it in her bones. 'I need a flake from that statue. I can try to date its weathering when I get back to Jackals.'

If the eight universities allowed her to. Jigger them, she could set up her own college with the size of the fee Quest was paying her.

Ironflanks pointed one of his four arms towards an opening in the jungle behind the statue-topped obelisk, a doorway of crushed trees. 'That's the trail to the freshwater spring. Neropods drink from it too.' He noticed the look on Amelia's face. 'Plant eaters, my little softbody friend. They'll crush you if you try to bring one of their pod down, but if you ignore them they'll leave you unmolested.'

Amelia glanced along the deck. Veryann's mercenaries were assembling an iron raft to shuttle them to the shore, a small rotary paddle on the rear powered by a steam engine. They had swapped their carbines for long bulky rifles, each tipped by a bolt resembling the sharp petals of a steel flower. Hanging off their unnaturally drug-swollen shoulders were heavy quivers of replacement bolts.

Ironflanks saw Amelia peering at the odd-looking rifles. 'Abraham Quest's ingenuity runs to more than hiring my services as your guide, it seems. The commander claims their weapons are designed to break the scales of a thunder lizard, penetrate the flesh and rotate inside their organs, inflicting maximum damage.'

'Have they ever been tested?'

'Not by Liongeli,' snorted Ironflanks. 'I sense the symmetry of your transaction engines in their modelling.'

Amelia shrugged off the disdain in the steamman's tone. 'Are our transaction engines so different from the minds of the Steammen Free State?'

'One third of my contempt is reserved for the slow-turning drums of your softbody calculating machines,' said Ironflanks. 'I reserve the remaining two parts for your people's understanding of the jungle and its life. This place is an organism, a system. You cannot model its complexity from the bones of thunder lizards glued back together in Middlesteel Museum, you cannot understand its language by leafing through tomes of flora and fauna pulled from the shelves of your Royal Society. Even our river is alive. You could boil it nine times over and when you drank from it after the tenth time, the fevers would claim your life in a single night.'

He let out a strange hoot and from inside the canopy came a reply annoyed at being disturbed, louder and fiercer. 'That is the language of this place.' He patted the cannon-sized firearm hanging from his shoulder. 'And this is my translator. If you wish to hear the jungle's whispers, come with me to the spring. You think this statue is a curiosity to behold? You'll love the relics inland.'

Amelia cursed the steamman under her breath. It seemed it was not just the language of this green hell he was fluent in. He knew well enough which levers he needed to press inside her.

It took eight sailors from the *Sprite* to pull the cart – a flatbed with eight empty barrels for wheels – through the passage and towards Ironflanks' freshwater spring. On the way back it would be slower going due to the gallons of drinking water they would be carrying. Led by Bull Kammerlan, the sailors had the burden of their tridents and capacitor packs to contend with as well. Ironflanks had argued against the unnecessary weight, claiming the wild energy would as like annoy the larger of the thunder lizards as bring them down, but the convict crewmen could not be dissuaded. Of the Catosians' strange rifles, the steamman made no further comment. Picking her way over the trail of crushed vines and ferns, Amelia found it hard to ignore the assault of smells that accompanied their passage. From rotting vegetation at the ground level, to plants as tall as their Catosian escorts, still dripping from a recent rain and emitting honey-like scents to attract insects for food. Liongeli was alive with a vibrancy of colour and life that was jarringly different from the bleak moors and dark oak forests of Jackals.

Amelia looked at Bull sweating under the weight of his brass capacitor pack and he noticed the disdain on her face. 'You needn't get sniffy about these, girl. They kept the feral shells off your hide long enough for the *Sprite* to slip away from Rapalaw Junction.'

'It's wild energy.'

'And that's what I like about it. You're as careful as that old grandmother Black – or should I use the commodore's *real* name?'

'Not unless you want everyone to use yours, you damn fool,' said Amelia.

'You know who he really is, as do I. Most of the men on the *Sprite* served with the royalist fleet in exile and these—' Bull indicated the line of Catosians—'these bloody foreigners don't give a hoot about Jackals or anything else other than their beloved patron Abraham Quest. As for old Blacky, he won't mind if anyone out here speaks of him as Solomon Dark. He was a duke in the fleet, and me just a lowly baron's son. He likes to lord it up, doesn't he, the big man on his big boat, not that our titles meant much when Jackals' airships came calling for us.'

'You like to live dangerously, don't you, Kammerlan? One of your people might turn you in for the reward on your head. In fact, *I* might . . .'

'You should turn me in, dimples,' said Bull. 'There's more noble blood in my veins than in those half-breed squires' daughters your parliament keeps locked up in their royal breeding house. Lucky for me, my census record is as fake as the commodore's.'

Amelia shook her head. 'If the commodore hears you mouthing off . . .'

'He's soft,' said Bull. 'They all were at court, all the way up to the Lord Protector in exile. Living like privateers rather than rebels. Taking the fat, easy cargoes. Sparing the crews we captured.'

'The commodore told me why he drummed you out of the fleet,' said Amelia.

'Fear is a weapon. The House of Guardians understands that. I just played the game on the same terms as parliament. I put the officers and crews I captured in their own life boats, then I towed them along the margins of the Fire Sea.'

'You covered them in seal fat first!' said Amelia.

'The smell of burning fat attracts ash eels – it was quicker for them than waiting for their rafts to burn and sink.'

'You're a merciful son of a bitch,' said Amelia.

'The royalists lost the civil war six hundred years ago,' said Bull. 'I was just carrying on the fight using Isambard Kirkhill's rulebook. We went from being rulers to being fugitives in one easy stroke. I didn't ask for this life, dimples, I was born to it. My noble blood made me a fugitive from before I could walk, like my mother, like my grandfather before me – an escaped slave for any topper or mug-hunter to collect, dead with my scalp removed, or alive to be tossed into parliament's stud menagerie of royal freaks. The fleet in exile was all we had left, and Black and his soft friends at court allowed parliament to track us back to Porto Principe – let them catch us on the surface before the city could be submerged and our pen doors locked down. The RAN came for us loaded with special fire-fins that could drop through the ocean and detonate on the seabed. It wasn't a battle, it was a slaughter.'

'The commodore saved you,' said Amelia, 'when he drummed you out of the fleet. You weren't at Porto Principe when the attack began.'

'The irony of that hasn't escaped me,' said Bull. 'Now what's left of us have abandoned the cause and we serve only ourselves. We used to make a good living out of selling the feral craynarbians on the Cassarabian slave block, but I daresay the treasure of this ancient place you're taking us to will be worth a few shillings, eh?'

'Nothing you could pawn back on the lanes of Middlesteel, Kammerlan. It's knowledge we seek, the secrets of the perfect society.'

'Is that so?' laughed Bull. 'Abraham Quest didn't get to be the richest Jack in Jackals by sinking his nose in philosophy books. We already had the perfect society in Jackals, until Isambard Kirkhill stirred the passions of the mob and stole our throne for your council of shopkeepers.'

'Watch what you say, slaver.'

'And who I say it to, Guardian's daughter? What did your father ever get out of Jackals' democracy of hawkers and street merchants? A bullet through the head and—'

Amelia grabbed the submariner by the throat and shoved him against the cart, his sailors raising their tridents against her while Veryann's mercenaries snapped their long rifles up at the crew. 'I should crack your throat, you maggot, and finish the job the Royal Aerostatical Navy began at Porto Principe.'

'That's gratitude for you,' choked Bull. He struggled frenziedly, but could not break the grip of the professor's unnaturally large arms. 'Next time you're thick with craynarbian savages, I'll let them fillet you up for their pot.'

Amelia dropped the coughing seadrinker to the ground. 'You mention my father again and that's not going to be nearly enough to keep you alive.'

Bull rubbed the red weal on his neck. 'Spoken like a true parliamentarian, girl. I'll be sure and remember that.'

Both forces let their weapons fall and the journey to the spring resumed. Their broken trail of crushed trees and vines eventually opened up into a flat clearing at the foot of a hill that held a large tarn fed by the course of a waterfall. To the left of the clearing a single line of columns jutted out of the pool and, as Amelia approached, she saw that the spring's waters had covered over a mosaic floor, gold-flecked marble steps leading down into an artificial pool. Just like the statue back at the *Sprite's* mooring on the Shedarkshe, this was from no period of history she was familiar with.

Stepping into the shallows, Amelia took out her knife and tried to prise a piece of the mosaic out, but her blade proved unequal to the task. Fascinated, she peered more closely at the mosaic images – ignoring the u-boat crew's pump being lowered into the opposite end of the pool and the wheeze of their labours at the piston. She was peering at illustrations of the race of man; people intermingled with animals in human form. The hybrids looked like they might be the bizarre breedings of Cassarabia's womb mages – but both the people and the hybrids were dressed in the same Jackelian-like clothes she had seen carved on the statue in the river. Wading a little deeper, Amelia tried her luck on the roofless columns rising from the water. Here too her knife could not even scratch the material, let alone claim a chip of the substance for dating.

'You will not be able to cut it, Amelia softbody,' called Ironflanks behind her. 'It's like no material known to the people of the metal, nor your kind. It has outlasted the rise of the hill and the formation of this spring.'

Amelia ran her fingers down a line of sigils imprinted on the column, their calligraphy both ethereal and precise. It put her in mind of something, but not any of the ancient languages she had seen in the university library. Simple, the language of the transaction engine men. It was a derivative of the symbols on a punch-card writer. 'This is a machine language, Ironflanks. Look at the flow of it, the cadence. These are instructions for a transaction engine.'

Ironflanks stamped closer, lifting the rim of his hat for a better look. 'Why, I do believe you are correct, professor of mammals. But it is no language set known to me, nor I suspect any of your mechomancers back in Jackals. King Steam carries the memory of many lost things, perhaps he—'

Amelia pulled a note pad from her pack. 'I shall take rubbings of the symbols, Ironflanks. This is amazing – an entirely lost civilization.'

But Ironflanks was no longer listening. He had spotted a brown bobbing shape being nibbled at by tiny fish in the spring. 'Get out, professor!' Ironflanks' voicebox shuddered at maximum volume. He waved his four arms frantically at the sailors filling the water cart at the other end of the pool. 'Get back from the water's edge!'

'Ironflanks?'

'A tauntoraptor has given birth in this pool – that is the youngling's faeces.' Ironflanks unstrapped his thunder-lizard gun as he waded towards the professor kicking back to the shore. 'When the youngling is newly born, a tauntoraptor is an—'

Something dark lashed out at the shadow of the sailors on the water, a screaming seadrinker ripped from the shore.

'—ambush predator.'

Shouting in terror and anger the sailors fell back, raising their tridents at the bubbling water where their comrade had disappeared.

'Don't shoot,' yelled Ironflanks. 'By the beard of Zaka of the Cylinders, hold your fire. Let me kill him with my rifle.'

Ignoring the steamman's entreaties the sailors let loose on the pool with their tridents, wild energy flickering over the surface of the water. There was a popping sound as insects exploded, then a flurry of burning fish convulsed to the surface. As they continued to empty their capacitors, a dark bony shape broke the surface, a lizard-rhinoceros with a human leg still hanging from its razor teeth. All the sailors concentrated their fire on the howling green thing and it flipped back, smoke steaming out from under its scales, mewling like the fox song that haunted Jackals' moors. Veryann's fighters were within range now and they finished it off in a hail of flower-headed bolts.

'Damn fools,' shouted Ironflanks at the u-boat crew. 'You've cooked him.'

'A fine meal for the next thunder lizard that comes along,' laughed Bull.

Out of the jungle echoed a terrifying rumble, similar to the death song they had just heard, but amplified a hundred fold.

'That *is* the next thunder lizard coming along,' cursed Ironflanks. 'And you've just boiled up her hatchling for her to smell out. Tauntoraptors hunt by scent, not sight.'

Veryann waved her fighters back from the rainforest's tree line, the furious crashing of falling trees growing louder and louder. 'Form two lines, independent fire.'

'Don't run,' Ironflanks cried at the milling crewmen, a few of whom were already sprinting back down the trail 'Force of fire is the only thing that will bring this beast down. Form up flanking the soldiers. We'll see how well your seadrinker forks fare against an adult tauntoraptor.'

Amelia unholstered her Tennyson and Bounder. Her heavy pistol felt like a child's catapult here in Liongeli. Laying his thunder-lizard gun across a fallen tree, Ironflanks took position, the massive iron barrel of the rifle fixed on the tree line. The expedition members suddenly faced the full fury of the enraged mother, smashing through trees and ferns towards the pool, as large as an elephant, with overlapping knife-edged armour and devil-like horns. Her polished bony head pushed down as she speeded up in the open, the glass-crack reports of the rifles and the hissing of the tridents lost in the howl of her rage.

There was not much in the jungle that could murder one of her hatchlings, and the tauntoraptor did not class these uniformed monkeys as a threat. That was a mistake. A wave of flower-headed bolts pin-cushioned her skull, ingenious explosive-driven steel rotating through her armour and cutting into her flesh. Charging in disbelief, the novel flare of pain running through her brain, the tauntoraptor made her weight count, piling through the line of Catosian soldiers as bodies were hurled into the air. One of the mercenaries thrashed, her torso impaled on the creature's horns.

A tail capped with a bone mace curved around, Ironflanks leaping over the swinging wall of toughened flesh as the tauntoraptor's weight flattened one of the sailor's capacitor packs, a stream of blue energy forking up into the air as if his life force was being emptied into the firmament. The steamman was whistling in mimicry of a winged petrodactyl, one of the few denizens of the jungle's sky that could trouble

187

Stephen Hunt

a tauntoraptor, and, enraged by the insults, the thunder lizard turned – just as Ironflanks had intended. He pushed his cannon-sized weapon underneath the earflap of her monstrous head and the gun boomed, the thunder lizard jerking then folding down on her four elephantine legs. With a detonation of mud the creature collapsed, her second brain – buried towards the back of her stubby neck – shredded by the steamman's rifle.

Amelia stood shivering an inch from where the thunder lizard had been felled, her pistol empty, the drip of blood from the impaled Catosian drumming slowly down across the tips of her boots. There were howls of victory from the sea-drinkers as they climbed up onto the beast's side, machetes drawn to saw off its horns.

'We'll grind them down to powder,' one of them shouted. 'Something to keep the ladies of Rapalaw awake when we return rich!'

Veryann looked at the cavorting u-boat crew with disgust. She drew her knife and walked to where the free company fighters that had been trampled lay in the arms of their comrades.

Amelia realized what the commander was about to do and ran over. One of the soldiers grabbed the professor. 'Do not interfere. It is our way.'

'You can't!'

'Do I have my honour?' asked one of the wounded fighters.

'You have your honour,' answered Veryann, plunging her dagger into the woman's throat.

'We can put them on the cart,' shouted Amelia, 'take them back to the *Sprite* for treatment.'

'Catosia has no surgeons,' said Veryann, repeating the ritual along the line of wounded. 'You have your honour. No doctors, and no citizens living with the shame of their weakness. You have your honour. No cripples or ill to sap our bloodlines of their strength.'

Amelia struggled in the grasp of the soldier holding her back. 'You're a bloody barbarian.'

Veryann's work done, she wiped the blood off her blade on the side of her britches and then sheathed the knife. She indicated Amelia's over-sized arms. 'We allow no perversions of the flesh save those which can be achieved through our own exertions and the blessed herb shine. No imperfections worked by womb mages, surgeons, worldsingers or the fates of battle. Our bodies must be perfect.'

'Your bodies—' Amelia was astonished '—your body may be perfect, but your soul is insane. What about your fallen? Circle's teeth, are you just going to discard them here without burial?'

'Toss them into the water of the pool if their sight offends you, Jackelian. They are not dead to my people; they live on in the fear-filled nightmares of their enemies and the memories of our free company, as they should. They are immortal now.'

Amelia shook her head. Between their convict u-boat crew capering around the fallen monster and the callous ice maiden in charge of the psychopaths meant to be protecting the expedition, she felt like the lone visitor to an asylum on Circle Day. Just two pennies, damson, to prod the lunatics in their cages with a stick.

A noise like a hunting horn blew in the distance, and there was an explosion from the jungle as a thousand winged creatures took to the air squawking, hissing and buzzing in panic.

Ironflanks' head turned slowly, his telescope eyes shadowed by the rim of his hunter's hat. 'It cannot be!'

'What is it, Ironflanks?' Amelia stared towards the horizon, the cliffs of a plateau squatting in the far distance. 'That noise came from quite a distance out, didn't it?'

'She never hunts this far east, her territory is fixed,' said

Ironflanks. The hunting horn sound came again. 'No, she knows I am here.'

'Who are you talking about, Ironflanks?'

'Queen Three-eyes, Amelia softbody. The Steamo Loas have cursed us this day.'

'Another thunder lizard?'

'The queen of them all, professor of mammals, a kilasaurus max. She knows I am here.'

On the wind the horn song seemed to be speaking.

'*Hateyouhateyouhateyouhateyoupunishpunishpunishpunishyouyou.*'

'How can that thing know you are here, Ironflanks? It's just a big damn lizard.'

'By that criteria, so are the lashlites,' said the steamman. 'She can follow a scent from a hundred miles away and well does she know the smell of my stacks.'

Amelia listened to the stream of hatred being sung over the jungle, almost words. 'It's talking. It knows Jackelian. Sweet Circle, how intelligent is this thing?'

'I doubt if she has a grant of letters from the eight universities, professor, but she understands revenge well enough. The k-max mates for life, and I took Queen Three-eyes' companion in a hunt six years back. That's when she taught herself Jackelian – listening to the hunting parties as they sat around their campfires at night. Anything to discover more about her enemy, more about *me*.'

Again, the horn.

'*Metaljiggermetaljiggermetaljiggermetaljiggercrushyoucrushyoucrushyoucrushyou.*'

'Take what water you have,' shouted Ironflanks at the expedition members. 'Back to the boat. NOW!'

Amelia broke her pistol, ready to insert a fresh round. She sprinted after the steamman, slipping in another crystal charge from her belt. 'We should form up into a battle line. Quest's lizard killer guns worked well enough just now, and if you managed to kill this thing's mate . . .'

'A male kilasaurus max is a quarter the size of the female,' said Ironflanks, his stacks pouring smoke into the air as they fled down the trail. 'Those big cannons on the walls of Rapalaw Junction, they are not for the feral craynarbian tribes, you understand? Dirt-gas sinks before it climbs as high as the head of a k-max.'

'And you killed that thing's mate?'

'I led the hunt,' said Ironflanks. 'I would not have brought the k-max down, as old and as sick as he was, I know better. Those fastblood fools who paid for my services did not live long enough to regret their decision – I was the only one to make it back to Rapalaw's gates from that safari.'

Animals scattered under their feet and past the escaping expedition members, the trampled passage to the spring alive with terrified jungle creatures fleeing the rampaging monarch of their realm.

Two of the u-boat men suddenly ran at Amelia. 'Strap her to a tree – leave the Jonah here, leave her to feed the beast's hunger. She's called the beast to us.'

Amelia kicked one in the gut. The other fell forward as a rotating steel bolt erupted from his striped shirt. Veryann reloaded her rifle swung it towards Bull Kammerlan. 'Our steamman scout has given you the only order you need to heed – keep running. I will cut down any of you filthy jiggers that dares to lift a hand in mutiny towards an officer.'

Her cold blue eyes bore into the sailors and whether it was due to the Catosian guns or the screams of the k-max, the crewmen fled for their miserable lives.

A dark shape grew visible in the distance above the canopy and there was a crashing avalanche of trees as the thunder lizard pushed through the press of darkest Liongeli. They were less than halfway back to the *Sprite*. Amelia increased her speed, the water cart lying abandoned behind them. The sacrifice of their drinking supply would not be enough. They were as good as dead.

CHAPTER EIGHT

It was said even a blind man could tell when he had walked into Steamside, and Cornelius Fortune believed it. While the evening sky above the steamman enclave of Middlesteel might not have been filled with a thousand spears of hearth smoke like the quarters of their fast-blooded neighbours, the people of the metal carried their own stacks, and the smell of high-grade boiler smoke rose up to envelop Cornelius in the rooftop nest where Septimoth had landed them. It was like sitting in a drawing room where the gentlemen had all simultaneously reached for their mumbleweed pipes.

The current focus of Cornelius's attention rested halfway across Adam Metal Square, waiting still and silent at the heart of Steamside, in the hub of a network of narrow alleys that had never once been widened in Middlesteel's history. Lanes that had remained untouched when King Felix broadened the streets of the capital after the great plague in the year of 901, just as they remained unaltered when Isambard Kirkhill began his great programme of public works after winning the civil war for parliament. No wide new avenues in Steamside to stop the Levellers raising barricades, no new boulevards constructed to mop up the unemployed rowdies of both sides' disbanded regiments. Steammen suffered their own plagues and were the most loyal of the capital's constituencies – being slow to anger and measured in pondering the troves of their long memories.

It was the owner of the longest of those memories that Cornelius had come to observe. In any other area of the city, Cornelius's surveillance would have been easy. He could have walked round the square, dipping in and out, returning each time with a fresh face borrowed from the locals. But imitating a steamman was beyond even his powers morphic.

'It is growing quieter,' observed Septimoth. 'Night will soon be upon us.'

Cornelius nodded. It was still relatively busy down below. Steamside had a high population density, the people of the metal able to approximate sleep standing up a dozen to a garret.

'And this steamman will just stay there, in the square?' asked Septimoth.

'So Dred Lands would have it,' replied Cornelius. 'Dred assured me that Bunzal Coalmelter has been standing down there in that same spot for over a hundred years.'

Septimoth's hunting eyes focused in on the old steamman below. Weeds had grown up around his legs and a chest assembly that had once been painted a brilliant red had been reduced to a few crumbling flecks of dye by the capital's rain and smog. Even with the lashlite's incredible powers of magnification, he could only just discern the flicker of a single point of yellow light behind the creature's vision plate, pulsing with the faintness of a mouse's heartbeat. Lands had told Cornelius that the locals had tried to polish and clean Bunzal Coalmelter in the old days, but he had cursed his fellow steammen for fools and refused to dispense his wisdom until they had left him alone. Now Coalmelter was more statue than steamman, an iron sage rusting away into a monument in the middle of Steamside.

'You watched him all last night,' said Septimoth. 'You should let me take this night's duty. Return to Dolorous Hall for some rest.'

'*You don't need rest,*' whispered his mask. '*Not when you are wearing me. The sun is losing its power and I am gaining mine.*'

'I don't need your power,' spat Cornelius.

Septimoth looked curiously at his friend.

'I mean to say we shall both stay here,' said Cornelius. 'They will come for him tonight. I am sure of it.'

Septimoth knew better than to underestimate his human companion's sense for such things. Sometimes it was as if he possessed a third eye himself. There was a touch of the lash-lite about Cornelius Fortune – perhaps there was more to their friendship than just a life debt owed?

'I could fly down there and ask Coalmelter if he thinks his kidnap is likely,' said Septimoth. 'There seems to be no shortage of people who seek his counsel.'

'Much good may his words do them,' said Cornelius. And it was true. Many of the visitors – steammen, graspers, cray-narbians, the race of man – who had come to the square during the day, went away with disappointed looks on their faces. For every piece of advice Bunzal Coalmelter uttered, there were as many insults thrown at his petitioners – '*work it out yourself, jigger*' – '*you are too fat*' – or sometimes he turned to the obscure and the indecipherable – '*the finger that points at the moon is not the moon.*'

Whether the ossifying creature of the metal possessed real wisdom was a moot point, Cornelius knew that Coalmelter possessed cogs and crystals as old as any to be found in a steamman grave – and that should be enough to attract a different sort of seeker of knowledge this night. He was sure of it. Or rather, the part of him that was Furnace-breath Nick was sure of it, which was good enough for the hermit of Dolorous Hall.

'Remember, we let them take the steamman when they come,' said Cornelius. 'It is the organ grinder we seek, not his monkeys.'

'An apt choice of words,' said Septimoth, 'given that rascal hatchling Smike said the hand of the Catgibbon is involved in this.'

'I doubt the flash mob's interest extends much beyond the guineas they receive for the thugs they have been supplying. Robur is behind the missing steammen corpses, of that much I am certain. Let us see if Middlesteel's gutter scum can lead us to him.'

Down below, the evening crowd had dwindled to a single group of steammen playing a game of chess on a table outside the temple of Legba of the Valves. That was when Cornelius saw it. A coal cart pulled by two giant craynarbians, a pair of vendors walking ahead of the creaking transport – a small rat-like coalman with fingerless gloves trailed by a bullet-headed colleague almost as large as the craynarbians.

'What do you think, Septimoth?'

The lashlite's eyes focused on the sword arms of the two craynarbians, the bony appendages swinging casually as they hauled the weight of the coal cart. 'Chipped and worn – I doubt through honest labours. Those sword arms have been sharpened against a grinder in a muscle pit.'

'Who will buy my high-grade boiler coke?' called out the small coalman. 'Smokes up as fine as mist, Pentshire mined and graded. Who will buy my lovely coke?' Approaching the group of chess-playing steammen, the coalman dug out a pail of coke and proffered it to the table. 'A free sample, good sirs. Once you've tried Pentshire fine grade, you'll never want anything else.'

Iron hands reached out for the free samples, then clicked open furnace chutes to imbibe the fuel. As the steammen started juddering and fitting where they sat, rat-face's bulky companion pulled out an anti-steamman grapple from under the cart and put a bolt straight through Bunzal Coalmelter's boiler heart.

'Quicksilver,' said Cornelius. 'They've laced the coke with magnesium.'

'And they obviously do not require the old steamman alive,' said Septimoth.

So stiff with age was Coalmelter, that even impaled, he did not sink to his iron knees. He remained swaying there, the grapple point showing through the back of his spine shell, crystals fizzing as black oil leaked out from ruptured pipes and onto the moss growing around his feet units. Working calmly but rapidly, the two craynarbians pulled back a false bottom on the cart, hauling the dying steamman out from the square and hiding him under the planks. Then the killers covered over the coal cart with their black produce, all four of them wheeling the corpse away. The murderous abduction was completed in a matter of seconds.

Cornelius snarled. It sat badly with him letting the flash mob do this, but it would have been difficult for the two of them to react fast enough to have saved the steamman, even forewarned, even if they had been there solely to act as Coalmelter's guardian angels.

'There are a hundred crimes as bad as this each night in Middlesteel,' said Septimoth, noticing his companion's hackles rising. 'The weeds of your society. Thefts and petty murders. We are not mere vigilantes. We serve our people's memories, we serve the song of the dead.'

'All the same, some weeds demand to be cleared away,' said Cornelius. 'Take me up, Septimoth. We follow them.'

Outside the temple of Legba of the Valves, only the hallucinating steammen were on hand as witnesses to a lashlite launching himself into the sky with a human passenger. Septimoth carried the man as his people had carried their prey for thousands of years. Only the two of them and the lashlite gods of the wind knew that the true prey was yet to be claimed.

'There is the location,' called Septimoth, the wind and rustle of the silk wings supporting Cornelius masking the man's reply.

The towers of Middlesteel drifted beneath, layered with smog. This high up, Cornelius was reliant on his friend's sharp eyes, which were nearly as powerful in the dark as in daylight. Septimoth dipped down, extending the harness tether, Cornelius's kite wings gliding behind the lashlite as if the man was a pet monkey with the gift of flight. Closer to the truth in this aerial realm than Cornelius liked to admit.

Looming out of the darkness of the Gambleflowers was the largest jinn palace Cornelius had ever seen afloat on the river – a tiered illuminated wedding cake bobbing in the tidal flow. So, the Catgibbon still retained her fondness for a river view.

'You have seen them go inside?' Cornelius called forward.

'They took the coal cart into a warehouse first, switched the cover of coke for a few hogsheads of jinn,' shouted Septimoth. 'All four of them went into the boat by its lower boarding ramp. The steamman's corpse is still in the cart, judging by the effort it took the four of them to pull a few barrels of drink.'

'Cut my line,' cried Cornelius, slipping his Furnace-breath Nick mask off and tossing it up to his friend. Stealth would serve him better than force this night. 'I'll go aboard and see if our old friend Robur has made himself a home by the river.'

'*Take me,*' pleaded the mask. '*I can still be of use to you. You are stronger as Furnace-breath Nick than as a mere man.*'

'I *am* a man,' shouted Cornelius.

'I do realize that,' Septimoth called back. 'You are far too heavy to be any lamb I have scooped up from a farmer's field. I should circle, you may yet need my assistance.'

'With a full moon tonight? Too dangerous. Lashlites don't frequent drinking houses and if they see you up here, they may take you for a spotter for Ham Yard, or worse, a scout for a gang of rival bludgers.'

Septimoth swished his devil's tail in annoyance. 'You are too reckless.'

'I have stolen into the fastness of Darksun Fortress under the Commonshare's very nose, old bird. I am sure I can safely penetrate a gang of Middlesteel cut purses. Go home to Dolorous Hall and tell Damson Beeton I will be returning shortly.'

Septimoth whistled his disapproval and then released the towline for Cornelius to glide down towards the roofs of the docks. Cornelius used his flight silks proficiently well for a wingless monkey.

Watching from the shadows of a tannery, Cornelius waited for a suitably sized reveller to leave the jinn house, then he slipped behind the man and gassed him before he could reach the line of waiting hansom cabs. He dragged his victim behind a warehouse and removed his cloak, jacket and cane, before binding and gagging the unconscious dupe. Cornelius's features flowed like melting wax into a facsimile of his victim's face as he donned the stolen clothes. Cornelius chafed at the high collar of his victim's tunic – it was lined with a ring of metal, sewn into the cloth to protect its owner's neck from the garrotte gangs that robbed worthies in the less salubrious parts of town. He tested the handle of the cane and sprung the sword concealed inside. Courtland Town steel – this fellow was not short of a penny or two.

Cornelius's destination was moored far enough away from the affluent heart of the capital that the visitors to the jinn house were in no danger of being spotted by anyone other than their fellow revellers. He noted that the jinn house's iron hull had once belonged to a fire-breaker. A decommissioned colony boat, no longer fit to skirt the Fire Sea, not now that her decks were fitted out with additional pagoda levels, flammable oakwood rising by the light of a constellation of paper lanterns. Her new silver nameplate had been riveted proudly above the entrance. The *Ruby Belle*.

On the boarding ramp the two whippers nodded at the face Cornelius was wearing, passing no comment that one of their regulars had changed his mind and decided to try his luck again. The ship's interior bore out the impression of wealth that Cornelius had derived from its patrons' dress. No ha'penny tumble this for dockers, riverboat crews and rookery dwellers. Her cramped colonist hold had been cut out, replaced with a set of stairs leading down to a floor of lush red carpet covered by gaming tables, mirror-backed bars and marble-surfaced drinking stalls. Another line of stairs swept up to the pagodas. The transparent silk shifts worn by the two women waiting by the flight of steps, as well as the oiled chests of the guards standing behind them, left little doubt as to the entertainments that were on offer above.

'Canes to be checked at the door, sir,' said one of the jinn palace hands, making it clear that they expected all their patrons' canes to have a razor-sharp utility beyond fashion.

Cornelius moved aside for a press of braying quality, rich ladies with their stud retainers close at hand. 'Of course.'

'Back for another crack at the whist tables, sir?'

Cornelius handed over his cape and cane. 'Yes. I believe my luck may be about to change.'

He took a step up onto a brass dais and received a numbered wooden coin from the cloakroom assistant, noting that the room behind her was racked with purse pistols, shoulder holsters, garter guns and sword sticks. The patrons might be slumming it in this end of town, but they were careful with it, preserving their dignity – and their life – while about their sport.

'Would you care for a masque, sir?' asked the cloakroom assistant, indicating a range of velvet-lined masques hanging to the side. 'To preserve your anonymity?'

Cornelius shook his head. 'I left mine at home today, I don't believe I would care for another.'

'As you will, sir.'

Down below, the gambling tables were frequented by a mix of merrymakers – some concealed by masques, others openly revelling in the wickedness of the house and probably hoping they would be recognized. Plying the tables, spinning the wheels of chance and turning cards, Cornelius moved across the connected series of chambers, mapping the layout of the *Ruby Belle* and locating the corridors and doors used by her staff. Taking a long glass of sweet wine, he slipped out onto the promenade, bypassing laughing clusters of patrons engrossed in their own amusements. He found the blind spot he was looking for and put down his glass. Pushing on his artificial arm with a finger, he drew out a metal cord, looping it around the railing, then lowered himself down the hull of the boat on her river side. His boots pushed him out in looping arcs, quietly swinging him down the outside of the jinn house.

Stephen Hunt

This should be about where the boarding ramp lay on the port side of the craft.

From his thumb he extruded a rubber circle that rolled out into a dome, a thin copper wire trailing back into his arm. He hated using this, the mechomancy so obviously imperfectly reverse-engineered from a steamman's architecture. He willed the device into action and it began to amplify the vibrations of sound in the hull, crystals in his arm flaring up as they fed the information along his nerves, a fire like heartburn withering his guts. But along with the fire came words – a male voice growling about his attentions being rejected by a croupier. Using the large rivets as footholds, Cornelius moved along the hull, flakes of paint and iron rubbing against him as he eavesdropped on the conversations and peeped in through portholes – safe enough with the darkness of night and the lapping waters of the river Gambleflowers behind him.

Midway across the hull he found them. The two flash mob enforcers that had bundled Bunzal Coalmelter into their false-bottomed cart. They had changed out of their coke vendors' rags, and were inspecting the ruin of the steamman's cracked chest casing as parts were being gingerly teased out into a pool of dark puddling oil. Damn. It was not Robur working on the grave robbers' dark business – instead, some gangly beanstalk of a man was poking around the steamman's body.

'Careful now,' said rat-face. 'The parts have to be preserved, removed without cracking the crystals.'

'For that I need to concentrate,' said the mechomancer performing the forbidden autopsy. The man spoke annoyingly quietly, his words barely carrying through to Cornelius's vibration amplifier.

'There's good coin in this for you,' said rat-face. 'You do this job *right*. The client needs the parts shipped out tomorrow, cleaned and each organ labelled.'

The larger of the two bruisers cracked his knuckles. 'You do it badly, and it'll be your parts that'll need work. This is the last of the steamers on our list. You won't get a second chance now.'

'This is delicate work,' whispered the mechomancer. 'Leave I to it.'

They laughed together at the sport of needling the quiet hireling, then left, shutting the door to the room. Cornelius was about to trigger the retraction wheel on his grappling line when he realized that the mechomancer was mumbling to himself. The Circle bless a mumbler. He dialled up his listening device to maximum to catch the hissed mutters, ignoring the lancing pain.

'Turds, turds, the way they treat I. But they have no brains, no wit.' He stuck his lips out like a fish that was about to start whistling, scratched at his head as fiercely as if he had nits, then delved back into Bunzal Coalmelter's guts. 'Not clever. The client wants it tomorrow. *They* want it tomorrow, get to stuff their face at Whittington Manor, see all the quality. All the pretties. Should be I that goes. It is I that is working for him, not the stupids. The way they treat I . . .'

Whittington Manor. Cornelius had heard that name recently, or had he read about it in the *Middlesteel Illustrated News*? Was that where Robur was holed up, playing him for a fool and possibly planning his mischief for Quatérshift's First Committee? He willed the retraction wheel into action and, with a low hiss, he was hauled back up to the *Ruby Belle's* promenade.

Picking up the fluted wine glass, Cornelius moved across the gaming floor, his mind revolving with the possibility of finally tracking down the slippery refugee from the Sun King's broken court; so focused on his quarry that he only noticed the two whippers when they stepped out in front of him – both a head taller than Cornelius.

'Excuse me, sir, the floor master would like a word with you about the settlement of your debts.'

'My debts?' Another two whippers emerged out of the crowd around the tables, taking position behind him. Four was not such a big number, but an ordinary patron killing them would spook the flash mob. Robur might be moved somewhere else as a precaution. Damn his unlucky stars, of all the customers he could have chosen to mimic, he had to have selected a welcher. Let them have their say, then. He should be able to buy them off for at least a night with the wad of money thickening his borrowed wallet. A night was all that he required.

'What foolishness is this?' protested Cornelius. 'I have money. You must have the wrong man.'

A vice-like grip laid itself on his shoulder. 'I am sure the floor master will be glad to discuss that with you, sir. Right away.'

They led him to a door padded with rich red leather. 'This way, sir.'

He found himself in a small lifting room, little more than a dumb waiter for the cooks and floor staff. Yellow gas started spraying up out of a grille on the floor as they closed the door on him, vapours warm to the skin and cloyingly choking to the lungs. Cornelius stumbled back, smashing into a wall of mirrored glass. The lifting room was neither sinking nor rising. He tried to lever open the door, but the foul cloud swilling around the chamber was sapping his strength. If this was their way of reclaiming money out of their clients' pockets, the flash mob might find debtors' prison a more effective approach. Whatever happened to breaking a couple of fingers first?

Fresh air poured in suddenly as the doors were drawn back,

someone catching him as he lurched out. His arms were pinned behind him and a pile driver of a fist sucked the last remaining breath out of his gut. A warning, then. Traditionalists after all. Pocket manacles were clamped around his wrists and the thugs dragged him along the corridor like an empty crate of jinn bottles. The stinging gas's residue made Cornelius's eyes stream, a swirl of locusts swarming across his vision as one of the whipper's boots slammed down onto his left leg.

He could barely see when they shoved him down into a chair, but he recognized the voice of the soft-spoken mechomancer he had spied scavenging inside Bunzal Coalmelter's corpse. The mumbler sounded no louder in person than he had through the hull of the floating jinn palace.

'Intolerable. How can I get on with the job I must do with all these distractions?'

'Just set it up,' growled a whipper.

Cornelius's borrowed forehead was scraped, a sharp-pointed tiara pulled down hard over his hair. Circle's teeth, it was a crown of thorns they were fitting him for. A circlet made up of small, imperfectly cut shards from the mother stones that allowed Jackals' crystalgrid network to function. But these crystals did not need senders to operate them, and the only communication they could relay was limited to a single message. Pain. Raw pain. A victim in a crown could be tortured for weeks leaving no physical evidence, until their brain started to fracture into multiple selves, in a vain attempt to protect the mind. It was said that while one person would go into a room wearing a crown of thorns, a dozen would come out.

'I'll pay you,' said Cornelius. 'I have the money.'

'You'll pay, jigger,' said a thug, securing Cornelius's feet to the chair. 'We'll make sure of that.'

'Get the floor master,' said Cornelius. 'This is pointless. I've already told you that I'll pay you. How are you going to clear my debts if you put me inside an asylum with this contraption?'

A stinging slap across his face served as his initial answer. 'You can shut your gob. We don't want your wallet. We already have that. We want to know who you are.'

'Who I am? You know that!'

Another slap. Far stronger this time.

Mumbling-boy was still assembling the crown of thorns, but they probably would have slapped Cornelius anyway. You couldn't beat a little physical degradation thrown into the mix. Six months as a prisoner in a Commonshare organized community had taught him that, sharing a cell with that bloody insufferable wolftaker, Harry Stave. At least most of the people with the education to assemble a crown of thorns within Quatérshift had ended up being pushed inside one of the shifties' steam-driven killing machines at the start of the revolution.

'Who are you *really*, jigger? Under that false face of yours, who are you?'

The crown started to vibrate on his scalp, tearing into his skin, close to full activation. They knew! But how? Somehow, his game had been rumbled by the flash mob.

From somewhere far away, he heard his mask laughing, dangling from Septimoth's belt as the lashlite headed home; the telling, mocking retribution of Furnace-breath Nick. '*Just a man. You're just a man after all.*'

Cornelius's punishment beating had just turned into something immeasurably worse.

Each step Amelia took closer to the *Sprite of the Lake* seemed to increase the weight of her boots, until it seemed that she was sprinting towards the u-boat with lead weights on her feet. Out of the jungle canopy, the insult-howls of the k-max chased after the fleeing expedition members. Was it something in the thunder lizard's screech that was slowing down her escape – a natural paralysis mechanism?

'Noescapenoescapenoescapeforyoumetaljggermetaljigger-metaljigger.'

Each time the k-max howled, more creatures flushed out of the jungle, bursting past at speeds that only served to remind Amelia how far they still were from the safety of the *Sprite*. This sluggishness had to be something in her mind. She had fled equally dangerous threats in her rascal's career – packs of hunting pecks in the capital's undercity, the Caliph's scent-seekers in Bladetenbul, Count Vauxtion's well mannered but deadly attentions in the alleys of Middlesteel, the bandit army of Kal Ferdo out on the Kikkosico pampas. She had not come this close to the lost city after a professional lifetime of heart-break, rejections and ridicule, to end up inside the gut of a six-storey lizard with a grudge against their half-insane steamman guide.

As Amelia sidestepped a panicked toad she saw something at the other end of the trail, two silhouettes against the afternoon sun, running towards them down the passage trampled through the jungle. Sweet Circle. She imagined all the disasters that could have befallen their boat while they were out in search of fresh drinking water. She knew from the size of the silhouette that it had to be Gabriel McCabe running out to meet them, yes, accompanied by one of Veryann's Catosian soldiers.

'Professor,' shouted Gabriel, sprinting towards them, 'we are betrayed.'

'We've got problems of our own,' panted Amelia. 'A big hungry problem the size of the Bells of Brute Julius coming down in our direction. Betrayal we don't need.'

'The thunder lizard is the betrayal,' said Gabriel. He held aloft a broken vial of dripping green liquid.

'Where did you get that?' demanded Ironflanks.

'It was placed smashed by the entrance to the trail. One of Bull's men found it while out collecting fruit. He knew what this filth would do . . .'

Amelia took the broken vial, smelling it.

'It's the gland milk from a kilasaurus max,' said Ironflanks, slowing down his pace. 'Parties out of Rapalaw Junction use it to lure the larger thunder lizards away from a safari area, so they have the hunt to themselves.'

Amelia cursed under her breath. And it looked like it worked well enough in the opposite direction too, if you were fool enough to use it. Or a traitor who wanted to bang the dinner gong for a thunder lizard.

The Catosian soldier unslung a signal rocket from her back and Gabriel motioned that she should set the small clockwork fuse turning on its mixing chamber. Veryann dashed up to them, the last of the water party's stragglers running past.

'You have mortars set up?' Veryann asked the soldier.

With a crack of glass the firing head on the rocket released blow-barrel sap from both chambers and the missile swept towards the sky above them, exploding out into a magnesium star shower.

'Yes, First.'

From the direction of the river a series of explosions answered, a sound like fresh logs popping on a fire grate. Round shells burst in the air above the retreating expedition members, streamers of smoke spiralling out before being smeared across the roof of the jungle.

Veryann nodded in satisfaction at her subordinate's efficiency. 'Let us see if this creature can find us as well inside a wall of smoke cover.'

'Circle bless the Catosian military,' said Amelia, resuming her pelt down the trail. And Circle curse the traitor in their ranks. First the sabotage of their u-boat's gas scrubbers and now this. Someone badly wanted to stop them reaching their destination. But anyone who knew anything about Camlantis must know that their civilization had reached the peak of moral evolution. Who in their right mind would seek to deny the ancients' secrets to the flawed, feuding nations that had succeeded Camlantis in the millennia since? That left ignorance as the motive. Which one of them wanted to stop the expedition finding Camlantis so badly they were prepared to murder half the crew to do it? Surely one of Bull's crew wasn't so afraid of ending up a slave of the Daggish that they were willing to sacrifice half their own shipmates' lives to force the *Sprite* to turn about? They wouldn't earn a pardon that way.

From the direction of the river, the mortars lined up on the u-boat continued to pour a rolling barrage of covering smoke behind them, matching the pace of their sprint with an uncanny accuracy. The howls of the k-max behind them became a confused mess of snarls lost in the acrid smoke as the welcoming sight of the long dark hull of the *Sprite* hove into view, sitting just ahead, fixed in the river current. Commodore Black waved from the nearest of the two conning towers. Helping the Catosians, the u-boat crew were desperately breaking down the mortars, tossing footplates and barrel piping down into their open hatches. The *Sprite* was close enough to the jungle that the barge they had used to reach the shore was more useful as a boarding ramp now. A roar echoed through the smoke. Uncomfortably close.

Commodore Black helped Amelia up the last few rungs of the hull ladder. 'You were meant to be bringing drinking water back with you, professor, not that rare fierce pet of yours.'

'You know how it is,' said Amelia, 'a girl sees it in a shop window along Penny Street and she has to have it.'

The commodore looked over at the shore; the remaining

u-boat crew were scrambling across to the *Sprite* in an undisciplined rabble while Veryann's mercenary company were falling back in formation, flower-headed bolt rifles at the ready. 'Well, I'll not be feeding the wicked thing for you. Veryann, board your people on the *Sprite* – I'll be pushing my bishop across our board by myself if you try and lock horns with a k-max.'

Amelia turned to see Ironflanks clanking down the hull. 'Can your friend out there wade into the water, old steamer?'

'A kilasaurus will not cross the Shedarkshe,' said Ironflanks, clutching his thunder-lizard gun and peering at the smoke-shrouded jungle. 'They have no taste for swimming.'

The last of the mortars was disassembled and the Catosians on board when a head appeared through the thinning fog, a freakishly small razor-lined snout twitching to find Ironflanks, a massive green-scaled body as large as a Middlesteel tower following behind, a tongue snicking out of a second mouth in her chest. This second maw sported a circular buzz-saw rim of teeth opening and shutting in an eager gnashing. Three good eyes and one scarred hole settled on the *Sprite* and the thunder lizard roared her rage, a sound so raw that it made Amelia's rib cage vibrate under its fury.

'Down ship,' yelled the commodore into the conning tower. 'Take us out, full speed forward.'

So frenzied were they to put the steel hull of the ancient u-boat between themselves and the thunder lizard, the remaining members of the expedition threw themselves down any hatch left open. Queen Three-eyes saw the steamman disappearing into one of the conning towers and her snout lashed around, aiming for the hatch where Ironflanks had vanished. '*METALJIGGERMETALJIGGERRIPANDKILL-ANDRIPANDKILL.*'

Amelia was barely through the conning tower door, followed

by the foetid heat wave of the monster's breath, when the submarine started sinking, water bubbling up past the turret's portholes. Reaching the pilot room, Amelia saw Commodore Black had got there first, hanging onto the periscope's arms, twisting the scope around towards the bank. 'Sweet mercy, Ironflanks, it's coming into the river after us.'

'She can't swim,' said Ironflanks, borrowing the periscope. 'Her forearms are meant for hooking down prey, not paddling.'

Unfortunately for the expedition, no one had told the thunder lizard, carefully keeping her balance as she manoeuvred into the Shedarkshe's currents.

'Full forward. Down inclination two degrees.' The commodore turned to his first mate. 'Flood tube one. Put a fish in the water, Mister McCabe.'

'You expect me to hit that thing, skipper?'

'Timed fuse, one hundred yards detonation. Ironflanks is right about one thing; that's no slipsharp coming after us. Unbalance the beast, give the wicked creature something to think about other than smashing the *Sprite* to pieces.'

Gabriel nodded. 'Aft tube, guns. Timed fish with a hundred-yard screw, number two head to load.'

'Aft tube, aye. Flooding now.'

Amelia watched the gunnery station sailors plotting in a firing solution and flooding the tubes as their loaders reported in. She could almost feel the shadow of the kilasaurus on the boat as their expansion engines vibrated along the hull plating, dragging them fast against the Shedarkshe's current.

Blind Billy adjusted the controls on the side of his large silver phones. 'The beast is wading after us.'

'Clear tube one,' ordered the commodore.

A clang and a hiss and a torpedo squeezed past the *Sprite's* screws, trailing backwards from the submarine.

'Fish in the water,' said guns.

'She's running smooth,' reported Billy. 'And she's running straight and true. The thunder lizard has seen the trail and is trying to move . . .'

The torpedo's explosion was a dull echo on the *Sprite's* hull. The commodore clung onto the periscope. Wading through the water after them and already up to her chest mouth, Queen Three-eyes lost her footing in the treacherous flow as the fountaining water from the blast unbalanced her, and spun her away downstream.

Her howl of fury swirled after the *Sprite* as the tips of the double conning towers disappeared up river. '*Comingback-comingbackcomingbackforyoumetaljiggermetaljigger.*'

'So you were right after all,' said the commodore to Ironflanks. 'The wicked thing isn't made for the water. But let's put a few leagues between ourselves and the beast all the same.'

'Will it come after us?' asked Amelia.

Ironflanks pushed the rim of his safari hat up. 'I am uncertain. We will be in Daggish territory within a week. Normally she would not be foolish enough to trespass on their lands.'

An uneasy silence fell over the pilot room. The expedition was moving into the heart of darkness with a traitor on board, a turncoat willing to dangle their shipmates out as bait for creatures like the k-max. The *Sprite* had felt safe once, a refuge from the jungle outside. Now the u-boat was in a vice. A vice being tightened by an unknown hand.

The *Sprite's* refectory was long and narrow. Its two huge tables were made of Jackelian oak that had been polished so much by generations of galley boys using leftover cooking oil that you could slide a plate along them, like skating pebbles across a pond.

Amelia entered the galley and glanced around. She had long

since stopped being sensitive to the smell of unwashed crewmen now their water was being reserved for drinking rations and the u-boat's overstretched cooling system. One of the Catosians who had spurned the submariners' advice and tried bathing in the river still had a rash to show for it. There were smaller predators in the river than devilbarb fish and crocodiles, and only a craynarbian would want to take a bath in the Shedarkshe. Amelia squeezed past Bull's off-duty sailors and sat next to T'ricola and Billy Snow.

'You've heard the commodore's running orders, now we are getting close to where Daggish seed ships patrol?' Amelia asked.

'Many times,' said Billy, taking a sip of yellow liquid juiced from fruit Ironflanks had discovered during his last rainforest sortie. 'I don't need to be told how dangerous these waters are. I can still hear the voice of that poor devil from the comfort auction back at the trading post, parroting his lines at his wife and daughter.'

'It's one way to survive in Liongeli,' said T'ricola. 'Join the Daggish, become part of the jungle, cooperate rather than compete.' She rubbed at her armoured forehead in discomfort.

'Are you all right?' asked Amelia.

'Headaches,' said T'ricola, 'I'm not sick. It's the jungle. My body knows Liongeli is out there. I'm changing. I must have grown two inches since we started this damn journey. None of those scrotes that Bull's assigned me for engine room duty wants to say two words to me now; they think I'll slice them with my sword arm if they even spill oil on the decking.'

'I'm sorry,' said Amelia.

'Don't worry,' said T'ricola. 'It'll be a while longer before I strap a pair of antlers to my head and start worshipping thunder lizards down in the engine room.'

'There's nothing to worry about – your body is working with nature,' said Billy. 'The same as if you were carrying a child.'

'Don't wish that on me,' said T'ricola. 'Out here I'd give birth to a dozen or more young shells rather than a couple of offspring.'

Billy reached out for a refill for his mug, Amelia pushing the jug across towards his fingers. 'Were you born blind, Billy?'

'No,' he smiled. 'In my younger days I could see just fine. But I caught the waterman's sickness off the Gambleflowers when I was a lad.'

'I thought that was fatal?'

'Usually it is. If you are lucky enough to survive, this is the price.' He waved a hand in front of his blind eyes. 'But my ears? I can hear the wind turn the pages of a book and tell you what page number it's blown open on. There was only one trade really open to me. My family were eelers, selling river crab and water serpent to the submarines that travelled up to Middlesteel docks; they had enough seadrinker friends to make sure I got a job as the phones-man on a boat.'

At the galley hatch, old cooky banged his spoon against the pan to indicate their stew was ready. The off-shift crew mobbed the hatch while Billy Snow stood up and collected a plate of boiled potatoes and green salad leaves, manoeuvring back around the benches as easily as any of the fully sighted crew. Cooky slopped out the mutton, laughing at the sonar man's slim fare.

Amelia looked over at T'ricola. 'Is Billy not feeling hungry?'

'Same reason he doesn't drink blackstrap or rum rations,' said T'ricola. 'Billy has his funny ways. I think it might be religious.'

Amelia shrugged. There were extreme Circlist sects that did

not eat meat, but most Jackelians had a hearty taste for a good steaming plate of red meat and roast potatoes drowning in gravy. Out in the shires, the doctors were known to prescribe red wine and hot roast beef to sickening children.

'My ways are not that funny,' said Billy, sitting down again.

Sweet Circle, he must have heard the two of them talking halfway across the room.

'Despite what Bull's pirates think to the contrary. It never sat well with me, that the price of my existence should be the end of something else's.'

'And the juice in your mug rather than a tot of rum?' asked Amelia.

'I like a ration of rum as much as the next man, professor, but when you're running shy of a sense, you take trouble not to dull your remaining ones,' said Billy. 'Besides, you're a fine one to be speculating about *my* funny ways. Most academics would be happy enough blowing the dust off journals back in Jackals, not dreaming of some ancient paradise that may or may not be lost beneath this green hell we are sailing through.'

There was a weight of things Amelia wanted to reply to that, but she had long since grown weary of trying to haul them out of her past – all the long evening conversations about Camlantis with her father, huddled under a blanket by a snug fire grate while hail tapped against their window – trying to find a way to reawaken that dream, that memory in her present. It was so hard, made her so cursed exhausted, attempting to explain the dream, attempting to justify it. Amelia speared a lump of stewed mutton in her bowl. 'I guess you'll just have to think of the lost city as my plate of salad at the spit-roast, Billy.'

Damson Beeton pursued Septimoth down the corridor. 'What do you mean, the master's delayed? His supper is waiting for him as dry as a Cassarabian sand garden inside my oven.'

'His business is keeping him in Middlesteel this evening,' said Septimoth.

'Oh it is, is it, you old bird? Appointment with his tailor overrunning? You two will be the death of me.'

'I am sure we will not, damson.'

'So *you* say.' Damson Beeton produced a bone pipe from beneath the folds of her pinny. 'If so, then why did I nearly trip over this and crack my skull outside?'

'My flute!' Septimoth's folded wings nearly expanded into their glide position. The seers of the crimson feather had made their decision, and returned his bone flute as a sign. Things must be worse than he had imagined, then, for them to turn to him for help.

'Your ma's old spine. Left on the top step of the main hall. I was going into the herb garden and nearly came a cropper tripping over this.'

Septimoth took the flute back and tucked the instrument into his belt. 'Thank you, damson, I had mislaid it.'

'Your poor mother,' said Damson Beeton. 'I thought her bones were meant to be holy and precious to you. If this is the way you treat them, then you can do me the favour of letting my spine rest in the grave when I move along the Circle, thank you very much. No. No lute for you stripped out of my poor weary back, you careless old bird.'

Septimoth bowed in acknowledgement and made to leave; he was grateful, too, that he wouldn't have to be called on to perform his people's death rites on the human housekeeper. Her corpse would be as tough as vulture meat, no doubt.

'Hang on there,' cried the housekeeper. 'You haven't told me where the master is, or what time I'm to be expecting him back?'

'Do not worry, I'm sure he will return presently.'

The housekeeper tutted as Septimoth walked away. 'Where is he, Septimoth? Has he accepted one of the invites to society I've been so carefully piling up?'

'I'm sure he's enjoying himself,' Septimoth called back.

'Are you enjoying yourself?' whispered the mumbler as Cornelius writhed in the chair. 'It's a clever device, the crown of thorns. Not many working parts to go wrong. No.'

Cornelius had to wait for the rogue mechomancer to turn off the crown before he could reply. The trick of surviving a crown was to grit your teeth – so you didn't bite your tongue off and bleed to death. If these thugs had been professionals, then they might have known that and given him the courtesy of a mouth guard to bite on. 'Why are you doing this?'

'You can drop the act,' said one of the thugs. 'The, *oh sir, let's just settle the debt and be out of here* bit. Which worldsinger changed your ugly features?'

'I don't—'

The thug grabbed Cornelius's face and viciously squeezed it. 'The plate in the floor you stood on by the cloakroom is connected to a transaction engine. Faces are easy to mimic with worldsinger sorcery – but weight? Your weight's changed by two pounds, you idiot.'

Cornelius silently swore to himself. They weren't the gang of simple bludgers he had taken them for. Smarter than the revolutionaries across the border in Quatérshift, certainly. He had badly underestimated the sophistication of the flash mob.

'You must be new in town,' said the thug, 'if you think you can come onto the *Ruby Belle* and count cards at our tables. You think that our boss likes to be swindled? You think she goes to bed with a big smile on her face knowing that scrotes like you have been dipping your hand in her pockets?'

217

His companion waved a sheaf of illustrations and real-box pictures in front of Cornelius; face after face of known card counters and cheats. 'So here's what you're going to do, new boy. You're going to give us the name of the back-street sorcerer that did your mug for you, then you're going to tell us the system you were planning to use to swindle the house, and finally, you're going off to meet the eels in the Gambleflowers.'

'You three are good,' said Cornelius. 'They should have you upstairs as the entertainment.'

One of them backhanded Cornelius. 'You're the amusement, jigger. Tell us what we need to know and we'll make your death a little easier.'

'You're not thinking big enough,' said Cornelius. 'I'm not here to count cards; I'm here working for a rival crew. And the rest of what I've got to say is for the Catgibbon's ears only.'

That stopped them short.

'I *could* tell you, but the Catgibbon is as like to kill you, when she finds out that you know what I have got to say.'

'Get her,' ordered the thug; then he turned to Cornelius. 'If you're playing us false . . .'

'I know. Little pieces; eels; feeding.'

He smelt her before he saw her, the faint scent of honey, a scent designed by womb mages to drive men wild. The Catgibbon. An ugly name for such an alluring creature; but none of her other names would have done. Not for a high lord of the flash mob.

'Hello, Jasmine,' said Cornelius.

The creature that had entered the room looked at him with anger on her face, brushing back the light dusting of fur that covered the golden skin on the nape of her neck. 'You had better have something good for me.'

'Will a greeting do?' said Cornelius, his face melting back

to an approximation of his natural features. Damson Beeton might not have recognized him now, but there was more than a touch of Cornelius Fortune in the old face he was wearing.

'You look good, for someone who's been dead for nearly thirty years.' The Catgibbon turned to the others in the room. 'Get out.'

The tone of her voice indicated that she was not inviting debate. The whippers and the crooked mechomancer hustled out.

'You look good, too,' said Cornelius. He inclined his head to indicate the boat. 'And you seem to have done well for yourself. You took over Dirty Porterbrook's crew after he died, I presume.'

'And a few others besides,' said the Catgibbon.

'You always were the brains behind the operation, Jasmine. Everyone always used to look at you and stop with your body. They never bothered to wonder what was inside that head of yours.'

'Brains enough that I never believed that body we found in the rookeries of Whineside was yours. I always knew you would disappear one day without a word. Just change your face and vanish into the crowd. It must be a constant temptation with your talent.'

'We are what we were born to be.'

'Yes, quite. Neither of us would have risen so far or so fast in Cassarabia, would we? Too many people who would recognize what we are.'

'My father was Jackelian,' said Cornelius.

'Of course he was. But how happy would the caliph's womb mages be if they knew that one of their tailor-made assassin bitches had escaped to Jackals and started breeding wild with the locals? I can still smell the half of you that's your mother in your blood.'

'Well, you smell as sweet as ever to me,' said Cornelius. 'Even if I am immune to the wiles of your sweat.'

'Where did you go, farm boy?'

'I tried my luck in Quatérshift, before the troubles began.'

'The court of the Sun King? Rich pickings, for the capital's greatest thief.'

'Actually,' said Cornelius, 'I tried going straight.'

The Catgibbon laughed at the idea. 'That I would have liked to have seen. But now you're back in Middlesteel. I can't blame you. What have the shifties got left that's worth stealing now? They can't even put food on the table, let alone set it with silver plate to eat off. You're not really working for a rival crew, are you?'

'No,' admitted Cornelius.

'No. You barely tolerated working under Dirty Porterbrook's patronage. But even you and your pliable assassin's face couldn't have afforded to have both Ham Yard and the flash mob hunting you down; which rather begs the question . . .'

'What I'm really doing here? You've grabbed a friend of mine. A steamman friend. I was hoping to find him.'

The Catgibbon looked puzzled, then her delicate golden-furred face split into a most unladylike laugh. 'Is that it? Is that all? No wonder I haven't been reading news sheet tales of paintings and jewels mysteriously going missing from the residences of the quality. Sweet Circle, that's a turn up for the books, you really have gone straight. What happened to you, Cornelius, what happened to the reign of crime of the Nightshifter?'

'Allow that a year held in a Commonshare organized community changes a man's perspective.'

The Catgibbon stroked his face, a cruel look settling on her face. 'Poor you.'

'Why is my friend lying in pieces on a table in your jinn house?'

'Nothing personal, farm boy. He's just a job, one that is paying handsomely at that.'

'Grave robbing? You used to only take on jobs that amused you. The years have changed you.'

'We're no longer those two young greenhorns that arrived in Middlesteel without a guinea to our names,' said the Catgibbon. 'And the Nightshifter I remember wouldn't have cared three turds for some senile old steamer that's been nothing but a pigeon rest for most of the century.'

Damn it. She was too canny to spill the beans on the steamman's fate, even with Cornelius tied up and at her mercy in the jinn palace.

'I don't suppose you'll let me go then, for old time's sake?'

She grinned at him, but not fondly. 'I would love to, but you know how it works. If I let you go, everyone's going to be talking about how the Catgibbon caught a card counter and went soft on him. Then the smaller crews will stop sending me my percentage and start sending me toppers with daggers down their trousers and strangle-cords sewn into their cuffs.'

'I thought you might say something like that.'

She fingered the crown of thorns on his head. 'I'm going to do exactly what you did to me. I'm going to walk out on you. Without a word. Without looking back. Then I'm going to let my crew turn your mind into a beef broth with our crown of thorns. You always liked wearing all those different faces – by the time my boys have finished with you, you'll have a fresh new personality to go along with each of them.'

'It irritates you, doesn't it,' said Cornelius, 'that I'm as immune to the wiles of your body's perfume as your old owners back in Cassarabia.'

'You're nothing but a halfbreed desert assassin,' said the

Catgibbon, 'and if you wanted to keep on bloody living, you should have stayed back in Quatérshift.'

Cornelius smiled. 'It's odd that you should say that, because part of me did stay behind in their death camp. I'd say round about the two extra pounds you spotted on your ingenious set of scales. Let me show you . . .'

He sent the flex command to his arm and the limb went rigid, snapping the cords binding him to the chair. She was diving for the door even as her whippers outside were piling back inside. But Cornelius wasn't planning on leaving by the grand entrance. One of the double nozzles that had emerged from his artificial wrist sprayed the porthole with a circle of blow-barrel sap and he ducked as a squirt of ignition chamber liquid left his arm. The explosion scythed out above Cornelius, knocking the Catgibbon's thugs back into the corridor while he flopped sideways out of the torn hull, the cold waters of the Gambleflowers slapping into his face as the Catgibbon's scream of rage chased him down.

Lead balls bubbled past him, the pistol shots' velocity broken by the black river waters. He swum downwards, watching the crown of thorns carried away towards the darkness of the river bottom, chased to the deeps by the flash mob's volley. A gutta-percha tube snaked out of his arm and Cornelius took a greedy gulp of air as his feet beat him down deeper into the grasp of old mother Gambleflowers. The tidal flow quickly sucked him out west, the jinn house nowhere to be seen when he finally broke the surface. He must have been carried a mile downriver at least. Cornelius's life would be far more dangerous now that the head of the flash mob knew he was alive and living in Middlesteel. But there was nothing to connect his old life to his solitary existence on Dolorous Isle. Nothing to connect a ghost-like thief that had made fools out of Ham Yard with the demon of vengeance stalking Quatérshift.

The man had won without the mask.

'*You were lucky tonight,*' the words drifted down the river from Dolorous Isle.

'I let myself be captured to find out more about their plans.'

'*Keep telling yourself that,*' whispered the mask.

Hotter each day, the *Sprite of the Lake* followed the Shedarkshe southeast. The hull of the u-boat seemed to sweat tears of coolant, the creak and crack of the heat exchangers the expedition's constant companion. Nerves were on edge now – fights and squabbles a daily affair – as they charted waters that had never been inked on any explorer's map. The commodore marked their progress with a compass and cartographer's nib, the blank expanse on the neatly lined roll of paper a reminder of how deep into the unknown they were sailing.

'No sign of any seed ships yet,' said Commodore Black. 'We'll be running into their borderlands soon. I hope our blessed steamman knows what he is about.'

Amelia stood behind the two pilot seats and gritted her teeth. If the mercurial Ironflanks didn't know where they were going then the whole expedition was in trouble.

'The Daggish are out there,' said Bull Kammerlan. 'If they're not patrolling this far west, it's a measure of their strength, not weakness.'

'I thought it was only Ironflanks who had ventured this far out?' said Amelia. 'What do you know about it?'

Bull grinned. 'The craynarbians around the fringes of the greenmesh worship the Daggish. When you think the gods protect you, you tend to get careless. Easy pickings.'

'You really are disgusting,' said Amelia. 'How many thousands of lives did your slavers ruin in Liongeli?'

'The way I see it, girl, we were giving them a step up.

You've only seen a taste of what it takes to survive out in the jungle. Life on a Cassarabian slave block looks pretty sweet after you've survived out in this hell for a few years.'

'That must be why you had to gas their village,' said Amelia, 'rather than selling the tribes a passage downriver.'

'You may be sniffy now, dimples, but it's my crew's knowledge of the Shedarkshe that's kept your skull connected to your neck so far, rather than shrunk down to the size of an apple on some war chief's necklace.'

'That's enough, Bull,' said the commodore. 'Your river lore's got you and your rascals out of a water sentence back in Bonegate, so be thankful for that.'

'Aye aye, *sir*,' said Bull. 'The water is where we both belong, one way or another, eh?'

'Old time's sake only goes so far,' warned the commodore.

'Yes, I do seem to remember you saying that at my court martial.'

'Channel is splitting up ahead, skipper,' called Billy from his station. 'Three courses.'

'Stop, full,' ordered the commodore. He pulled a speaking tube out of the wall and dialled Ironflanks' quarters on the panel. 'Up to the bridge with you, old steamer. You never said anything about a choice of tributaries in the river.'

Commodore Black looked puzzled. There was no answer from the speaking tube.

'I'll find him,' said Amelia, swinging out of the pilot room.

Find him she did, lying in a pool of dark oil that had vomited out between the seal joins around his boiler, the smell of magnesium in the air as his legs jerked and twitched in the delusion of his quicksilver dreams. His trip did not look like a good one. For a moment she didn't know whether she should feel pity or revulsion for the creature of the metal. She called the master of arms on the room's speaker tube and Veryann turned up with two of her fighters fast behind her.

'By the blood of Forman Thawnight,' swore Veryann, seeing the half-comatose steamman lying on the floor. 'I thought we had confiscated his stash of quicksilver.'

'He must have had some more hidden away,' said Amelia. She ran her finger along the tell-tale trail of white-veined coal dust that lay on a folding table in the corner of the cabin. A terrible thought occurred to her. 'The quicksilver you confiscated from Ironflanks after he boarded, what did you do with it?'

'Master of arms gallery,' said Veryann, 'locked inside one of the rifle lockers. The armoury is guarded by my people, day and night both.'

'Let's go.'

Veryann led Amelia past a sentry and through the u-boat's narrow training range. A second sentry stood guard over the ship's small arms store, but despite the Catosian's vigilance, Amelia's heart sank when she saw the empty locker that was opened for her.

'This is not possible,' said Veryann. 'The sentries are rotated. There is no shift when this room is not locked and guarded.'

'Maybe a ghost stole it,' said Amelia. Damn the traitor's eyes. The turncoat in their midst had done it again, wrecking their chances as surely as they had burnt out the gas scrubbers. 'Oh, Ironflanks, why did you have to pick now to be weak?'

'I should have flushed the narcotic overboard,' said Veryann. 'But I thought it might come in useful as an inducement if our steamman scout started becoming uncooperative.'

Amelia checked the grille on the air vent in the ceiling. It was loose. If someone knew the *Sprite's* layout well enough . . . 'Yes, you should have flushed that filth down the head.'

'The steamman may not have known there was quicksilver in his coke supply,' said Veryann. 'The traitor might have poisoned his coal bins.'

Amelia shook her head. 'No, Ironflanks knew what he was doing. I don't know what he's trying to escape from, but whatever it is, he didn't need to be fooled into taking quicksilver. Just leaving it on his table would have been enough.'

Veryann looked at her two soldiers. 'Lie the steamman in his bunk. His dream-state could last for days.'

'Put a double guard on Ironflanks' room,' said Amelia. 'Nobody to be left alone with him. Two at all times.'

'Does that include you, professor?'

'Me, Commodore Black, every jack in this crew.'

'I didn't bring nearly enough free company fighters for this expedition,' said Veryann. 'There's not a cabin or hull plate in this underwater antique we're not guarding now.'

'And there was me thinking Quest was being a touch paranoid when he put marines on board,' said Amelia.

'The cleverest man in Jackals?' said Veryann. 'No, I think he was being just cautious enough. There's a saying in the city-states: *just because you're paranoid, doesn't mean they're not out to get you.*'

Amelia looked over at poor Ironflanks, his voicebox murmuring in some low-level language that sounded like static over the *Sprite's* speakers. 'Damn it, you fool of an old steamer.'

His quicksilver-induced nightmare continued. Theirs was just beginning.

Commodore Black dripped sweat on the pilot room's map table. The only thing the cartographers knew for sure about the river Shedarkshe was that it continued southeast and eventually ended up at the sea-sized lake that lapped against the shores of the Daggish capital city. 'Well, Bull, you're our river man, what do you know about these channels?'

'The channel on the right doesn't go as far as the river's source. The one in the middle is said to be the shortest route and its waters are the widest, but it's going to be hairy with seed-ship patrols sooner rather than later. The one on the far left steers nor'-east and is reputed to be the long way round, narrow waters at points, but it eventually rejoins the main trunk of the Shedarkshe. It's out of the way, but that's where I'd put my money.'

'It isn't your money,' said Amelia. 'It's Quest's.'

'His money but my blessed boat,' said the commodore.

'And I'd like to survive this fool's voyage with my hide intact enough to spend the bonus that Quest promised us,' said Bull.

'We should wait for Ironflanks to recover,' said Amelia. 'He knows the greenmesh better than any of us.'

'Right now he doesn't know his metal arse from his tin elbow, girl,' said Bull. 'You want to lay down here for a few days, you might as well run up a signal buoy with an invite to the first seed ship that sails out this far. We need to wait for night, surface, clean our air, then its deep sailing all the way until we've got the lights of the Daggish nest glinting in our periscope.'

'Better a moving target, right now,' said Commodore Black. He had made his decision. 'Mister McCabe, Mister Snow, rig stations for narrow waters. Ahead slow. If that lunatic steamer has his wits about him when we tank for air, we'll ask his opinion on our course. Right now, left channel it is. Long and easy sounds mighty fine if we are to be dealing with these mortal terrible jungle lords.'

Amelia said nothing. She could sense the danger lurking for them down this tapered offshoot of the Shedarkshe. She couldn't put her finger on it, but there was something desperately wrong about the commodore's long and easy channel. And whatever it was, they were sailing straight for it.

Commodore Black pushed the periscope back into the ceiling. 'Cloudy and moonless, a good night to sit on the surface for a while. Take us up, Mister McCabe. Tank for air. Let's clean my beautiful girl's lungs out before we put our necks on the block for these wicked Daggish.'

The *Sprite's* nose erupted out of the dark waters of the Shedarkshe like a whale surfacing for air, the rest of the u-boat following. As she settled on the surface of the tributary, hatches along her port side opened and started venting stale air while hatches on the starboard side sucked in clean air from outside, febrile and scented with night flowers from the thick jungle.

Amelia checked on Ironflanks, but he was still in no state to gainsay their passage down the river's fork. Lying on the bunk, he was making strange whistling noises with his voicebox – partway between a song and some call of one of the jungle creatures. Last chance to stretch her legs topside. She exited via the nearest conning tower. Others in the expedition had the same idea. Gabriel McCabe was sitting with his legs hanging over the *Sprite's* hull, his dark fingers tapping a mumbleweed pipe on the side of the boat.

Amelia sat down next to him. 'The crew is nervous.'

'They have good reason to be, professor.' The first mate pointed down the river. There was a night mist on the surface, the *Sprite* gently pushing against the current towards it. They might as well be sailing through the gates of the underworld denied by the Circlist faith. 'If anyone has ever sailed further upriver than Bull's slave raiders, they never made it back to Rapalaw Junction to boast about it.'

A line of crewmen in diving gear left the conning tower in front of them, ready to give the u-boat's diving planes and hull a final check before they embarked on the last leg of their perilous voyage.

'I know it's a risk,' said Amelia. Damn, but it had seemed so much less of a risk when she had been looking at map tables in Abraham Quest's offices, drawing up their supply lists and making plans for the *Sprite's* recovery and resurrection with Fulton's submarine engineers. 'But we have to believe it's worth it.'

'Are you following this dream for your sake, or the sake of your father?' asked Gabriel McCabe. 'Even if we make it to Lake Ataa Naa Nyongmo without being blown apart by a Daggish patrol, there are no guarantees that you will find a clue to the position of Camlantis in the heavens.'

'Water preserves crystal-books,' said Amelia. 'The best records we have of the Camlantean civilization have been fished out of ancient shipwrecks.'

'You know in your heart we will find nothing but the ruined, drowned basement levels of their city, full of nothing but the skeletons of any who were left behind for the Black-oil Horde to slaughter.'

'They wanted their legacy to survive,' said Amelia. 'They knew the time would come when another civilization would transcend the dark ages, would be ready to embrace their society and its learning.'

'Is Jackals that society, professor?' asked the first mate.

'We are!' said Amelia. 'Like Camlantis, we are a democracy. Like Camlantis, we have held the power for hundreds of years to conquer every other nation on the continent, yet we have used that power only to preserve our society and keep our people safe.'

'The ancients did not hang children outside Bonegate for

dipping pocket-books and stealing silk handkerchiefs,' said Gabriel McCabe. 'Nor did they dirt-gas thousands of innocents in Quatérshift from the safety of a fleet of aerostats during the great war. We are not, I think, ready for their knowledge.'

'You don't understand; we can use their teachings to change Jackals,' said Amelia, 'to make things better. We can use it to end hunger and starvation, end poverty, end disease, end conflict. They had such a society, why should we deny ourselves that chance?'

Gabriel McCabe relit his pipe. 'For myself I am happy enough to have a berth on a seadrinker, serving under an honourable skipper, rather than being beached back in Middlesteel; even sailing up the Shedarkshe is better than such a fate. But I have a feeling you will be disappointed by what we find. I do not know much about archaeology and history, professor, but I know people well enough from all my time in the confines of a u-boat. We are not big enough for your ideas.'

'I hope you are wrong, Gabriel,' said Amelia. 'We will have come a long way for nothing if you are correct.'

The first mate's pipe began to grow as he tapped his old weed out, twisting and turning on the deck like a wooden serpent. Amelia looked at it in horror. 'Gabriel, what kind of sorcery is this?'

'Kiss the pipe,' said Gabriel McCabe, 'the mumbleweed will feed you, give you strength.'

'Get it *away* from me,' said Amelia, stepping back. Leaves sprouted out of Gabriel McCabe's face, his dark limbs twisting upwards towards the sky. 'Your face, your face!'

'I'm becoming a tree,' said Gabriel McCabe. His bones cracked as they splintered. 'The moon is too cold to go under the water again. My roots will drink from the Shedarkshe.'

Amelia stumbled into the conning tower. Two Catosian mercenaries fell out of the door, their shine-swollen muscles no longer able to be contained by their armoured jackets. Belts snapped and fabric tore, showering the deck with crystal rifle charges as the women changed into dog-things, balls of taut muscle snuffling and scratching at the hull of the u-boat. She tried to push them away but she noticed her own arms were becoming squid-like tentacles, slimy and wet and flopping off the Catosian dog women. Amelia tried to scream but her mouth was a cone of clawed teeth and all that came out was a chatter of bone.

Pulling themselves out of the river, the repair crew climbed the ladder back to the flat deck of the *Sprite*. Bull Kammerlan prodded one of the Catosian soldiers crawling across the decking with his trident. She mewled, her hand trying to catch some imaginary shape in front of her. Satisfied, Bull booted her unconscious with a lash of his weighted diving boots. Laughing, he reached for Amelia's collar and hauled her into the conning tower, his divers marching in front and giving the wild crewmen of the u-boat a mild taste of their capacitors to clear the way.

Circle, but it was good to be back in the slaving business.

CHAPTER NINE

Cornelius was certainly attracting glances from the other passengers drawn up in the lane leading to the great house, but he was the centre of attention for all the wrong reasons. While everyone else sat in stylish horseless carriages, hand-crafted copper boxes gleaming in the moonlight, or lounged inside the leather opulence of barouche-and-fours drawn by well-brushed horses, he rested his feet in a dusty mail coach. His fiction of a coat of arms had been fixed onto its two doors, but that was the only concession to remodelling that the ancient vehicle had received. He had even kept the original ship-style name painted on the rear, the *Guardian Fleetfoot*.

It hardly helped that Septimoth held the reins above, on a seat that had been intended to accommodate both a driver and a guard with a blunderbuss. Or that the footplate to their rear stood empty of retainers. The *Guardian Fleetfoot* was kept in a stable Cornelius rented across the river from Dolorous Hall; the ideal accompaniment for the face he was wearing this evening. Almost his own, but slightly altered – just a touch of the crazed eccentric, features that he had styled on an insane but very wealthy composer he had robbed many years ago in

Middlesteel. It was what people expected of a hermit, and there was always a value in giving the audience what they expected.

At last the horseless carriage in front of him had disgorged its passengers and pulled away with a hum of high-tension clockwork. Cornelius stepped down in front of the mansion's entrance, not waiting for Septimoth to dismount and open the door for him as was proper. 'Off you go now,' Cornelius called up at Septimoth. 'Wait around the back with the others, and no flying off now, do you hear?'

'As you say, sir,' said Septimoth. With a crack of the whip the four horses pulled away and Cornelius brushed down his cape, then looked up at the mansion.

He was not the only one parading his eccentricity, it seemed. Whittington Manor had once been better known as Fort Whittington, an ugly, squat, thick-walled castle, constructed during the civil war and filled with parliament's cannons staring out over the downs of the west from its commanding promontory. Abraham Quest had bought the derelict, half-abandoned place and spent a small fortune adding the façade of a graceful villa to its brutal walls. The manor house was of a distance from town that any status-conscious member of society would never have classed its grounds as part of the capital, yet still they came out here, lining up their expensive clockwork vehicles in his drive. Attracted by the flame of Quest's genius and the vast amount of money he had accrued.

At the open door, the red-coated major-domo gave Cornelius a quizzical glance as he handed over the cream invitation. It was the major-domo's job to recognize all of the capital's quality by sight and greet them personally like long lost relatives. How could it be that there was someone standing here with an invitation he had never seen before? Then he read the beautiful calligraphy of the name. Cornelius Fortune! His eyes opened in understanding and the major-domo looked at

Cornelius as if he had just discovered a mythical creature on his doorstep. 'Mister Fortune! A rare pleasure, sir. I do not believe we have ever had the honour of your attendance at Whittington before. Allow us to take your cloak for you . . .'

Cornelius shrugged his hand away. 'I get cold, man. Do you want me to pass away of the fever in your corridors?'

'That would never do, sir. Please, come inside. You will find warmth and a special buffet cooked by our own chef, a man who once attended to the culinary needs of the Sun King personally.'

'Very good, very good.' Cornelius stumbled inside, ignoring the solicitations of the other staff and the tremor of interest that ran through the crowd as his name was announced. So, this was Whittington Manor? He should have brought Damson Beeton, she would have appreciated it. A peculiar resting place for the stripped-down components of antiquated steammen turned out of their graves and kidnapped by the flash mob. But this was the location that the mechomancer on the *Ruby Belle* had given as the destination of their dirty graveyard trade.

Cornelius walked through a series of ballrooms until he came to the buffet tables, as many staff waiting to serve behind them as there were platters in front. 'This is all foreign muck. Don't you have any eels, or a nice lamb pie? Nothing spicy, mind, my plumbing is delicate.'

So, it appeared, were the sensibilities of the other guests. They seemed to vanish as the uncouth newcomer moved along the table, piling his plate with boiled potatoes, scraping off the buttery cream sauce and shovelling it onto a spare plate.

'The meat on the river crab is very good,' a voice announced. 'If you can get under its shell to catch it.'

Abraham Quest. Word of Cornelius's presence had been discreetly passed to the master of the manor and his curiosity had no doubt been piqued – as well as his ego flattered – that it was at one of *his* functions that the hermit of Dolorous Isle had finally surfaced.

'It's a tough shell to get past,' said Cornelius.

Quest picked up one of the long, tongue-like silver forks from the table, a single edge serrated and as sharp as a scalpel. 'But not impossible. As long as you have the right leverage. Do I have the honour of addressing the Compte de Spééler?'

'That's not a title I use anymore. I prefer plain Mister Fortune.'

'I'm not surprised,' said Quest. 'My experts in heraldry tell me that your title never actually existed, outside of the pages of a three-hundred-year-old adventure novel written by an obscure Quatérshiftian author.'

'I believe the writer used my family's title in her book,' said Cornelius. 'There were so many small titles and noble grants in Quatérshift . . . and then the revolution came.'

'Yes, the revolution, and so much of the ancient regime's history and documentation went up in the smoke of the Carlist book burnings,' said Quest. 'Interestingly enough, the word speeler has a different meaning in Jackals. In the argot of our criminal underclass it means a thief or a cheat.'

'Really? I have never heard that before. Spééler is a small mountain village in the north of Quatérshift, quite close to the border with Kikkosico.'

'Your accent, if you don't mind me saying so, sounds more rural Shapshire than Quatérshiftian,' said Quest.

'I married into the family,' said Cornelius. 'I was born in Jackals.'

'And now you are back. That can't have been an easy journey.'

'No,' said Cornelius, 'that it was not.'

'Well, the only Carlists we have in the capital are the ones we've elected along with the Levellers to parliament. They seem a fairly harmless bunch in comparison to your revolutionaries in Quatérshift.'

Cornelius gnawed greedily on a chick leg as if he was a hound. 'I trust that they will stay that way.'

'I trust they will, also. A little change is always good for the system.'

'While a lot of change is better described as a cancer,' said Cornelius, 'something to be dug out with a surgeon's blade.'

'Or a trowel, perhaps?' said Quest. 'Someone with your name published a paper in the *Horticultural Journal* many years ago on the care of trees struck by Ferniethian willow disease.'

'You have a good memory.'

'I have a freakishly unique one,' said Quest, 'although truth to tell, I find it a curse as much as it is a blessing. I can tell you the colour of the apron of the serving boy in the first drinking house I went into at the age of six. I can describe the conversations I heard there. I could tell you all of the drinks we consumed and in what order and how many pennies each of us paid for them. But, alas, all memory is dust without the wisdom to apply it. I haven't noticed any papers published by yourself for quite a while.'

'I like to spend my time in my garden on the Skerries on more practical pursuits,' said Cornelius. 'I still read the *Journal*, but I am afraid I haven't had the inclination to pick up a pen since I departed Quatérshift.'

'Capital,' said Quest. 'Most of the people I meet at my functions think that gardening is what you do when you order the head groundsman to take the lawn roller out of the shed.'

'You are telling me that the richest man in Jackals spends his Circleday afternoons in the rose beds behind this fortress?' Cornelius was amused.

'More or less,' said Quest. 'I have a conservatory on the

roof and a collection of rare orchids up there. Their maintenance and care helps me relax. I am surprised you haven't seen
the cartoons lampooning my pastime in the Dock Street news
sheets.'

'I prefer the Quatérshiftian press,' said Cornelius.

'Really?' Quest raised an eyebrow. 'I'm astonished there's
anything still coming over the border. I thought it was closed.'

'Oh, you might be surprised at what makes it over the
cursewall. One way or another.'

'I'm sure I would be surprised by nothing where human
nature is involved,' smiled Quest. If he had been unsettled by
Cornelius's comment, he did not show it. 'Are you familiar
with orchids, Compte de Spééler?'

'I was raised on a farm,' said Cornelius. 'My upbringing
gave itself over to more practical horticulture. Manure and
irrigation; the nurture of apple orchards, pearl barley, pear
trees . . .'

'I was raised in the alleys of Middlesteel myself,' said Quest.
'Cheap jinn and sleeping in the gutter with the other urchins.
I was running with a bad crowd when I was younger. But I
used to love the plants at Driselwell Market, the small flash
of colour in the smoke, the traders from countries with names
I couldn't even pronounce, let alone locate in an atlas. It was
one of those traders who gave me my first break – gave me
an honest job and taught me to read, gave me the numbers
I needed to help keep his ledger.'

'From market-stall boy to all this,' said Cornelius, indicating the ballroom. 'That can't have been an easy journey,
either.'

'Surprisingly easy,' said Quest, 'and diverting enough along
the way. In fact, I rather think I enjoyed the journey more
than the destination. When I was homeless on the streets, I
couldn't have afforded the price of the pot my orchids came

to market in to piss in, let alone one of the flowers. Now I possess the rarest collection in Jackals. Perhaps I can convert you to my cause.'

'Me?'

'To a fancier of orchids, Compte de Spééler.' Quest pointed up to the roof. 'I am sure I can find time for a tour, for a fellow *Horticultural Journal* subscriber.'

Rare orchids and a chance to nose around for evidence of an even rarer trade in vintage steamman components. How could Cornelius refuse?

While the other drivers, footmen and assorted cabbies tossed a set of dice in the illumination of their coach lamps around the rear of Whittington Manor, Septimoth had moved to the inside of the old mail coach rather than perching on the step. He had tied up the horses inside the manor's stables, all four of them used enough to the lashlite that they were not unsettled by his presence, not worried that he might swoop down from a height and bury his talons into their backs. This was slow work, following the precognitions of the seers of the crimson feather, trailing across Middlesteel after the corpses of steammen. How much purer was his vengeance. How much simpler to swoop out of the skies of Quatérshift and pay their murderers back the blood debt he owed his clan. Killing revolutionaries and dropping the devil of Furnace-breath Nick into their midst to stir up terror and fear. That was satisfying. Almost as fine as flying on the wing of a hunt with his people.

Septimoth had thought that the hatred he felt for his people's executioners would have faded over time. But it was only the memories of his family that seemed to diminish. He could no longer conjure up the remembrance of his mother's face, or the features of his life-mate and their four children. He could recall events he had shared with them – his children's first moulting ritual, the joy he had felt at their birth, their pride when he was appointed ambassador to the court of the Sun King, teaching his children the monkey-throat language so they might have an advantage in trade or service to the flight. He could recall their hatchling voices singing the tone teachings, but not their faces as they sung. How strange were these malicious games of memory. As his recollections faded, his longing for his family had increased, his hatred becoming harder, purer each week, a shining diamond seeded in the blasted wreckage of his soul. The blood of his foe no longer eased his pain, but at least vengeance distracted him from the memories. And the lack of them.

Septimoth's trance was interrupted by voices outside, including one that he recognized. His hunter's mind moved through the thousands of tones he had heard this year and matched them to its owner. The short thug who had led the team responsible for the kidnapping of Bunzal Coalmelter. A coach not dissimilar to the *Guardian Fleetfoot* was being pulled out of a passage cut into the angular walls of the manor, the original utility of the thick concrete barely concealed by the veneer of brickwork cladding. On the driver's step sat the bludger who had led Septimoth and Cornelius to the flash mob's riverboat in the Gambleflowers, holding the reins next to a second man he didn't recognize. Septimoth's ears trembled. The two were bickering.

'Did you see the quality of the bawdy in that place?'

'Those women were Catosian, man. They'd rip your jewels out of your trousers for staring at 'em sideways.'

'Well, we missed out on the food tonight, too. Dragging these cargoes across half of Jackals. If I'd wanted to run a bleeding coaching business . . .'

'What, you thick or something? They aren't going to trust this lot to the penny post, are they? We're being paid.'

'Not enough, mate, not enough.'

The wheels of the departing coach were muffled with rags, an old coachman's trick; not out of concern for the sleeping residents of the villages they would pass through, but to avoid giving advance notice of their approach to any highwaymen that might be out plying their trade this evening. Wherever they were heading, it wasn't the Catgibbon's floating jinn palace; they were making for somewhere far further out than that.

Septimoth unfastened the door on the far side of the coach and silently slipped out, vanishing into the darkness of the gardens before launching himself unseen into the air. He had a feeling that Cornelius would be driving himself back to the Skerries tonight. The wind above the downs lifted Septimoth up, buoying him effortlessly higher. He tilted his wings, feeling the glorious run of air across his feathers and scales as he glided behind the coach, a black dot below on the bare gravel road. He could hear the crack of the whip over the train of horses. The pair were driving them hard. They obviously wanted to make their journey at night under the cover of the moonless sky. Much better for avoiding awkward questions from any county constabulary, now stabled and sleeping along with the keepers of the toll cottages on the crown roads.

But a cloudy night was better for a stalking lashlite, too.

Cornelius followed Abraham Quest out of the series of ballrooms, four Catosian soldiers saluting him as they raised an old iron blast door leading into the main body of the manor house. Quest had the women dressed in the cherry tunics of a Jackelian fencible regiment, private auxiliaries ready to assist parliament in times of war. Without the padded war jackets favoured by the free companies, their shine-swollen muscles made the fencible uniforms look five sizes too small, as if someone had dressed them in children's clothes.

'You value your privacy,' said Cornelius.

'What, my girls? They're here to preserve my life, not my privacy. They're very effective. I haven't had an attempted poisoning or assassination attempt for months. Toppers very rarely get as far as we are standing these days.'

'Who would have thought it was so arduous, being the richest man in Jackals?' said Cornelius.

'It isn't my money that brings the assassins. I have no heirs, and if I should have an "accident", how long would my commercial concerns survive in their dominant position beyond my tenure? I have no illusions about the longevity of any empire built on the hope that the children may prove to be the equal of their parents. If I had offspring, I wouldn't wish them to follow my path, even if they could. Any venture predicated on bloodlines is doomed to fade to dust eventually, including my own. It is my labours and the course of my life that has set me here – nothing more.'

'Thank the Circle for our great democracy over monarchy, then,' said Cornelius.

'Yes,' Quest smiled. 'Thank the Circle for that. Do you have any children, Compte?'

'I had a wife who was with child once.'

'Had?'

'The revolution in Quatérshift.'

'Ah,' said Quest. 'I'm sorry. As you said, thank the Circle for Jackals and our democracy.'

They entered the heart of the old fortress, an atrium with a view of four storeys rising above them. A railing ran around a pit ahead of them, fencing off a dizzying vista – level after level dropping down beyond the illumination of the gaslight. The architects who had remodelled the fortress as a manor house had done their best to soften the functional lines of the ammunition lifts and military gantries, but no amount of

241

hanging plants and ivy trellises could fully conceal the building's severe original purpose.

Quest led Cornelius past a line of food trolleys, being wheeled from the kitchens to the party via an inspection station running random tests for poison. Quest wasn't the only powerful notable at the manor tonight and it wouldn't do to have some Guardian or commercial lord dropping dead on his floor.

It wasn't the food that caught Cornelius's eye, but the woman supervising the testing team. She glanced up, saw Quest, and nodded towards him, failing to notice the staring guest by the mill owner's side. Not that she would have recognized Cornelius, given that the last time they had met he had been concealed underneath the mask of Furnace-breath Nick. It was Robur's supposed daughter, no longer wearing the coy bonnet of a child desperate to have her father returned to her, but dressed instead in the crimson officer's uniform of Quest's fencibles.

'I'm glad to see you look after your guests,' said Cornelius, looking at Robur's daughter and the poison tests.

'What kind of host would I be if I didn't?' said Quest. A glass-fronted lifting room was descending down an iron rail into the atrium. He pointed at the testing station. 'I take it you don't have to go to these lengths on your island for a decent meal?'

'Just the risk of my housekeeper's cooking,' said Cornelius, 'and she's really rather good.'

They stepped into the lifting room and Quest inserted a key to access the private arboretum level at the top of the manor house. 'You can see everything from here.'

Cornelius stared out at a line of deactivated catapult arms, their grips open and still, like the claws of sleeping birds of prey. In the old days they could have risen to the roof and whirled drums of flammable oil out of hidden hatches, turning what was now the topiary gardens into a molten hell for any attackers to cross. It was a good view, but no, he could not quite see everything. Wherever the flash mob's delivery of steammen corpses had ended up was well concealed, Cornelius had no doubt of that. Quest should have no conceivable use for their grisly remains, but then he should have had no need either to surreptitiously engage Furnace-breath Nick to spirit out Quatérshift's court mechomancer from that revolution-wracked land. Quest had helped the Levellers to power in the last general election, with Ben Carl at the helm – the father of Carlism. But old Ben Carl was no shiftie committeeman; he had proved his credentials on that matter when he had led the Jackelians in repelling the invasion from Quatérshift.

Cornelius looked at his host, hiding his suspicions. Was Abraham Quest dissatisfied with the progress of the Levellers in the House of Guardians? Had Quest secretly been hoping for a bloodbath, one party dictatorship and the declaration of a Jackelian Commonshare? Surely not; for all his model work villages and paternal manufactory conditions, Quest was still the man who had nearly acquired the whole nation in a single burst of his freakish intelligence. If the radicals were to set up their Gideon's Collars in Jackals, then Cornelius's eccentric host clearly had a place at the head of the queue of those who would be escorted into one of the wicked steam-driven killing machines.

The lifting room opened its doors to a blast of heat, a miniature jungle hidden under acres of botanic glass. The scene was more ordered than it first appeared, curved planting troughs twisting away on neatly planned paths, a riot of colours stretching out into the distance, orchids the height of shire horses, blossoms as large as the wheels of a hansom cab.

'What do you think?' asked Quest.

'I can only name a fraction of these,' said Cornelius, genuinely impressed. 'They're rare, I haven't even seen them as plates in *Cheggs' Encyclopaedia of Flora*.'

'Taken from wherever my factors have travelled on the house's business,' said Quest. 'Southern Concorzia, Liongeli, Thar. Not kept in a single chamber, but in many interconnecting arboreta – each with its own humidity and temperature. A little piece of home so that each species may prosper. Do you read the scientific journals? The scholars call such a miniature world an *ecos*, a system of life bound together.'

'Incredible,' said Cornelius. 'Even the Botanic Gardens have nothing as sophisticated as this.'

'Interesting that you should say that.' Quest walked across to a silver tank. 'It was my first visit to the Botanic Gardens in Middlesteel that gave me the insight I needed to create my original fortune. The interconnectedness of all things, how the economy of Jackals resembled the complex systems we see in life, in the ecos, each market with its own predators and prey, an intricate ever-evolving environment supporting them. If a foreign garden can be transported and captured under a palace of glass, I thought, why not a simulacrum of the markets of Jackals held on the drums of a transaction engine?'

'The whole world in your hand,' said Cornelius. 'And now your trading house is the top predator in the savage land of commerce.'

'Ah, but I only ever held a shadow of the economy in my transaction engines,' said Quest. 'As for real predators, let me show you . . .' He banged the side of a glass tank and lifted its lid. Inside, hundreds of mice flowed desperately away from his hand, climbing over each other in living mounds, each of them trying not to be the creature he would select. His hand dipped down and a frantic white mouse was removed by its tail. Quest took the rodent and tossed it over a gated enclosure. On the other side, a bed of orchids lashed out with whip-like fronds, shield-sized petals turning in search of their prey. The mouse scurried between the wavering tongues, slipping back until one plant seized the small creature and tossed it into the air, straight into the digestion sack around its roots. The squeaking died away as the mouse sunk below the poisonous gluey liquid, hundreds of tiny barbs impaling its body, preventing its struggles from tearing the sack wall.

'Now there's something you don't see in the Botanic Gardens,' said Cornelius.

'Not for lack of demand, if the seats sold at our cock fighting pits are anything to judge by,' said Quest. 'We all love a spectacle, do we not? For me, however, this is a salutary reminder of the intricacy of our own ecos. Almost everything that exists is either the meal or it is the diner, often both at the same time. It is these complexities that engage my interest these days, far more, I can sadly say, than people.'

'Your reputation as a humanitarian suggests otherwise,' said Cornelius.

'I cannot abide the cruelties of our people, the poverty and the misery we tolerate in our world,' said Quest, 'but alas, that is not the same thing as an endless store of empathy for those who suffer. I am not that good a person, and such a store would have to be deep indeed to cope with our world. I cannot abide our miseries because they are *unnecessary*, they are symptomatic of a total failure of imagination and intelligence on the part of those who shoulder the burden of leading Jackals. A different ecos could produce a different outcome, could ensure no one else would have to grow up seeing the things I did. How many times have you stepped over a body lying in the street at night wrapped up in rags, shivering and hungry and cold? How many times have you looked the other way when the street children run up to your carriage in the lanes of Middlesteel, their skeletal hands stretched out begging for a few pennies to buy them enough jinn to blot out the emptiness of their lives? How many news sheets have you turned a page on when you got to yet another story of wars, massacres and famines? How many times, Compte, how many times can you bear to see that, before you do something?'

'I don't get out that much,' said Cornelius, 'and I had my fill of utopias in Quatérshift. I found utopia wanting.'

'Something about you told me that you would be a philosopher,' said Quest. 'Quatérshift is broken because their Commonshare runs contrary to human nature. It expects people to be noble, to put others before themselves – all for the community, nothing for the self – and it is then psychotically disappointed when its citizens fail to live up to that impossible ideal. We are selfish monkeys capering around in clothes and you cannot take a corrupt autocracy, murder its wolves and expect the sheep to run everything without other predators emerging to seize control of the flock. Certainly not when the fools in their First Committee think that issuing a piece of parchment in triplicate stating that the people are to be fed is the same as actually feeding them.'

'Are we still talking about Quatérshift?' asked Cornelius.

'Of course,' smiled Quest.

'If you can't change the state . . .'

Quest shrugged. 'Then you must change the people, or at least, what the people believe in.'

Smashing glass above them interrupted the mill owner's musings. A dark figure dropped down through the hole in the ceiling and kicked off a line of steam pipes, setting the valves hissing as heated water spread across the mosaic floor. An assassin swinging down on a drop cord with a gun in his hand! Cornelius shoved Quest out of the way and ducked, the pistol shot missing both of them. The intruder arced through the spot where Cornelius had been standing, Quest recovering his balance and seizing the attacker, the two of them swinging up towards the conservatory roof.

Cornelius was rolling over, bringing his artificial arm up to shoot a string of gas globes at the attacker – then he saw the gas mask on the assassin's face, protecting him from the house's defences as well as Cornelius's arm. But their host was proving surprisingly resilient for a mere merchant. Quest had seized a girder with one arm and converted the assassin's momentum with all the skill of a trapeze artist, bringing the pair of them into a support strut, letting the intruder take the brunt of the impact. Both of them began tumbling down towards the ground, the intruder falling with the dead weight of a sack of cannon balls, Quest turning gracefully in the air, angling his body for a bent-knee landing.

They crashed into the display of carnivorous plants, a lashing frenzy of spines and razor fronds, the assassin trying to disengage from the man-eaters long enough to spring to safety, Abraham Quest pin-wheeling through the attacking vegetation as a raucous clamour sounded across the roof. Bells! The manor house's bells were ringing – the old fortress's towers had sentries, then, and they weren't asleep on the job. A rush of Catosian guards emerged out of a doorway behind Cornelius, soldiers armed with crossbows. Cornelius lowered his weaponized arm as the heads on the crossbows detonated, steel nets weighted with copper spheres wrapping themselves around the intruder as he tried to dodge away. A shower of sparks danced around the attacker's chest, timers on the spheres in the netting jolting their victim with bursts of wild energy – the power electric.

More soldiers poured into the arboretum, armed with long

poles tipped with pincers, their hands safe inside insulated gloves to protect them from the wild force being expended around the intruder. They were taking no chances. Soon a ring of cherry-uniformed guards had the assassin pinned to the floor with their immobilizing poles, the assassin still struggling forlornly between each burst of energy. Cornelius stood almost forgotten on the sidelines, none of the soldiers noticing the fingertip barrels of his artificial arm sealing shut.

Quest brushed away the spined leaves that had embedded themselves along his velvet jacket's arm. He hadn't even worked up a sweat. 'That was fast work. Well done, ladies. You have upheld the honour of the free company as capably as always.'

'You said downstairs you hadn't had an attempted poisoning or assassination attempt for months,' said Cornelius.

'Yes, foolish me, tempting fate. I was long overdue,' Quest noted.

'What are you going to do with him?'

'What I normally do when I find trespassers on my land,' said Quest. 'Hand them over to the constabulary. Ham Yard can ascertain which of my competitors paid for his services.'

'You know why I'm here! You didn't find us all, you jigger,' yelled the assassin, his words muffled by the gas mask before he was shocked into unconsciousness by the Catosian soldiers' weapons. One of the Catosians pulled his mask off, revealing a thin face with round spectacles. An unlikely looking assassin: always the best kind.

'Ah,' said Quest. 'Mister Zaker Browne, which I think we can now take is not his real name.' He turned to Cornelius. 'One of my clerks from my counting house in Middlesteel. That explains how he got into Whittington Manor with such ease.'

'Somebody must want you out of the picture very badly indeed to go to the trouble of infiltrating your staff,' said Cornelius. 'Toppers very rarely play the long game. They prefer the direct approach.'

'My enemies are learning subtlety at last. Well, as always Ham Yard will have a tediously long list of suspects to interview. I must apologize to you,' said Quest. 'Normally my guests have a much more pleasant experience at Whittington.'

'Not at all,' said Cornelius.

Not at all. He knew a lot more than when he had come to this grand house on the edge of the capital. But he still didn't know *why*. And that, unfortunately, was just about the most puzzling piece of the jigsaw to be missing.

Watching the lifting room door close on their master and his guest, the Catosian soldiers lifted up the unconscious prisoner. One of them pulled out a knife to cut the assassin's throat, but their officer stayed her hand. 'Did you not see the master's hand signal before he departed? We need to secure him with the others. We are to keep him alive, at least for now.'

'This one will make for a very dangerous hostage.'

'Nothing of value can be won without danger,' said the officer. She looked at the pale face of the assassin. 'Cleverer than the others, to avoid detection among us for so long.'

'He would be less clever dead,' said the soldier, pushing her knife back into her belt.

'You have your orders! Obey them.'

It was not the place of a free company fighter to voice such doubts, so the officer kept her peace. But inside she agreed with every word of her soldier's sentiments. Some hostages were far better off dead.

CHAPTER TEN

Amelia could tell her arms were shackled even as she was waking up. She could barely remember where she was through the waves of nausea; but the line of trussed-up Catosian free company soldiers lying comatose in the low-roofed chamber brought it all back to her. The *Sprite of the Lake*. And it wasn't just the mercenaries bundled down here – there was Billy Snow, his grizzled old head lying sprawled unconscious on one of the Catosians, while at the far end she could just see Gabriel McCabe and an armoured set of foot claws that had to belong to T'ricola.

'Breathe deep, lass,' said a voice. 'You took a bad lungful of the vapours out on the deck.'

'Commodore? Jared, are you here?' Amelia tried to peer down the dimly lit chamber, but then she realized the voice was coming from behind her.

'Where else would I be, professor? Captain of my own boat and now master of nothing more than this old storage hold.' The commodore wriggled into the corner of her vision, his legs tied and arms bound like Amelia's. 'What do you remember?'

'I was outside on the deck and reality was breaking down. People were changing into things, becoming monsters, even parts of the boat were coming alive.'

'It was no more than your mind breaking down, lass. We sailed into a wall of river mist – but it turned out to be something more potent, a defensive wall of gas laid out to snare anyone foolish enough to come visiting.'

'A Daggish weapon?' said Amelia. 'But that makes no sense. They have living creatures in their cooperative, animals that would be affected by the gas. And where are the sailors, where are Bull's people?'

'Who do you think led us into the trap? Ah, they played me for a fool, so they did. Us on the surface venting the stale air out of our corridors. Bull and his cronies in suits, scraping off barnacles below our hull, knowing they would have all the time in the world to seize the boat when we ran into that wicked wall of vapours. Snug in their wet suits while the rest of us were out of our gourds.'

'Whose wall of vapours, Jared? Whose, if not the Daggish empire's?'

'Bull was in here gloating an hour ago, but he did not say, although I have a terrible idea who it may belong to. Something that would not be affected by any amount of madness-inducing vapours. Our mutual friend Coppertracks used to hint at an evil that dwelled in Liongeli, when he dared, when he was off his guard . . . something so fearful he would never say much more.'

'That gas didn't come out of one of your old steamer's ghost stories,' said Amelia. Circle, her head was throbbing now. 'It was real enough.'

Like most steammen, Coppertracks had never been given to exaggeration. A thought occurred to her. 'Where's Ironflanks?'

'Off flying with the tree monkeys,' laughed a voice.

It was Bull Kammerlan, three of his sailors behind him, now armed with the Catosians' carbines.

'We've kept him on the sauce, as much Quicksilver as he can snort into his boiler, bless him.'

'You filthy jigger,' spat Amelia. 'You were the traitor! Poisoning the old steamer and wrecking the *Sprite*.'

'Me?' Bull smiled. 'Well, I spiked your scout, there's no denying that. We could hardly have Ironflanks warning you that the channel we were taking had a nasty surprise halfway up it, could we? But am I your traitor? No. I'm not that. It wasn't me behind the games on the *Sprite*. I'd not want to damage the old girl, would I, dimples? She's my boat now, and the old gang are back in business, I should say.'

'Don't do this, Bull,' pleaded the commodore. 'You have a pardon waiting for you. You and the lads can be free, as legal as the powder on a magistrate's wig back in Jackals.'

'Free!' Bull roared. 'Free! Free to pay taxes on my beer to the rabble that turned our families off our land and stole everything we owned? Free to bend my knee to their law and kiss their populist arses once a five-year at the ballot? You've forgotten what we once were, old man, hiding your real name and pretending that the cause is dead.'

'It is dead, Bull – you, me, a few others scattered to the winds, we're all that's left of the royalist fleet now. We need to survive, you and I – why do you think it was old Blacky that sprung you out of Bonegate?'

'I intend to do more than survive,' said Bull, 'I intend to live! If Quest was going to pay you for a few antiques scraped off the bottom of Lake Ataa Naa Nyongmo, then he'll pay us too, I fancy. What with his money and the coins we'll raise from selling these killer Catosian princesses on the block down Cassarabia way, I reckon we'll have enough loot to kick off the cause again in a grand old style. Guns and boats and a whole ocean's worth of Jackelian shipping to plunder. They'll curse my name in the House of Guardians for a thousand years after I have made them bleed, after I cut off their precious trade and shake the pennies from their dirty, thieving pockets.'

'Bull, I'm begging you . . .'

'And don't think I don't like the sound of you doing it.' The u-boat man turned to his sailors. 'Just remove the people I talked about, boys. You'll get your chance to "survive" now, commodore, that's the least I owe you for giving me the *Sprite* and setting us back on the water and back in the game.'

The guards pulled up Amelia and the commodore. At the opposite end of the chamber they picked up the unconscious forms of the other expedition officers – Billy Snow, Gabriel McCabe, Veryann, T'ricola – carrying their limp forms out like sacks of coal.

'What are you going to do to us?' Amelia demanded.

'You ever fight a snake, dimples? Best way to stop it quick is to cut off the head, leave the rest of it wriggling on the dirt. Especially you, commodore. I know there are secret passages on this boat, pieces of equipment hidden away in chambers with private activation codes – secrets handed down from generation to generation by the captains. I leave you tied up in my brig, I'm as like to wake up to find my cabin flooded and the pilot room locked on me. No, I think we'll be sailing with our own officers in charge of things from now on.'

Hauled at gunpoint to the deck, Amelia saw that one of the shore boats had been taken out, Ironflanks' passed-out form already inside it, twitching in the bright, clear sunlight. Sailors carried the unconscious bodies of the other officers down the ladder, tossing them next to the steamman.

'Marooning us, are you?' the commodore said.

'More of a chance than you gave me when I was exiled from the fleet,' replied Bull. 'There's pistols in the boat, water and victuals. We'll toss some charges on the shore upriver for your guns. There's a couple of holes in the shore boat, but if you're quick at rowing, it'll stay afloat long enough to get you out of the river and into the rainforest.'

'Nobody has ever come this far up the southeast fork on foot and survived,' said Amelia.

'Not true,' said Bull, pointing at the drugged steamman. 'He has. Of course, he didn't return to Rapalaw Junction with anyone else!'

That drew a laugh from the ring of grinning sailors.

'Besides, what do you care?' He shoved Amelia back. 'You're staying here. I just brought you topside so you could say goodbye to this old dog . . .'

'No, Bull!' shouted the commodore, but he was kicked to the deck then pushed down the ladder towards the other officers.

'I don't know too much about fishing antiquities off lake beds,' said Bull, 'so you're going to help make me rich, dimples. And if we don't get that far and have to turn back, well, I'm sure there's someone in Cassarabia who likes to buy them in large for their harem.'

There was a ripple of unease through the crew. One of the stripe-shirted sailors stepped forward. 'She's got the hex on her, this one. Leave her, Bull. Leave her here with Blacky and his friends.'

Bull's hand wavered over his pistol holster. 'We've just got rid of one skipper – any of you think you can do the same to me?'

'We're not challenging you, captain,' said the sailor, 'but she's trouble, this one. I can feel it. You've seen what happens around her. She draws death to her like wasps to sweet cider.

If we carry her along with us, this'll become a voyage of damned souls.'

Bull turned to his men. 'How damned are we, then? Freed from the tanks at Bonegate, treading the decks of our own war boat again? A full cargo of flaxen-haired moxies trussed up in our holds – treasure before us, and the fool that drummed us out of the royal fleet quaking on his fat feet at the thought of being stranded out in the jungle. If that's bad luck, I'll take a barrelful of it any day. And unless any of you jacks became experts in ancient civilizations while you were treading water back in Middlesteel, we still need the Guardian girl's knowledge to make us wealthy.'

They seemed mollified and Bull cut the line holding the shore boat. It began to drift back as the *Sprite's* engines pulled the u-boat away against the current.

'You'd break your mother's heart if she was alive to see this,' called the commodore as the flow of the Shedarkshe seized the small craft and carried it away.

'She hated you as much as I did, even before you court-martialled me,' laughed Bull. 'Say hello to the sleekclaws and tree spiders for me, *uncle*.'

'A seadrinker's curse on you and for paying back my mercy like this,' shouted the commodore. 'But not on your head, Amelia. When Bull's dogs are struggling in the water, cursing the day they stole the *Sprite*, the river dolphins will come for you and carry you to safety.'

'Not unless they've developed a taste for this Liongeli soup,' roared Bull. 'You take care, uncle, try not to poison the pot of the first tribe of craynarbians you come across with your fraud's swagger and your landsman's belly. I'll take care of your boat and your women for you while you're off exploring.'

'Jared, I'm sorry!' Amelia turned aghast to the new master

of the *Sprite*. 'He's your own family and you're doing this to him?'

'It was only our bloodline that kept the fleet-in-exile going,' said Bull. 'Leastways, it was until his dim-witted courtier's ways brought your RAN aerostats calling over the free isles.'

'You're not going to make it without him and the other officers.'

'You think?' Bull gave a final mocking wave to the drifting shore craft. 'Well, we'll be doing a lot better than your friends will when they wake up and find out where we've marooned them.'

Rifle muzzles shoved Amelia back as she tried to grab Bull. 'What do you mean?'

'Blacky can ask your friend Ironflanks. He knows,' said Bull, amused. 'That wall of gas is about to become the least of their problems. Your fate has taken a turn for the worse too, girl. Take her below and keep her out of my sight.'

Ironflanks was the last of them to emerge from the effects of his sedation and the uneasiest with it, all four of his arms shaking as the effect of days of quicksilver abuse wore off.

'We're not on the u-boat any longer, then?' noted the steamman, his metal body smoking with condensation as the sun sliced through the canopy, burning off the morning dew from his hull.

'You tell us,' said Gabriel McCabe. 'You're the expert on this damned jungle.'

'Your bender has seen us marooned,' explained the commodore. 'While you were out of your metal skull, Bull and his gang of pirates ran us up a channel and into a wall of gas that had us barking at the moon as if we belonged in an asylum.'

'A wall of gas?' Ironflanks hissed what might have been a

sigh out of his voicebox. 'Then I know where we are, and it isn't anywhere we want to be. What supplies do we have?'

Veryann pointed to the two pistols, a belt of charges and a pile of water canteens behind them.

'The pistols are enough to annoy most of what we will encounter in Liongeli,' said Ironflanks. 'No boiler-grade coke for me?'

The commodore shook his head.

'Excellent,' said Ironflanks. 'I do so *love* the taste of wet leaves burning inside my body.'

'Where are we?' asked Veryann. 'I thought we had entered Daggish territory?'

'We are near their border, at the edge of the nest's patrol area. But there are some things that even the greenmesh does not want to absorb into its hive.'

Ironflanks stared past the commodore's bulk to where Billy Snow was holding T'ricola, the craynarbian engineer shaking worse than he was. 'She has acclimatization sickness?'

'My armour is expanding,' said T'ricola, 'I'm moulting all over.'

'You are nearly at your full jungle height,' said Ironflanks. 'Direct exposure to Liongeli is accelerating your body's natural cycles.'

'I detest this place,' moaned T'ricola.

'Then it is fitting you survive it,' said Ironflanks.

'You know the route back to Rapalaw Junction from here?' asked T'ricola.

'We are not going back,' said Veryann. 'My company is on the *Sprite* and my mission is at the source of this river.'

'Your mission is over,' said Gabriel McCabe. 'Your people are slaves that haven't been sold yet, and even if we caught up with the *Sprite*, the six of us are not going to be able to storm the boat and take her back.'

'Gabriel is right,' said the commodore. 'I would walk to the end of the Shedarkshe if I thought I would get my precious *Sprite* back and free our friends, but Bull's rascals would raise lances and fry us like eels in a frying pan if they saw us clambering over her hull. Our best hope is to make it back to the Junction and send word to Quest. With his resources we can lay an ambush downriver, wait for the *Sprite* to return and net her on Jackelian territory.'

'You may be correct,' said Ironflanks. 'But you are missing one thing, my softbody friends. I am not going back to Rapalaw Junction. I am taking myself and any of you that want to accompany me to Lake Ataa Naa Nyongmo. Quest will not pay me for a missing u-boat and a failed expedition.'

'It was difficult enough sneaking up the river in the safety of my lovely boat. What chance do the six of us have on foot, against an empire? What will you be doing with Abraham Quest's blessed coins?' demanded the commodore. 'Melting them down to make yourself a set of gold-plated arms?'

'If you only knew,' said Ironflanks. 'You are welcome to try to return to Rapalaw Junction by yourself. Follow the river northwest, walking along the west bank – avoid any and all villages you come across. In fact, avoid anything that is bigger than you.'

'Quest's money cannot be that important to you,' said Gabriel McCabe.

'As I said, you have no idea,' replied Ironflanks.

Veryann picked up one of the water canteens and looked meaningfully at the group.

'We should go with them,' said Billy. 'See our mission through. Let's face it, the chances are we're going to die either way, and I'd rather have it said that I passed along the Circle running towards danger than running away from it.'

'Is that it, then?' said the commodore. 'I am to finish as a pile of bleached bones hidden in the jungle, used as a nest for snakes while my friends back home in Tock House raise a glass to poor old missing Blacky each Midwinter, his genius as lost to the world as the temples of ancient Camlantis.'

'The free companies have a saying,' said Veryann. 'You are not dead until you have taken a hundred with you.'

'Ah, lass, I'll follow you to the heart of the dark territory of the Daggish. For you and my blessed *Sprite* I'll go. But I've killed a hundred or more in duels when I was young and had a temper as red as the blood that runs through my veins. So don't be surprised if poor old Blacky gets carried off by a petrodactyl or trampled by a tauntoraptor; I've got my hundred lined up in the halls of the dead waiting for me to fall into their dreadful clutches.'

Billy Snow got up, leaning on his old cane which the *Sprite's* new masters had contemptuously tossed into the raft before casting them off. 'Sometimes I'm glad I can't see what we're getting ourselves into.'

They set off and the jungle closed around them. Something like a snake crawled out of the bush, its metal carapace scraping along the floor, turning a single jewel-sized eye towards the trail left by the departing officers from the u-boat. Normally the gas would have been enough to finish the intruders off. How foolish of these creatures to forsake the safety of their craft for the embrace of deepest Liongeli.

Switching its sight to heat vision, the metal scout slithered silently after them.

Cornelius pushed open the door to the banqueting room of Dolorous Hall, largely empty except for the rows of mirrored suits of armour, Damson Beeton's reflection distorted in the breastplates as she busied about, sorting the day's delivery of victuals from Gattie and Pierce.

She noticed Cornelius's entry into the room. 'Don't even bother turning up for breakfast, you and that old bird both.'

'I was out late last night,' explained Cornelius. 'The final evening of the House of Quest's big function. I thought you would be pleased I had accepted one of the society invites at last.'

'If you accepted a few more, perhaps you would develop your manners enough to come down in time to see the now-cold fare I cooked for you when the sun was coming up.'

'Thank you, but I am not hungry. Have you seen Septimoth this morning?'

'Pah.' Damson Beeton dismissed his inquiry with a cursory wave. 'No. And I have to sort through these boxes. They've either forgotten to send the salt, or that crooked delivery boy has cheated us out of it. Next time he rows this way, I'll give him what for. How can you cook without salt?'

'How indeed?' Realizing he wasn't going to get any sense out of the housekeeper, Cornelius beat a retreat to the lifting room and rode the chamber up to the aerie. Septimoth was waiting inside, resting his back with both wings unfolded against a y-shaped wooden frame that had been built in facsimile of the lashlites' simple pine furniture.

'If you were my coachman, I would release you from my service,' said Cornelius.

'If I were your coachman I would ask for danger money,' said Septimoth.

'Where did you get to yesterday evening?'

'Our friends in the flash mob were at Quest's residence,' said Septimoth, lifting himself from the frame and pulling his massive leathery wings in. 'They left with a cargo of eviscerated steammen.'

'That would explain why I didn't find anything at the mansion,' said Cornelius. 'You followed the thugs from the flash mob?'

'I did,' said Septimoth, 'until my wings ached from it. They switched horses at staging posts twice and rode across two counties. They finished their journey at the airship works at Ruxley Waters, and waiting for them was the same mouse I scooped up for you by the cursewall in Quatérshift.'

'Robur!' Cornelius swore under his breath. 'So, Quest's money *is* paying for the grave robbing. It was our handsomely moneyed friend who set Furnace-breath Nick up to grab Robur from the Commonshare, too. I came across Robur's so-called daughter at Quest's house, nicely fitted out in the cherry uniform of one of his fencibles.'

'The woman in the jinn house?'

'The same,' said Cornelius. 'Good for more than making fools out of us, too; they earn their keep, those ladies of his. An assassin paid an uninvited visit to Quest's reception last night, broke a skylight and came sailing down a cord like a spider. I thought the topper was after me for a moment, but he'd come for Quest – who's been suspiciously well trained in the art of combat, by the way. His Catosian fighters were on the assassin like a hunt falling on a fox. Fast enough that I wager they were expecting trouble. So then, what mischief do you think that Quest and Robur are up to at the airship works?'

'I know only two people guaranteed to have the answers to that. We should snatch the merchant,' said Septimoth. 'If he is an agent of the Commonshare I shall enjoy myself finding ways to make him talk.'

'Quest is too well protected,' said Cornelius. 'I saw some of his set-up at Whittington Manor. He has an army salted away up there, with blood machines at sentry points inside.

I can change my face and body within limits, but I can't mimic flesh at a fundamental enough level to fool a blood machine.'

'Whatever his plans, there is a sure way to stop them. If we can't get close enough to seize Quest, we can get close enough to kill him,' said Septimoth. 'I can drop you past his close-quarter protection – he travels in the open, he has commercial concerns to run, he can't stay inside that fortress of his forever.'

'It may yet come to that,' said Cornelius. 'But this isn't the same as taking our vengeance against a Commonshare leader, this is one of our own we are talking about. If I put a bullet in Quest's skull, we'll have the Ham Yard crushers and the army after us, possibly the Court of the Air's wolftakers too, no more sanctuary inside Jackals for the pair of us. We cannot bring down the Commonshare on the run, hiding in barns and travelling on false papers.'

'You forget our blood oath, Cornelius Fortune. If this merchant is abetting the Commonshare's designs, I shall tear his heart out myself.'

'If Quest was in the pocket of the First Committee, he wouldn't have needed to trick us into freeing Robur. The mechomancer could have been quietly smuggled out to Quest, dropped off on the coast by a shiftie submersible.'

'And yet the seers of the crimson feather have been prodded out of the cave of the oracle to seek out a disgraced outcast such as I. This is not happening merely because a Jackelian trader thought his commercial concerns would profit by having a Quatérshiftian tinker broken out of the camps and employed on his staff.'

'Robur,' said Cornelius. 'This mystery started with that damn mechomancer and he is the key that will unlock the puzzle.'

Septimoth flashed his talons. 'Then it is time to pay Ruxley Waters a visit.'

'Not me,' said Cornelius, pulling out the mask of Furnace-breath Nick and slipping it down over his skull. 'But *me*!'

The dark laughter faded inside Dolorous Hall's banqueting room as Damson Beeton's remote viewing spell dwindled away to nothing. In the old days, the people of Jackals would have burnt her as a witch for such tricks. She chuckled and resumed sorting the day's delivery of food. It was about time those two lackwits started making some progress on this affair.

Damson Beeton suspected their instinct was a good one, though. Robur *was* the key, and if he was secreted away at the airship works at Ruxley Waters, then that was a revelation she could use. The thing that worried her most was the assassin Cornelius had spoken of. The description of the methods used in the assassination attempt sounded worryingly familiar, but not so worrying as the fact the assassination had failed in the first place. That spoke of desperation, foolhardiness from quarters that should have been coldly calculated in their choreography of such a murder.

Her mind was awhirl with the possibilities, until she found the missing bag of salt under the cabbage and swore. Now she would have to apologize to the damn delivery boy tomorrow morning.

The two sailors dragging Amelia into the commodore's old quarters were careful to keep their carbines at the ready as they pushed her in front of the large hardwood navigation table. Bull Kammerlan looked up, prodding aside a pile of papers in irritation – not charts but mission documents, carefully compiled by the House of Quest's researchers and added to during the voyage by Amelia.

'Have you developed a taste for archaeology?' asked Amelia.

'Have you developed a taste for quarters other than a hold filled with resentful Catosians?' Bull retorted. 'I brought you along to make sense of this rubbish, to do the job Quest paid you to do.'

'I may be on Quest's pay book, but I wasn't mounting this expedition for him,' said Amelia.

'Leave off with the nobility of science speech, dimples,' retorted Bull. 'You're a looter of tombs, a history thief with letters after your name that were paid for by your rich family. I know the way Abraham Quest's mind works better than you do, and a man like him isn't doing all this to fill the bowls of the poor with milk and honey.' Bull leafed through the papers in exasperation 'There were wonders in that ancient time, things we can only dream of now. That's the knowledge your rich shopkeeper friend is after. Artificers' tricks to swell his pockets.'

'Quest is already the richest man in Jackals,' said Amelia. 'He doesn't need more money.'

Bull shook his head sadly. 'He doesn't need it to pay his pantry bill, girl, but he *needs* it all right. Needs it like an itch – because it's how his kind keeps count.'

'Even if we make it to Lake Ataa Naa Nyongmo, even if we unearth the location of the city in the heavens from those ruins on the lake bed, what makes you think he'll pay you for it?'

'Oh, he'll pay all right, Guardian's daughter. I wager he won't even ask what happened to poor old Blacky, or you, or his army of golden-haired killers. He'll just ask if we have the location of Camlantis for him. Then he'll whistle up the lads from his counting house with as many bags of Jackelian guineas as I have a care to ask for.'

'What if he won't pay?'

Bull smiled. 'Then it won't just be your companions down in the hold that I sell on the trading block in Cassarabia. What do you reckon the caliph will pay for the location of Camlantis?'

Amelia recoiled in disgust. 'You'd betray Jackals.'

'My Jackals stopped existing six hundred years ago. I'd sell the location of Camlantis to the First Committee in Quatérshift if they had enough gold in their vaults left to buy a loaf of bread.'

'And what will you do with your newfound wealth? Rebuild Porto Principe? Pay for the daughters of the new regime to lay down with you in your underwater kingdom?'

'I've never needed to pay for it, girl,' said Bull, 'and it might shock you to know that not everyone finds arms as large as a side of beef appealing.'

Amelia walked to the bunk and patted the blankets, then rested her hand on the dolphin-encircled ornament there. It would need to be easy to find, for a skipper surprised in his sleep by a mutinous rabble, but not so easy as to be obvious. 'Of course you don't need to pay for it. Not with a hold full of Catosians who're going to end up on the slave market anyway.'

Bull started to laugh a retort, but Amelia found the cover and the switch hidden underneath, the slaver's words turning to a yelp as a hidden capacitor fed the copper-veined marble floor with its charge, a sheet of blue energy scything across the chamber, tossing the two guards into the wall as Bull's chair was hurled back with the force of his convulsing muscles.

Amelia's boots stood on the square of thick woollen carpet surrounding the bunk alcove – more than just insulation against the cold seas the *Sprite* had passed through, as the three unconscious figures sprawled across the commodore's luxurious quarters attested to. 'You were right, Jared, the river dolphins did come to my rescue.'

Amelia scooped up one of the carbines and unclipped the belt of charges for the gun. Her mind raced with the possibilities. One woman against more than ninety of Bull's crew. She could try to even the odds by releasing the Catosian fighters, but their hold was the most heavily guarded position in the *Sprite*, she had already seen that. Bull's people were rightly paranoid that the fighters would chew their way out of their manacles and throttle the crew in their sleep. Revenge was a matter of principle for a betrayed city-state free company. She could take Bull Kammerlan hostage – put a gun to his head and demand the Catosians' release. But perhaps not. The slavers would as like allow Bull to swing, then gleefully knife each other for the vacant position of skipper.

If only Commodore Black were here, he'd have a way to even the odds. A second secret pilot room able to override the first, a hidden tank of gas just as vile as the ambush mist Bull had ridden them into – but the other secrets of the *Sprite* were as lost to Amelia as her friends marooned out in the jungle.

Amelia made up her mind. The bathysphere attached to the *Sprite's* hull. If they lost that as well as her knowledge of Camlantis, the expedition was as good as over – unless the slavers fancied blundering around the ruins on the lake bed in their diving suits, trying to distinguish ancient crystal-books from two-thousand-year-old rubble. She would scupper their chances and use the bathysphere as an escape capsule at the same time.

As Amelia stepped out of the commodore's quarters, the corridor's lights changed from the standard yellow to a muted crimson hue. Was this to do with her escape? There were no claxons, though. Unless the sudden surge of capacitor juice had thrown an alarm somewhere, drained the boat's power, nobody outside of the thugs lying shocked in the skipper's quarters should know she had activated Black's secret switch.

Amelia crept through the corridors, as silent as the rest of the boat. The *Sprite* had stopped moving now, her engines stilled. Pulling herself up the cold steel of a ladder, Amelia climbed two decks, heading for the rear conning tower. At one point she passed the *Sprite's* engineering bay and risked a glance through its slightly ajar hatch. The bay's lathes and workbenches were at a halt, maintenance work quieted while the crewmen inside nervously held onto the ceiling pipes. It was as if by stunning Bull Kammerlan she had cut the marionette cords on the rest of his gang of slavers; they were just waiting there in the stale tinned air for their leader to awake kraken-like from his slumbers.

Her luck did not hold. Amelia dipped into the passage leading to the bathysphere and a sailor at the other end saw her, then did a double take as he realized she should be locked up below in the hold with the Catosians. He grabbed for a holster on his belt and Amelia let him have the round in her carbine, the sailor bouncing from the wall and collapsing in front of her – she had hit him square in the chest: he was dead before the crack of the stubby rifle had finished echoing down the boat. There goes caution, Amelia sighed. She teased another charge from her ammunition belt even as she ejected the broken crystal from the first onto the deck. Slid the new shell into her carbine.

Amelia found the entrance to the bathysphere barred to her – a simple rotating combination lock. With no hope of guessing the sequence she placed the muzzle of the carbine an inch from the metal and turned her head as the blast from the short rifle jounced off the hatch. Hot metal lanced her hand. The lock was mangled, but it still held. She beat the butt of the carbine on the hatch, exposing the locking mechanism. Curse the *Sprite* for being so well built by its long-dead royalist engineers. Desperation grew in Amelia as she heard stirrings from the lower decks. She smashed the rifle as hard as she could against the lock, shattering the wooden butt with the impact. On Amelia's last blow the *Sprite* shook violently as if a fire squid had scooped up the u-boat from the river to rattle it around, a muffled detonation that knocked Amelia off her feet, and landed her across the dead sailor. Then all was still again, an unnatural silence tinted only by the eerie crimson light.

A head popped up through the floor hatch – it was cooky, the grizzled old chef still wearing his oil-spattered apron. He looked down the corridor, took in the dead sailor and the carbine still in Amelia's grip, then pulled himself up, running terrified to the bathysphere hatch, practically sobbing when he saw the ruin that was all that was left of the locking system. Amelia got to her feet, covering him with the carbine, but he was so horrified that he showed no sign of even being aware of the weapon.

'Did you not see the red light?'

Amelia glanced up at the illumination strips. 'The red light?'

'Silent bloody running,' moaned the crewman. 'There's a pair of seed ships above us and your gunshots have blown us to them. They've depth-charged our engines, we're dead in the water.' He started pulling distraughtly at the door, but it was beyond use. There would be no escape that way. A hissing sound came from inside the rear conning tower.

Old cooky gave up, slumping to the deck in despair. 'Jonah. Jonah. We never should have kept you here.'

She glanced down the corridor. There were screams and shouts coming up from the lower decks as the crew realized what was happening, all thoughts of silent running abandoned as they began to panic. Amelia turned around. Cooky was reaching for the holster of the sailor she had killed. 'Don't do it, cooky. I'll shoot you if I have to, I swear I will . . .'

He continued to fumble with the flap and slid the pistol out. 'Save the last shell for yourself.'

Amelia sighted her carbine before she realized what cooky was doing. The pistol barrel slid into his mouth and he exchanged a luckless look with the professor before he pressed the trigger and whipped into the wall of the corridor, the explosion taking off the rear of his head. Amelia felt like being sick. She had made Billy Snow promise she wouldn't end up like those poor soul-scrubbed zombies swaying empty on the block of Rapalaw Junction's comfort auction; but Billy Snow wasn't here. Whatever death in the jungle was awaiting the officers of the expedition who had been marooned, it was looking like they had got the best of the bargain. She pointed the carbine at her own heart and willed herself to squeeze the trigger. Just a small squeeze, that was all that was needed. Tighter, tighter. As she tried to find the resolve to do it, a weight seemed to press down on the weapon, lowering the barrel away from her body.

'I took that way, and I was very wrong to do so.'

'Father!' Amelia called into the empty corridor, but there were only the dead bodies of the sailor and cooky to hear her. She was going mad, justifying her gutlessness with echoes from the past.

Above Amelia the hissing grew louder. The mindless drones of the Daggish Empire were cutting their way into the u-boat.

They needed fresh flesh for the hive.

It was sweltering work, hacking through the green deeps of Liongeli, avoiding the trails favoured by the land's lumbering predators. Ironflanks led the way, his four arms cutting back the vegetation. The others quickly realized that his habit of whistling in mimicry of the jungle's creatures was born out of his stacks overheating – better to release pressure in a way that sounded natural, rather than announcing his presence with a full piercing lift of his boiler's whistle.

'Can we not rest?' wheezed the commodore. 'We've been an age breaking our way through these infernal green halls.'

'An age?' said Ironflanks. 'We have hardly started our journey, Jared softbody.'

'There was a call from the rear of the line. Billy had found something, his fingers tearing a scrap of canvas from a bush by his side. 'This is not a creeper.'

T'ricola took the cloth from the blind sonar man and sniffed it through the three olfactory holes in her head armour. 'It's burnt and it looks like – no, it cannot be . . .'

The others gathered around to examine it.

'It's a piece of catenary curtain,' said T'ricola. 'Burnt off from an airship hull.'

'The RAN do not fly missions this deep into the interior,' said Ironflanks. 'Rapalaw Junction counts itself lucky if Jackals' aerostats answer the garrison's siege alarm.'

'Yet here it is,' said T'ricola.

Commodore Black pushed his head between the trees behind them. 'There is more through here, and a terrible sight it is to behold, too.'

Bearing the officers' pistols, Gabriel McCabe and Veryann pressed through the bush, emerging into a clearing where the jungle was growing back over hacked-down trees and felled ferns. The others came through after them.

'It's the remains of a camp,' said Gabriel.

'Not just a camp,' said the commodore. He pointed at a wall of unopened crates lying buried by Liongeli's green mass. 'I recognize those blessed things: it's a mobile fortress. They didn't even have enough time to bolt it together.'

Ironflanks cleared the vegetation back. White bones lay amid the debris, picked totally clean by legions of scavengers. 'I don't believe I am familiar with the term.'

'That's because your people have been fighting the brigades of Quatérshift and not the red-coated devils of Jackals,' said the commodore. 'And count yourself lucky for it.'

'It is a conceit of their parliament's new pattern army,' said Veryann. 'A modular construction system Jackelian regiments use on campaign. A walled fort that can be raised or dismantled in a period of hours; a ridiculous toy that encourages defensive thinking and belies the very name, "mobile", that it sports.'

Billy Snow rapped one of the boxes with his cane. 'The wood on these crates hasn't rotted through. They've been here less than a year I would say.'

T'ricola pulled out more catenary curtain sheeting from the vegetation, blackened and brittle. 'So an airship came down here and the survivors were trying to build a camp? But celgas is not flammable, so why would the hull end up so burnt?'

'Celgas may not be flammable,' said Ironflanks. 'But an airship will burn all the same if it tries to pass low over Daggish territory. Their flame cannons would scratch one from the sky for daring to pass over the nest.'

'Perhaps the stat's navigation and steering were wrecked?' mused T'ricola. 'They could have drifted over the greenmesh by accident and been brought down. The RAN fleet was pretty well scuppered when Quatérshift attacked Jackals; this could have happened during the war.'

'I saw the fleet brought down over the hills of Rivermarsh,' said the commodore, 'when the wicked shifties were given a drubbing in the skies true and clear by King Steam's forces, assisted in no small part by my own genius. I don't recall

271

seeing any Daggish there, nor any airships making a run for it towards Liongeli.'

'It was a big battle,' said Veryann. 'It was said that the shroud of cannon fire remained over the downs like a mist for a week afterwards. You can't have seen all the action.'

'Aye, it was thick work,' agreed the commodore. 'There was the rebel leader's army of demons, the treacherous shifties and half our own people fighting against us. A hard pounding, that day, for poor old Blacky, wading through the blood of our brave boys with a sabre in one hand and a pistol in the other. But the steammen knights boarded the fleet when it was turned against us and cut the airships up from inside, using King Steam's fighters as cannonballs and boarding parties both.'

'Well, there you are,' said Veryann. 'No doubt this is the remains of one of those RAN vessels. Broken during the war and left to drift on the winds of fortune.'

'And drift a rare long way it did,' said the commodore. He looked at Veryann with a knowing glint in his eye. 'And where were you and our expedition's beloved benefactor during the invasion of 1596?'

'On a paddle steamer halfway between Jackals and the colonies. We were tending to the house's business in Concorzia.'

'You were lucky, then,' said the commodore. 'Safe on a boat is where I would have liked to have been during that wicked conflict. But curse my unlucky stars, fate was not so kind to me that year.'

T'ricola bent over the trailing creepers, picking at the debris. 'I see no Quatérshiftian uniforms here.'

'I see no uniforms left at all,' said Ironflanks. 'And that is what I find the most disturbing fact of all. Let us quit this place now, back to the trail.'

Ironflanks had taken only a single step back into the dense press of the jungle when the cry echoed through the trees. '*Smellyouyouyoumetalmetaljiggerjiggerjigger.*'

'Tell me that is not what I think it is,' said the commodore.

'You know the answer to that question,' said Ironflanks.

Gabriel McCabe glanced down sadly at the pathetic pistol in his hand. 'I thought we had lost the thunder lizard.'

'Queen Three-eyes knows enough to be able to follow the river upstream,' said Ironflanks. 'And it is the scent of my stacks she is following now.'

'We have about a quarter of an hour,' said Billy Snow, 'judging by the strength of her cry, before she is on top of us.'

'Not on top of us,' said Ironflanks. 'On top of *me*. It's my hull she is coming for, so it is my old hull that will lead her off.'

'We won't last a day in the Liongeli deeps without you,' said the commodore.

Veryann took her knife out and threw it across the clearing, embedding it in the skull of a giant python that was slipping down a branch towards T'ricola. 'Survival is a secondary concern to the success of our mission, and that has a minimal chance of succeeding without a scout to lead us to Lake Ataa Naa Nyongmo.'

'Then we must run,' said Ironflanks. 'Follow me into the deepest bush and hope that it is enough to slow down Queen Three-eyes.'

They ran. Without the safety of a submersible to escape to and with the long cries of the kilasaurus max growing louder behind them. Into the dense heat of the rainforest, through walls of orchids that quivered and shot out streams of super-heated pollen juice, past trees covered in running brown liquid glue where trapped animals shrieked desperately at the fleeing

273

party, across coffee-coloured creepers that had bridged a small ravine in their search for sunlight free of the competition under the canopy. Billy Snow proved surprisingly dextrous, leaping through the twisted vines with his machete, cutting down walls of greenery and opening passages through the trees as if he had been born a feral craynarbian tracker. At times it was not clear whether T'ricola was leading him, or the blind sonar man was leading her.

Ironflanks was getting slower. He was trying to keep his stacks from venting fully, to throw Queen Three-eyes off their trail. But the effort of recycling the exhaust of his furnace was sapping his strength. If he continued at this pace, he would poison his brain with the fumes and be left with a grip on reality even more tenuous than it already was.

Ironflanks stumbled and the commodore caught him. 'You've got to let it out, old steamer, or we're going to be carrying you the rest of the way.'

Ironflanks' voicebox trembled as he tried to find the words. 'She will smell it.'

'If the thunder lizard hunts by scent she will already have ours,' said Veryann. 'Your incapacitation will not serve us.'

The steamman stood up and his stacks whistled as a column of foul-smelling smoke lanced through the canopy above them. As the last trace of smoke left the trail, Queen Three-eyes' voice sounded in answer, so loud that the ribcages of the u-boat officers shook in their chests.

'I am sorry my softbody friends, I have doomed us all,' said Ironflanks.

'Blame my nephew rather than yourself,' said the commodore. 'For it's his dark treachery that has left us marooned out here. Or blame fool old Blacky for giving him a second chance in the first place.'

'Are you the dregs from a Jackelian jinn house?' shouted

Veryann. 'We are not dead yet. Not while we have blood in our legs and weapons in our hands. Now run, or I'll shoot you myself.'

Menaced by the unsteady pistol of the Catosian commander the party stumbled into life again, Gabriel McCabe taking the lead and putting all the strength of the self-proclaimed strongest man in Jackals into the swings of his machete. Gobs of green sap splashed out across them as they piled ahead, splattering their uniforms with a mess of sticky residue and then, suddenly, they were free of the press of the jungle, a clearing of grassed hills and tall emerald meadows waiting for them. Ironflanks stumbled out and looked around as if recognizing the territory. Then the howl of the kilasaurus max roared behind them. '*Gettingclosegettingclosetoyourendend-endmetaljigger.*'

'Head for the forest on the other side,' called Veryann, checking the charge in her pistol. 'We can get off a few shots when the thunder lizard comes into the open. Aim for the creature's eyes.'

Knee-deep in grass, they were plunging down one of the hillocks when the trees at the ridge of the hill flowered open, spouting white jets of liquid into the air. For a second the commodore thought that they had triggered some devilish man-eating hardwood into feeding, but the white fountain solidified into a net, scooping up the expedition members and sweeping them off their feet. They were hanging between the trees like a hammock, bound to the sticky material and swaying seven feet off the ground. Just the right height for an offering to Queen Three-eyes. T'ricola thrashed, trying to turn her sword arm on the material, but the harder she struggled, the more the netting seemed to tighten around them.

Crashing through the jungle, the kilasaurus max splintered through the last of the towering trees. She emerged in the clearing; her undersized lizard's head darting about before settling on the direction of the hills, her nostrils flaring and snorting like those of a stallion. Sensing the ensnared presence of Ironflanks, the thunder lizard dipped down then stretched to her full height and roared at a volume that shook the netting the expedition members lay pinned against. Billy Snow dropped his machete from his left arm to his partially free right hand and tried to saw their cords of bondage but the material turned slippery, oozing a soap-like liquid that made his blade slip. 'What is this stuff?' he growled.

Veryann attempted to lower her pistol arm enough to get a shot off against the thunder lizard, but the gun discharged wide, the bullet disappearing over the horizon.

'This is a rare old mess and no mistake,' said the commodore.

The webbing of their snare trembled as Queen Three-eyes advanced towards them, roaring gusts of fetid hate from the second mouth in her chest. Reaching the foot of the hillock, Queen Three-eyes' snout snaked around as she detected a movement in the corner of her field of vision. A line of boulders at the bottom of the hill was swivelling towards her, tracking each thumping footstep. She backed away, sensing the oddness of this place – a clearing so purpose-made for animals to graze across, yet so bereft of local life. Where tiny prey that should be running instead lay paralysed. Where rocks came alive. Too late. Slits opened in the boulders, iron spider's legs sprouting out, the suddenly mobile rocks spraying Queen Three-eyes with an orange liquid that solidified on contact with the air and sheathed the thunder lizard in a rubber bubble. She pushed against the foul glutinous substance but only succeeded in unbalancing herself, falling over and rolling back down the slope. Now the mightiest creature in the jungle lay as helpless as a toy figurine embedded inside the glass of a child's marble. The legs in the rocks retracted and the monarch of Liongeli was left thrashing futilely inside the orange enclosure.

'What is this, Ironflanks?' demanded the commodore. 'This is no Daggish trap. Those blessed rocks are machines.'

There was no intelligible reply. Something inside the steamman had snapped and he spouted a static screech of raw machine code, in the same inhuman voice as his people used to sing hymns to the Steamo Loas in their mountain fastness.

'Look,' called Veryann, 'look behind us.'

On the other side of the clearing a line of dark shapes was emerging from the twilight shadow of the rainforest. Metal bodies with the edges of their arms, wheels, legs and tracks filed down to razor sharpness, their rivets extruded into spikes. Iron hands clutching spears frilled with the shrunken heads of thunder lizards, craynarbians and the race of man. One of the figures crouched like a monkey and pointed at the full net containing the *Sprite's* officers. The arm indicating the catch was slipped through the bloodied sleeve of an airship captain's uniform: the fate of the shattered aerostat's crew had become clear.

'Steammen,' said the commodore. 'By my stars, they're steammen.'

'No,' said Ironflanks, recovering his higher functions, 'they're not.'

It was the first time any of them had heard a citizen of the Steammen Free State sob.

CHAPTER ELEVEN

Damson Beeton waddled down the front garden of Dolorous Hall, whistling and happy to be up with the larks. Red fingers of sunrise fringed the skyline behind the capital's pneumatic towers, most of the city's mills silent, not yet throwing the dark miasma of commerce into the air. The barge from Gattie and Pierce was pulling towards the isle's landing, using its single sail to keep down the cost of gas for the boat's expansion engine.

So much easier to get a start on the day's tasks this early in the morning. Cornelius and Septimoth were both pretending to be asleep, when in reality they were on the riverbed level of the isle, rattling around the old museum, planning their next move in the great game they had been sucked into within Jackals. All in all, Damson Beeton preferred it when they were causing their mischief across the border in Quatérshift. She had more time to herself, then. Not to mention lighter duties and the run of the place when empty.

'Morning, damson,' called the delivery boy at the prow. 'Two boxes for you today, right? And a quart of milk in the jug.'

'Fresh, I hope, young man,' said the housekeeper. 'Where's Master Jerry Cruncher today?'

'Called in sick,' said the delivery boy. The barge bumped gently into the landing and the boy started tying up.

She looked at the man on the rudder and the two bargemen tackling the sail. 'Not night-fog chest again, poor lad?'

'Beer-night head is more like it, I reckon,' laughed the delivery boy, stepping onto the isle with two crates balanced under his arms.

'Empty boxes are over there,' said Damson Beeton. As the boy looked towards the end of the pier, the housekeeper reached out and snapped the lad's nose bone back through his brain case. Instant death. 'The correct counter phrase was "that night-fog is the devil," young man.'

The three assassins abandoned their pretence as the crew of the delivery barge. They were reaching for secreted weapons, fingers wrapping around pistol butts and marlinspikes, when Damson Beeton stepped across the gap with a grace that belied her near seventy years. Targeting the fastest of the bargemen she kicked the pistol he had managed to draw out into the river, then cart-wheeled past, placing a needle kick just above his heart on the way towards his two friends. Just as he was wondering why his heart was no longer beating, the old woman's hand chopped out, breaking the heavy marlinspike in his other hand in two, converting her motion to embed a foot in one of the remaining two killers' guts. The last one standing punched out towards where her throat should have been. He was quick. And trained. A style that marked him as a topper, one of the elite cadres of assassins that floated around the capital's orbit.

She seized the two halves of the marlinspike as they fell and slammed them against his eardrums, then swivelled as his winded companion launched himself at her side. Oh, they were good. A normal man would have been left rolling on the floor of the boat, clutching his sides as the internal bleeding left him incapacitated. This one just came back for more. Luckily, she had more to give. She used his own momentum to break his spine against the sail, then gave mister no-hearing a little something to take his mind off the pain in his ears, seemingly brushing his knee with the tip of her boot. It was enough to collapse him down towards the barge's seat, where she pulled the hidden garrotte wire out of the sleeve of his river-man's jacket and twisted it around his neck, tightening it until he turned purple.

'Who do you work for, dearie?'

He gargled something unintelligible and she placed a boot on the seat of his trousers for extra purchase. 'Come on now, young man. You know enough to turn off the pain centre to your ears. Give me my answer.'

'Here's your answer,' said a voice behind her, as the dart buried itself in her back.

Damson Beeton just had time to turn to see the squat conning tower of the small river submersible rising on the other side of the pier, behind the figures in diving rubbers. One of the divers pulled off her mask, giving the unconscious housekeeper a prod with her boot.

'She was expecting someone else.'

'Obviously,' said the second diver, replying in fluent Catosian.

'You didn't say anything about this,' moaned the sole survivor in the barge, untangling the strangle cord from his neck. 'She was fighting in witch-time. She could have killed us all.'

'Yours is a risky profession,' was all that the diver on the pier had to say. Then to her comrade, 'Check her empty crates for hidden signals. She was expecting a courier exchange.'

'You are aware of what she is?' asked the other diver. Behind them, their submarine was discharging a row of soldiers in heavy padded uniforms onto the isle.

'Yes, but ours is also a risky profession.'

A lone man stepped out onto the pier, flanked by female soldiers. The only sign of his identity were the scars on his forehead where the purple flower tattoos of a worldsinger had been badly removed. The dive commander looked at the ex-worldsinger with distaste. Anyone willing to sell out his allegiance to his own people was not to be trusted. A necessary evil.

'How many left?' she asked.

'Just two that I can sense,' said the turncoat sorcerer. 'A lashlite and a man. The man's body is not normal. I have felt nothing like him before.'

'Interesting. It appears like the Catgibbon was telling the truth about him, then. You are sure there are only two more?' She looked up at Dolorous Hall. 'In a place this size?'

'That is what I sense. But they're not up in the house. They're below the water: the island extends out onto the riverbed.'

'Clever,' said the diver. 'They obviously value their privacy, but I wonder how good the seals on their construction are?'

'We need them alive,' said the other raider.

'If their maid of all works here is anything to go by, I think we shall settle for alive and wet.'

Cornelius was looking at the county map for Ruxley Waters when Septimoth's head swivelled. His hunter's sense had detected the first crack of the glass above them, but Cornelius did not need to be a lashlite to hear what followed. A wall of water burst through the shattering glass, landing on their stolen transaction engine then smashing over statues of royalty long dead and curiosities milled hundreds of years before. The old Middlesteel Museum was rejoining the other submerged buildings beneath the Gambleflowers as a breeding room for river crabs and eels. The two of them scrambled for the corridor leading to the isle's concealed lifting room, trying to keep on their feet as waves of water fountained past their legs, rising higher with each second.

'The crystal can't have cracked,' shouted Cornelius, evading a man-sized vase flowing past with the force of a battering ram. 'I designed it with sandwich layers to withstand five times the weight above us.'

'Your calculations seem to be a little at fault,' said Septimoth. One of the glass skylights in a side hall gave way and a second wave rode in with tidal force, sending both of them sprawling towards the rear of the museum. Behind them another wave of the Gambleflowers loosed its way across the museum. Buffeted in the crosscurrents, Septimoth spun away to slam into a wall, the press of water dislodging a display of swords on top of him, large cutlass-style affairs with clockwork driven rotating teeth raining down. Cornelius could tell his friend was unconscious by the way his wings unfolded limply out, a leathery stingray spiralling around on top of the water pouring in. Cornelius ejected the gutta-percha breathing tube from his artificial arm, biting down on the mouthpiece, then swam out towards the lashlite, each second pushing him higher towards the ceiling of the hall. Would the lifting room work with this amount of water in its mechanism, even if he could reach it now? He doubted it.

Cornelius grabbed his friend and pulled him close. Septimoth was oddly buoyant. Of course! The lashlite's nostrils had closed, the two air humps on his back filled and sealed. In unconsciousness his body had triggered his high flight reflex, a useful gift of nature when hunting skraypers in the airless upper atmosphere – higher even than RAN aerostats could climb. If Cornelius could swim them both to the surface they wouldn't drown. With only a foot of air left in the flooding chamber, Cornelius dragged them both down. It was devilish hard work with his lashlite friend inflated like a puffer fish, and Cornelius had to use the wall to pull them towards the shattered skylight. Kicking out the remaining shards of crystal so they were not eviscerated escaping the museum hall, Cornelius launched them out, using Septimoth as a buoy to lift them towards the surface. There was just enough light this deep underneath the Gambleflowers to see the remains of the flooded quarter of Middlesteel, slimy black buildings that had once been shops and homes, fish swimming out of broken windows while river crabs scuttled across gaping doorways. Cornelius tried to hold Septimoth back as they rose to the surface. He was uncertain about lashlite physiology, but he had heard enough tales in the submarine sailors' taverns along the waterway to be wary of the bends should they ascend too fast.

Something was wrong, he could feel it. Then they appeared. Two figures swimming out from behind the spire of a Circlist chapel, the spear guns in their hands the same golden colour as their dolphin skull-moulded helmets. Now Cornelius had sighted them, he didn't even need to look behind him to confirm the presence of the others rising up from concealed positions around the roof of the submerged museum. The warning shot of a spear powering closely past his chest was largely unnecessary. He and his winged friend were surrounded, and even if he could make a break for it without being pin-cushioned with spearheads, he would not abandon Septimoth. One of the underwater ambushers pointed to the two of them and then gestured to the dark hull of a small river submersible sinking down behind the spire.

Cornelius lacked the free air to sigh. He let himself be led to the submarine. A prisoner.

Most of the Daggish that had captured Amelia looked like walking cacti. Except that cacti did not have a single cyclopslike eye slit and their hard bark-like skin was not covered in a fuzz of foul-smelling green moss. But it was not these walking plant-animal hybrids that disturbed Amelia – not their rotting-plant smell, nor the dagger-sharp spines that they liberally applied at the first sign of disobedience among their prisoners; not even their disconcerting habit of suddenly stopping still and emitting chattering clicks at each other as if their minds were infected by crickets. It was the things they had with them that unsettled Amelia. Shambling sleekclaws that were allowed enough of their original minds to lope off as scouts, their beautiful coats veined green and putrid. Moss-covered gorillas that would stare with inhuman intelligence at the *Sprite's* crew, before lumbering off with their backs bent by baskets filled with ripped-out instrumentation from the u-boat. While the *Sprite of the Lake* was being towed by two long seed ships into the heart of the Daggish realm, the crew were kept split up, locked in random rooms in the submersible, giant plant-soldiers standing sentry outside.

Once during the trip, Amelia had been removed from the old supply room where she was confined alone and taken across to the nearest of the seed ships. They had shoved her in a room with a table-like globule extruded from the floor, covered with the logs, maps and crystal-book copies she had taken on the expedition. One of the room's walls had a strange sheen and she knew the Daggish were watching her from the other side, even though she could not see them. Theirs was an intelligence so different from the race of man's that she could not begin to imagine what they expected her to do. How had they guessed her position in the expedition? Did they presume that as one of the few females in their hands she must be some kind of matriarch? None of these creatures appeared either able or inclined to communicate with her in any tongue she understood. Perhaps they had taken one of the crewmen and absorbed him into their slime-drenched co-operative, stripping his thoughts as casually as she peeled the bananas Ironflanks used to bring back from the jungle? Terrifyingly, that was the most likely option. Amelia flipped open the notebooks and studied them for signs of damage. The copied crystal-books seemed intact, but without reader machinery they were only good for bookends.

After half an hour of fiddling with the material that had been left out, the hidden watchers seemed satisfied and two Daggish guards opened a bone-like iris into the room and silently carried her away, careless of how easily their spines cut her dirty uniform. Off the ugly living craft – as much a part of their cooperative as the twisted animal servants and intelligent plants – and back into the reassuringly man-made corridors of the *Sprite*, all plates, pipes and rivets after the pulsing, throbbing curves of the seed ship. As Amelia was being taken back to her makeshift cell, she crossed paths with a group of sailors being moved by a larger escort. When the crewmen saw Amelia they began to hurl abuse at her, ignoring the spined Daggish arms smashing them back, chains rattling as they were knocked down, screaming like banshees at her.

'Jonah!'

'Bitch!'

'Killed us all!'

Then she was shoved into the solitude of the storeroom. Isolation she was glad of, now she had been reminded she was not the only passenger on the ghost ship the *Sprite* had become. With the cries of hate still echoing in her mind, she remembered a conversation she had had with her father many years ago, when she had asked why so many of Jackals' neighbours seemed ready to invade, held back only by the ingenious floating navy of the RAN – their famous wall of cloth. In answer, he had not explained about the politics of envy, or that outside the checks and balances of Isambard Kirkhill's perfect democracy, the point of power was simply the accumulation of more power. He had not explained that the Jackelians' insular, contented nature was mistaken for decadence and weakness by kings, caliphs and warlords. He had not explained how ridiculous the rituals of the House of Guardians, the games of four-poles on the village green, or the shopkeepers pottering around their rose beds, trowels in hand, looked from the shores of rulers used to being able to stretch dissenters on racks. Rulers who would mangle the bodies of opposing voices in the scented torture gardens of the south, or shove them into the steam-driven killing rooms of the east. All these things he had expected her to have already learnt. His answer was far simpler. *'Amelia, they don't like us and we don't care.'*

She sat down and laid her back against the bulkhead, the tears streaming down her face. Was it the failure of the expedition; the memory of the father that had meant so much to her; the loathing of the crew for the Jonah that had brought certain death down on their heads; the loss of her friends, cast away to die in the jungle – probably dead now? Had chasing her dream wrought all this? Perhaps the superstitious sailors were correct. She was a Jonah. Her personal life had been cursed, her professional life ruined. She was akin to a leper in academia, a joke told at luncheons in the university refectories. Whatever happened to Professor Harsh? Why don't you know, dear fellow? Rumour has it she slipped into Liongeli on some mad expedition and died there, rambling through the jungle when her food and water ran out. Never heard from again.

Amelia buried her head in her hands. She should have listened to the advice of that insane witch in the dunes back in Cassarabia. *The true kindness would have been to let the sands of Cassarabia suck the marrow from your bones.* But wasn't it better to die trying to follow a dream, rather than experience the death of a million cuts she would have endured back in Middlesteel? Slowly suffocated by the cant and ritual of academia, the way things had always been. The received wisdom. She drifted into sleep and the worries, fears and regrets swirled around her, keeping her tossing on the hard metal floor.

Amelia was back in Jackals, in the grand old house along Mouse Place that had been sold off after her father's suicide. But the great financial crash hadn't happened yet. Had she imagined her family's fall? She was reading in the library when her father entered. She felt an enormous wave of gratitude to see him, such happiness. But he hadn't died yet, so why should she feel such joy?

'Amelia,' he said. 'What have you done to your arms? They look like they belong on a butcher, not a professor with letters after her name.'

'I needed to be strong, father.' Should she tell him about the dig in the foothills of Kikkosico, where she had nearly died at the hands of the bandits; when she vowed she would never let herself be captured like that again? No, it would just worry him. 'I can lift a horse with these. It wasn't womb magic that changed them, I went to a worldsinger here in Jackals, used the power of the earth.'

'It's a thin difference,' said her father, the disapproval evident in his voice. 'We should move along the Circle as we were born to it. We are not Catosians to fill ourselves with the herb of shine, or Cassarabians to curse our children's line with the mutations of womb magic.'

'It's something I had to do,' said Amelia.

'So it seems.'

'For the dream,' said Amelia. 'To find Camlantis.'

'I rather think this is the dream,' said her father, indicating the house at Mouse Place.

'Please be real,' begged Amelia.

'I cannot.'

'Are you a ghost now? You told me they exist.'

'Not all of us moves along the Circle,' said her father. 'Some of our pattern is left imprinted on the one sea of consciousness, the universal soul, before we are drawn back into the realm of the many and the fragmented.'

'Then you are a ghost. You're dead,' sobbed Amelia. If this was a dream, why were there colours? You couldn't have colours in a dream, everyone knew that. The shelves seemed brown, polished Jackelian oak, and the books . . .

'No,' said her father, 'not dead. You know better than that. I just swapped one pair of clothes for another.' He reached out to touch her hair. 'I live in here, in the bees on the flowers and the gnats over the meadow and in a thousand babies born since. When a cup of water is poured into the stream, then refilled, is the cup filled with the same water or with different water?'

'The water is movement,' said Amelia. 'The stream is flow. It is change.'

Her father smiled. 'I am glad to see the time you spent listening to our Circlist vicar in her pulpit was not entirely in vain.'

'You never liked the church,' said Amelia. 'You said you only went along because your constituents packed the building each Circleday.'

'I never particularly liked the people in the pews,' corrected her father. 'A habit I am sad to say I passed down to you, living more for your books than for those who might have shared your life with you. The church's beliefs I did not have a problem with. I was always rather fond of the fourth koan:

288

"When you hurt another creature you hurt yourself." It always seemed we never paid enough attention to that one.'

'I never dream of you. Some mornings I can wake up and I can't even remember what you looked like. Please stay with me,' Amelia implored.

'In a way I will and in a way I will not,' said her father. 'Even an echo must end. You are afraid to wake for fear of the trials that await you, but you should not be. You must free your mind and burn your beliefs.'

'But Camlantis,' said Amelia. 'I'm trapped, so damned useless here. Camlantis is so very close now and the dream . . .'

'. . . Is closer than you know,' said her father. 'All flesh is a prison and your desires are its bars. Dreams, desires, the burdens of the flesh, they all seem so distant to me now. Just remember that the dream you chase is not the dream you find.'

'What will I find, father? What will I find in the land where Camlantis once lay?'

'A hole filled with a lake. Life always gives you what you need, but never what you want. I think you might find the truth.'

'My truth or yours?' Amelia asked.

'Now that's my girl talking,' said her father. 'The one who knows that nothing can be achieved sitting around feeling sorry for yourself.' He walked out of the library, his shape becoming fainter with each step. 'Is there anything else I can do for you, before I go?'

'Do you ever see mamma?'

'You know, I find her every damned where I look,' said her father, his voice as much an echo now as the pattern of his soul. 'In the rustle of the trees and the song of decaying carbon, in the sway of a newborn colt and the froth on a jar of beer. But mostly I find her in you.'

He was gone.

'Well, that's reassuring, given that she bloody died in child-birth.'

Her next dream slipped into her mind, but she was not to remember it.

Amelia was starting to think the Daggish had forgotten about her. Left her in the u-boat's storage room to starve, although that might have been a blessing, given the food they had been bringing her once a day up until then. Long green bricks that resembled compressed, dried peas, but tasted more like zinc, full of crunchy pip-like things. Even washed down with cold water it tasted no better. No doubt designed to be perfectly balanced to meet the bodily functions of the Daggish army of organic slaves, it only underlined their alien nature.

She used a paste made from the food to count a line of days across her metal walls, each long smear another wasted day in captivity. The motion of the *Sprite* had ceased a couple of days ago – she had marked that day with a cross. If they were waiting in an attempt to wear down her nerves, it was working. Each hour all she could think about was the living death that was existence for those absorbed by the green-mesh. The pitiable freed slaves of the Daggish being sold off in the comfort auction back at the trading post. And they, supposedly, were the lucky ones, recaptured by their own people. What would it be like to have all individuality and personality subsumed to the dictates of the super-organism that dwelled in the heart of the jungle? Were the slaves aware of what they once were? Was there a small seed of humanity watching out through Daggish eyes after you were made part of the hive? A feverish dream you could never wake from.

Finally the Daggish came for Amelia, dragging the bloody body of Bull Kammerlan, his stolen captain's uniform – inexpertly re-tailored from a fit for the commodore's frame – now ripped and pierced by his captors' spines. Amelia had just enough time to take in the scene when the guards reached for her and pulled her out into the corridor.

Bull coughed and shook his head in sadness when he saw the identity of his fellow prisoner. 'You think I've taken a kicking, you should see the other guy.'

'Where's the rest of your crew, Kammerlan?'

The silent guards showed no sign of recognizing that their prisoners were communicating, let alone objecting to it.

'Beats me, girl. They had me locked up on my own. At one point they threw in one of the Catosians – a centurion, a real hellcat. That lasted an hour, until they grew tired of us both trying to kill each other. Then they took her away and I've been on my own ever since.'

More Daggish appeared, carrying weapons that resembled a Jackelian uplander's sack-pipes, except that the uplanders' musical instruments did not squirt fire that stuck like treacle to the flesh. The new guards marched in front of Bull and Amelia.

'Rank,' said Amelia. 'They've separated us by rank. You were the u-boat skipper when they took the *Sprite*. I'm the expedition head – the centurion was the senior officer of marines after Veryann. Ironflanks said the Daggish had different castes, like insects.'

'All I've seen are these cactus-skinned bruisers and a few animals dripping in that filthy green moss,' said Bull. He turned to the Daggish soldiers. 'Where're my people, you bark-faced bastards? What have you done with my crew?'

The guards showed no response to his words.

'They can't talk,' said Amelia. 'Only that clicking noise.'

'I've heard enough of that to last me a lifetime. Like crickets in the meadow, chattering at each other during the night. What a bloody waste. I could have been rich. Quest would have coughed up half the silver in his counting house for what we could have salvaged from the lake bed.'

Amelia didn't point out that Kammerlan's dreams of riches were as far away as her chances of discovering where Camlantis drifted in the heavens. With a clang, one of the forward hatches was flung open and Amelia found herself blinking in the bright sunlight. As her eyes adjusted, she saw they were moored on the shores of what looked like a sea. No, not a sea. She could just make out the green-covered mountains rising above the opposite shore. Lake Ataa Naa Nyongmo. Behind her squatted the Daggish nest city, flute-shaped towers given life and allowed to breed to the plans of a madman, sweeps and angles that no architect from Jackals was capable of mimicking, and everything overgrown – or perhaps intermingled – with lush emerald vegetation.

But it was not the bizarre city that caught Amelia's eye; it was the range of mountains behind the jungle and the ruins that lay between two of the peaks she was gawping at. 'Do you see that? No wonder . . .'

Bull followed her gaze but saw nothing of note. 'What is it?'

'Look, between the two peaks of the mountains. Those are the remains of a wall. Haven't you seen something similar to that before?'

'It's manmade?' Bull said in wonder. 'Nobody can build a wall that large.'

'That's what people say about the dyke wall at Hundred Locks back in Jackals. A freak of geology, smoothed by ancient storms to resemble an artefact of the race of the man. Look at its design, it's the same!'

'There's no water to hold back here,' said Bull.

'Not now, but thousands of years ago, before the skin of the earth had turned, there would have been water. The

Camlanteans were mariners, explorers. Their country wouldn't have been landlocked under this green hell.'

The Daggish escort pushed them across a boarding ramp and onto a pier that might have been formed from the hardened secretions of a giant snail.

'Well, this cursed place is under new management now,' said Bull.

'No wonder the lake formed here,' said Amelia. 'When the Camlanteans generated the floatquake to rip their city into the sky, the dyke would have been destroyed, the waters they had dammed here would have flooded over the ruins of Camlantis.'

'I thought you said these ancients of yours were pacifists,' said Bull. 'Doesn't sound too friendly to me, dimples, drowning the invaders of your land through your own suicide.'

'They had decided to deny the riches of their high science to the Black-oil Horde,' said Amelia. 'I would imagine the rest of what happened here was accidental damage. Dear Circle, I wish those dolts on the High Table could see this. Incontrovertible proof that their precious "natural phenomena" back at Hundred Locks is nothing of the sort. Not only artificial, but also built by the same civilization that they have staked their fusty reputations on denying all these years. There were Camlanteans in *Jackals*, there had to be.'

'I'd like to see that with those dolts of yours, too,' said Bull. 'Because it would mean I wouldn't be stumbling around some jungle city at the beck and call of a bunch of walking trees.'

'You've spent your last few years selling on any feral craynarbian you could snatch to the caliph's people,' said Amelia. 'I would say there's a certain amount of justice in what they're going to do to you. From slave trader to slave, in one easy step.'

'You think so?' Bull spat. 'Well, at least I'll know that you're going to be drooling blank-eyed about two steps behind me after they've stolen my body.'

Their guards picked up the pace and Amelia and Bull had to trot to keep up with the Daggish soldiers and avoid the stinging spines that would come their way if they showed any signs of slacking. They scurried past massive black shells shining like beetle-armour, twin barrels protruding from the house-sized pods. Bags at the back of the pods pulsed with green liquid, the same natural flammables that the guards carried in their sack-pipe weapons, Amelia noted that with interest. So, these were the batteries protecting the city nest that Abraham Quest had warned her about. The death of any airship that dared pass over the heart of Liongeli. Most creatures in the jungle would be terrified of normal fire, let alone the clinging, burning treacle these brutes could spit. Thunder lizards would not make the mistake of straying into Daggish territory more than once, Amelia suspected.

The streets of the Daggish nest were like no city in Jackals – not Middlesteel or Aribridge or Strathdrum. There was none of the random arbitrariness of trade or the bustle of those scampering about with the necessity of making a living. Everyone and everything that moved through this metropolis raised out of the jungle did so with single-minded purpose, whether they were working on the sides of the towers, polishing them with spittle-like resin, bearing loads on their backs in eerily coordinated columns, or waiting silently in front of water-filled troughs for the liquid they needed to stay hydrated in the harsh heat. Even ants marching in a line showed more individuality than the drones of the Daggish Empire.

Occasionally a series of hornpipes suspended from the bone-like buildings would emit a song in the clicking code that the Daggish drones appeared to use as a language and the inhabitants would stop instantly, taking on board whatever instructions the noise was imparting, standing and swaying quietly, before resuming their activity. This was the only sound; the rest was a terrible silence. None of the clamour of an honest city crowd: the hum of horseless carriages, the clatter of hansom cabs on cobbles, the hawkers' cries and the crack of the great mills. Amelia and Bull might as well have been walking through a cathedral at morning meditations; sleek-claws that should have filled the jungle with their roars padded past without a snarl, gorillas that should have called to each other with grunts quietly propelled loaded carts. All slaves. All moving as one.

Following the silence into the centre of the city, their quick-step escort ran them to a ramp cut into the ground of a building constructed of coils of polished bone-like resin. It was the largest building Amelia had seen in the city so far, a pipe organ that had gone into a mating frenzy and expanded out in a hundred directions. Iris doors admitted the two prisoners from the u-boat – taking them into a labyrinth of tubes. No furniture or ornamentation, just succession after succession of doors with Daggish guards standing sentry by them. At one point they were led into a tube with a blue liquid bubbling along its length. Was the heart of the building flooded? But the guards took a walkway along the side, making Amelia and Bull wade shoulder high through the liquid.

Bull shook his head in disgust. 'I've smelt better urinals on my boat.'

'I guess your rebels didn't keep flocks of sheep in the royalist fleet,' said Amelia. 'This is a dip. They're delousing us.' She slapped the surface of the thick liquid. Black dots were rising to the surface, dead mosquitoes and other insects that had settled in their shabby, sweat-drenched clothes.

Bull laughed. 'Well, don't that beat all. You might be right.

They're scrubbing us up before putting us on the auction block.'

'Who are they going to sell us to?' Amelia asked. 'They are all the same creature, and if Ironflanks is to be believed, their only interaction with anyone outside their empire is to eat, kill or absorb.'

Dripping blue gunk on the floor they were to meet their new owner soon enough. The last door irised open onto a domed chamber, revealing a cavernous interior, dim and cool and pierced in a hundred places by shafts of light from ceiling slits. Plants grew inside, crawling over each other, shaped and crafted across millennia to perform specific functions, organic machines tended by compliant creatures – tree monkeys and tiny thunder lizards with dextrous hands – all covered with the green slime that marked them as slaves of a single will. The architect of that will sat on a raised dais at the far end of the chamber, surrounded and obscured by an arc of sentinels. These were not the river-guard caste Amelia had seen on the u-boat and in the seed ship; they were hulking beasts, trees that had metamorphosed into fanged predators the size of elephants, with twisted, bark-hard skins. As Amelia got closer to the dais she caught a brief glimpse of the master intelligence of the Daggish through the gaps in its bodyguard, the cold intellect that dwelled in thousands of stolen bodies and circulated through the sap-like blood at the heart of the dark jungle. The emperor of the Daggish.

As high as an oak tree, the ruler of this living empire should have looked taller, but age after age of renewed bark had left the torso of the intelligence as wide as the watchtower on a fortress. How many rings would she count, Amelia wondered, if she took an axe to this monster? A small army of attendants crawled over it, little marsupials with their fur matted by the control algae that patterned their skin, wiping the crevices of their master's bark, trimming the parasitical growths that gnawed at it after an age on the earth. The emperor sent a silent command and two of its troll-sized guardians moved aside so it could gaze at Amelia and the mutinous skipper of the *Sprite*. On one of the ridges that circled its bulbous head there was something fixed to the bark, almost a crown. Something that looked familiar. Amelia ignored the penetrating stare of the Daggish ruler and gazed above its eyes at the coronet. Where had she seen that before? Then it came to her. The crystal-book in Middlesteel, Abraham Quest's startling discovery. It was similar to the headdress that Pairdan, Reader-Administrator of Camlantis had been wearing in his recording. A relic from the fall of the city. But why should such trinkets matter to this hideous entity?

As the ancient intelligence turned to look at the wall of green machinery that lay behind the dais, a warthog-sized creature trotted forward, its lips and mouth distorted so that they were unnaturally large and shaped like the orifice of one of the race of man. Even before it opened its ulcerous mouth Amelia knew its purpose. A translator. Something that still possessed enough of a spark of the race of man's template that it could communicate with a human-sounding throat. The fact that whatever spark of humanity rested in their old crewmates had been so extinguished by the Daggish absorption process that they could no longer serve for such a task was far more terrifying than this shambling substitute's presence.

'You have defiled the methods of nature,' warbled the pig-like beast. There was no doubt now whose voice it was articulating.

Amelia looked at Bull. Were they expected to answer? 'Methods of nature?'

'You have entered the territory of the purity.'

'You are the purity?' Amelia asked.

Daggish drones behind Bull and Amelia pushed them rudely to the floor; as if they were outraged such a question could be asked.

'Your breed only dares to violate the territory of the purity if it perceives great gain to be within reach.' Fronds of leaves spiralling around the emperor's arms went stiff at the thought of such an outrage. Drones came forward, bearing an open chest filled with Amelia's expedition notes, maps and crystal-book translations pillaged from the u-boat. 'You are thieves, invaders who have discovered the location of the source.'

The dome was filled with the chattering of the Daggish, a sudden eruption of hammering clicks giving voice to their emperor's offence at their brazen attempt to steal into its fast-ness and remove objects from the lake bed.

'You know of Camlantis?' asked Amelia. 'You know of the ancients who lived here?'

'They were the source,' translated the pig creature. 'The purity is descended from the source. The purity is ancient, older than the chaos of that which has not been joined with the purity and made clean and given order.'

'I've seen her notes, too,' said Bull, 'and if you're a Camlantean, then I'm the God-emperor of Kikkosico.'

One of the Daggish shot a spine into Bull's leg and the slaver yelled, squirming about on the floor before yanking the spine out of his flesh.

'If you had read all of my notes,' hissed Amelia at Bull as she helped him to his feet, 'then you would know that one of the reasons we have so little from the Camlantean age is that their tools were living things, a more advanced form of the same twisting of nature the caliph practises in Cassarabia.' She tipped her head at the Daggish. 'What do you think happened to all their engineering when the Camlantean gardeners that carefully tended it blasted their civilization into the heavens?'

Bull gazed at their massive jailors, the strange lines of the organic machinery. 'I saw an abandoned village on the banks of the Shedarkshe once, plague, everyone dead and the craynarbians' hunting hounds gone feral.'

She looked across the dais. 'Imagine that village many thousands of years later.'

'Damn, but the tree monkeys are running the jinn house,' said Bull. He scratched at his unkempt hair and chased out a couple of flies that had survived the chemical dip. The Daggish emperor twitched in agony at the sight of the flies and one of the guards came running forward. Amelia thought that the creature was going to burn them to the ground, but his sackpipe weapon discharged a jet of the delousing substance towards their heads, its foul-smelling stream madly stinging her eyes.

As she rubbed away the burning liquid, the translator creature shuddered violently in front of them. 'Not pure – not pure. Filthy unclean thieves with their filthy crawling parasites.'

'You're the jigging impurity, here, Tree-head Joe!' Bull yelled, giving the Daggish ruler the inverted 'V' of the Lion of Jackals with two of his fingers. 'You're nothing but a rotting hulk of talking wood decomposing in the heart of this rotting jungle.'

The misshapen translator creature announced his meaning to the chamber and behind Bull the troll-sized throne guards went into apoplexy at his abuse towards their ruler, smashing him to the ground and raising cudgels not much shorter than the slaver himself to finish the job of beating him to death. They only held off when Amelia leapt between them and the man they were about to murder.

'You need him alive. You need *us* alive for something. All that trouble you went to separating us out on the u-boat, feeding us . . .'

The throne guards hesitated as the pig-like creature translated her words into the drumming language of the Daggish, reluctantly moving back as the fronds of the emperor wavered across in silent command. 'Your place is to obey, not to criticize,' piped the translator. 'If you forget your position again the stain that is your existence will be scoured from the purity.'

Bull was stunned by the quickness of the assault and Amelia had to pull him back to his feet. He glowered resentfully in the direction of the Daggish emperor. 'Touchy beggar, isn't he?'

'Hold your tongue,' hissed Amelia, 'or you're going to get us both killed here.'

Bull spat a gob of blood from his swollen mouth onto the floor in defiance of their captors. 'You saved my life, Guardian's girl.'

'That was just a temporary lapse of judgement, I assure you.'

Spined arms forced Amelia and Bull towards the side of the dome and a section of the smooth wall fell away, revealing a low chamber, sailors and marines from the *Sprite* lying in a field of wavering fronds, hair-thin green roots undulating snake-like into the ears, mouths and nostrils of the comatose crew. Amelia had to choke back her own vomit at the sight of Veryann's fighters and Bull's sailors crawling with the living filth of the greenmesh, over a hundred of them resting zombie-like under the wan emerald light while their bodies were erased of every last vestige of their humanity.

'You should be cleansed,' barked the translation creature, its monstrously oversized human lips dribbling with saliva. 'You should be made uncontaminated within the purity. But there is the need, the need . . .'

The ring of Daggish guards and drones shoved them back in front of the dais.

'If you're going to fill my mind with your moss, you decaying cabbage, get on with it,' Bull demanded. 'Because you're bloody boring me, and I hate being bored.'

'You fear the purity,' trilled the pig-like beast on behalf of its owner. 'You value your insignificant life span, barely longer than those of the parasites you harbour.'

'Do not all things?' asked Amelia.

'Then you shall do as you are bid, as you value your exclusion from the purity,' instructed the translator. 'You were correct in your appraisal of the purity's *temporary* need for your services. You shall take your construct for navigating the lake of deep waters and undertake a sacred duty for the purity. In the event of your success, the purity shall consider your exclusion from the perfection of form you fear.'

'The bathysphere?' said Amelia. 'You are talking about taking our bathysphere down to the bed of Lake Ataa Naa Nyongmo?'

'Jigger your archaeology. The thing I care about is the bit about our exclusion from the "perfection" of this bark-faced monarch of the jungle.' Bull waved a fist at their captors. 'What about my bloody crew?'

'Your thieves are already complete within the purity,' warbled the translator.

'Twenty years we survived,' sobbed Bull. 'Twenty years after the destruction of Porto Principe – we survived Liongeli, survived being hunted by the RAN and Jackals' men-o'-war, survived trading with those treacherous double-crossing jiggers down in Cassarabia. What did we survive for? This!'

'They survive still,' said the translator, 'within the purity. They survive evolved and clean and whole.' The hog-like creature waddled up to Amelia. 'Observe the crown.'

On the dais one of the Daggish emperor's ape servants pulled off its crown from the ridge of bark and held it aloft.

'It is from the Camlantean age,' said Amelia. 'Ancient.'

'There is another like it, underneath the deep waters outside our nest,' said the translator. 'Recover it, return it to the purity.'

Amelia frowned. But that made no sense. Why would this entity not fill hers and Bull's skulls with the green filth that the rest of the crew had been exposed to? Why would this callous intelligence not wish to control their explorations of the lake bed, make them puppets of meat within its hive mind? If it knew what it was looking for, what use had it for the free intellect of a Jackelian academic and the treacherous impulses of Bull Kammerlan?

'I have questions,' said Amelia.

'Your compliance shall serve the purity better than your inferior intellect,' warned the translator. A wave of clicks swept the dome, the Daggish drones signalling their agreement, or perhaps their impatience with the two outsiders.

'You shall be provided with the coordinates of the probable location of the crown. Retrieve it, salvage it for the purity as you value the brutish, brief flicker of your life span.'

Amelia exchanged glances with her companion in this predicament, the man she would least trust to watch her back now that Abraham Quest had been supplanted as the patron of their expedition and traded for an inhuman emperor with chlorophyll for emotions. Whatever the reasoning for sending them into the lake rather than risking its drones, Amelia was fairly certain the welfare of two prisoners factored fairly small into the equation, if at all. And despite the emperor's hollow-sounding promises, Amelia was also fairly certain that their fate, once they had dredged the lake bed and located the missing crown, was not going to involve a fond farewell from the Daggish nest as she and Bull sailed off down the Shedarkshe back to Jackals.

CHAPTER TWELVE

Fumes from the liquid below – a dark oil that steamed and bubbled up from the well – kept the commodore coughing and cursing his fate as the others clutched onto the bars of their cage, trying not to make the box swing on the end of its precarious cable. It would not do to hit any of the other cages lowered into the pit on tethers. Not that the other occupants would mind. Whether as a warning, or simply out of pure neglect, their nearest neighbours hanging over the oily well were the carapaces of three craynarbian warriors, flesh long since rotted away through starvation. The smallest of the craynarbians had the sword arm of one of its fellows piercing its thorax, testament to how they had turned to cannibalism in their last desperate days.

'I shall never complain about the wicked fogs of a Middlesteel peculiar again,' said the commodore, 'not if I have to walk through the mills of Workbarrows on a hot summer's day without a linen mask, then swear in front of a magistrate that the air there is as sweet as the scent of the lilies along the hills of the western downs.'

'I think the chance of you ever standing in front of a magistrate in Middlesteel are looking distinctly slim right now,' said Gabriel McCabe, staring at the corpses in the other cages.

'We know very little of our captors' motives,' Billy Snow pointed out. 'Although I think we can presume they are not benevolently disposed towards us.'

'Damn feral steammen,' said T'ricola. 'I wish Ironflanks hadn't been taken away. He might have had a few answers for us.'

'They are not steammen,' said Billy Snow. 'I can hear the difference in how they move. Steammen have an honest clunk about their walk; those things that captured us move like panthers in armour, they're light on their feet, almost organic.'

'It's answer enough for me that they dragged Ironflanks away whistling in terror,' said the commodore. 'The old steamer recognized those monsters. He's had prior dealings with them for sure.'

'Our captors are the beasts that slaughtered the survivors of the airship crash we found,' said Veryann. 'Ironflanks intimated in the jungle that the masters of this territory are the architects of the gas wall the *Sprite* encountered. You do not have to smell the rot from the other cages to know that this metal tribe are a hostile and formidable force.'

The commodore clutched a handkerchief to his nose. 'Ah, Coppertracks, my fine old friend, I should have listened to you back in Jackals. He said there were dark things in Liongeli that he would not speak of and fool that I am I ignored his mortal advice – left the comforts of Tock House and plunged into this green hell blinded by the inducements of the great Abraham Quest.'

'He offered you what you wanted,' said Veryann. 'He offered all of you what you wanted. For you, Jared Black, a chance to get the *Sprite* back, for your officers a chance to serve on a seadrinker vessel again when no other master would take them onto their pay list.'

'And what did he offer you?' T'ricola asked Veryann.

'My honour and my life,' said Veryann. 'For the soldiers of a free company the two are indivisible.'

'There we are then,' said the commodore. 'We've all got what we wanted, fine and sure now. For Ironflanks his chest of silver Jackelian guineas he will never spend, for me a beautiful boat that has been stolen away by my scheming nephew, and for you, your warrior's death at the hands of some feral steamers.'

'I do not welcome death,' said Veryann. 'But I do not fear it.'

The commodore took off his jacket, his shirt covered in sweat from the heat of the pit below. 'Noble words, lass, but it'll break old Blacky's heart to see your golden head dangling like a shrunken apple on the necklace of the terrible beasts that have taken us.'

There was a jolt on the cage and it began to be lifted out of the steam of the bubbling black oil, raised high on its joist. As they cleared the wall of petrol mist they saw the village of their captors stretched out below, geodesic domes in the same style as the encampments the steammen knights set up when on campaign, covered by creepers and jungle bush. It had been raining an hour before, a deluge that had left puddles in the mud, each pool broiling now with the return of the febrile heat. When the arm holding them swung across to the ground, they had a brief glimpse of a second pit next to theirs, deeper, but not filled with oil. The head of Queen Three-eyes turned towards their cage, a brief look of recognition in her eyes as she caught the scent of her fellow prisoners, followed by disappointment that her mortal enemy Ironflanks did not count among their number. She may have been free of the bubble-like substance that had trapped her, but the queen of Liongeli was as much a prisoner as the officers from the *Sprite*.

On the ground a small party of natives waited for them, their metal bodies filed down, sharp razors visible on any hull-part not covered by animal furs and shell armour scalped from craynarbian tribesmen. All but one of their reception committee were hulking things, steel gorillas that hissed steam from outlets along their armour while they waited. The odd tribesman out was a quarter of his companions' size. He wore a cheetah cape and a segmented metal tail swung behind him as he capered to and fro, poking at the air with a rusty iron staff topped with an eagle sculpture. Dirty water leaked across the cage floor as the box thumped down, one of the tribe inserting his hand in the door lock – interfacing with the cage and springing their door open. The commodore looked on with interest. He knew a thing or two about locks, and the primitive appearance of their captors belied the sophistication of the cage the expedition members had been held in. These tribesmen might look like feral skull hunters, but there were few properties back in Middlesteel that had such well-protected doors.

'What have you done with our scout?' Veryann demanded as she stepped out. 'Why have you separated Ironflanks from our company?'

The small steamman danced in amusement. 'Ironflanks is an old friend and now he is an uneasy rider.'

'Uneasy rider? Are you talking about the Steamo Loas, is Ironflanks being ridden by one of your blessed spirits?' said the commodore, shuddering. The steamman gods had always made him nervous. Ever since one of the Loas had ridden Coppertracks and his warrior mu-bodies on the Isla Needless, driving off an attack of the rock-like creatures that bided there. The steammen gods were fickle things and numerous – you could never tell which of them might come calling when invited in during the Gear-gi-ju rituals.

The commodore's question seemed to tickle the little metal creature, steam shrieking out of his stacks. 'Once a Loa, once a Loa, you fat hairless monkey.'

There were no more half-answers forthcoming and the expedition officers were led into a passage deep into the jungle covered by steel netting over arched girders – the rib bones of a mechanical whale holding out the press of the forest. Billy Snow had been right, there was something animal-like about these things. They had a strutting gait quite unlike that of the calm, meticulous steammen found back in Middlesteel. Their path through the jungle led them to a rocky hillock, a crumbling temple carved into the rock face. Whoever the original architect of the construction might have been, their artifice had been chiselled over and carved out with new statues and bas-reliefs – crudely done, but obviously remade into the form of steammen.

'I thought your people lacked an eye for art,' muttered the commodore.

'Not to be confusing us with the people of the metal in your monkey land,' said the guide. 'We follow the true path of Lord Two-Tar.'

'And I'm sure a fine path it is too,' said the commodore. 'But how about you let us leave now, rather than be bothering about a miserable small band of travellers just making their honest way through Liongeli?'

'But you are our guests,' giggled the little creature. 'We have a duty to entertain you. Or is it the other way around? It is so easy to be confused.'

Inside, the temple corridors were lit – barely – by jagged green crystals wired to chemical batteries in braziers, the steam and fizz of wild energy lost as the sound of drums grew louder. The officers were jabbed forward into a wide shadowed chamber under the centre of the hill, straight into the middle of a frenzied celebration – creatures of the metal ducking and turning in front of a pit filled with red molten coals. Many of the wild steammen had worked themselves into a manic frenzy and were detaching limbs – arms, legs, vision plates, voiceboxes – and fixing them on a spiked totem pole, then grabbing other pieces of assembly and pressing their new components into the burning coals before thrusting them into their empty sockets and continuing their dance. As a result of this insane limb-trading some of the tribesmen were loping on arm pincers or swinging legs from their shoulder sockets.

The expedition members found themselves in front of a pool containing the same black oil that had filled the prison pit. A steamman luxuriated on his back – almost corpulent in his design, a massive belly slick with oil, round lines broken by a brush of golden metal curls running down the side of his frog-like mask of a face.

Raising a goblet spilling with oil, the bathing steamman seemed to toast them. 'So, these are the hairless monkeys that were on Queen Three-eyes' supper menu? Mark me, they hardly look fit to be an appetizer for the thunder lizard.'

'And don't think we are not grateful to you for rescuing us,' said the commodore. 'You can have the thanks of old Blacky before we continue on our way in peace.'

'Silence!' The guards struck their prisoners with their needle-lined fists. 'You do not address Prince Doublemetal without his permission.'

'Well. Perhaps this fat ape might give Queen Three-eyes a few mouthfuls before he is made deactivate,' mused the corpulent steamman. 'Though in truth, I grow weary of what sport there is in seeing thunder lizards rip apart softbodies. It is all over so quickly. What do you think of that, fat little monkey, do you think that you might run fast enough to last more than a few seconds in the pit?'

'I'm a great one for running,' said the commodore. 'I've something of a royal title myself and it's made me a mite unpopular back in Jackals, although I have found the steammen back home to be a little more forgiving in that regard than the race of man.'

The chief of the wild things sat up and oil dripped off the gold curls moulded onto his chest assembly. 'Oh ho, do not dare compare the siltempters with the people of the metal, my noble-titled monkey friend. We have advanced far beyond their meagre ambitions. We call Loas that they shun, receive wisdom that their slaves' boiler hearts are too small to contain. We change our own bodies, swap parts as it pleases us – why, I even allow the most courageous of my siltempters to function with cogs and crystals that have once been part of my own august being!'

'Very wise,' agreed the commodore.

Prince Doublemetal raised an arm out of the bath and pointed it accusingly at the expedition members. 'What do you want with the sixth?'

'The sixth?' said Commodore Black 'There's only five of us.'

'Do not play games with me, you portly softbody scum!' roared the prince. 'I know why you have defiled our realm. Has King Steam sunk so low that he now sends such as you to continue the war between our two people, to steal our relics? Does the Free State have no more steammen knights brave enough to travel to our land?'

The commodore looked at Veryann, T'ricola and Gabriel McCabe, but it was clear they had no idea what this mad frog-faced machine was talking about. Billy Snow held to his silence, grimly.

'You'll have to forgive me, your highness,' said Commodore Black. 'The steammen back home don't really talk about your fine kingdom out here in Liongeli – save a passing mention with a little trepidation.'

'And well they should fear us. They have memories long enough to remember the schism between the siltempters and the steammen, even if it has faded from the frail minds of meat and water possessed by your kind.' Prince Doublemetal gestured to his warriors. 'Let these filthy softbody liars see the sixth they have come stealing into our realm to seize. Let them tremble at its splendour.'

At his urging a section of the floor rumbled back, a platform rising slowly into the chamber. Mounted like a jewel in a coronet on the platform was a cube of the same material that had been sprayed around Queen Three-eyes, imprisoning the thunder lizard. But this confinement glue held no organic creature – instead, a battered white globe was set immobile inside – a machine – the material of its spherical skin quite unlike anything of this world, save where its surface had been blackened and scarred, and there it resembled a copper-coloured lava.

'Behold, the sixth,' said Prince Doublemetal. 'Tell me now you have no idea what this holy of holies is. Let me hear the lie tumble from your lips. Let me hear that you were not paid by King Steam to rob the siltempters of this glory of ours.'

'I have never seen such as this before,' said Veryann. 'Although it is obviously damaged, a war machine – perhaps part of a steamman fighting frame?'

'Sweet Circle preserve me, but I have seen one of these terrible things before,' whispered the commodore. 'And heard a little more of it from my Molly back at Tock House.

Something like this appeared during the battle of Rivermarsh and helped break the army of demons conjured up by that madman Tzlayloc. Seven of them, there were. Seven Hexmachina to preserve the world. But I thought they were all dead, all save Molly's one curled up sleeping snug in the veins of the world deep below Middlesteel.'

His news seemed to alarm the siltempters, the little cheetah-cloaked one scampering back, squealing as it clutched its sound baffles.

'Calm yourselves,' called the prince. 'Of course this hairless monkey knows of the Hexmachina. Even a softbody can press his ears to the dirt and feel the throb of power of the holy of holies within the earth. There are two Hexmachina left – and we have one of them!'

The commodore looked doubtfully at the broken thing they had captured – or preserved – inside the amber-like cube. If this was their talisman, it showed none of the raw power of the thing he had seen intervene in the invasion of Jackals when the god machine had tossed Quatérshift's demon allies back through the pit of hell they had crawled out of.

'We have not come for your treasures,' said Billy Snow. 'We are bound for Lake Ataa Naa Nyongmo and the ruins of Camlantis.'

'Pah,' said Prince Doublemetal. 'The realm of that brooding cabbage who rules over the creepers contains nothing but ancient dust and rubble. Do you really expect me to believe you are not in service to King Steam and his minions?'

'Your ancient enemy has nothing to do with our voyage,' insisted Billy. 'Have you not discovered as much from Ironflanks?'

'Ironflanks,' said Prince Doublemetal. 'Dear Ironflanks. He is almost family to me. Let us see what he has to say.' He clicked his iron fingers and a heavy frame was lowered from one of the temple levels above, Ironflanks hanging limply from the mesh, his shredded safari suit clinging to his body like peeling flesh. 'Not that I would be inclined to believe too much of what he says. Poor exiled product of the Free State. Desperately trying to amass enough money to pay a mechomancer from the race of softbodies to extract the superior components we so kindly donated to his inferior architecture the last time he was our guest.'

Ironflanks' telescope eyes extended weakly out – oil dripping like drool from his head. Too weak to speak in a higher language after hours of torture, his voicebox emitted a pitiful squawk of static in machine language.

'You see,' said Prince Doublemetal, refilling his goblet with oil from his pool. 'You see how ungrateful he is. We brought him into the fold, gave him components from our holy bodies and how does he repay us? He escapes from his cage and goes running back to the mongrel traders of Rapalaw Junction. Could they help you, weak little fool? Would King Steam lift a finger to correct the "corruption" of your architecture? It pains me, Ironflanks. My own components sparking inside you, my own design imposed on your pattern and how do you repay your new father? You reject me for that weak monarch of compromise, that ruler of the maybe and the middle way you foolishly call sovereign in the Free State. Tell me that you were not coming here in search of the Hexmachina again, tell me you do not recognize the armour of the steammen knights you once dared to lead here now adorning the bodies of my warriors.'

Instead of answering with his voice, Ironflanks extended two fingers out from one of his manipulator arms and made the shape of the inverted 'V' – the lion's teeth, the traditional Jackelian gesture of defiance.

'There, do I lie?' Prince Doublemetal sighed with regret;

sad his words had been borne out. 'An ingrate. But there are better ways of getting to the truth. Where is my tosser of the cogs?'

'Here, your highness.' An emaciated siltempter emerged from the shadows of the chamber, a dark cloak covering his tall, mantis-like body. As he loomed closer, the commodore saw the cloak was a patchwork map of different skins – pard, sleekclaw, craynarbian – oiled and shiny. A tripod of legs clacked him across to the bath of oil. Prince Doublemetal topped up his goblet and passed it to the shaman. As he did so the siltempters behind the expedition officers seized the arms of the softbodies, vice-like fingers clamping their iron tightly around muscles, giving the commodore and his friends not an inch to squirm.

'Which of these do you require to perform the ritual?'

'I have no preference, your highness,' said the shaman.

'Take the craynarbian woman, then. I never tire of hearing the crack of their shells.'

Gabriel McCabe struggled in the grip of the metal apes binding his arms, trying to stop them dragging the engineer away. 'Let T'ricola go – if you have a challenge, let me face it.'

'A challenge?' laughed the shaman. 'Do you know nothing of Gear-gi-ju? We do not require your sport to invoke the Steamo Loas!'

'I have seen the rituals of Gear-gi-ju,' said the commodore. 'Coppertracks draining his own oil and throwing his cogs to read the future in their patterns.'

The shaman lifted the goblet of black liquid his prince had passed him. 'Here is our oil – holy sap of our bodies – it has been filtered through each of us here. But Lord Two-Tar does not come riding for such as this, though it still be required for the calling.'

Prince Doublemetal waved a languid pincer hand in the direction of Gabriel McCabe. 'Take the big one at his word, then. Keep the craynarbian woman for the thunder lizards – she will be mauled as well under their jaws as she will in the calling. You'll get more system juice out of the giant, besides.'

'Gabriel!' T'ricola cried as the metal savages dragged the first mate away from his friends. Gabriel struggled with all his strength, but the beetle-shelled machines held him tight and dragged him towards an altar, pushing his spine down to the stone. The strongest man in Jackals was no match for the strongest siltempter in Liongeli. Leather straps were lashed down across his arms, chest and legs. When they were finished the nearest siltempters started lurching around the altar, forming a drunken circle, their voices chanting in the machine language. Whether activated by their dark hymn or by an unseen switch, a stone block in the ceiling began to crunch down, lowering inexorably towards the first mate.

Prince Doublemetal's amused laughter drowned out the shouts of anger from the struggling officers. Now the purpose of the blood-encrusted rivulets in the altar had become clear, the channel at the foot of the stone leading to a stained granite basin where goblets could be filled with the oil – or blood – of their sacrifices.

Gabriel McCabe was staring in terror at the crushing press only a foot above him, the gap closing every second, when Billy Snow broke free of the grip of his captor, the ape-like machine turning in the air as if it had become the cog in an invisible machine. The blind sonar man moved his feet as if he was following the footsteps of a dance that had been sketched onto the chamber floor, gracefully avoiding the frenzied wave of sharp-edged siltempters reaching and thrusting for him with their spears. His cane had split open, expelling a shining swordstick that licked out, severing steel limbs and opening iron chests with deft flicks. Where Billy Snow danced the warriors fell back, clutching their metal bodies, crystals sparking fire and tubes pumping dirty oil onto the floor.

He was almost at the altar, his blade raised to plunge into the stone control panel, when a steamman with a large pepper-pot gun connected by tubes to his boiler came out of the crowd, a hail of darts pin-pricking the sonar man's legs. Billy Snow collapsed, paralysed by the wicked poison on the dart-tips. The last look on Gabriel McCabe's face before the press bore down on him was one of incredulity at the blind sonar man collapsing by his side – as if he had glimpsed the meta-morphosis of his friend into a deadly butterfly. Then the rock ground down and there was a brief, horrific scream, followed by a sickening wet crunching sound, the first mate's blood draining out in a dark river down the channels of the altar.

'Sorry, Gabriel,' whispered the commodore. T'ricola was sobbing with anger even as the shaman began filling cups with their shipmate's blood, chanting and mixing the remains of the first mate with the oil from the tribe's own bodies.

'Excellent,' applauded Prince Doublemetal from the pool. Two of his people dragged Billy Snow's paralysed form back to where the surviving officers stood. Prince Doublemetal extended his hand out for Billy's sword. 'You poor miserable hairless monkeys have no idea how hard it is to surprise me, to relieve the monotony of my exulted, long-lived existence.' He rotated the sword in his hand. 'Living metal, a witch-blade. Of course it can cut through our armour. Not one of those poorly smithed blades from the east either, this is ancient. Who was responsible for searching the prisoners?'

A siltempter crept forward, his vision plate averted from the sword the prince was gesturing with. 'The sightless one needed his cane to move around without being led by our warriors. To remove it would have inconvenienced the guards.'

'Yes, I see that,' said the prince.

Three of the hulking siltempters dragged their colleague to the side of the prince's oil pool, forcing him to kneel by the edge. Prince Doublemetal lashed out, severing the steamman's head from his shoulder hull, before pushing the blade into the unfortunate lackey's chest, a jet of superheated steam cleansing the blade of the oil smeared onto its silvery surface as he found the boiler heart. 'Well, there we are. Sorry to "inconvenience" you.'

He indicated that his guards should drag the corpse over to where the shaman was finishing draining Gabriel McCabe's body. 'Waste not, want not.'

Laying the goblets out at the points of a floor-chalked dodecahedron, the shaman spilt an offering of the mix of oil and blood at each corner of the shape. A hush fell on the chamber as the emaciated shaman entered the centre of the diagram and began a slow gyratory dance, calling the Steamo Loa from the hall of spirits to ride his body. Mist seeped upward from the goblets, liquid spilling out as they frothed with an unholy energy. Coalescing into the shape of something horned and angular, the mist seeped around the rivets of the shaman, cloaking him with a transparent nimbus. Behind the commodore, the crowd let out gasps of awe from their voiceboxes as the shaman started to convulse, his dance moving into a fit of juddering metal limbs. He straightened up, filled with a power that made the folds of his hull creak and pop as he capered around the inside of the diagram, his fingers shaking, and pointing at the warriors in the ancient temple.

The shaman's words made no sense to Jared Black, they were raw machine code, but a code mixed with something else – the crackling of furnaces, the pop and splinter of the ovens where steammen components were melted down. This was their hell. This was their death communicating with them.

Steam leaked from the shaman's voicebox as he accused and insulted in the ancient tongue. Then the shaman pointed up at the grille where the tortured body of Ironflanks hung limply and began clanging his tripod legs on the floor as if the spirit that had possessed him was trying to drum out a message. Around the perimeter of the dodecahedron the goblets were melting, the heat of the steaming blood and oil too much for the copper vessels.

'You said you share your residence in Middlesteel with a steamman,' Veryann whispered to the commodore. 'Is this their usual form of their worship?'

The commodore dragged his gaze away from the crushed remains of Gabriel McCabe. There was the rest of the crew to think of, those with lives still left to lose. 'That it is definitely not, lass. The people of the metal record the future by reading the cogs they toss in their own oil and the Steamo Loas come calling to ride them of their own accord. This Lord Two-Tar must be a standoffish spirit – I believe he is shunned by the people of the metal back home, for I have never heard my friend Coppertracks speak of him, nor come across any wicked temple to him in Steamside.'

At last, the possession of the shaman was at an end and the sorcerer was left trembling inside the pattern, his wasted form shrouded by the fizzing remains of his offering to Lord Two-Tar.

'What knowledge have you gained while you were ridden?' demanded Prince Doublemetal. 'The mighty lord was not pleased with us, he cursed us all and called down terrible blessings in his song to us.'

'These monkeys are telling the truth,' said the shaman, recovering his composure enough to talk again. 'Ironflanks was guiding them to the realm where the writ of the Daggish runs.'

'That turnip,' hissed the prince, 'that ruler of the walking trees. What has he that is worthy of the journey to steal? The siltempters have the holy body of one of the Hexmachina – what does the empire of the Daggish have to offer?'

'Life,' said the shaman, 'and death!'

'They shall find the latter here, without troubling to travel across our border with the Daggish.'

'Lord Two-Tar counsels us to put these softbodies to death at once. Their deaths may lead us to great power very shortly.'

'Wonderful news,' said Prince Doublemetal. 'The softbodies' part in the great pattern shall end in the gut of Queen Three-eyes. I have a new thunder lizard to feed.'

'Their immediate death is required,' said the shaman. 'It would not be wise to keep them for the arena.'

'Wise!' Prince Doublemetal furiously tossed a goblet at the shaman. 'If the Loa disagrees with my wisdom let it ride me now, let it impart its vision in this matter to me! No? Then I shall decide for us. I decide that a spear plunged into these dogs' softbody bellies is too quick and affords me no amusement. They shall die between the jaws of the thunder lizards. These water-filled organics have invaded our realm, led by this ingrate Ironflanks – a traitor who has spurned my gifts to his architecture – a traitor who keeps on coming to our land leading our enemies fast behind him. First with King Steam's knights, now with the Free State's Jackelian allies. We shall give them to the thunder lizards for breakfast tomorrow and watch such sport as they might provide, scampering about in the pit before they are consumed. I understand Ironflanks and Queen Three-eyes are old friends. Let them be re-acquainted tomorrow.'

Ironflanks' semiconscious body was lowered from the ceiling and had to be dragged across the chamber floor with the paralysed form of Billy Snow by his side.

'You're no prince worthy of the name,' shouted the commodore. 'You're just the king of the loons out here.'

'While you, my fine, fat friend, are kilasaurus fodder,' giggled Prince Doublemetal. 'We'll see how full of puff and monkey bravado you are when you swagger out onto the sand to face my new pet.'

'For the death of our comrade,' said Veryann quietly, with a coldness that left no doubt it was not an idle boast, 'with no sword in his hand, with no honour when he had offered you combat, I shall watch your death throes, you dirty steamer.'

'Yes, yes. Of course you will.' The prince waved the prisoners away, his languid gaze returning to the carnival frenzy of the dancing warriors, swapping components in their unholy revelry. 'Be seeing you all for breakfast.'

Prodded by the spears, the surviving members of the expedition were taken back to their cage, leaving behind the stench of Gabriel McCabe's smouldering blood and the siltempters' insane celebrations.

CHAPTER THIRTEEN

Water bubbled over the oval hull of the bathysphere, the view of the small armada of seed ships on the surface rising behind Amelia and Bull as Lake Ataa Naa Nyongmo covered over their vessel.

Amelia rested a hand on the thick armoured walls of the craft, built to withstand depths that would have crushed the *Sprite*. 'Have we got the range to make a run for it?'

'Not in this bucket, girl,' said Bull. 'We're good for a poke on the lake bed, up and down. But this is intended for slow delicate work with a base vessel near by. A canoe and a couple of strong oarsmen could chase us down if we tried to scarper, let alone seed ships loaded with depth charges. Our best bet is to find Tree-head Joe's crown and hope it makes good on its word to let us go.'

'You've got to be kidding me,' said Amelia. 'That monster's going to toss us into its conversion chamber with the rest of our crew as soon as we've got what it wants. We'll be drooling moss from our lips an hour after we've handed over the crown.'

'The Daggish haven't done for us yet.'

'No, they haven't.' And that bothered Amelia almost as

320

much as the thought of actually being absorbed into the Daggish hive. Why did the Daggish controller require their humanity for its errand? If she and Bull died and they were part of the hive, did the Daggish Emperor feel their pain? Was this mission so dangerous that it could not stand to suffer its drones' failure and death? The murderous entity was made of tougher stuff than that, she suspected.

Amelia grabbed a handhold on the wall as the bathysphere lurched. Bull made a small corrective motion on the stick.

'I thought you could pilot this thing.'

'I can pilot just fine, first or second stick back on the *Sprite*,' said Bull, 'but it was your Catosian friend who was trained by Quest to pilot this tub. Look at our controls: your rich shopkeeper designed this – nothing is where it should be.'

'Veryann?' That was strange. On a ship full of experienced submariners, why would Quest pick one of his mercenary warriors to pilot the bathysphere? 'Quest told me the *Sprite* had been refitted by Robert Fulton,' said Amelia. 'I thought he was a legend in your line of work.'

'Blacky's old boat might have been patched up by him,' said Bull, touching a line of control boxes, 'but this exploration ball surely wasn't. Fulton didn't put this on the pilot's station.'

Amelia looked at what Bull was indicating. Iron boxes, solid as their hull. 'What is it?'

'That I would like to know myself,' said Bull. 'Whatever it is, I'm locked out. I don't even understand what's turning our screws – this tub takes expansion-engine gas, but there's no scrubbers running that I can see.'

'He's a clever man,' said Amelia. 'And as long as it works . . .'

'Oh, he's a sharp one,' laughed Bull. 'Sharp enough to buy us to sail up the Shedarkshe and do his dying for him.'

'You planning on living for ever?'

'Just long enough to see the head of every Guardian on a pike outside traitor's gate and maybe your parliament turned into something useful – like a barracks for the royal cavalry.'

'For that you're going to need immortality,' said Amelia.

As they sank deeper with each second, the last of the light from the surface was lost, replaced by a stygian darkness broken only by the occasional small silver fish darting out of their way. With the last of their natural visibility gone, Bull pulled a lever activating a circle of high-intensity gas lamps on the surface of their craft, checking the dial on the expansion gas reservoir to make sure they weren't burning fuel too fast. A whine sounded and Amelia looked behind her to try to locate the source of the noise.

'It's the waldos,' said Bull. 'The arms on the back of the sphere. I'm putting the clockwork under tension while we've still got gas to burn.'

Amelia spotted the rubber circles surrounding two holes for her arms. 'How do you see what the manipulator claws are doing?'

'Just pull back the cover from the aft porthole, you'll see well enough.'

Amelia slid the iron lid to the side and saw a strip of triple-layered crystal looking out onto the darkness. Two large clamp arms hung folded in the water outside. She pushed her arms through the holes – a tight fit for her muscled biceps – and found a metal frame inside with leather straps for her fingers to slot into.

'Is there a dial near your thumbs inside there?' Bull asked.

'Got it,' confirmed Amelia. 'Ridged like a copper ha'penny.'

'That'll be your power amplification,' said Bull. 'Keep it dialled down when you're poking about in the silt. If by some miracle we find Tree-head Joe's crown, those claws will crumple it like paper on the highest power setting.'

Amelia unfolded the arms outside their submersible and practised moving them from side to side, clenching the frame to manipulate the pincer claws. Something dark floated past at the periphery of the illumination and Amelia jumped back from the glass port.

'I saw something, Kammerlan, something big floating out there at the edge of the lights.'

Bull leant on the pilot stick and rotated the craft around sixty degrees. 'Those two waldo arms are all the weapons we're packing, dimples. If there's a tussle between us and one of the Shedarkshe's critters that's swum into the lake, you are going to need to dish out a walloping.'

Amelia said nothing. If it came to a prolonged fight between the bathysphere and a school of underwater thunder lizards, the amplification on the arms would bleed their power fast. She returned her gaze to the lake waters. There! Something drifting at a strange angle in front of the pilot's porthole. Bull edged the sphere forward, manually swivelling the inclination on their main gaslight to throw a circle of illumination across the shape. A bone-hard shell, bleached white.

'A sunken seed ship,' gasped Amelia. There were tears along its side, clean, straight rents, as if the holes had been carved open on a lathe.

'That's no normal seed ship,' said Bull, guiding the bathysphere slowly about the wreck while their lamps tracked along its hull. 'There's no top deck, no flame cannons, no pod bulbs for its depth charge seeds.' He pointed the main light at a silvery dome glittering like a compound eye on the wreck's side. 'And that isn't anything like the patrols that used to chase my crew down. They've sealed the seed ship at every point, made it watertight. Tree-head Joe's been making himself a u-boat.'

'I knew there was something wrong!' Amelia cursed the controlling mind of the Daggish. 'Cutting deals with us, when all it wanted to do was cut into our skulls.'

'Sweet Circle,' Bull whistled, turning the craft around. 'It's worse than you know. Will you look out there . . .'

The bathysphere was drifting through a graveyard of seed ships – all different designs, some craft barely larger than their own and decayed down to barnacle-encrusted shells, others long torpedoes of modified surface craft. A dead history of Daggish nautical evolution.

'Erosion like this,' said Amelia. 'Some of those wrecks have to be over seven hundred years old. How long has it been trying to find its crown?'

'Old Tree-head Joe is desperate all right,' said Bull. 'Desperate enough that it'll sully its perfection by dealing with the race of man. It must have thought that Midwinter gift-giving had come early when it netted the *Sprite* and her bathysphere – a Jackelian seadrinker with its very own expert on Camlantis on board. But what is worrying me is what killed the damn boats out there? Look at them – that's not any engineering failure. Something cut them up like mince on a butcher's slab.'

Amelia didn't hear Bull. Her mind was turning over the ramifications of the Daggish emperor's obsession. 'All this! Persisting and persevering for hundreds of years just for a *crown*?'

'It probably thinks the bleeding thing is holy,' said Bull. 'The crown of its creators or some equally fool notion. Maybe it thinks that having the crown will allow it to talk to its god. It may be a hive, but the Daggish acts like a single organism. Tree-head Joe needs something to believe in, doesn't it?'

'Societies do many strange things when religion is involved, I'll grant you,' said Amelia. 'But the Daggish Emperor didn't strike me as having any deep, unfulfilled spiritual needs.' She was trying to think like an archaeologist again. Getting inside the minds of those long lost to alien times wasn't so different from trying to understand the Daggish. Look at what it was doing, analyse its behaviour. 'So, what does it want?'

'The jigger wants to kill us,' said Bull. 'Cover us in slime and clean our brains like a teacher wiping chalk off the blackboard.'

'You've got it,' said Amelia. 'What does it want? It wants to expand. To grow its territory.'

'It can't,' said Bull. 'There was a lot of useless blarney about the Daggish down in Rapalaw Junction, but one thing everyone agreed on . . . the greenmesh never expands. It has a range, the reach at which everything inside the Daggish empire acts in unity. I saw a craynarbian once that had been grabbed back from the greenmesh by comfort auction traders – she was blank: she could breathe all right, could be fed liquids and mush, but there was nothing left inside of her. You might as well chop your finger off, toss it away, and expect it to come running back to you in gratitude. I reckon Tree-head Joe is the centre of it all, the spider in the middle of the web. Its drones have got to stay close to it to take their orders and the coward isn't moving anywhere. You saw how spooked it got when it saw the bugs in my hair.'

'The emperor wants the crown to expand its hive,' said Amelia. 'Trust me on this. I've spent a lifetime trying to get inside the minds of cultures and kingdoms that last existed millennia ago from only the faintest of clues. I don't know how exactly the crown will help it, but growth is what the Daggish emperor wants, it's all that the hive wants.' She looked out at the graveyard of broken ships. 'And it's been trying a long time to get it.'

Bull started lowering them beneath the field of broken

vessels, checking the depth readings as they sank. 'Tree-head Joe's already got itself a crown; it hasn't done the Daggish much good so far. Beyond its symbolic value, what's so special about a king's crown? Those trinkets were two-a-penny at the court-in-exile at Porto Principe and none of them did us any good when your parliament came a-calling with its aerostats. It's power that counts, not the robes that you wear.'

That was true. Something about the crown was nagging at Amelia, but what? Something she had seen in the crystal-book back in Jackals. Something obvious. Her archaeologist's sense was on fire. The rush that she got when she was close to un-covering one of history's misplaced secrets. 'It's not a king's crown. Camlantean society didn't have a hierarchy or aristocracy. The crown is from a reader-administrator, a coordinator of knowledge. Imagine a head librarian crossed with the civil servants at Greenhall.'

'No king, not even an elected thief like your First Guardian?' Bull said, incredulous. 'How did your Camlanteans decide how things got done, who was quality and who was taking the orders?'

'The most knowledgeable person on any subject made the decisions for that area,' said Amelia. 'If someone came along who knew more about it, who was wiser, the incumbent would step aside. If there was a fundamental disagreement about a certain issue, everyone in the city who felt they had enough experience to make an informed judgement would vote on it.'

'You're joking,' said Bull. 'That sounds as jiggered as the anarchy the city-states have up north in Catosia. No law, mob rule, the strong blade survives . . .'

'Camlantean society had no war, Kammerlan, no hunger, no poverty or crime, they possessed a level of engineering expertise that makes the kingdom of Jackals look like a tribe of feral craynarbians scratching a living along the banks of the Shedarkshe. The secret of achieving that is what we came looking for in Liongeli, not bags of silver from Quest's counting house.'

Bull shook his head sadly at the professor's gullibility. 'And who recorded these accounts of a perfect society, dimples? It wouldn't happen to be the same "coordinators of knowledge" who were looking after the shop, would it?'

'Camlantis was mentioned in awe in every scrap of contemporary history we've ever uncovered from her neighbours. It wasn't propaganda.'

'Right.' Bull rolled his eyes in amusement. 'Well, the nature of the race of man sure has changed a lot over the intervening millennia, and not for the better.' He pushed his face closer to the pilot's porthole. 'And out there, I reckon, is all that is left of your flawless society now.'

'All that is left on earth,' corrected Amelia. The professor gazed out with disappointment at the ruins their lights had revealed. But then, what was she expecting? What would Middlesteel look like if a great chunk of it was ripped and sent skyward by a floatquake? A crater with exposed basements and a few chopped up atmospheric lines, rained on by rubble as the city lifted up to the heavens. Now leave that to rot for ten thousand years under the floodwaters of a collapsed dam the height of a mountain and what would you have? Something very similar to what they were slowly drifting over. An underwater rubbish dump.

Amelia tried to cheer herself up. Some of the greatest discoveries Jackelian archaeology had ever made had been found in the dust pits of fallen civilizations. Bull grabbed an iron wheel with a wooden handle and began to rotate it fast. 'That's your collection nets out. Keep your eyes open at the rear port. If we come across whatever did for Tree-head Joe's toy fleet, I'm going to bounce our buoyancy tanks, send us to the surface like a flying fish running for its life.'

'You know what'll happen if we surface without the crown,' Amelia said.

'Reckon we're dead whichever way you look at it,' said Bull. 'But an hour or two more is worth having. Let's get to work.'

Amelia extended the waldos and began to pick through the debris on the lake bed. There were shreds of things that could have been pieces of machinery, rubble with a single side carved by the hand of man. In other circumstances she would have been filling her nets with such objects, anything that could expand Jackals' knowledge of the Camlantean civilization. Crates of antiquities that could be labelled, stored and analysed by teams of researchers at Jackals' museums and colleges. The purpose of most of what she recovered might lay undiscovered for decades, centuries even, before it could be cross-referenced and its function teased out. But she didn't have the luxury of repeat trips. This might be her only chance to explore down here on the good graces of the Daggish emperor. The frustration welled in her, the minutes of fruitless searching, minutes turning into an hour. How much air did they have left?

Then it hit her. She was thinking like an archaeologist. The best advice she had been given for this kind of situation had come from a Chimecan tomb raider who specialized in under-city work. *Follow the traps. The traps mean plunder.*

'Traps,' said Amelia. 'Traps mean treasure. Those broken up Daggish submersibles. How did they all get to be clustered in the same place?'

'Currents, girl,' said Bull. 'It ain't worldsinger sorcery that put them there, just the currents down here.'

'Follow the currents.'

'I've been avoiding them,' said Bull. 'Whatever killed those Daggish boats is as like living somewhere along the flow.'

'That's what I'm counting on,' said Amelia.

'Well, why not,' muttered Bull, turning the bathysphere into the pull of the undercurrents. 'Why not face the monster of the lake in its den. Least it'll be something to see before we go.'

As they tracked against the push of water across the lake bed, Amelia noticed that the water outside appeared to be becoming lighter, the darkness of their depth lessening until the jagged outcrops of rock below started to cast shadows towards them. Bull checked the depth readings on his control panel, tapping the glass above the dial, but the hand remained hovering at eighty fathoms.

'We're not rising,' said Bull. 'This isn't natural. Look at the light out there, we might as well be diving for pearls off the Fire Sea corals.'

'Light at the end of the tunnel,' said Amelia,' except we're not in any tunnel. Keep going. This is what we're looking for, I can feel it in my blood.'

After five minutes they crested a rise of rubble, their small craft's gaslights hardly needed now. They were drifting over the centre of a basin, while down below a ring of monoliths traded waves of rainbow light between each other, wide sheets of energy undulating slowly through the water. The dark granite giants lay surrounded by a litter of sliced-apart seed-ship wreckage.

'Jigger that,' said Bull, 'jigger that for a game of soldiers.'

'Head for it,' said Amelia. 'Head for the centre of the stones and the light.'

'Not in a million years,' said Bull, pushing the pilot stick away from the basin. 'That's a death trap – you want to know how a fish feels when it gets sucked into a boat's screws, you dive into that mess of light. It's nothing we need.'

'It is,' said Amelia. 'Can't you feel it, feel the song the city is singing for us?'

'You've lost it, dimples, you've lost your mind.' He glanced across at Amelia and nearly fell out of the pilot seat – the professor was glowing, a faint echo of the rainbow sheets outside rippling along the surface of her torn and tattered clothes. He checked his own hands but the bizarre radiance was only covering her body, not his.

'Turn the craft,' said Amelia.

As if in response to her voice there was a violent lurch in the bathysphere's direction. Bull slammed the pilot stick and pushed the pressure on the expansion engine up to the red line on his dials, but even at maximum power the craft was still getting sucked in towards the stone circle.

'Stop it!' Bull yelled. 'Look at the wreckage out there. It's a siren's song – you're pulling us into the butcher's mincer.'

Amelia's eyes were glazed with the power of the radiance. It was home. They were going home.

Bull smashed the lever to blow the lake water out of the main ballast tanks, trying to trigger an emergency surface, but the control deck was no longer responding to his directions. Something else was in control, and it sure wasn't him. Behind Bull, the waldo arms screamed as the engine began to put its springs under intolerable tension, the dial hands under every circle of crystal on his instrument panel turning in angry loops, the craft shaking the slaver fit to rattle his teeth. They struck the plane of rainbow energy and the field flowed through the reinforced walls of the bathysphere as if they were made of glass. It was dissolving the walls of the craft – so bright, pain plunging directly into the back of his skull.

Bull yelled and tried to cover his eyes with his arms.

Anything to deaden the pain. The last sound he heard was Amelia laughing like a possessed demon.

Cornelius rolled over. Something was wrong. His arm had no weight. It felt like a feather by his side. Blinking his eyes open, he watched the walls of the cell focus into view, the dark shadow by his side solidifying into Septimoth. An alien noise faded out of the range of Cornelius's hearing, the lashlite tucking the bone-pipe of his dead mother back into his belt, halting his mediation song to the gods of the holy winds.

Cornelius tried to speak but his throat was sore and a gargle came out instead.

'Rest yourself,' said Septimoth. 'You were gassed.'

Cornelius could remember nothing. 'How?'

'We were inside the brig of a submersible and you tried to escape, running a bypass on a transaction engine lock with your arm. Our captors detected the attempt and flooded our cell with a poisonous vapour. I held my breath as long as I could, but the gas got me eventually.'

'My arm!' It was coming back to Cornelius now. The flood at their hidden rooms in the old Middlesteel Museum. Being captured by the divers and taken into a small river submersible. Their housekeeper lying unconscious in the brig with them. 'Where are we – what have they done with Damson Beeton?'

'She was gone when I woke up,' said Septimoth. 'We are no longer on the submersible. There is no movement or pressure differential in the atmosphere here. We are being held on land now, I think. Yesterday the soldiers took you away and when you were returned here your arm had been tampered with.'

'Naturally.' A disembodied voice echoed around the cell. 'Your artificial limb was far too dangerous for us to let you keep it as it was designed. A work of some craftsmanship, by the way. My compliments to whichever mechomancer you patronized.'

Septimoth nodded towards fluted trumpets in the four corners of the cell. For listening in and talking, both, but Cornelius didn't need to see the face to recognize the voice.

'Robur!'

'Indeed. I am glad my people had a chance to find the hidden store of Furnace-breath Nick masks on your isle, otherwise I would never have known who to thank for my liberation from Quatérshift.'

'You've a strange way of showing your gratitude,' said Cornelius.

'I am grateful,' said Robur, 'not suicidal. Your friend's talons are still as sharp as an eagle's, even if I have tensioned down the strength on your false arm. I removed the weapons and lock picks and all the other gimcracks that had been packed inside it, too. Who would have thought you could fit so much inside such a confined space?'

'What have you done with Damson Beeton?' Cornelius demanded. 'For your sake she had better still be alive.'

'Hah,' Robur's voice snorted. 'You keep an odd household, Cornelius Fortune.'

'She's just an old woman,' said Cornelius. 'She has no part in this. You can let her go.'

'That "old woman" killed five of Middlesteel's finest and most expensive toppers on your island,' said Robur. 'If I had to choose whose cell to be locked up in, I'd take my chances with you and your flying lizard over that old crone any day.'

A panel in the wall slid back, revealing an abacus with a hundred rails, thousands of tiny squares hanging on the copper tubes beginning to spin, forming an image. It was a Rutledge Rotator, a transaction-engine screen – still rare outside the engine rooms at Greenhall – Cornelius had briefly considered stealing one to go along with the engine he had rebuilt in Middlesteel Museum. The image on the wall of flickering squares revealed a woman held upright in a prison frame, her mouth gagged and her eyes blinded by a leather mask.

'We're holding your wolftaker friend hostage to ensure your cooperation. If you try and escape again, the gas we flood her cell with won't be a somnic. It will be something far more lethal.'

Cornelius's eyes widened. 'A wolftaker?'

'Did you really imagine your activities would escape the attention of the Court of the Air?' Robur asked. 'How typically Jackelian – a secret police so secret that even your political masters live in fear of them, the lethal shepherds of your conscience – truer guardians of Jackals' much vaunted democracy than the politicians who wear that name in parliament. You must have looked like a wolf to the court, Cornelius – the Sun Deity knows, you looked enough like a wolf to the new rulers of Quatérshift. Even at Darksun Fortress your name was legend, the prison guards lived in fear of a visit from you. But as happy as the Court was for you to be making mischief for their ancient enemy across the border, I still don't think they trusted you; so it seems you and your winged friend got your own shepherd to ensure you didn't start preying on the wrong flock.'

Septimoth looked over at his friend. 'Damson Beeton was recommended to our service by Dred Lands as I recall.'

'So she was.' Cornelius cursed his own stupidity. And the proprietor of the Old Mechomancery Shop along Knocking Yard was so perfectly connected into the heart of the Jackelian underworld, so perfectly equipped with illegal equipment and banned lore. The Court of the Air could look a long time before they found such a well-connected informer in Middlesteel – except that they obviously hadn't needed to.

'The watchers in the sky,' said Septimoth. 'My people avoid that cold place where they dwell. Perhaps it was to be expected. You always warned me that the Court could be monitoring us.'

'You must have thought you were very clever,' said Robur. 'Your little palace of tricks hidden under the waters of the Gambleflowers. We use submersibles where we can to avoid their gaze ourselves, as it happens.'

'Dear old Damson Beeton. Well, if the Court of the Air was using me to do their dirty work for them, then I was using them in exchange,' sighed Cornelius. 'They let Furnace-breath Nick flit back and forth across the cursewall like a wine merchant pushing bottles of brandy in a cart. But who is your "we", mechomancer, who are *you* working for?'

'So you were using them, were you, eh? A privateer, not a pirate – an admirably practical attitude. As for myself, you might say I am now working for the greater good of the race of man.'

'Not Quatérshift, then,' said Cornelius.

'You dare ask that!' Robur's voice exploded in anger. 'After you saw the conditions they had me living in at Darksun Fortress. I could tell you things, Jackelian, the crimes I saw in that place and others like it, before. The things those monsters did to families that had fallen out with the First Committee and their revolutionary barbarians. To my friends, to their own supporters in the end . . .'

'Save your breath, I have already seen the blessings of the revolution,' said Cornelius, 'as has Septimoth. I didn't lose my arm in a milling accident – it was cut off as a punish-ment, then tossed into the fertilizer pit of an organized commu-nity not so very different from your camp.'

'Then you know, you understand.' It sounded like Robur was crying.

'Yes,' said Cornelius. 'I know. So, mechomancer, who is it paying for the greater good of the race of man, these days?'

'That I think you also know. Shall I confirm it for you?'

'Abraham Quest,' hissed Cornelius.

'Yes, indeed. When the Catgibbon passed on word of an old friend of hers returning from the dead with an interest in missing steammen, it wasn't too difficult to match her description to a reclusive hermit with no obvious means to show for his wealth suddenly showing up at Whittington Manor brandishing a party invite. Compte de Spééler – the Count of Thieves. That little wordplay may have cost you your life. Your methods are both hasty and unsound.'

'My methods saved your life,' said Cornelius.

'That is the main reason why you and your companion are still alive,' said Robur. 'We are working on the same side, really. You in your small limited way. Myself in mine – but my methods are played on a grander stage. You are never going to change the Commonshare by slaughtering Carlists and the revolutionary leaders one by one. Your horror – as effective as it is – can never equal the great terror the revolution has imposed on Quatérshift. What is a single angel of death dropping from the sky, one agent of vengeance, what is that compared to the constant fear of the knock at the door in the middle of the night by the Commonshare's thugs? What is the terror invoked by the voice changer in your mask compared to the screams of your neighbours as their children are fed into a Gideon's Collar?'

'One death at a time is all I need,' said Cornelius, 'to slake my vengeance and give me a little peace at night.'

'There we are, then,' sighed Robur's disembodied voice. 'You are looking to punish those who wronged you, one grave at a time. I am looking to change society so that such evil can never be allowed to take hold again. You crudely treat the symptoms; I wish to eradicate the disease itself.'

'There speaks a mechomancer,' said Septimoth, his wings shivering in anger. 'The race of man treating the sum of the world like a machine that can be fixed by tinkering with its components, by providing a different instruction set for the transaction engine.'

'My talents will help usher in a new age,' said Robur 'An age where the crimes the Commonshare inflicted on my people in Quatérshift will never be repeated.'

'The Carlists were infected by the same meme,' said Septimoth. 'I heard identical noises from your monkey throats, even as the Commonshare practised genocide against the people of the wind when we would not turn from the old ways. I trusted your kind's grand intentions once. I shall never do so again.'

'You are not going to usher in a new age by robbing the decaying remains of steammen from their graves,' Cornelius interrupted. 'I fail to see how that is going to topple the regime in Quatérshift.'

'Of course you fail to see it, you dolt,' said Robur. 'And I am afraid I will be unable to enlighten you for a few days yet, as unlike you, I am anything but hasty. All will be revealed in good time.'

'What about us?' said Cornelius. 'Do we have a place in your shining new society?'

'We shall see,' said Robur. 'We shall see.'

The speaker in the ceiling fell silent.

'Well, what do you make of that?' Cornelius asked Septimoth.

'I think, on reflection, we should have interviewed more than one candidate for the position of maid-of-all-works when we set up home in Jackals.'

'Robur was fishing,' said Cornelius. 'He wanted to find out if we're working with the Court of the Air. He's worried how much the Court might know about his little game.'

'Let us hope the Court knows more about his schemes than we do,' said Septimoth, 'for both our sakes.'

Cornelius did not reply. The last time he and Septimoth had been held captive it had been he who had come up with the plan to escape: his brains and freakish assassin's face to break them free, Septimoth's wings to carry them to freedom. But Robur was not a blunt instrument like an organized community inside the Commonshare. And relying on the old woman lashed to a frame in the cell next door and her deadly celestial employers to rescue them wasn't much of a plan. If that was what they were relying on, then they truly were in trouble.

Blood-bats circled the cage at night, making passes that carried them uncomfortably close to Commodore Black. The commodore ignored the squeals of the large rodents as T'ricola massaged life back into Billy Snow's legs, the paralysis toxin finally losing its effect. Ironflanks was with them now, and while no one wanted to speak of it, the absence of valiant Gabriel McCabe – the strongest man in Jackals no more – still hung over them like a ghost at the feast.

'You are an unusual sonar man,' Veryann said to Billy as she looked down on the bats sweeping through the petrol mist beneath them. 'One who fights uncommonly well for a blind man. And a submariner.'

'I crewed my way across the oceans to Thar when I was younger,' said Billy. 'They know a thing to two about blade work and empty fist fighting out there. You can even study the skill at their monasteries.'

'Did they also smith witch-blades at their monasteries?' Veryann asked.

'It was considered something of an art,' said Billy.

'Quiet, Billy,' said T'ricola. 'Your throat muscles are as weak as every other part of your creaking body. You need to rest.'

'I can rest when I'm dead,' said the sonar man.

'That fate will come soon enough,' said Commodore Black. 'Along with the wicked spectacle the mad prince of this jungle hell is planning for us.'

'At least the end will be quick,' said Ironflanks. 'The five of us pitted weaponless against a kilasaurus max. It will be quick.'

The commodore laid a hand on the steamman's shoulder. 'For the love of the Circle, can't you be telling the prince that you have changed your mind and that he's a fine fellow who should be letting his new friends go on their way?'

'You mistake him for one of my kind,' said Ironflanks. 'Doublemetal and his siltempters haven't been part of the Free State for many thousands of years. They worship the foulest of Loas, Lord Two-Tar and his minions, and the Lord of Deactivation has driven all compassion from the siltempters' boiler hearts for those whose threads are woven alongside their own in the great pattern.'

'The prince said you escaped from this place once before,' said T'ricola. 'Can you not break the cell's locks and get us out of the pit?'

'That was an age ago,' said Ironflanks. 'And I had help. I was a knight steamman, ranked errant among the Order of the Pathfinder Fist. I led a party of knights here – King Steam had heard rumours that the siltempters had captured one of the last remaining Hexmachina, a wounded and nearly de-activate model. We were to find it and free it. But we had not realized how the jungle had changed the siltempters over the millennia. They had grown into monsters here. They slaughtered us, those who did not run. A few of us survived, tortured while our architecture was violated by the same prince that King Steam had once cast out of Mechancia by his own hand.'

'But still you escaped,' said Commodore Black.

'It was Bronzehall who broke the codes on our lock in the temple's torture rooms,' said Ironflanks. 'He was a sly one, Bronzehall. A knight of the Commando Militant with a hundred ways to demolish any construction, and a thousand more to break into it. He was one of the last of us to die when we were pursued through the jungle by the siltempters, the only steamman other than I not to be recaptured.'

'What happened to him?' Billy Snow asked.

'We had almost reached Rapalaw Junction when the components the prince had violated our architecture with began to change our bodies. When Bronzehall realized how badly he had been afflicted, he could not bear the shame.'

'A warrior's death,' said Veryann.

'Yes, a warrior's death. If we had succeeded in bringing back the Hexmachina, then perhaps King Steam would have helped us, instructed the hall of architects at Mechancia to do what they could to restore our bodies to the righteous pattern. As it was, banishment and the isolation of the unclean was to be my reward.'

'You are still a steamman,' implored the commodore. 'Can you not help me break this cunning transaction-engine lock?'

'Bronzehall could,' said Ironflanks, 'but not I, my softbody friend. I wish that I could, but I am as much a part of the jungle now as I am of the metal, which is why Liongeli's dark realm speaks to me at night and fills my thoughtflow with the whispers of the canopy.'

Commodore Black stared forlornly down towards the bubbling lake of oil. 'Then I will tease the blessed thing open myself. My genius versus the mocking black boiler hearts of the siltempters. Let us see if Prince Doublemetal is as canny as he thinks he is, the lord of the loons, filing down his rivets like a walking razor and crushing the bones of honest travellers that fall into his clutches.'

'Let me help you,' offered Billy Snow.

'I know machines,' said T'ricola. 'I'll take over from you when you tire.'

The commodore bent down to examine the lock, the sonar man and the chief engineer of the *Sprite* by his side. It was a race against time. Only a few hours remained until dawn splintered the star-filled night and ushered in their appointment with the thunder lizards in the fighting pit next door.

'Oh, this is clever,' said the commodore. 'This lock is a work of art. The codes on this merciless thing are resetting themselves every few minutes – at random intervals, too, as best as I can see. You come up with a system to crack the lock and the wicked thing changes the game halfway through.'

'What good will springing the doors do?' said Ironflanks, pointing to the steaming oil below.

'We can climb our cell's tether,' said Veryann, 'or swing ourselves cage by cage to the edge.'

'Let me try, let me try,' the commodore muttered to himself, making wincing noises and grumbling as the lock matched its cunning with his. T'ricola observed his work while Billy Snow listened to the tumble of the mechanism inside, learning the clicks and clacks that preceded the apparatus resetting itself.

The commodore grew more frustrated, each small victory overturned as the lock altered its state. 'Oh, you beast. You dark piece of work, built to play with my skill and break my hopes upon the sharp crags of your wicked construction.' He was distracted by the distant howls from the arena next to their prison pit; a grim reminder of their fate if they failed to break the lock. 'What are they, now? Blessed wolves howling at the moon, or thunder lizards? Can they not keep quiet? Must I crack this infernal device while listening to their song too.'

'Their chains are fed with wild energy,' said Ironflanks. 'To torture the creatures and goad them into a killing fury before a contest. I saw many of my order sacrificed in such a way the last time I was held here.'

'Are the odds not unequal enough already?' moaned the commodore. 'Poor old Blacky and his brave legs made slow by the years and what meagre crumbs of comfort I was able to salvage while living with my friends in Tock House. Thunder lizards do not need goading to feast on my weary bones . . . every mortal creature we've come across in Liongeli has already been clicking its jaws in fierce anticipation of the walking meal wearing the skipper of the *Sprite's* uniform that they've found.'

Time was running out beneath their feet, an hour turning into two, then three. When the commodore's hands were shaking and cramped, T'ricola took over and began to play the system, her bony craynarbian manipulator arms twisting and turning the mechanism with swift decisive strokes where the commodore had instead teased it like a musician playing his instrument. She was still attacking the lock when the cage heaved and began to rise out of the oil pit.

'No!' T'ricola cursed. 'We're so close. It's still night, the sun hasn't even broken the horizon yet.'

'You would think that toad-faced prince would be a late riser,' whined the commodore. 'Soaking himself in the oil of his own people, a nice bath for his wicked steel bones before he takes it into his head to throw us into his deadly arena.'

Yet still their prison rose. Past the cages filled with rotting corpses and the bones of craynarbian tribesmen who had strayed too close to the siltempters' territory. That was not to be their fate. They had a far more active demise than a slow starvation in the petrol mists awaiting them.

As soon as the package had been slid through the feeding hatch of their cell, the voice of one of their captors – not Robur, this time – came out of the speaking trumpet.

'Open the box.'

Cornelius unbolted the lid of the crate. What choice did they have? A viewing slit in the cell door opened to ensure he and Septimoth were following instructions. Inside the crate there was a mess of leather straps and buckles and two large gloves, padded and oversized.

'Put the gloves on the lashlite first. Then strap the harness around the lashlite's wings.'

Cornelius hesitated and a female voice behind the viewing slit barked at them. 'Do as you are instructed. A rifle ball in the head is your alternative.'

Septimoth held out his arms and Cornelius sheathed his friend's talons inside the large gloves, then began strapping on the harness.

'I am insulted,' said Cornelius. 'Am I so insignificant that you don't have a set of manacles for me?'

'You are just a man,' said the voice outside the cell. 'A one-armed freak with your artificial limb deactivated. Your large friend is quite another matter. We don't want him attempting to fly away, or shredding us to pieces with his formidable-looking talons.'

'They have the measure of you,' said Septimoth, his beak twisting into an approximation of a smile as Cornelius worked the harness buckles around his body.

'Just how tight do you want to be trussed?'

When Septimoth's wings and talons were made safe, the

cell door opened, an officer with a pistol beckoning them into a corridor where more soldiers waited with rifles. They wore the cherry uniforms of the House of Quest's fencible regiment and their commander was Robur's so-called 'daughter'.

'So, you have joined the family business after all,' said Cornelius.

'We could have rescued Robur ourselves,' said the Catosian, 'assaulted Darksun Fortress from the air. But such an action would have attracted attention. You were already operating across the border in Quatérshift with a high degree of efficiency. Convincing you to rescue Robur from the Commonshare was the obvious choice.'

'A part you played extremely well,' said Cornelius. 'And I do understand why you played me for a dupe. I'm sure the First Committee would have been most curious as to why one of the city-states of the Catosian League had declared war on them just for the sake of kidnapping a single prisoner.'

'It was not the reaction in Quatérshift we were concerned with,' said the officer. Another cell door opened, a figure weighted down under the armour of a hex suit emerging into the corridor. 'It was *her* people . . .'

'Damson Beeton!' Cornelius only just recognized her under the mass of the midnight-black shell, silver sigils traced across every inch of the metal. Whatever sorceries the Court of the Air had taught her, she wouldn't be practising them in that sheathing, customized to nullify her talents. 'Sink me, are you all right?'

Her eyes gleamed angrily from underneath her visor. 'What, apart from being shot full of shellfish toxin, kidnapped, imprisoned, and made to stumble around sweating under enough armour to keep a steamman knight happy?'

'Yes, apart from that.'

'Just dandy,' she spat.

'Good, because I'm afraid I'm going to have to release you from my service. Moonlighting on my time is a serious offence.'

'That's no way to treat an elderly woman,' said Damson Beeton. She looked at Septimoth, bound tight under the harness with his heavy gloves hanging by his side, then at Cornelius without even a set of manacles. 'They've got the measure of you, then.'

'Oh, I have it on reliable authority that we are all on the same side,' said Cornelius.

'Take these hex plates off me, dearie,' said the housekeeper, 'and I'll show these Catosian dolly-mops whose side I am on.'

'Enough of your prattle,' said the Catosian commander. 'Follow us.'

Cornelius stared at the rifle muzzles pointing at them, then at his friends; a lashlite who couldn't fly, an old woman who could barely walk under the weight of her mobile prison and himself: a one-armed freak. Perhaps they were going to be displayed as a carnival attraction?

They were guided through long corridors and chambers carved out of the rock. In one of the chambers, stacks of supplies were being loaded into a capsule by the lock of a miniature atmospheric system and Cornelius revised his estimate of the size of the complex. If they needed an airless transport system to move victuals about, the place might go on for miles. He glanced up. Walls of rough granite towered above them, held in place by iron girders and massive mining pins.

'Ruxley granite,' said Cornelius. 'We must be at Ruxley Waters. We've made it into your airship works after all.'

Robur's 'daughter' shot him an angry glance.

'The works' hangers extend back into the hills,' said Damson Beeton.

'I would say they have been excavating a little more than a few aerostat chambers,' said Cornelius. 'To see this place, you'd think Quest believed that another coldtime was returning and he was digging himself an underground hold to see out the centuries of winter.'

They climbed a set of stairs that had been carved into the rock, passing dumb waiters carrying up copper cylinders marked with the celgas symbol. There looked to be far more canisters of the strictly controlled celgas than Abraham Quest should have had access to. At the top of the stairs, a window in a narrow corridor looked down on a chamber containing an engineering-frame hung with models of various airships – some based on the Jackelian aerial navy, others blue-sky designs, outlandish shapes of connected hulls with battleship-like under structures. A rotating propeller driven by a compact steam engine was simulating a powerful wind down the length of the test frame.

Damson Beeton turned her head to and fro despite the weight of her hex helmet, drinking in all the sights the airship works had to offer. Stolen celgas. Unauthorized airship designs. Military forces far beyond the company limits allowed to fencible regiments. There was enough evidence down here to see Abraham Quest and his staff take the drop outside Bonegate for the amusement of the Circleday gallows crowd a dozen times over.

The granite walls gave way to narrow wooden corridors, as if they were walking along the inside of a steamship. At one point they had to form into single file to cross a wooden gangway across a cavern, rope nets covering store rooms below, the space being loaded high with sacks and crates by a column of Quest's workers.

Prods from the fencible soldiers' rifles kept them moving, apart from a brief halt when a squad of retainers came striding across their path. They all looked of an age in their green uniforms. There was a flicker of inquisitiveness in their eager eyes as they passed by the motley prisoners, but they kept on marching in a disciplined formation.

'Young,' noted Septimoth.

'From his academies, no doubt,' said Damson Beeton. 'The homes for street children and urchins that the House of Quest sponsors.'

'They look more like soldiers than poorhouse sweepings to me,' said Cornelius.

'I'm sure their training is superior to that of the army's regiments,' said the housekeeper. 'A better deal than parliament's silver shilling and the taste of the lash more often than the taste of grog rations.'

'The cadets are trained by the free company,' said the Catosian, the pride evident in her tone. 'At least, in matters pertaining to military instruction. They want for nothing when it comes to honing their bodies and their minds.'

'Philosopher-kings,' whispered Cornelius. 'He has raised an army of philosopher-kings.'

'I doubt that Quest found much time for tutoring them in philosophy,' said Septimoth.

'You are wrong,' said the officer, watching the last of the column of cadets pass by. 'Without a perfect mind to drive it, a perfect body is reduced to barely competent muscle. A soldier must understand what is worth dying for and what is worth living for, and the distinction between the two.'

Damson Beeton frowned. The wolftakers of the Court of the Air lived by a similar code. 'Now that sounds worryingly familiar.'

'You will have the opportunity to hear it again,' said the Catosian. 'Very shortly.'

They entered a round chamber with polished wooden

decking but no natural light, recessed gas lamps hissing gently with a yellow radiance. Steps on either side led down to pits where retainers tended transaction engines and monitored illuminated dials. Dressed in aprons similar to those worn by Greenhall engine men, the staff regulated their machinery's pressure by working wheels set along racks of copper pipes.

At the end of the chamber stood Abraham Quest and Robur, a handful of fencible officers in attendance – some obviously Catosian, others more of his academy sweepings. Quest turned, smiling, when he noticed Cornelius and the other two prisoners from Dolorous Isle. 'A little different from the last tour I gave you, Compte de Spééler.'

'All in all, I preferred the orchids,' said Cornelius. 'Even the ones that ate your mice.'

'You three were coming close to uncovering my real game,' said Quest. 'So close that I thought I would spare you the trouble of breaking into my airship works and the undignified business of sneaking around my premises.'

'Or the trouble I was taking to update the whistler network with my last report,' said Damson Beeton.

'You mean the Court of the Air doesn't know about me already? You needn't underplay your organization's curiosity about my ambitions,' said Quest. 'I appreciate the interest the Court has been taking in my activities, wholly predictable as your people's predations are.'

'I've been called a lot of things in my years,' said Damson Beeton, 'but never predictable.'

'Please,' said Quest, 'no false modesty. I am one of the few people in the world to grasp the amount of transaction-engine power it takes to model the whole of Jackelian society, to structure the quiet but deadly interventions of your wolftakers. How does the House of Quest and myself appear in the maths turning on the Court of the Air's transaction-engine drums, I wonder?'

'Leakage,' said Damson Beeton. 'Pure leakage.'

Quest's lips tightened into a thin smile. 'Well, what's sauce for the goose is sauce for the gander. I have been putting my own theories of transaction-engine modelling to good use.'

'Using deceased steammen components, perhaps?' Cornelius said.

'You're not even warm,' said Quest. 'No, I used my transaction-engine rooms to model the pattern of what should be the behavioural norm for my employees. Here's what came up as abnormal—' Quest gestured at one of the workers in the pit and a Rutledge Rotator spun into operation on the wall. The image pixellated into a row of coffins, heavy armoured affairs gleaming black, with silver sigils sketched across them. The angle of the picture altered to show human heads visible at the other end of the metal coffins, mouths gagged with the same style of restraining mask Damson Beeton had been wearing. The old woman hissed as she recognized some of the faces.

'Normally I admire persistence,' said Abraham Quest. 'You can accomplish so much with simple persistence. Give it enough time, and the wind can wear away mountains with a breeze as gentle as a whisper; but the Court of the Air's tedious desire to infiltrate my concerns has really grown into something of an irritation for me now.'

'You really think you can do *that* to the Court's agents with impunity?' asked Damson Beeton.

'I've already had a taste of your reprisals. One of your sleeper agents managed to escape my attentions. He tried to eliminate me when he discovered I had captured your colleagues, but in one of life's little ironies, I was pushed out of the way of his killing shot by your employer.' Quest laughed, and looked across at Cornelius. 'Would you save me again if the opportunity arose? It is interesting, is it not? For all the havoc you inflict across the border running around wearing a Furnace-breath Nick mask, when you had to act on pure instinct, your first reaction was to save life, not take it. I would say there's hope for you, yet.' Quest pointed up at the image of the restrained agents. 'I'm sure there will be repercussions, damson. Wolves prey on sheep; wolftakers prey on the wolves, but who preys on the wolftakers? I do believe you will find the Court of the Air's position in the ecos has just changed.'

'You think you're the top of the food chain now?' said Damson Beeton. 'Circle preserve us all, then. What do you intend to do with our agents?'

'Your colleagues are alive,' said Quest. 'Albeit a little limited in capacity, currently. I didn't want to find out their level of proficiency in the worldsinger arts the hard way, so I devised the hex boxes as a way to curtail the Court's witchery and sorcerer's tricks. I modelled the hexes on a transaction engine too – another first, I believe. They are very complex. I doubt whether there are many agents in the Court capable of breaking them. As to your colleagues' fate, I am sure I can find a good use for them. As bookends, perhaps?'

A retainer in an elaborate blue uniform came up to Quest, whispering something in the mill owner's ear. Quest looked at Robur, nodded, and the mechomancer descended into one of the instrumentation pits, both his hands reaching out to yank down a lever. As he threw the lever, the entire room started to tremble, the wall behind Quest lowering to reveal an arc of armoured glass stretching from the floor to the ceiling. There was only darkness behind the glass, but it was getting lighter, the growing illumination accompanied by a massive crunching sound beyond their room.

Septimoth covered his sensitive ears with his glove-covered talons. 'That noise . . .'

'Pneumatic pistons,' said Quest. 'Extremely large ones.'

With a heavy jolt their chamber was raising itself from the earth, the dark rock face outside falling away as they passed iron tubes pushing back the Ruxley granite in gushes of steam. Then they were raised clear of all obstructions, left with a view of a line of fertile green hills outside the glass. On the opposite slope, the rocky crest of a hill was flowering open to give birth to a monstrously large airship – three globes bound together in a steel frame, the under-structure of a Jackelian man-o'-war hanging embedded into her hull units. To the side of them a second hill was opening, releasing another giant aerostat into the sky, gusts of smoke from the pneumatic engines billowing out underneath the craft. With a start, Cornelius realized they were standing on the bridge of a third such vessel.

In front of the sheet glass, two ship's wheels had risen from the floor, retainers in striped airship sailors' shirts taking the wheels, while an elaborately uniformed man – the captain of the vessel – paced behind the elevator and rudder helmsmen. Cornelius shook his head. The skipper should be nervous. They had just declared war on Jackals. The House of Guardians maintained an absolute monopoly over their power in the skies. The RAN flew alone, as guarantor of the realm's freedoms. No other nation had celgas. No other nation had an aerial navy – and the Jackelian state would severely punish anyone who dared to try to alter that happy equilibrium.

'You have gone too far this time,' said Cornelius.

'These three vessels are high-lifters,' said Quest. 'You'll find our journey has only just begun.'

'Jackals has dealt with science pirates before,' noted Damson Beeton. 'Underwater raiders like Solomon Dark and aerial menaces like the Marshal of the Air. If you think these three oversized toys of yours are a match for the hundreds of airships the RAN has on her lists, you will find yourself sadly mistaken. The first city you attack, the four fleets of the navy will be mobilized to hunt you down.'

'Do you really believe my vision is so limited?' said Quest, sadly. 'I helped design half the vessels serving with the Jackelian navy today – I know their weaknesses and their strengths – I could give them quite a run for their money, if that was my intent. But it is not. The *Leviathan* here and her two sister ships are not vessels of war, they are vessels of exploration.'

'I glided past many Jackelian aerostats when I hunted,' said Septimoth, 'but I have never seen anything like these craft.'

'No,' said Quest, turning to the elderly wolftaker, 'but you have, haven't you, damson? When you've visited the Court of the Air. A configuration of modified aerospheres bound together in an aerial city. All the better for keeping the celgas under pressure, every square inch of extra lift we can squeeze out of our ballonets.'

'How high are you planning to take us?' demanded Damson Beeton.

'A little further than the Court of the Air's station in the sky,' said Quest. 'I intend to find Camlantis with my three explorers of the heavens.'

'Cam—' Cornelius could not believe what he was hearing. 'You've lost your bloody mind. Camlantis is a penny dreadful tale – bad history that makes for good novels. You might as well fly off to find the cottage of Mother White Horse or the ancient kings of Jackals sleeping under their hill.'

'Scholars said the same about the city of Lost Angels before its ruined towers were discovered rotting under the ocean,' said Quest. 'In fact, people say something very similar about you now in Quatérshift, Compte de Spééler . . . that you are a myth, not a man: *They seek him here, they seek him there, the furnace-breathed killer with the demon stare.*'

'You declared yourself an outlaw when you launched your three stats,' said Cornelius, fighting down the urge to yell. 'You've thrown away your entire commercial empire in Jackals. And you've done all that for the sake of a child's tale?'

'Easy come, easy go,' said Quest. 'You think I had true wealth, the man who bought Jackals, only to have his bill of sale cancelled when he presented it? I was never rich, before now. I just had piles of trinkets to spill onto my grave like some dirty great barbarian chief. What's inside our minds, what we think, what dreams we can achieve, that's our true wealth. With the secrets of the ancients unlocked, we shall rewrite not just our understanding of prehistory, but the face of the world itself!'

Cornelius looked at Damson Beeton and Septimoth. The lashlite seemed entranced by the scale of the high-lifters they could see turning slowly against the sky. Damson Beeton shook her head sadly, only her ancient eyes visible under the heavy visor. Abraham Quest was quite clearly insane – his wealth, his reputation, all his holdings – he had destroyed his entire life on a mere whim and the three of them were now being pulled along in the jet stream of his preposterous obsession. Prisoners, until they plunged down ice-heavy from the airless heavens, or were shot to pieces by squadrons of RAN vessels enraged by these three interlopers threatening Jackals' carefully crafted balance of power on the continent.

CHAPTER FOURTEEN

Commodore Black clutched tightly onto the cage's bars as they swung out of the petrol mists and over the edge of the pit. That was odd; the normal reception committee of iron apes did not seem to be waiting for them. Instead it was the small siltempter with a prehensile tail and a cheetah cloak working the winch mechanism below, alone.

'It's that capering fool,' said the commodore. 'Maybe his job is to give us breakfast and fatten us up before we are fed to the thunder lizards.' His stomach grumbled at the thought. They hadn't been fed in days 'A nice slice of jungle boar with plenty of crackling on the side for me to crunch through, and a little blessed cold wine to wash it down with.'

'They feed their boilers with tar-soaked charcoal,' said Ironflanks. 'I doubt if any of the siltempters have much experience with the murdered meat you softbodies consume.'

'They can pick fruit from their trees, can't they?' whined the commodore. 'Just a little energy, to help us run around their infernal fighting pit. That's not too much to ask, is it?'

'I can feel something,' said Billy Snow. 'A presence. Can you not sense it, too?'

'The hunger is playing tricks on your mind,' said the commodore.

But it was not in his mind.

'Something is not as it should be,' said Veryann. 'Look at the siltempter.'

Their cage lodged on the mud in front of the small metal creature – his dark hull faintly illuminated, not with the glow of the fireflies that flitted above the burning oil in the prison pit, but with a light that was pure white, whiter than anything had a right to be.

'Keep your voices down,' said the siltempter. 'Most of the tribe are deep in thoughtflow. Only the perimeter pickets are awake.'

He extended his iron fingers and white light flowed from the tips of his pincers, suffusing the transaction lock with its glow. As the light entered the lock, the tiny transaction-engine drums inside the construct started rotating at a blinding speed, steam rising from the metal as they spun so fast they began to melt. There was a dull thud as the cage door opened, the remains of the lock engine dripping molten tears onto the mud, coalescing into a cooling steel puddle.

'Ayeeee,' Ironflanks bowed – half in reverence, half in fear. 'You are no siltempter, you are ridden. Which Loa . . .?'

'Quiet, Ironflanks of the Pathfinder Fist,' instructed the siltempter. 'I am not from the halls of your ancestors – no Loa, I.'

'I have been party to a steamman possession before,' said the commodore, 'on the Isla Needless, when I was on the trail of the treasure of the *Peacock Hearne*, and you will beg my pardon, sir, if I point out that you appear to be no siltempter now.'

'He is inhabited by the spirit of the wreckage they have imprisoned in the temple,' said Billy Snow. 'You are the Hexmachina.'

'I see that I am recognized,' said the possessed siltempter. 'Well met, Snow of the race of man.'

'You live!' Ironflanks hissed in surprise through his voicebox. 'I thought you fully deactivate.'

'You have the measure of me, then, for I am spent,' said the Hexmachina, 'close to death. Once I could cross the walls of the world and beard the darkest of gods in their dens. Now I only have enough life force to watch from my cage and perform parlour tricks on weak minds such as this vessel I ride.'

'Why?' begged Ironflanks. 'Why come for us now? You never appeared before, you never came for us when a whole order of steammen knights perished to free you from the siltempters.'

'There was not enough of me left to free,' said the possessed siltempter, 'and you had the means to escape among your own number. I do not expend my last reserves of energy for the sake of a party of innocent travellers, Ironflanks of the Pathfinder Fist. My centuries imprisoned here have seen countless slaughtered who did not deserve their fate. There is more to your mission than your personal survival. I see a disturbance in the great pattern surfacing on the paths of probability and your threads are bound tightly to it. Much rests on your survival. More than your mere existence – and more than mine.'

'I must rescue you,' said Ironflanks. 'I still carry the charge from King Steam for your release.'

'Your mission is over,' said the Hexmachina. 'I am fading now. Follow your own path on the great pattern.'

The diminutive siltempter stumbled to his knees, a single arm reaching for something he had tucked under his cheetah cloak. He pulled out Billy Snow's cane sword, with its hidden witch-blade. 'I am dying, now; my hold on this vessel weakens. This form cannot be allowed to raise the alarm.'

Billy Snow's hand reached out for the cane, receiving it in his grip with an uncanny accuracy.

'You see truly, Snow of the race of man. You know what must be done.'

Ironflanks realized what was happening and tried to stop it, but the little siltempter's arm pushed weakly out. 'What must be, must be. All things have their season and my age has passed away, now, along with most of my kin. The age of gods has been replaced with a cold new age of reason and the need for god-slayers in this land is small.'

The possessed siltempter looked up at Billy Snow, his vision plate leaking white light towards the old sonar man. 'I believe you understand what that feels like.'

'I believe I do,' said Billy Snow.

His blade was unsheathed almost too fast to follow, looping around once as the siltempter's head spilled from his shoulders and slapped into the mud, severed crystal shards sparking as the body tumbled over, oil pumping out from a handful of cables quivering inside the ruin of his neck.

Veryann loosened a machete strapped to the corpse and looped the strap over her own back. 'It won't protect us against their kind, but it will serve well enough in the jungle.'

The commodore bent over the corpse. 'And then there was one, again. I wish we could bury your true remains inside the body of the world, Hexmachina, where your lover the earth could blow lava to warm your strange soul and bring some comfort to you in this mortal winter of reason we have created.'

Ironflanks seemed deeply disturbed by what had happened. He stood there, swaying, as if his mind were locked in a recursive loop. This god-machine had been his life – the reason for his banishment and his life's purpose before that. Now the Hexmachina was gone. Ironflanks was truly alone, the last of an order of steammen knights reckless enough – coura- geous enough – to attempt to free the holy machine from their ancient enemy.

T'ricola laid one of her four arms on the steamman's shoulder. 'He freed us for a reason.'

'To find a softbody city abandoned an eternity ago?' Ironflanks waved his arms in desperation. 'What reason is that?'

'Reason enough to go on,' said Veryann. 'Are you still my scout?'

'I—'

'Think about Abraham Quest's fee,' pleaded the commodore. 'Enough to pay Jackals' finest mechomancers to remove the lord of the loons' wicked components from your body.'

'Why not?' said Ironflanks. 'What else is left for me, now? Let us go. The Shedarkshe is south of here. It served me well enough once, leading me northwest and home to Rapalaw Junction. If we follow its course southeast we should reach Lake Ataa Naa Nyongmo within a week.'

Veryann looked at the sonar man. 'May I see your witch-blade, Billy Snow?'

'It was fashioned to respond only to my touch. In your hands it would just be dead metal.'

'I thought you would say something like that,' said Veryann, her eyes gleaming suspiciously.

Behind them came a howl of anger – half animal, half machine-screech. It was a siltempter wearing the bleached skull of a thunder lizard as a helmet, emerging from a box-like building overhanging the arena next to the oil lake. As the siltempter screeched, the caged thunder lizards in the arena behind him howled and shook the bars of their cages. The keeper of the lizards ran back towards his building even as

Billy Snow sprinted towards him, casting out his arm. Billy's witch-blade shifted form into a spear that hummed as it sliced through the air, striking the running siltempter in the spine and passing straight through his chest to embed itself in a wall. The lizard-keeper stumbled and grabbed hold of a wheel fixed to the wall, rotating it as he fell deactivate into the mud. Above the building, a cap on a whistle lifted, blowing a piercing screech across the darkened pre-dawn compound. Feeding time had started early in the realm of the siltempters.

Still dazed from emerging early from thoughtflow – the trance-like pseudo-sleep of the steammen – metal tribesmen began stumbling out of creeper-covered domes in the jungle in response to the din.

The commodore cast around for a direction free of awakening siltempters, but there was no clear passage that he could see. Razor-edged horrors were coming out from all directions. Roused by the noise outside, Queen Three-eyes pulled against her massive cast-iron chains down in the sand of the arena, her rage and fury roaring across the siltempter community.

Amelia was shivering when she awoke. A cold floor and the drip-drip-drip of water tapping at a puddle close to her head had replaced the warmth of the cramped bathysphere. Groaning, she turned over. She was in a large, grey room with smooth walls made out of some glossy substance she did not recognize. Behind her was the bathysphere, dripping water from its battered lake-weed-covered surface onto the floor – and the prone body of Bull Kammerlan stretched in its shadow.

How had they arrived here? There were no doorways or hatches visible in the chamber. It was as if someone had disassembled their vessel piece by piece, then rebuilt it in this place. That was the kind of prank that first-years loved to play on their professors. Stealing the giant clocks from the college towers and rebuilding them in one of the don's lecture rooms. But whoever had done this to them possessed no playful streak, she suspected. Amelia pulled herself up, ignoring the stiff pain of her limbs – had someone taken her to bits then put her back together, too? She lurched over to where Bull lay. She checked the pulse at his throat with her fingers – he was still warm. Still alive. The luck of a damn slaver.

Amelia looked around the chamber. No doors, no windows – the flat, gas-lightless walls were generating their own illumination somehow, with no visible source. Cupping the puddling water from the bathysphere she splashed it onto Bull's face. He blinked and she gave him another dousing, which had the intended effect.

'You back to normal, dimples?' Bull coughed.

'What do you mean?'

'You were laughing like a mad woman back on the boat, dragging us towards the mincing machine that had done for Tree-head Joe's vessels,' said Bull. 'I wasn't expecting to wake up at all, let alone in here. Where is "here" by the way?'

Her head hurt. She remembered the radiance of the stone circle under the water and the longing for it. But nothing else.

'I'll be cast off the Circle if I know where we are,' said Amelia. 'There doesn't appear to be any way to get inside here . . . or out again.'

Bull pulled himself up and laid his hands on the bathysphere, ducking his head under the hull to check its condition. There was a clunk as he popped the hatch, then he reappeared a minute later, brandishing a metal rod. It was a poor weapon, but it was all he could detach from the interior of their craft. 'The hatch was locked from the inside. I had to use the diver's emergency release to get into her – but someone got us out of the cabin, right enough.'

Amelia looked around. Something about the chamber –

something she could not quite put her finger on – reminded her of the seed-ship observation room she had been locked up in by the Daggish. But the walls down here were like nothing she had seen in the nest city. And if they had been returned to the not-so-tender clutches of the Daggish emperor without his precious crown to placate him, they were more likely to have woken up with moss fronds creeping down their throats and crawling inside their eardrums, than in this chill alien place. Yes, there was definitely something about this chamber. A sense of familiarity, as if she had visited here before.

'Here we are!' Amelia shouted into space. 'What are you doing with us?'

There was no reply. Bull snorted. 'Nobody visiting the zoo today, then?'

Amelia checked the collection nets behind the bathysphere. They had been emptied of all the debris she had collected from the bottom of the lake, but there were still fronds of wet lake weed wrapped around the wire mesh. Giving up on the boat, Amelia prowled the boundary of the chamber, feeling the walls for any sign of a hatch, an exit. When she approached the final side of the chamber, a section of the wall disappeared, simply dissolved as if it had never existed, the newly formed entrance revealing a corridor receding into absolute darkness. Jumping back in alarm, Amelia watched the wall become solid again as she moved away. Bull came running over, laying both of his hands on the section of the wall that had vanished. It was rock hard. Nothing happened as he thumped it. Amelia stepped forward and the wall vanished again, the corridor illuminating this time, as if it was encouraging her to enter.

'It likes you, girl,' said Bull.

Amelia glanced around the chamber holding the bathysphere. 'There's nothing for us here.'

'Well, I'm not staying around here on my lonesome,' said Bull, stepping closer to her, as if he was fearful that the wall might close up and leave him trapped behind.

'I thought you believed I was a Jonah?' said Amelia.

'Stuck in Circle-knows where, with half the Daggish fleet waiting for us at the other end, what would make you think that?' Bull said. 'Besides, I'm a practical man. Something created this – and it sure wasn't Tree-head Joe or the spirit of Lord Tridentscale. What was it you said about traps?'

'They mean treasure.'

'That's the part I like,' said Bull. 'You can tell me more about that.'

'They also mean death concealed in a hundred different cunning ways,' said Amelia, annoyed by his flippant tone. 'I've worked with a lot of people over the years – none of them have lasted the course.'

'Yeah, I can tell,' said Bull. 'But you haven't worked with a superior pedigree like mine before. I survived life in the fleet-in-exile, I survived working the river along Liongeli and the holding tanks of Bonegate. All this—' he gestured down the corridor '—is just meat on the bone to a man like me.'

'You're poured from the same pot as Jared Black,' said Amelia. 'I can see that much from your boasting.'

'He's a useless old man who gave up on what he believed in,' said Bull. 'That's not something I would ever do.'

Amelia indicated they should go into the corridor, the slaver first. 'The commodore cut his cloth to fit the times. I would take that as a sign of intelligence.'

A couple of seconds after they had passed through, the wall solidified behind them. She resisted the temptation to walk back and see if it would open as willingly for her again as it had when she had been inside the chamber.

Halfway down the corridor, and the air around them seemed

to be getting warmer – a tepid wind playing down the passageway. Amelia stopped, suspicious now, and checked the floor and the walls. They were as featureless as the chamber holding the bathysphere.

'What is it?' said Bull.

'It's getting hotter.'

'You expecting us to be chased down the corridor by a wall of fire?'

'At the very least.' She traced her hand across the wall, not quite enamel, not quite glass. 'No dust down here, no leaks of water, no dirt. Just like our chamber. This could have been cleaned a couple of minutes ago.'

'The walls here are a different colour,' said Bull, tapping the side of the passageway. 'It feels different to the touch too.'

The sides of the passage changed even more as they progressed down the corridor – from the strange smooth grey material to something that resembled green glass. Amelia was walking with her finger running down the cool surface when the glass turned completely transparent. Bull whirled around. Dazzling light flooded the corridor, multiple oblong-shaped sheets of green glass rotating on the other side of the now translucent wall. As they watched, the revolving oblong planes began to be filled with scenes, images and sounds of the world beyond – grey rain-filled clouds scudding over the pneumatic towers of Middlesteel, a drover leading a flock of geese down a small country lane. There was no order to the images, some familiar, others scenes from nations so exotic that Amelia could only guess at their identity.

'There's the town square at Coldkirk,' said Bull. 'I stayed there for a winter, when I was on the run from the crushers in Jackals.'

'And Cassarabia, too,' said Amelia. 'The royal water gardens at Bladetenbul. They're like the imagery from a crystal-book.'

She pressed her hand against the barrier. Not even a smear was left on the surface. 'But with this wall, I think it's the glass that holds the recording.'

Bull pointed at the scenes of Jackelian life floating on the sheared planes beyond. 'That's no ancient record from a crystal-book. That's happening *now*.'

As they moved further down the corridor the scenes began to transform. Subtle changes at first – streets from Jackelian cities, but with their fashions slightly off kilter – women wearing Quatérshiftian bonnets and soldiers on leave strutting about in brigade blue rather than the wine-red coats of the new pattern army. Further still, and the clothes changed to an austere parliamentarian cut, the kind of fashion favoured hundreds of years earlier – but updated in a sinister military style. The streets of Middlesteel grew darker, less colourful. The buildings taller and more imposing, but all individuality of dress vanishing from the citizenry – a sea of grey and black, as if everyone in the capital was serving in the army.

'What is this?' hissed Bull. 'This isn't Jackals.'

Amelia's head had begun to throb again. 'It is. Look at the streets, the buildings. It's the capital.'

In the vision floating in front of them, a massive roaring sounded from the crowds lining the boulevard, the silhouettes of a fleet of airships thrumming across the sky. Their hulls were not painted in the chequerboard colours of the RAN, but were instead pitch black, apart from a single circle filled with a blood-red gate – the gate of parliament, solitary, without the lion that flew on the true flag of Jackals. Along the boulevard marched the Special Guard – black cloaks instead of red, their muscled arms wearing armbands bearing the same crimson gate that adorned the aerostats. Their sweeping march, so precise and strong, was made menacing in this vision. Stamping the road, shaking the street. Between their ranks were carts loaded with cages full of prisoners – starved, broken wretches still wearing the rags of other nations – Cassarabian gowns, Catosian togas, Kikkosicoan ponchos. The crowd bayed their hate, soldiers accompanying the carts striking through the bars with their whips when the mob had roared loud enough to be rewarded with blood.

A Cassarabian woman hidden under black robes shielded her daughter, the whip cracking across her back. 'Whip the child,' someone yelled from the pavement. The call was taken up by the mob until one of the Special Guardsmen yanked the mother back to expose her ten-year-old girl to their fury.

'No,' Amelia moaned, 'that's not us, that's not Jackals.' Her words were lost in the fury of the vision, a sea of standards bobbing in front of her tear-stained eyes, each bearing an eagle clinging to the sharpened teeth of parliament's gate.

'What is this cursed place?' said Bull.

Words came to Amelia in answer, but it was as if they were drawn deep from something ancient lurking within her. 'These are the corridors of else-when, that which might have been, the resonance of the parallel path.'

Bull stumbled past a revolving plane where cavalrymen with royalist feathers in their caps galloped past a burning hamlet; huddles of refugees mixed with suspected Leveller insurgents watching their lives disappear in a furnace of heat. 'These are visions sent to drive us insane.'

'No, this is the great pattern that the people of the metal talk about, but alternative threads on it. The same story told by different authors, with endings just as diverse.'

'Who would do this thing?' asked Bull. 'Create this hall of horrors?'

'I think this is for humility,' said Amelia. 'To remind us that we always have choices and our choices have consequences. To be mindful of the harm that we might cause others.'

Bull gazed hypnotized by the plane he was watching. A royalist regime, killing and burning and punishing any dissent displayed towards the whims of a dark queen. He could not bear to look at the coat of arms worn by the secret police tossing the night's curfew breakers into the torture rooms at Ham Yard – not the hedgehog symbol of the honest crushers of Middlesteel, but the unicorn and lion of his mother's house. *His* house.

'We ruled for the people,' whispered Bull, 'for them, not over them.'

The two of them pushed deeper down the corridor, trying to avoid looking at the walls now, catching only glimpses as the scenes deviated further and further from the comfortably reassuring world they knew. A Jackals filled with craynarbians, polishing their exo-skeletons while their cousins from the race of man laboured in the fields, clad only in slaves' loincloths and shivering under the overseers' whips. A Middlesteel empty and abandoned, the capital's streets buried by ice and snow – the coldtime returned early to make a world of frozen emptiness. Then a land of sands blowing in hot from a furnace sun, only the tip of the solitary bell tower of Brute Julius protruding from the drifting desert to mark the fact that this world had ever been inhabited at all – a lone figure in Cassarabian sand-rider's garb on his knees in front of the lost tower, praying to the hundred aspects of the blessed Cent. No green and pleasant realm for Jackals here, just a sea of endless dunes.

At last the corridor of cruel possibilities came to an end, opening out onto a colossal chamber. The vista reminded Amelia of the Chimecan undercity beneath Middlesteel in its scale, but the statues carved into the entrance wall behind them were far more ancient, and the valley before them was not filled with the massive fungal forests of Middlesteel-below, but an entirely different kind of woodland. Mounds of living machines! Some, bamboo fields of tentacles and throbbing anthills, others spreading out from oak-sized limbs to form an undulating canopy.

Bull's arm rose as he found his metal rod from the bathysphere tugging itself towards a small orange sun burning in the sky above them.

'The sun is trying to snatch my club.'

Amelia shook her head. 'It's no true sun. It's a source of power, like an expansion engine or a steam boiler. There's a field of magnetism containing it – release your club.'

Bull opened his fingers and the rod left his hand, spinning out and up towards the sun; a minute later there was a tiny splash of light as it hit the surface of the globe and was incinerated.

'Are you possessed again, Guardian's daughter?'

No,' said Amelia. 'It's as if I know this already. It's as if all of this is a memory.'

She turned to look at the pair of statues shielding the entrance to the corridor of visions. Carved out of white stone, they were heavily stylized, cubist arms joining together to hold up a roll of parchment above the door.

'The twins. Knowledge standing on the left, and the wisdom to use it appropriately standing on the right.'

'If you can "remember" a way out of here that doesn't involve us being pursued by half the greenmesh, I would consider that mighty useful,' said Bull.

Her mind was filling with information. As if her existence here was awakening long-dormant memories of a house she had once lived in. But this was an ancient place. She had never seen anything like it – not in the university archives, not in the crystal-books her father had saved from the bailiffs' clutches and left to her. So how could all this seem so familiar?

'Through that forest of machines,' said Amelia. 'Our way lays through there.'

'Isn't there another track?' asked Bull. 'Even a corridor showing more horrors of the might-have-been . . .?'

She shook her head.

'It's the spit of Tree-head Joe's throne room down there—'

Was that where she had seen this before? No. Her memory wasn't from the chambers of the Daggish hive. It came from somewhere deeper.

'There's a reason for that. I think the Daggish are the feral descendants of the Camlanteans' living machines. Not much of a legacy to leave behind, are they? This is the way. Let's follow my instincts,' said Amelia, stepping down the slope towards the machine forest.

Bull sighed. 'And it looks like I'm still following you.'

He cast his eyes around nervously as the two of them entered the forest. While the engineering of the Daggish had seemed bone-like and shell hard, the machine forest was smooth and organic, tentacles extruding from trunks to stroke other machines – exchanging information and function, then reshaping to whatever exotic design they were working to. Delicate transparent devices like butterflies fluttered between the various limbs of the organic machines, orange light glinting off their milky scales. There was a spray like dew raining from somewhere overhead, keeping the living engineering cool and supple. Some of it fell on Amelia's face and she tasted it on her lips. Sweet, sugary – it contained the nourishment the growing flesh needed to renew itself. Renewing it forever, perhaps, or for as long as the manufactured sun providing it with life-giving light continued to burn in its magnetic hearth.

The two of them pushed through the forest, deeper into the dream-like realm. Amelia's dream. She was close now, she could feel it with every iota of her being, and the determination of seeing her life's work fulfilled drove her further into the alien land.

Billy Snow pulled the spear out of the wall of the building, the witch-blade shifting back to its sabre form, quivering in delight at having tasted the system oil of the impaled siltempter.

The first tribesman to have been roused by the arena's whistle leapt at Ironflanks, but the scout had anticipated the move and closed in, using the momentum of the siltempter's attack to twist him about, slamming him down into the mud. One of Ironflanks' four arms punched in, piercing the siltempter's hull and bursting his boiler heart.

Commodore Black scooped up the dying creature's machete attachment, brandishing it like a crab's claw, as if just its presence was enough to avert the charge of siltempters running towards them. 'There!' He pointed to a section of the jungle wall still clear of fighters. 'Run for that, my brave boys.'

Glancing around, the commodore saw Ironflanks racing away from them, towards the arena. 'What are you doing? This way.'

'It is time,' shouted Ironflanks as he sprinted towards where the thunder lizards' keeper had died. 'Time to make amends for my thread on the pattern.'

Commodore Black cursed the steamman. Had the Hexmachina's expiry from this plane of existence sent Ironflanks off the deep six?

Billy Snow moved in front of T'ricola; cutting the head off the spear a siltempter was using to try to disembowel the craynarbian. They were ancient enemies, the siltempters and the craynarbians, living shell-to-hull as they did in the depths of Liongeli. The mutate steammen knew every trick of piercing craynarbian shells, breaking them open like lobsters and

368

bringing them pain. Snow's blade dipped low and the siltempter fell forward, all three of his tripod of legs severed below the knee joints, three spears left sticking up from the mud while the decapitated body twitched unbelieving in front of T'ricola.

Commodore Black reached the building overlooking the arena. Its door had been staved in and was hanging off its hinges. Inside, the warmth of the previous day had been preserved within its thick walls. Ironflanks was standing in front of a plane of transparent crystal overlooking the arena floor. The steamman heaved at a wheel set on a panel, looking nothing so much as the master of a vessel, trying to turn the building about onto a new course. Commodore Black caught a glimpse of the arena below. Something like a drawbridge was dropping towards the sand and the commodore suddenly understood what the steamman was doing. Exactly how he intended to make up for his perceived sins on the great pattern.

'Ironflanks, you idiot of a steamer, you cannot . . .'

'Oh, but I can!' Ironflanks said. 'My waters are hot, commodore softbody, and now I'm running fit to boil.'

Beyond the screen of glass, the head of Queen Three-eyes hove into view – her single ruined pit and three good eyes focusing on the steamman behind the glass. She roared her contempt of the siltempters, that these little metal devils could chain her, starve her and think that her will could be broken by such artifice. As she howled her rage, the panicked echoes of the other thunder lizards held in the arena joined her in a nervous chorus.

'*Metaljiggermetaljiggerwillwillwillyoufightmefight-memememeinthesandsandsand?*'

'I spent very little time in the court of the Steamman Free State,' shouted Ironflanks, 'but this I do know – a queen should never be humbled before a prince.'

'Don't be doing this,' pleaded the commodore. 'Have we not got enough blessed problems to be dealing with?'

Ironflanks punched the switch that released the chains on the kilasaurus max. Somewhere deeper in the building an alarm claxon sounded. Outside there was a whistling noise as the k-max wrenched her newly unlocked chains out of their stake rings so fast that they were sent flying across the arena sands, lashing into a series of benches in the wall and smashing them to splinters. Chains fell off the other lizards in the shadows of the stadium pit, steel teeth in the ground clanking open.

'Freemefreemefreeme?' Queen Three-eyes appeared astonished by the actions of her mortal enemy.

Commodore Black backed away from the viewing gallery; terrified the k-max would smash the glass and scoop them out. The steamman seemed to welcome such a fate, standing there with his four arms outstretched, as if he was beseeching Queen Three-eyes to end his aimless life.

It was a dreadful act of symmetry. Ironflanks had been cut from his life's purpose and the wreckage of his duty in the jungles of Liongeli – and now he had done the same for the queen of the thunder lizards. Killing Ironflanks was all that Queen Three-eyes had lived for since she had lost her life-mate, and now she was being offered the life of her mate's murderer on a plate.

'We are both free,' whispered Ironflanks' voicebox. 'We are both free, now.'

Queen Three-eyes looked across the arena at her fellow thunder lizards stampeding for the lowered ramp while it remained open, crunching underfoot the massive bleached bones of their brethren who had been captured before them, made to starve to sharpen their appetite for the games. Her sly eyes narrowed in a cold fury, the sting of oily smoke from these metal devils' stacks a foul affront to the natural scents of the jungle. This was not the way of things. Other thunder lizards bowed before her and backed away from the claw marks on the plateaux that surrounded her territory. It was time to remind these metal intruders why *she* was the monarch of Liongeli.

Ironflanks followed Commodore Black back outside the arena building, the first of the thunder lizards to stampede – a tauntoraptor – thumping geysers of mud into the air as it pawed the ground and lowered its horned head towards the siltempters, the metal tribesmen thrown into confusion by the release of the arena animals.

Some of the siltempters had been trying to outflank blind Billy Snow and his deadly morphic blade and noticed the new arrivals too late – outflanked themselves. They tried to throw themselves out of the way of a charging pentaceratops, but delayed by fatal seconds, the bone-clawed hooves flattened their hulls in a pop of splitting steel and cracking crystal. Behind them more rampaging beasts followed, a petrodactyl scooping up a fleeing tribesman and lifting him high in the air before skimming the creature down towards a rocky outcrop, the brief explosion of his breeched boiler sending a shower of shrapnel across the jungle clearing.

Into this carnage strode the queen of Liongeli, her scaly skin flashing orange where the fires of broken siltempters burned in the pre-dawn light. A company of siltempters appeared with airguns, monstrously large iron barrels with ancient cables connected to the pressure of their own boilers. Heavy ammunition drums jangled on top of the guns, hundreds of lead balls queuing for gravity to drop them into barrels and speed them on their deadly duty. With a roar like splintering wood, the siltempters opened fire on the nearest thunder lizards, peppering the beasts with streams of hot lead while other creatures of the metal ran out with poison-tipped javelins, sharp injector reservoirs ready to jet concentrated shots of flying-fish toxin into the flanks of the huge, marauding creatures. A tauntoraptor swung its tail at the group of siltempters bringing it pain with their hail of tiny, stinging stones, sending three of them soaring back into the tree line with their chests crumpled and bleeding oil.

'Time to withdraw,' shouted Veryann, surveilling the siltempters as they emerged with increasingly heavy weaponry dug out from their jungle domes and the dark chambers of the temple. The siltempters' defences were concentrated in a ring around their territory and the released arena creatures had bypassed all of them; but the expedition's luck wasn't going to last forever. The siltempters were regrouping fast.

Ironflanks, still disorientated by the twists and turns of his fate, stumbled over a dead tribesman. 'This way, the river.' His words were interspersed with his voicebox's whistles and cries, the stampeding thunder lizards answering with similar calls, a few even moving out of his way – as if he was a calf of their own kind, to be treated with patience. The tree-high legs of a vulcanodon thumped past, revealing a group of trampled siltempter corpses half-buried in the mud. One of the bodies was still moving, trying to pull itself free while dragging two ruined legs, the alloy of both limbs burst and fizzing with the effort of hauling himself along.

Veryann recognized the corpulent form and the frog-like features of the face. 'Good morning, my prince.'

She pulled one of the poison-headed javelins free from the dirt, brushing down the mud from its shaft. Prince Doublemetal gazed up at the softbody standing over him, his vision plate pulsing in recognition at those who should have been the morning's entertainment in the arena.

'You don't have to do this,' said Billy Snow. 'We are different from their kind.'

'The difference is the free company's code,' said Veryann. 'And that demands vengeance against those who fight without honour.'

'Blood only begets blood,' said the sonar man.

'That it certainly does.' Veryann knelt down before the slowly moving body. 'And I made you a blood oath yesterday, my prince. Do you recall what I said, or were you too busy salivating oil over the crushed remains of Gabriel McCabe to listen to me?'

Prince Doublemetal tried to raise the volume on his voicebox and call for help, but only a burst of static emerged.

'Gabriel would not have asked for this,' said Billy Snow.

'The prince can ask him himself,' said Veryann, 'in the unlikely event his putrid soul should be granted entrance to the hall of the fallen.' She lifted the lance and leveraged it through the gap in the prince's hull where his left leg was hanging off, sliding it up hard through his abdomen. Her shine-swollen muscles bulged as she used every last iota of her strength to drive her makeshift stake inside the body of the siltempters' ruler. With a squawk, the crawling prince fell still, smoke pouring through the joints where his crushed legs clung uselessly to his body.

A roar echoed over the stampede, Queen Three-eyes, entering the jungle to crush the camouflaged geodesic domes of the camp, gutta-percha plates shattering as the enraged kilasaurus max slammed against them, terrified siltempters cowering inside as she scooped them out. Veryann nodded in approval at the butchery and tore the House of Quest's fencibles' badge from her tattered war jacket, shoving it inside the mouth slash of Prince Doublemetal's voicebox. So that they would know who had done this. And why. Not a rogue arena

373

animal, but the forces of the free company. Her payment for the slaughter of the strongest man in Jackals.

With the siltempters' community being torn apart by the creatures they had once tortured for their amusement, the five officers of the *Sprite* vanished in the confusion, leaving the crash of falling trees and the explosions of bursting siltempters behind them.

The cool, dark rainforest swallowed them up.

There was a discernible difference between the territory that fell on the siltempter side of the border and the greenmesh, a difference that went beyond the peculiar silence of the terrain controlled by the Daggish. In their realm, the jungle grew neater, to a pattern. Still wild, but with a purpose that was lacking outside their dominion.

Commodore Black was the first to comment on it. 'We might as well be walking through some wicked, wild green out here – like Peddler's Piece back in the heart of Middlesteel, but laid out by a deranged groundsman.'

'Peddler's Piece never felt like this dark place,' said T'ricola. 'It makes me itch. Everything about it feels wrong – corrupt.'

'Your instincts serve you well,' said Ironflanks. 'In Liongeli, craynarbians are born with the knowledge that coming close to this land means certain death.' The lack of animal calls was setting the steamman's nerves even more on edge than usual – no whistle-song of the birds of the canopy, no growls from hunting cats.

'I'm glad my moulting skin has proved of some practical use,' said T'ricola, 'beyond my sharp new sword bone for hacking back the bush.'

Billy Snow was at the head of the party, now. Ever since they had reached the edge of the greenmesh, it was as if the sonar man had acquired a whole new set of senses, leading them across trails where the massive tree-like sentries of the Daggish had been marching only minutes before. Stopping them in silence at times – sometimes for up to an hour – waiting tensely in the Liongeli heat, moisture rolling down their skins, shell and boiler, while the u-boat man sat cross-legged, meditating on the best path to take. No one commented on this unnatural turn of events, not even Ironflanks, who had warned them it was next to impossible to penetrate the greenmesh by land without alerting the Daggish – without coming across some creature or sentient plant cluster that would pass on its warning to the others in the hive.

Billy Snow might have been denied the services of the *Sprite* to steal them into the waters of Lake Ataa Naa Nyongmo, but he was acting as his own sonar now, a living echo sounder. It was said that craynarbian witch doctors possessed the ability to dream walk into the territory of the Daggish without becoming absorbed into their living empire. But as for old Billy, where had he acquired such a talent? While Billy Snow was still in meditation, Ironflanks set his voicebox to low, whispering his suspicions that the sonar man was using a witch doctor's skills to lead them past the nodes of self-aware jungle that would have alerted the hive to their presence. Nobody seemed willing to raise this with Billy, as if questioning his strange ability might awaken him from his dream and bring Daggish patrols crashing down around the expedition.

Only Veryann appeared to have qualms, her body language revealing the suspicions she harboured towards Billy Snow. But perhaps that was the Catosian way? Trust nothing save that which can be slit with a dagger. His abnormal flowering of abilities was not to be trusted, at least not until it could be understood.

When they reached the course of the Shedarkshe, Billy raised a finger to his mouth. He had led them within a stone's throw of a seed ship, moored against a pier that looked as if it had flowed out of the skeleton of a hippopotamus that had expired in the water. It was a small vessel of its type – just the right size to carry a border patrol of Daggish warrior drones to the edge of the greenmesh. Or to take the five of them into the heart of enemy territory. Billy pointed to the seed ship and held up three fingers: three Daggish crew left on board.

'If we attack, won't these fiendish creatures be able to call for help?' whispered the commodore.

Billy Snow shook his head. No. He did not voice it, but his meditations had a more practical purpose than merely stilling his noisy mind.

They were fast across the bone-hard pier when the first of the enemy sailors appeared from an iris hatch at the rear of the vessel. It was unarmed and clearly not expecting to blunder into five impure animals not blessed with the harmony of their hive mind. But then, why should the race of man be trespassing on Daggish territory? Creatures such as these were dragged screaming and fighting to their absorption chambers. They did not venture near the Daggish of their own inferior will.

It had barely begun to chatter an alarm when it realized it could no longer communicate with the others on the ship, Billy Snow's witch-blade – in sabre form now – slashing through the bark-like torso of the thing, cleaving its sensory organs from its trunk and hewing the drone in half. The two drones inside the craft were quicker to realize that they were no longer in communication with the others of the coopera- tive – the death of their comrade outside suddenly registering on their consciousness – and filled the air with the hammering of their native tongue. Drones had a reflex fear of being out of contact with their fellows. A healthy survival instinct, to stop them from wandering away from the protection of the hive. They knew enough to recognize that they were under assault, though, and one of the drones had the wherewithal to scurry to the wall where the patrol's spare flame squirts were racked.

It had just pulled the sack-pipe-shaped weapon off the wall when the intruders burst into the cabin, Billy Snow tracing a fatal gash across the creature's bark-thick chest, before pirouetting and ripping down to sever the weapon's combustion sack. The dying Dagga tried to trigger its gun but the weapon made an empty hissing noise like an angry cat, the floor puddling with its unlit ammunition.

T'ricola charged the other Dagga, her bone-knife arm swinging in an angry arc and taking a wedge out of the drone, all the pent-up chemical anger of her body's changes releasing itself in a sudden flurry of strikes. The Dagga stumbled back, shaken – no soldier caste fighter this, but a symbiote navigator for the living boat. Veryann finished the drone off from behind, driving her machete through its brain-bulb and letting the thing fall to the cabin floor, the chattering inside its trunk dying away as its hammer-like tonsils lost their life force.

'The patrol may be back any second,' said Veryann, lifting an intact flame weapon from the wall.

'They are a long way from the boat,' said Billy, 'and that weapon you have taken will not work for you. It has a mechanism inside it that serves a similar purpose to a Jackelian blood-code machine – it will fire only for members of the hive.'

'There's a cunning thing,' said the commodore. He kicked the deck of the seed ship. 'A clever race would make sure this strange seahorse of a craft operated in a similar way.'

'It does,' said Ironflanks. 'It will not travel the Shedarkshe for us.' The steamman pointed to the dead navigator drone lying sprawled across the floor. 'Only for one of those.'

'The seed ship has a brain,' said Billy Snow. 'A wonderful thing, grown from a nubbin no larger than a ha'penny. Right about *here*.' Billy's witch-blade cut down, fizzing with delight as it sliced open the living decking, then transforming itself into a trident which the sonar man plunged down through the opening. The ship trembled at the strike, the trident's fangs growing longer and penetrating deep into the nautical creature. Water churned up from the rear of the craft, bone-like hydro tubes convulsing with misery as it emptied propulsive air behind their stern, pulling against the pier's anchorage. The craft grew still as the witch-blade extended into the boat's brain matrix, poisoning and infiltrating the seed ship, much as the Daggish subverted other creatures into their own hive. Turnabout was fair play, it seemed.

'The craft is ours now,' said Billy.

'How are you doing this?' demanded T'ricola. 'That witch-blade of yours is no sword that ever saw the shores of Thar.'

'This vessel and its breed were made to serve people, once, not the other way around. It just needed to be reminded.'

'Will your blessed seahorse carry us to Lake Ataa Naa Nyongmo?' Commodore Black asked. 'Will it carry us, Billy Snow, without alerting the other seed ships and Daggish to our presence?'

'I believe it will,' said Billy. 'Although we should rip some vegetation from the shore first to rub over us, if we want to pass for Daggish slaves at a distance.' He looked at Ironflanks. 'And you will have to stay out of sight at all times. These creatures possess no means to absorb steammen within their hive – or siltempters, for that matter.'

'It is almost as if you have been absorbed by the Daggish already, Billy softbody,' said Ironflanks. 'The House of Quest might have been better advised to have contracted you for your services as a guide, rather than a u-boat man.'

378

Billy Snow pointed to his milky unseeing eyes. 'Who would trust a blind pathfinder, old steamer?'

'Who indeed?' said Veryann. 'Does your mysterious new-found reserve of knowledge extend to whether the *Sprite* and her mutinous crew have already achieved the expedition's objective and sailed back past us on the Shedarkshe?'

'The *Sprite* has not sailed back down the river,' said Billy. 'I fear that things have not gone too well for the u-boat.'

'My boat. My precious *Sprite*,' moaned the commodore. 'Don't say that she is wrecked at the end of this river of damned souls?'

'It is not the u-boat's condition I speak of,' said the old sonar man. 'It's our crew's. Apart from those standing in this cabin, I can sense only two other souls from the race of man unabsorbed by the Daggish. And speaking frankly, they don't appear to be holding up too well at the moment!'

Two Catosian soldiers escorted Cornelius down a corridor along the airship's starboard side. The exploration vessel had stopped moving now, the immense aerostat holding station at whatever position they had reached. The portholes along the gallery offered little clue to their location – save the fact that they were high. Clouds drifted far below them on the other side of the iced-up glass, the heavens were birdless, and the airship's jack cloudies wore woollen jerseys over their striped sailors' shirts. Little puffs of warm fresh air were injected from grilles in the ceiling every couple of minutes, followed by a wheeze like an old man as stale air was withdrawn. Unfortunately for Cornelius, Septimoth and Damson Beeton weren't there with him to speculate on where in the heavens they had ended up – they had been left behind in the brig when the guards came for him.

At one point, Cornelius and his escort passed a small glass

dome set in the hull, a sailor on a metal gangway using a gas-fired heliograph to flash messages across to one of their sister ships hanging in the firmament. The scope clacked as fresh communications landed in a wire basket from a pneumatic tube. Along from the signal station, Cornelius got the briefest glimpse of a hangar filled with engineers working in the shadow of something that looked like nothing so much as an oversized hencoop – a long queue of large iron capsules lined up inside racks, in place of eggs. Now, that was odd. An airship's fin bombs were made of crystal to contain the acidic blow-barrel sap, two chambers separated by a thin glass membrane in mimicry of the violently explosive tree seeds. Those capsules couldn't be fin bombs. The metal would corrode, detonating at random. What was this rogue airship fleet of Quest's up to? The shove of the guards' rifle butts hurried Cornelius past the open hatch. Had Robur constructed a legion of primitive steammen fighting machines to drop on Jackals, to make its people bend their knee to whatever strange Camlantean philosophy-religion his master Abraham Quest had uncovered in his crystal-books?

Cornelius was led to a portal with a pair of sentries waiting outside. The guards swung open the heavy doors – polished Jackelian oak – to reveal a stately dining room positioned underneath the airship's bridge. There was a substantial glass nose cone at the far end with panes of glass curving across the floor between embedded girder rails, allowing guests to stare down onto the clouds when the conversation stalled. There was only one diner – Abraham Quest – but a host of staff scurried around under the watchful gaze of Catosian free company fighters lining the wall.

Cornelius indicated the sentries standing guard over their master of the air. 'Are you expecting one of your crew to murder you?'

'You think me paranoid?' said Quest. 'Well, perhaps. But the Court of the Air may still have infiltrators working undetected among my staff.'

'I doubt it.'

'What makes you think that?' said Quest.

'The fact that we are still afloat. The Court's wolftakers are nothing if not thorough.'

Quest indicated the chair at the other end of the table. 'Perhaps they will be kind enough to allow us to finish our supper before crashing us.'

'A large table,' said Cornelius, 'for only two diners.'

'I had to construct the *Leviathan* and her sister stats under the pretence that they were proving craft for a new generation of RAN warships,' Quest apologized. 'My airship was to be a flagship design – while this was to be the captain's table, serving formal dinners for the crew's officers and visiting dignitaries. The Royal Aerostatical Navy does so love its ritual and its pomp. And foreigners are so easily impressed by the swell of our canvas hulls and the glint of shells from our fin-bomb bays.'

'The navy doesn't have airship hangars large enough to dock a craft of this size,' said Cornelius, watching as a seat was pulled out for him by one of the retainers.

'Admiralty House are planning a new statodrome,' said Quest. 'The invasion by Quatérshift and the ease with which they and their revolutionary allies seized our airship fields around Shadowclock unnerved the navy. They are planning to use Veneering's Rock as their new base of operations.'

'Veneering's Rock?' Cornelius frowned. That was next to impossible. A mile of prime Pentshire land ripped out by the Earth's fury and left to hang about the county, its heavy granite base keeping it locked above the downs, the land beneath dark in the shadow of the floatquake. There had been a famous cartoon forty years ago, in the *Middlesteel Illustrated News*. The head of the Jackelian order of worldsingers – the sorcerers whose first function was to tame the raging leylines – standing directly underneath the shadow of the sundered land, his hand cupped over his forehead searchingly; the speech bubble reading: *'I see no problem?'*

'The Levellers don't support the scheme, but the Purist members of parliament are pushing for it anyway. The expense will be prodigious, but for a fortress reachable only by airship, immune to the brigades of the People's Army of the Commonshare . . .'

'It's just a bigger stick,' said Cornelius.

'I thought you might approve – or do you prefer something less blunt to beat the shifties with; someone like Furnace-breath Nick, perhaps?'

In front of Cornelius, a retainer lifted the silver lid on a platter of roast pork floating in cider gravy. 'Furnace-breath Nick is feared by the revolution.'

'I think our conversation is coming back to where we were in my orchid house, before we were so rudely interrupted,' said Quest. 'A single man cannot fight an idea. Only another belief can slay an idea.'

'You sound like your toad Robur,' said Cornelius.

'He took very little persuading to join me,' said Quest. 'Anyone who has survived the hell of an organized community knows what the race of man is capable of, knows we have to change our nature if we are to prevent such atrocities repeating themselves with tedious inevitability. He is really very similar to you, in his aspirations.'

'Robur is nothing like me. He was only kept alive because the First Committee wanted him working on the revolution's revenge weapons. They needed his skills, much as you seem to.'

'He's an exceptionally clever man,' said Quest. 'In his own field of expertise, he makes my knowledge and advancements appear as those of a state school foundling in comparison.'

'Why?' Cornelius asked. 'Why do you need the Sun King's old court mechomancer? Is he helping you in your mad search for Camlantis?'

'In a manner of speaking,' said the mill owner. 'When you join me, I shall tell you.'

'Camlantis,' Cornelius tasted the word. 'Do you realize how insane that sounds? A lost land, a city that historians will tell you never existed at all.'

'It existed,' insisted Quest. 'Listen to me, Cornelius Fortune, Furnace-breath Nick, Compte de Spééler. I have studied all that we know about history and pre-history in the hope that I could learn lessons that might stop us repeating the errors of our past in the present. Everything I have found is the same cycle of war and devastation, for as far back as time is recorded. You think the blood of the revolution in Quatérshift you nearly drowned in is exceptional? Sadly, it is the norm. Every age has its Commonshare. The invasion of Jackals five summers ago, the Two-Year War, the civil war in Jackals six hundred years before that. Go back sixteen hundred years and you'll find the Chimecans ruling the continent from their underground holds and treating the frozen nations of the surface as nothing but food for their table. Every age, Cornelius, every age produces blood and famine and needless suffering. All save one. One brief glimmer of sanity where a group of people worked together in understanding and peace and achieved the closest thing to paradise the world has ever seen, before or since. Isn't such a world worth the search?'

'It won't work,' said Cornelius. His artificial arm was shaking with anger, the reworked mechanism unable to cope with the surge of emotions in its owner. 'It never does. Sink me, but I do believe you are quite insane.'

'Are you so sure in your prejudices?' Quest shook his head sadly. 'This is how you will defeat the great terror in Quatérshift. Not by the stalking of their committeemen and Carlists, but with a rival idea. The truth of Camlantis shall set the world free. You need to decide who you are and what your destiny is. Is it to end the horrors of revolution once and for all – or is it merely to torture those who once tortured you?' Quest lifted the mask of Furnace-breath Nick out from under the table. 'Are you Cornelius Fortune, or are you this? The man, or the monster?'

'This one doesn't deserve me,' whispered the mask. *'He is a butcher, not a swordsman.'*

None of the retainers was prepared for their guest's reaction. Cornelius shoved the table back, sending a soup tureen spilling over the glass of the viewing gallery.

'My face!' Cornelius lunged across the table, trying to claw at Quest. 'Give me back my face!'

On a hair-trigger already, the Catosian free company soldiers rushed forward and dragged Cornelius back. He kicked down, shattering one of the guard's knees with the heel of his boot, lunging out to try to stave in another's windpipe with the flat of his palm. She blocked the move and her comrades piled in, raining blows down with their rifle butts as Cornelius's fierce struggle ebbed away under their assault. They pulled him up, bruised and bloodied, and gasped as they saw his face had changed. It was now an exact simulacrum of Abraham Quest's own.

'The Catgibbon was right,' said Quest. 'You *are* a shape switcher. It's astounding the consideration Cassarabia's womb mages show when it comes to ensuring the caliph's rivals fall to his assassins' blades. And I understand your lineage is half-Jackelian, too. Imagine what you could do if both your parents had been blood-twisted. You were created with quite a gift, Compte de Spééler.'

'Isn't this what *you* wanted to create?' Cornelius snarled across the table at Abraham Quest. 'A twin of you, dreaming your dreams of an unachievable utopia. A compliant servant of the House of Quest, following behind your toad Robur to murder any vision save that which you have imagined first?'

'It's quite unnerving to see your own face contorted with rage, drooling spittle on someone else's skull,' Quest said.

Cornelius groaned with frustration as he tried to twist out of the soldiers' grip.

'Take me back, old friend,' hissed the mask. *'I'll make you strong. Strong enough to kill them all.'*

'This is *you*,' screamed Cornelius. 'This *is* your face. You give me back my face and I'll return yours.'

Quest sighed. 'So this really is all you are, the monster over the man.'

Cornelius tried to struggle free and nearly managed to escape his captors' grip, until he was winded by the fresh slam of rifle butts. The pain pacified him for a moment only. 'You're the monster, Quest. I've hunted enough of your kind across the border to have smelt your stench before. The smell of a new order approaching, and the blood in the fields, all the bones sticking out of the mud.'

'Take him back to his cell with the lashlite. Don't allow him anywhere near the Court of the Air's agent in the brig. Damson Beeton is dangerous enough as she is, without this madman's help.'

'Don't leave me,' pleaded the mask. *'This one is full of light and he burns so bright. I need to breathe the shadows.'*

It took five of the Catosian women to pull Cornelius away, his legs flailing as their shine-enhanced muscles bulged, restraining him with all their unnatural strength. The prisoner's counterfeit Quest-face was distorted in fury. 'Let me go back to my tree, Quest! I want to go back to my beautiful tree, my wife, and I want my face back; so full of light, burning. You're burning, burning—'

Then he was gone, his cries echoing fainter and fainter in the corridor outside, the two great doors cutting off his howls of anger with a heavy thump. The retainers busied themselves, cleaning up the spilled food and blood that had fallen across the observation glass. One of the staff lifted up the upset tureen. 'Tree . . . what tree was he talking about?'

Quest stood up from the table, wiping the soup off his shirt, and laid a reassuring hand on the retainer's shoulder. 'I doubt if we will ever know – or understand if we did.'

He lifted up the mask of Furnace-breath Nick, examining it from different angles, as if the answer lay in the sigils painted on its surface. Shaking his head he put the devil's mask down and left the chamber.

'And he had the audacity to think me insane.'

Amelia was starting to believe the deranged ramblings of that old hag in Cassarabia and the prognostications of Rapalaw Junction's witch doctor. If her life had a purpose, a point, a fixed resolution on the Circle, then investigating the strange pocket world they had been transported to from under the lake in the ruins of Camlantis was it. She reined herself in. When you started believing your own press in the penny dreadfuls, that was when you got sloppy . . . and sloppy in her trade meant a trapdoor falling onto a chute lined with steel stakes.

Amelia glanced across at Bull Kammerlan. 'The ruler of the Daggish seemed convinced its crown is down here. Let's see if we can find it.'

Bull glanced around. 'Which way?'

Under the land's artificial sun, her sense of direction wasn't as good as it normally was – but a part of her knew where they should be heading all the same. This was quite disconcerting. Did birds feel the same way when they quit a Jackelian winter for warmer climes, or did they just accept the knowledge of direction and the urge to travel, like they accepted the impulse to feed on an empty belly? At the edge of the forest the throbbing, waxy skin of the living machines gave way to a slope covered with structures that seemed to glisten on the hillside – an architecture that had last been seen on the surface of the world many thousands of years ago.

'There's a city,' said Bull, 'an entire city down here.'

Amelia sighed. 'Not quite.'

From their elevation she could see the entrance to other unexplored chambers beyond the floating, simulated sun. So, what lay through those? The two of them could explore for weeks down here, although with only the sugary rain for nourishment, Amelia suspected that her body would give out on her before her thirst for exploration did.

They walked closer to the city facing them, its architecture shimmering as their perspective changed; but *what* an architecture – as much art, as construction – raised from tiny germs of life and grown in accordance with long-lost principles of harmony, a perfect balance of space and light. Not meant to overwhelm like the palladian extravagance of the richer quarters of Middlesteel, nor thrown together out of hard necessity like the capital's poverty-stricken slums. This organic city possessed sweeps and curves that made the habitation of it as natural as living in a forest; brief glimpses of such places in a crystal-book could never equal the actual experience of walking through its boulevards.

Bull Kammerlan ran his hand through the wall of one of

the fluted towers, the sides flickering as his fingers passed through the material. 'A ghost town! But I can feel the surface.'

Amelia placed her own hand on a wall, the tower shivering as her fingers passed completely through it, horizontal transparency lines flickering while she walked along. She might have been running her hands through a waterfall, but she could feel the surface too: a resin – oaken wood that had been blended with the properties of a synthetic metal when it grew. Natural, but as hard as a steamman knight's hull. 'These ghosts remember. The projection contains the memory of what once was.'

'Projection?' Bull peered around them. 'This is a magic lantern show?'

'No,' said Amelia wistfully. 'The magic disappeared a long time ago. This is what is left of a dream. Unfortunately, I rather think the dream is mine.'

'There're no people in this projection,' said Bull. 'What's the point of a city with no people?'

'I noticed that too.'

Amelia did not say that the ghosts of this place could not bear to remember the missing, a whole civilization, as shining a zenith as the race of man had ever climbed – a million or more people who had sacrificed themselves so their legacy would not be corrupted.

She led them through the not-so-solid memories of what had once been, compensating for the tricks of perspective as the city rebuilt itself around them, taking them along boulevards that once towered majestically above the surface of Lake Ataa Naa Nyongmo; past river-sized aqueducts snaking under monorails; through gardens where abstract sculptures cycled from one artist's creation to another's – a cubist body lifting up a dancer in the air, before morphing into a knot of spheres that might have been a bird, then turning into an explosion of fused pyramids.

The ghosts were playing tricks on her. They didn't want to harm her, that much was clear, but they were trying to conceal what was at the heart of this apparition. The core that called out to her. She had a terrible suspicion of what she would find, and the decision she would have to make there. This chamber wasn't big enough to hold a thousandth of the glory that had been Camlantis. It was a maze resetting itself about them, trying to mask its true nature.

'This won't do,' said Amelia. She felt like crying. Everything she had seen suggested in every broken fragment of the past she had risked her neck for, it was all true. The Camlanteans' lives had been lived as art. Their skies filled not with the deadly pea-soupers of steam engines, but with delicate wisp-lines of mists from towers that converted rainwater into inestimable reserves of energy, or streets that drank their power from the endless light of the sun. All this lost, until now.

She switched direction, trusting her inner compass over the priceless glimpses she was being afforded into the long-lost culture. The ghosts of Camlantis cycled through more of their streets and scenes, faster, trying to entice them away from the small passages and back paths she was committing them to now. Amelia ignored the ghosts when they showed her an arena with controlled microclimates, the absent weather artists' creations playing to an empty stadium, or a vast square racked with rainbow-coloured rotor-like umbrellas that could be used to lift curious travellers into the air and transport them to any part of the city with a simple command. Whatever the wonders on display, she was no longer for turning.

As if sensing her determination on this matter, the apparitions gave up and finally opened their architecture out onto another square, a tower in its centre enclosed by slow-moving spirals of radiance.

'At last,' said Amelia, 'something real.'

She approached the tower and it began to descend into the ground. Ribbons of light twisted back up towards the reducing zenith of the tower, the entire city around them sinking towards the ground as if Camlantis was being submerged by a tide. With the last twist of light sucked into the tip of the tower, the fading illumination revealed a crown similar to the circlet worn by the Daggish emperor. This one had a single addition that immediately caught their attention – a crimson jewel the size of an egg sparking in the centre of the headpiece. The city about them had vanished. Only the tower remained, the column reset at the height of their shoulders.

'I've never seen a ruby that large,' hissed Bull. 'That has to be worth the price of a kingdom.'

'Well, why not?' said Amelia. 'The gem has a whole world inside it. This is what was projecting the vision of Camlantis.'

Bull looked around, only now noticing that everything about them had disappeared. They stood on a flat plateau, looking down on the machine forest below.

Bull reached out to lift the crown off the column, but Amelia slapped his hand back. 'Traps mean treasure, but the reverse also holds true.'

Amelia inspected the column carefully, looking for weight sensors and other triggers. There was nothing she could see, but then, Camlantean society had progressed to a level of super-science mere Jackelians could only dream of. There could be a thermal trigger, a light-grid – sensors that did not even exist on this plane of reality. And what sort of traps would pacifists build to protect an ancient projector? Was this the secret the ruler of the Daggish had been trying to recover for centuries? If the gem held the memory of Camlantis within its glittering planes, might it also contain the current location of the broken city among the heavens?

'You take the jewel, then,' said Bull. 'The doors here work for you, not for me.'

'I don't know. This crown is beyond price, we can't just pass it over to the Daggish.'

'Sod them, we're going to take it for ourselves.' Bull leered as if he had been handed the keys to the city of Middlesteel. 'What a bloody great jewel.'

'It's not a ruby,' said Amelia. She knew what it was now, bathing in its light. The jewel was illuminating her, feeding her. 'It's been grown from a single seed of data. Can't you feel the energy flowing from it? It's raw information, a nugget of absolute knowledge, compressed to a level of detail that has forged it into a universe within itself – this makes the Camlanteans' crystal-books look like a page of text scalpel-carved onto a wax tablet.'

'Then Abraham Quest will pay us for it,' said Bull. 'Even if it doesn't provide the location of Camlantis in the heavens, he'll pay us for it all the same. The Camlanteans are just like every other bugger that followed after them – all ego and self-importance. They couldn't bear to leave the world without scrawling a little graffiti on the wall, so we'd know that they'd been here and what they'd achieved. You know what this is, don't you? This is your rich shopkeeper friend's manual for his perfect, pacifist society, and he'll bleed money to get his hands on it. He'll bloody well need to, too.'

Amelia stared at her comrade-in-arms with disgust. The slaver's avarice was an affront to everything the ancient civilization that had created this miracle once stood for.

He saw her look. 'Don't give me that, dimples. Quest will get his jewel and you'll have the rest of your life to study the information inside it. And all the plaudits from your bookworm friends who didn't want you walking their college corridors.'

'I hope they accept Jackelian coin inside the Daggish hive,' said Amelia, 'because that's where we'll be thrown if we go back to the surface with this. No wonder the hive wants the crown. Whatever blood limiters the Camlanteans placed into their engineering to stop the ancestors of the Daggish breeding feral, the clues to removing the restrictions lie inside this gem. Imagine the Daggish armed with the knowledge of a Cassarabian womb mage – no limit to the hive's growth, able to project their drone armies hundreds of miles beyond Liongeli's borders, absorbing Jackals, Quatérshift, the Catosian city-states and Kikkosico. Adding our strength to its own, nation by nation – everyone on the continent converted into its slaves.'

'So what are you going to do?' said Bull. 'Leave the crown down here? You've seen how patient the Daggish are – like bulldogs with a bone. They'll keep on trying, keep on developing new u-boats. They've already absorbed my crew – they know more about u-boats than they ever did before. Sooner or later they'll bag some more explorers from the race of man and try their luck with them. Who is to say others won't just take the jewel and hand it over to Tree-head Joe? The hive knows how our minds work, too. Grab a mother or father with their children, keep the kids as hostages, make the parents come down here to get its precious crown back for it.'

'You're just saying that because it suits your greed,' said Amelia.

'Maybe, but you know it's true. All that's keeping that crown from the Daggish is a crater filled with water. Sooner or later, the hive is getting in here. We have to take the crown and make a run for Jackals. We can take it now, or Tree-head Joe's boys will take it later.'

'You said we couldn't outrun their seed ships in our bathysphere.'

'I didn't have the crown then,' said Bull. 'We'll sneak past them. I know a few tricks about silent running those walking trees and their moss-covered slaves have yet to learn.'

Her hand reached out for the jewel, hesitating just above the crown. If they failed in their escape attempt, she was condemning everything and everyone she cared for in Jackals to a living death. But then there were the seed ships, the graveyard of Daggish u-boats lying dead in the currents of the lake. Kammerlan was right. Leaving the gem where it was wouldn't deny it to the hive, just postpone the inevitable day when the Daggish broke in down here and took the knowledge they needed. The knowledge for infinite expansion.

'You think you can do it, Guardian's daughter?' said Bull. 'Then walk away. Let's go.' His hand clenched into a fist. 'Let's leave a hundred thousand crystal-books crushed into an object no bigger than my hand. Everything your life has been devoted to. Let's just leave the gem down here, dreaming its dreams of old Camlantis town, and go back to the bathysphere empty handed. We'll make a run for home all the same. And if we make it back to Jackals, well, you can return to digging out Wheat Tribe pottery from the plains of Concorzia, while old Bully-boy will take a berth on a Spumehead trader working the oceans for your shopkeeper friends: then we'll both be happy.'

Amelia tried to block out the slaver's voice. This had to be done for the right reasons; there was too much riding on the outcome for the decision to be made any other way. Jigger it. Her hand flashed out and she removed the crown from the plinth. Action over inaction every time.

'Let me hold it for a moment,' said Bull.

'Don't push your luck. Or mine. That was—' she noticed the tide of light rushing up the empty hill.

'—easy.'

The wave washed over the two of them, and, as it overtook them, their hill above the machine forest was rewritten with the flat, featureless walls of the chamber they had started out in. Only the dried-up pools of water around the bathysphere indicated that any time had passed at all. Amelia checked her hand – still clutching the crown with its near weightless egg-sized jewel of knowledge. Were the Jackelians ready for the wisdom it contained? Did the fact she had been allowed to take it at all mean she had been tested and the Jackelians judged ready to receive the precious knowledge of the Camlantean civilization? That had to be the purpose of the crown, this place, the ancients' legacy preserved for those who would walk the world after them.

There was no sign of the doorway down to the corridors of else-when. Amelia resisted the urge to walk over to the wall to see if she would be granted admittance a second time. Everything she needed from the wrecked basement world of Camlantis was in this crown.

'Make the bathysphere ready,' said Amelia.

Bull looked at the walls. 'There's no way back out to the lake.'

'Yes there is, we just can't see it, is all.'

Bull unlocked the craft and tossed out any loose objects that could be dislodged and make a noise falling, prepping for silent running, then emerged to adjust the screws at the back of the craft. 'We'll be running light, as gentle as a lady's fan at a playhouse. Just enough thrust to push us out into the currents of the Shedarkshe.'

'How capable is a seed ship's sonar?'

'Not so good,' said Bull, 'from what I've seen. Down here,

we'll probably be deep enough to avoid them, but on the river – well, at least we'll be running with the flow of the Shedarkshe at our back.'

The enormity of the risk they were taking was beginning to sink in. Bull was following the fires of his avarice, but what in the Circle's name was she following? Was this her dead father's dream, her dream?

'The Daggish aren't so sharp underwater,' said Bull, thinking the professor was about to change her mind about departing with the crown. 'They can't absorb fish or river lizards into the hive, only creatures of the land and the air. That's why they rely on seed ships on the Shedarkshe's surface rather than a navy of sliporaptors. Maybe that green muck of theirs don't work so well down here, or perhaps Tree-head Joe's commands don't get passed on as clear in the deeps. We've got a chance.'

Amelia bit her lip and ducked under the bathysphere to enter the submersible. The crown of the Camlanteans rested on her lap, so light as not to be noticeable. That was the best she could hope for, then, that the drones of the Daggish Empire hadn't learnt to swim properly. On such a premise did the fate of their continent rest. Kammerlan had only just begun spinning up the expansion engine when the burning light overtook them, dwindling away to be replaced by the cool, dark waters of Lake Ataa Naa Nyongmo.

CHAPTER FIFTEEN

It was unusual for the Stalker Cave to be filled with such a low noise – a keening more appropriate to the funeral feast of one of the lashlite flight escaping the beaks of those who waited motionless. It was even more unusual for one of the great seer's attendants to slip out of the inner cave without taking time to wash away the sins of the future-revealed in the pool that lay to the side of the holy of holies.

The four seers of the crimson feather looked up as one, uncrossing their legs and standing, the tallest lighting the small brazier of slipsharp oil that lay in the corner. His beak opened to blow out the match, fixing the attendant with his lizard's eyes. 'The great seer has seen true?'

'I fear so.' The attendant raised his hand to cover the nape of his neck and his true eye. A superstitious gesture, lest his seeing orb pollute the vision of those with greater sight than he himself possessed.

'And in her seeing, what stands revealed?'

The attendant hesitated, still too dumbstruck by what he had been ordered to do.

Reaching out, the seer of the crimson feather shook the

other lashlite. 'I do not have the luxury of three days to undergo the cleansing rituals and ablutions to pass through to the Stalker Cave. You must tell us what has been said, *now*.'

'You are bid to enter the great seer's chamber,' said the attendant. 'Without the cleansing rituals. To enter immediately.'

Their beaks hung open in astonishment. Abandon the rituals they had been raised to honour? Just walk into the great seer's chamber? Such a thing had never been sung of, not once in the memory of any of the people of the wind's poems. They would risk polluting her sight forever.

The attendant fell nervously to his knees in supplication and indicated the passage they were to take. The four members of the crimson feather reluctantly did as they were instructed. They were the great seer's disciples, what other choice did they have? The attendant fell in behind them, taking a torch from the wall to illuminate the darkness. Each time they passed one of the pools of meditation they faltered, resisting the instinct to fulfil their ancient rituals. To wash the dust of the cliffs from their feathers. To still their noisy minds. The air grew warmer the deeper they walked into the mountain, until at last a breeze like a sigh blew over their clawed feet, and the four members of the crimson feather and the attendant found themselves in the blackest of caverns. A darkness that was splintered by the attendant's torchlight glittering off mineral veins as he strode forward, a thousand quartz stars twinkling in the vast space. The four disciples waited by the entrance, feeling soiled for having forsaken the cleansing pools. Advancing, the attendant dipped his torch into a lake of oil and it erupted into flames, the light running up the cavern wall and, high above, revealing the great seer's wings stretched out from her perch in the rocks, moaning as the heat banished the rheumatism in her ancient hollow bones.

'Advance, children of the crimson feather,' she whistled.

They formed a line in front of the cavern's lake, their wings furled and wrapped around them to ward off the heat of the fire.

'Septimoth has fallen!' said the great seer, her voice reflected by the walls.

The four seers of the crimson feather quivered in shock at her words.

'Why did it have to be a miserable exile that was chosen?' moaned one of the seers, recovering his composure enough to speak. 'Why not a warrior of the flight? Why not a champion?'

'Septimoth still lives,' explained the great seer. 'But he dwells in the shadows of the bright realm, as does his companion from the race of man. Soon there is to be desolation, desolation everywhere – for the waters of the lake of the past have finally been parted. Our future is to be decided in the kingdom beyond the waves.'

Sensing her four disciples' trepidation, the great seer added, 'There is still hope. The future is disturbed. There are many paths narrowing to a beggarly pair. One path is the end of our people, the terrible chimneys of the dark wind, the end of everything. The other . . . the other might yet be bought with our blood and our bravery.'

'And what else is there, Mother-Future of the Stalker Cave?'

She flexed a weary talon in the direction of the attendant below. Her servant walked to the side of the chamber, across an undecorated rock floor worn smooth by the clawed footsteps of hundreds of his predecessors. He knelt by a wooden chest and undid its latch, laying four long, cloth-wrapped objects onto the floor – rolling out the fabric to reveal spears.

Long shafts of golden metal, cast by a smelting process long forgotten, their heads so sharply edged it was said they could be cast at a boulder and pass completely through without a scratch.

Still kneeling, the attendant solemnly passed one across to each of the four seers of the crimson feather as they advanced to receive their gifts. 'For the mountains of the north and the wind to warm your wings. For the mountains of the east and the wind to speed you across barren ground. For the mountains of the south and the wind to lift you across the dunes. For the mountains of the west and the wind to carry you across the sea.'

They stood there a moment, clutching their spears, overwhelmed by the enormity of what they were expected to do. There were songs of times such as these. When the spears made from the fallen star were distributed to the seers; but they were ancient songs, so old the verses had been made liturgy by their repetition. To be told that they were now living in such times . . . that they were living in legend . . .

One of the seers raised his spear and the other three followed suit, joining their tips in the centre of the great seer's cavern. There was silence, broken only by the sound of the oil burning in the lake.

'This is what there is,' said the great seer, though the words were surely passed in turn to her by the whisper of the winds and the grace of the gods. 'I have spoken.' The great seer furled her wings, her attendant stilling the fires in the lake beneath with the throw of a golden blanket, its threads woven from the rare star metal. The four seers of the crimson feather followed the attendant back towards the light of the first cave.

Alone once more in the darkness, the great seer let the emptiness of the future fill her soul. 'Oh, aweless throne, oh, all the cleverness and hopes of man.' A tear left the great seer's eye unseen, falling towards the lake below. 'Oh, Camlantis.'

As the four seers of the crimson feather gained sight of their eyrie's entrance the winged creatures broke into a sprint, leaving a short interval between each runner and the seer that followed. On the opposite cliff, the heads of a class of young flightlings looked up from their ledge, the shaman teaching them their tone poems irritated at being interrupted. Each seer fell from the peak, arrowing down until their wings extended to full width with a deafening crack. There were gasps from the children as the golden spears glinted in the sunlight. Their people's most ancient songs were always those that were taught first, but perhaps only the shaman teaching them truly understood what they were witnessing.

From the ledges of the nests above and below came whistles of alarm, more and more of the flight coming out of their cliffside dwellings to see what the commotion was.

Catching an updraught, the four seers of the crimson feather spiralled up above the line of mountains and broke formation. To the north. To the east. To the south. To the west.

To war.

CHAPTER SIXTEEN

Bull thrust the bathysphere hard to starboard as the seed ship's spine weapon flashed past leaving a trail of highly compressed air bubbles in its wake. The Daggish ruler had obviously grown suspicious during their prisoners' absence in the Camlantean underworld. Two of its latest submersible seed ships had been waiting in ambush for them when they exited the gate of light on the bed of Lake Ataa Naa Nyongmo.

'I thought they wanted the crown back in one piece,' said Bull.

'Whatever's in those spine heads, it won't damage the crown,' said Amelia, clutching onto her seat, 'you can be sure of that.'

'Poison, then,' speculated Bull. 'Dirt-gas, or their version of it.' He dropped the bathysphere, using the manoeuvrability of their vessel to push down towards the ruins. 'I don't want to find out the hard way.'

More shots came past, well wide, disappearing into the crater beneath.

'Kill the lights.' Bull's hands closed the illumination reservoir to the gas spots. 'Let's see how good their sonar is.'

'Better than ours.' Amelia peered out of the rear porthole. 'We don't have any!'

Beyond the glass she could see luminescent strips along the side of the submersible following them, a blood marker from whatever underwater creature the Daggish had used to create its seed ship design. Their craft were slow to turn due to their size, but that bulk meant they were carrying a lot more air than their small bathysphere. The two expedition survivors were down to half an hour's charge; even if they escaped into the Shedarkshe, the chase downriver was going to be over before it started.

'They're piloting those two boats like they've broken into the grog rations,' sneered Bull. 'It's small wonder their vessels have been ending up in the graveyard down here. They've got a dead hand on the stick.'

'Head for the river,' called Amelia, as a spine head from the second pursuer flashed past, 'or there'll be two corpses in this boat.'

Schools of tiny fish scattered as their bathysphere powered through the water, chased by the whale-like outlines of the Daggish submersibles turning after them with an organic grace, like fish themselves.

'We're nearly there,' said Bull. 'We're in the river currents now and—'

He yelled in alarm. A wall of anti-u-boat netting had been laid ahead, stretched across the wide entrance to the river. Bull turned the sphere, the expansion engines whining as loudly as Amelia had ever heard them. Missing the metal gauze by less than a foot, they turned away from the rigid mesh, running along the crater wall with the pull of the current buffeting them.

'Dead hand on the stick!' Amelia cursed the slaver. 'They weren't trying to catch us, just corral us in here.'

'I didn't see those nets on the way in,' said Bull. 'What's that jigger Tree-head Joe done that for? You'd think that he didn't trust us.'

'You were brigged on the way in, you lackwit.' Amelia looked through the rear porthole. The two Daggish craft were turning after them – they had only been slowing to avoid being caught in the nets. 'And they've absorbed enough feral craynarbians into the hive to know the tales of a u-boat making slaving calls along the river villages.'

Bull laughed, twisting the bathysphere around to face their pursuers.

'What are you doing?'

Bull slammed the pilot stick forward. 'Attacking!'

Amelia ran for the exo-claws at the back, pushing her arms into the control gloves. She'd had plenty of practice sifting through the debris on the lake bed. She dialled them up to maximum strength, the clockwork amplification feeding the claws with so much energy that they shook every couple of seconds as if they were possessed with palsy. Good enough. Taken aback by the attack of this minnow, the modified seed ships tried to pull to port, but they had slowed too much to avoid colliding with the anti-sub netting. The bathysphere's shadow passed over the nearest of the craft and Amelia lashed down with both her claws at the illuminated compound eye-shaped conning dome on the hull. Bull's words came back to her. *You are going to need to dish out a walloping with them waldos.* She had a brief glimpse of shattering panels, the pressure of the water imploding the dome, drowning Daggish drones, then the submersible's light flickering and dying.

The second seed ship had turned enough to bring her aft tubes to bear, two spine heads powering forward faster than they had any right to, a trail of bubbles in their wake. Bull dived their craft down, but the second of the spines glanced off the bathysphere's screws, smashing open the engine assembly. Pressurized expansion engine gas hissed out into the waters of the lake, spinning them around. Bull twisted the pilot stick and slammed his fist into the control panel but nothing he could do was making any difference to their gyrations.

'I'm going to blow the tanks,' shouted Bull. 'Grab hold of something and make for a hard rise.'

Amelia cursed the slaver. He should have held his nerve and left her to tear open the anti-submarine netting with their waldos. Now their fallback plan was to break surface and swim for it. To a shore where every organism they blundered into for a hundred miles would be controlled by the hive. As their ballast tanks emptied at high velocity, they found a new direction, corkscrewing upwards, erupting out of the lake in a spout of water before smashing back down to the surface. They had stopped their demented pirouette now, the bathysphere's engine fuel bleeding out into the air. Amelia caught a glimpse of the armada of seed ships on the surface waiting for them, her view blocked by the remaining Daggish submersible breaking the surface beside the bathysphere. Bull spun the wheel on the top hatch lock, pulling himself out, Amelia close behind, still clutching her precious crown. An iris door on the Daggish u-boat's conning dome was cycling open. It was searing outside, a wall of bright heat after their confinement in the cool, deep waters of the lake.

'Soldiers coming,' Bull called.

'That's the least of our problems,' Amelia replied, steadying herself on one of the sphere's gas lamps as the wake of a passing seed ship struck them. She stretched out to dive for the water, but the heat blast from the seed ship's forward guns knocked her back. Not directed at them, but towards the Daggish submersible, a visor on the boat's flame cannon twisting up as a stream of flame licked down the u-boat's hull. Incinerated drones were flung back towards the open iris, the submersible bucking in agony at the scorch marks blistering down its hull. Curving around the submersible, the patrol craft bore down on them. Amelia gripped tighter as the wash from the seed ship tidal-waved towards them.

Had civil war broken out among the hive? Some fundamental disagreement over what to do with the crown? Then Amelia saw a sight that she never thought she'd see on a Daggish patrol boat – a steamman, a four-armed steamman on the deck no less. Ironflanks! His seed ship cut through the lake waters, interposing itself between the bathysphere and the enemy submersible, the flame squirt on the prow whistling as compressed incendiary fire licked out along the length of the Daggish u-boat. Whatever prohibition stopped members of the hive from attacking one another had been broken by the prize vessel, and the seed ship was wreaking havoc in the confusion. Overjoyed at seeing Amelia still alive, Ironflanks spun in a frenzied tribal dance on the prow.

Bull spotted his uncle standing behind Veryann at the rear of the cabin as the seed ship drew up alongside the bathysphere 'You've got to be kidding me.'

'Who's piloting that boat, old steamer?' Amelia tossed across the bathysphere's guide rope so both craft could moor together.

'Billy Snow,' Ironflanks called back, his eyes extending telescope-like towards the Daggish armada on the centre of the lake, the enemy seed ships making full speed towards them.

Veryann leapt across the gap before the two craft tied up, landing on the bathysphere's hull. Bull stepped back, expecting an assault as payment for his marooning of her, but she ignored both Amelia and the slaver, instead diving inside the craft. None of the other expedition members looked as if they had been expecting the Catosian woman to plunge inside

Amelia's bathysphere, but Commodore Black had other fish to fry.

'Bull,' roared the commodore, hauling the bathysphere in to thud against the seed ship's bony hull. 'Bull, you treacherous stain on the House of Dark, where's my *Sprite*? Where's my beautiful u-boat?'

Bull thumbed at the hive's approaching fleet. 'Talk to her new owners, old man.' He slapped the top of the bathysphere. 'You can have this diving ball back for your troubles.'

Ironflanks and T'ricola had to restrain the commodore from trying to leap across at the news. Amelia jumped the gap, landing on the aft of the Daggish prize vessel. 'They've laid anti-submarine nets across the mouth of the Shedarkshe. We're going to need to break them to get out of here.' She glanced across at the Daggish fleet. 'Sweet Circle, how many ships have they got? And how did you know—'

'Billy softbody said you would be here,' answered Ironflanks. 'He told us he felt your presence.'

Amelia looked at the steamman as if he had lost his mind – if he had ever fully possessed it to begin with. Bull crossed the gap between the bathysphere and the patrol boat, making sure he stayed out of reach of the commodore. 'And I feel the presence of half the Daggish Empire coming down on us.'

Two explosive cracks from the bathysphere made Amelia flinch. It wasn't incoming fire from the Daggish. There was a splash as a metal panel ejected from the bathysphere and hit the water, followed by a boom as something fired out of their diving ball's hull.

'A rocket,' said Ironflanks, tracking the projectile heading towards the firmament.

'You don't carry rockets on a submersible,' said Bull, confused. 'You carry torpedoes.' He looked up. 'And that one's missed the fleet.'

Commodore Black made to throttle his nephew, before changing his mind and running to the patrol boat's rail. 'Veryann, get yourself out of that blessed sphere. Billy, hold your fire on the u-boat, she's dead in the water now. Can you—'

But Billy Snow had already abandoned the cabin and was coming out of the door, the seed ship left a mindless derelict with the controlling witch-blade in the sonar man's hand.

Amelia glanced behind him into the cabin. 'Billy, what in the name of the Circle is going on here?'

'A long tale for a less desperate time,' said Billy. 'I am glad that you survived, Amelia – but not to see you with that.' He pointed at the crown in Amelia's hand.

'This is what we came all the way out here for,' said Amelia. 'The things we've seen under the lake's waters, I can't begin to tell you. The crown holds the secrets to the location of Camlantis in the heavens, I can feel it.'

'It holds many things,' said Billy, 'but the location of Camlantis isn't one of them.'

'You can't know that.'

'Give it to me,' said Billy.

'What for?'

Billy extended his witch-blade, the evil thing thrumming, tasting the opportunity for fresh trouble. 'You know what I'm going to do. What you should have done, rather than bring that terrible thing back into the world.'

Bull rushed at Billy Snow, and the sonar man kicked out almost gently, tapping Bull's left leg above the knee. The slaver collapsed, howling as if Billy had cut off his limb, silenced into unconsciousness as the old sonar man ducked down and tapped him on the back of the neck.

'Have you lost your mind, Billy?' shouted the commodore. 'If that gem is a crystal-book, then it's what we rolled all the way up this wicked devil's river for.'

Billy waved his sword at the approaching commodore. 'You came for it. I only came to make sure you didn't get it.'

'Billy,' begged T'ricola, 'I don't know what this is about and I don't care, but while we're arguing the Daggish are getting closer.'

Amelia stepped back. 'The knowledge on this crystal—'

'You're not ready for it. Jackals isn't ready for it,' said Billy. He nodded at the approaching Daggish fleet. 'They're certainly not ready for it. Give it to me now. I don't want to hurt you, professor, but I'll take off your arm along with the crown to obliterate that terrible thing.'

'You can't destroy a crystal-book, you can't destroy knowledge. I was meant to find this!'

'Prophecy is a poor substitute for intellect,' said Billy, advancing menacingly. 'And that thing is not just a crystal-book.'

Ironflanks had been slowly trying to edge behind Billy, but the sonar man wagged a finger at the steamman. 'I may be blind, old steamer, but I know all about your militant order's fighting forms. Your voicebox won't work on me, my body is hardened against the frequency the knights steammen use for paralysis.'

'You were the traitor on the u-boat,' said Ironflanks accusingly. 'I thought it was the commodore's nephew trying to force us to turn about, but all the time it was you sabotaging the *Sprite*. Destroying the scrubbers, calling in the thunder lizard when we were filling up for water . . .'

'Billy,' pleaded T'ricola. 'That isn't true?'

'If you only knew what was at stake, you would understand.' Billy Snow lunged at Amelia, faster than the eye could follow, striking her wrist and capturing the falling crown. Amelia punched out with her massive gorilla-sized arm – the good one he had left her – but the sonar man wasn't there anymore. His boot kicked out and she got a taste of what Bull had received. Pure nerve fire pulsed along her left leg, as if the bottom half of her limb had ceased to exist. She fell back, trying not to scream.

'My steam is up,' roared Ironflanks, charging Billy while the sonar man was busy incapacitating Amelia.

Billy's witch-blade flexed to the diameter of a sewing pin and without turning around he stepped back, the tip of the impossibly thin sword emerging from the back of the steam-man's hull. Billy stepped forward and Ironflanks fell side-ways, grasping for the side of the boat and as weak as a kitten.

'I've sliced your circuit line for spatial balance,' said Billy, making the slightest bow in the direction of the fallen steamman. 'You should be able to reroute around the damage using your self-repair routines. But not—' he rested the crown on the boat and converted his witch sword into something capable of smashing a near-indestructible crystal, all claws and blades, '—before I've had a chance to account for this filthy thing . . .'

'My body,' begged Ironflanks. 'Please, I need that crown to pay for my body to be cleansed of my siltempter corrup-tion.'

'Not with this,' said Billy, raising his sword to strike. He hesitated as something like a meteor hit close to them, a whistling trail of heat, followed by a spout of lake water erupting into the air – then the firmament above was filled with fiery scratches impacting all around them. As Billy moved to smash the crown into pieces, a pair of weighted bolas wrapped around his abdomen, the attached net landing on his back and shimmering with a field of sparks. It was as if a wall had collapsed on top of the sonar man. He fell to his face with a single moan.

Veryann's legs were wedged around the bathysphere airlock, a discharged bola launcher resting against her arm. 'That was designed to paralyse a Daggish drone, but it seems to work as well on our unusually adept sonar operator.'

Amelia tried to pull herself up, massaging life back into her leg and ignoring the pain in her sprained wrist. Had the world gone mad? Billy Snow turning on them, a rain of fire falling from the heavens? On the distant shore, the Daggish nest's flame cannons were jouncing in their cradles, answering the volley coming down on them with streams of fire of their own. The objects Amelia had mistaken for meteors were surfacing across the lake in their hundreds, long iron capsules opening like metal flowers to give birth to boxy-looking landing craft. Periscopes, steam engine stacks and clockwork-stabilized cannons pushed out from the landing crafts' hulls, metal lobsters extending their claws.

Veryann leapt back across to the seed ship. 'Don't touch Billy Snow,' she warned the crew. 'Leave him in the incapacitator net. If anyone tries to free him, I'll kill him.'

More capsules came thumping down towards the edge of the lake, against a background of tinny explosions from the Daggish city, a pall of smoke rising above the jungle canopy of Liongeli and the twisted organic towers of the nest city. There was a second rain following now, silk chutes, detached from the engines of war they had been designed to slow, following in the invaders' wake like a rain of blossom.

Amelia shaded her eyes against the bright afternoon sun. The invaders were pushing out of the lake and up onto the distant shore – amphibious horseless carriages moving on caterpillar tracks similar to those some of the steammen favoured. Tiny figures dismounted from the rear and moved up beside them as they trundled along.

The commodore came to Amelia's side, helping her try to

raise Ironflanks back onto his feet. 'We're in the middle of a shooting war now, lass.'

'And I think I know whose . . .' Amelia looked with resentment at the Catosian officer.

'A raid,' said Veryann, 'not a war. With a very specific objective.'

On the centre of the lake the Daggish armada was scattering, heading for the shore to protect their city. Tree-head Joe must be in apoplexy by now – far more than a few gnats in danger of penetrating his sanctum and threatening his ancient purity.

'You can't beat the Daggish, Veryann,' said Commodore Black. 'They're like a blessed weed. You'd have to burn down hundreds of miles of greenmesh to finish them off.'

'We're just giving their kind something to think about,' said Veryann, picking up the fallen crown. 'Into the bathysphere, if you want to live.'

'What are you doing?' demanded Amelia.

'Preserving your crown's precious knowledge. We haven't got long. You have two choices. Enter the bathysphere and live, or stay on board the Daggish boat and die.' She tossed the prone weight of Billy Snow over her shoulders. 'Help the steamman to his feet. As for him—' she pointed at the limp form of Bull Kammerlan, '—leave him here like he left us marooned in the jungle.'

'I can't be doing that,' said the commodore. 'There's precious few of my blood left now, for me to be abandoning the mortal few that survive. Don't ask me to do such a terrible thing.'

'If he is truly of your line, you will be uncontaminating it by removing him from the breeding pool,' said Veryann.

'You may be right, lass, but your people follow a hard code – abandoning the runt of the litter on a mountainside is not something old Blacky can do.'

411

Amelia limped over and scooped Bull's unconscious body up, trying to avoid using her burning, sprained wrist. 'You help Ironflanks, Jared, I'll carry your damn nephew.'

'How can such a powerful nation be populated by such weaklings?' Veryann shook her head in disgust. 'You make a religion out of your softheartedness. The fact that Jackals has endured intact to this day without falling to one of your enemies is one of life's eternal mysteries.'

T'ricola and the commodore heaved the barely functioning body of the steamman across to the bathysphere, his limbs shaking as he tried to re-establish enough control to leave the seed ship.

'You appear to have been touched by some of our beliefs, then,' said Amelia, nodding towards the sonar man.

Veryann lowered Billy Snow through the hatch. 'You think saving his life is an act of compassion? I assure you it is not, professor. In his way, this old man may be just as valuable as your Camlantean crown.'

Commodore Black wheezed, half the weight of Ironflanks on his shoulder. 'I've seen those fighting tricks before, when Billy's kind come down from the sky to make a shambles of the honest rest of a poor old seafarer, long retired from adventure and danger.'

'Snow, an agent of the Court of the Air?' Veryann's lips pursed into a thin smile. 'He is no wolftaker, of that much you can be certain.' She tossed the man's inactive witch-blade into the bathysphere. 'Inside quick, I'm sealing the sphere.'

The interior of the bathysphere had changed since Amelia had abandoned it for the Daggish patrol boat – a whole new suite of hidden instruments had been exposed, while an open panel to the right of the controls revealed a previously concealed rack of weapons, an empty space for the Catosian's bolas launcher.

Amelia tapped the near-empty oxygen dial. 'We're not going far on three minutes' worth of air.'

'Further than you think,' said Veryann.

'We're crammed in here like blessed sardines,' complained the commodore.

'We'd be one lighter without your mutinous nephew,' said Veryann, kicking Bull's unconscious body in anger.

Amelia glanced through the porthole. Outside, the Daggish seed ship was turning in idiot circles on one hydro-tube, the mind of the craft trying to establish itself now it had been freed from the witch-blade's control. But it was hopeless – too much of the ship's brain had been overwritten by Billy Snow's strange weapon.

Veryann had their bathysphere's small periscope trained on the distant shoreline and after a couple of minutes she nodded in satisfaction and began to work the controls again. Amelia took the scope, pressing her face against the viewing hood. The Daggish city was ablaze. Neon-yellow smoke over-shadowed the haze of the attack, columns of it pouring into the sky. Amelia might have taken it for dirt-gas were it not for the fact that nozzles on their own hull seemed to be leaking the same vapour, tears of bronze dye forming on the bathy-sphere's portholes.

'Who are you signalling?' Amelia demanded.

'The long-range flame guns of the Daggish have been spiked now,' said Veryann. 'It's safe to be picked up.' She pulled on a lever, and two antennae with a cable strung between them rose above the dome of the bathysphere.

'Your troops are out there,' said Amelia. 'Is there enough space in this bathysphere for all of them?'

'They have achieved their objective,' said Veryann.

'Achieved . . .' Amelia stared in disbelief at the Catosian officer. 'You're leaving them behind!'

'Our losses in the nest will not be significant,' said Veryann. 'Our worst-case plan of battle was that the Daggish would attain the Crown of Pairdan and that a full-scale occupation of their capital would be necessary while simultaneously holding off an assault by the rest of the greenmesh.'

'In the name of the Circle, those are your own people out there!'

'They will have warriors' deaths, selling themselves dearly against creatures that would make slaves of our whole race if they could. If that was my duty, I would welcome such an end.'

Amelia pointed an accusing finger at Veryann. 'That Camlantean crown last saw the light of day when Catosia was a scratch on the map, yet you now suddenly value it enough to exchange a whole division of your troops! You guessed that Billy Snow was going to try to destroy the crown, too . . .'

'Of all people, professor, I would expect you to know the value of being well read. Now brace yourselves.'

There was a whining outside, growing louder. Just in time for Amelia to recognize it as the noise made by the rotating propeller blades of an airship. Then the floor of the bathysphere was pulled out from under their feet, the seven of them sent sprawling as they swung pendulum-like, ripped out of the waters of Lake Ataa Naa Nyongmo. Bull groaned when the dead weight of Ironflanks slid into him, Amelia barely hanging on as the commodore lost his grip and came tumbling towards her. Stability returned and they were rising. The hull of an impossibly large airship was just visible above them, cannons in rotating mounts jolting as they poured shells downwards. Three aerospheres bound together in a reinforced frame, short black stabilizer wings like the flying fish of the Shedarkshe. And damned if she could see any flag. Amelia gaped, wordlessly. This airship was clearly a man-o'-war, but she lacked the chequerboard belly of a RAN craft, instead sporting a curved black shell broken by gun ports and engine casings. There was a traitor's death waiting for someone back in Jackals. She glanced back down at the rapidly receding jungle below. If there were any Daggish gunners left with the wit to try to bring them down, Amelia could not see their answering fire.

Commodore Black stumbled towards the porthole, trying to snatch a last look at the Daggish nest and his u-boat. 'My *Sprite*, my beautiful *Sprite*. You're leaving her here.'

'No,' said Veryann. 'One of our assault craft has orders to scuttle her. The less of our engineering the Daggish have access to, the better we will like it.'

The commodore collapsed into the navigator's seat at the news. 'Lass, say that's not true. We can belay that order. With this mighty airship of yours you can pound the Daggish to pieces and winch my *Sprite* up to safety. I'll pilot her back to Rapalaw Junction myself with the help of T'ricola and Bull; maybe him in leg irons just to be safe.'

'I'm truly sorry, Jared,' said Veryann. 'I must abandon a division of my finest fighters behind, and you must leave your ancient craft. We only have a brief window of flight time while the Daggish flame guns are incapacitated. If we are still within range above the city when their cannons are repaired and re-crewed, our fate will not be a kind one.'

The hooks clamped around the bathysphere's catapult-like roof assembly began to winch them upwards into an opening hangar, the airship climbing for height as they were drawn into her belly.

'No,' said the commodore, an unruly glint in his eyes. 'No kinder than the fate of that burnt-up airship we found crashed by the borders of Prince Doublemetal's kingdom of loons.

That was no derelict blown in from Jackals' last war with Quatérshift, was it? That was your people, learning the hard way that an expedition by air to Lake Ataa Naa Nyongmo is a mortal dangerous thing to attempt. Far better to bribe poor old Blacky and his brave, foolish friends, to sneak into the greenmesh for you on the *Sprite*.'

Veryann said nothing, but her silence spoke volumes.

Amelia watched as they were hauled into the airship's hangar, rising up past gantries and empty launch rails for Catosian glider capsules. 'This is no RAN vessel. Has Quest gone insane? Parliament will declare him a science pirate – he'll be hunted to the ends of the earth as an outlaw for building this aerial folly.'

Veryann pointed towards the party waiting for them in the hangar. 'There he stands, you can tell him yourself in a minute. You've followed the path of your obsession, professor, as Abraham Quest has followed his. Whatever the cost to you both. Were it not for your gender, I believe I would find it hard to tell the two of you apart sometimes.'

With the bathysphere raised into a docking cradle, their hatch was popped, fresh air replacing the febrile mix that had been cooked up by the expedition members. Veryann was first on deck, then the semi-conscious forms of Ironflanks, Bull Kammerlan and Billy Snow were pulled out by the airship crew.

'Put these two in the brig,' said Veryann, pointing at Kammerlan and Snow. 'Chains for the old man and make sure they are strong – he can fight in witch-time.'

Abraham Quest walked over and grasped Veryann's arm in the Catosian style. 'You have it?'

She held up Amelia's Camlantean crown. 'Did you ever doubt me?'

'It was as dangerous a thing as I have ever asked you to

do.' He looked at the motley group climbing out of the bathy-sphere, drenched in sweat, their clothes torn by long months in the jungle. 'So few . . . did none of the others make it?'

'My boys are gone,' whined the commodore. 'Walking dead among the Daggish or made proper corpses along the way of our voyage, left rotting in that Liongeli hell. You promised me my beautiful boat back, but even that's gone now.'

'You might yet have it returned,' said Abraham Quest. 'Stranger things have happened.'

'Stranger things *have* happened,' spat Amelia. 'We've been shot at, gassed, imprisoned, seen glimpses of Camlantis at the bottom of Lake Ataa Naa Nyongmo, and had members of our own crew turn on us, all for the sake of that crown.'

'For which I apologize.' Quest looked at the prone form of Billy Snow being fitted with a metal cuirass, his arms strapped inside the steel straightjacket at a painful angle. 'He looks a little like the last one who came after us, don't you think?'

Veryann waved her soldiers forward to stand guard over Billy while he was being restrained. 'Like a brother, perhaps, if you shaved his beard off.'

'Who is Billy Snow, Quest? Who is he really?' asked Amelia. 'He claimed the location of Camlantis wasn't going to be found in the crown's crystal-book.'

'He's something ancient, professor. One of the texts mentioned something very much like him being grown in the old days.'

'What texts? I didn't read—'

'You read only what you needed for our expedition to succeed,' said Quest. 'Something else that you have my apology for.'

Amelia bridled at the deception. 'You were holding out on me? I risked my life for that crown!'

'And you will find the risk was worth it. I needed your passion to be pure, Amelia. The truth would have made you doubtful; you might even have refused to go in search of Camlantis. I risked everything I have on this throw of the dice, and my methods have not always been as honourable as I would otherwise have had them. Some of the crystal-books' secrets I kept back.'

'What secrets? What in the name of the Circle would have stopped me from going in search of Camlantis?'

'Camlantis is everything we thought it was and more, but its final days on Earth were not the best of times. Threatened by the Black-oil Horde, there was a schism in the Camlantean consensus on how to handle the barbarian invasion. The crystal-book I omitted showing you contains details of their civil war.'

Amelia's mouth hung open in shock. 'But that can't be. Their whole civilization was based on pacifism, they were not capable—'

'They were facing extinction,' interrupted Quest. 'Some of their people felt they had no choice but to take alternative action. That terrible decision tore Camlantis apart. It was no accidental floatquake that struck a looted and ruined city, and neither was their ascent into the heavens a noble act of mass suicide to prevent their knowledge from being perverted by the barbarians. The Camlanteans were at least as advanced in the worldsinger arts and geomancy as we are today. Camlantis was destroyed in a civil war. Leylines were strategically altered and the city blown into the heavens during the fighting.'

Tears ran down Amelia's cheeks. 'No!' But she knew it had the ring of truth. The pocket world under the waters of Lake Ataa Naa Nyongmo, its halls of else-when, a prophetic warning of the dangers of conflict. *This* was the warning from her father's shade, an admonition that had come true, *this* was the bitter laughter of a desert witch in Cassarabia.

'They sacrificed themselves, gave their lives rather than commit acts of violence,' Amelia whispered.

'Just another war, Amelia, a stupid senseless war and a small imperfection in an otherwise untarnished record. The Camlanteans lived for two-thousand years in peace and only faltered in their final months when they were nearly extinct – how can we judge them for that?' Quest held up the gleaming Camlantean crown. 'And look where your passion has led you.'

Amelia pointed at Billy Snow being dragged away across the hangar floor. 'I told you, he said the crown doesn't hold the location of Camlantis.'

'A half-truth,' said Quest. 'The crown does not contain the location of the city. It contains the key to unlock her gates.'

'A key? It's a jigging key! Then you already know where Camlantis is?' gasped Amelia. 'All this time and you *knew*?'

'You might say I know where it isn't,' smiled Quest. 'Which amounts to the same thing in this instance.'

'You're a thorough bastard,' said Amelia.

'I needed your knowledge and your expertise,' apologized Quest, 'and I preferred to limit the facts of the expedition's true objective to Veryann. If the Daggish had captured her, she had access to a herb that would have ensured the green-mesh did not take her alive. Would the rest of your crew have sacrificed themselves to keep the people of Jackals safe? Even the Camlanteans failed that test in the end.'

'Well, we've passed your blessed test now,' said the commodore, 'those of us who've made it back alive. We'll take our money and be on our way.'

'Really?' said Quest. 'Do you have no curiosity? You are all welcome to travel with me to Camlantis. You'll see sights that no one has seen in millennia, travel higher than any aerostat in the history of Jackals. This is your chance to touch the stars.'

'The only sights I want to see are the warm corridors of Tock House,' said the commodore, 'and the only things I want to touch are the fine bottles of wine I have stored away back in my pantry. You can keep your dead city with its dead secrets, Abraham Quest.'

T'ricola nodded in agreement and Ironflanks pulled himself straight, leaning against the craynarbian, his voicebox tinny after self-repairing his wounded systems. 'I will take the second part of the payment you promised me and leave with my soft-body friends.'

'Fair enough,' said Quest. 'It was money you all signed up for and if that is what matters to you, it is money you shall have. Triple the agreed fee if you wish. My holdings in Jackals have been, shall we say, liquidated by circumstances. Mere money is the least of my concerns now.' He glanced over at his airship's captain.

'We will be over Jackals in two days, sir, I would not advise flying low enough to be reachable by the cannons of the RAN fleet, though.'

'Load a glider capsule onto the racks,' ordered Quest, turning to the expedition survivors. 'We'll fire you off some-where out of the way. No one need ever know you were involved with the mad schemes of a rogue commercial lord.'

'That will suit me just fine,' said the commodore.

'And what of you, professor?' asked Quest. 'Our journey's end lies above the Sepia Sea. In four to five days' time you could be walking the empty streets of ancient Camlantis, touching towers and spires you have only glimpsed before in crystal-book images.'

'Damn your eyes, you know the answer as well as I do,' said Amelia.

'Don't go, lass,' pleaded the commodore. 'Sailing around the sky like the queen of the clouds, tweaking parliament's nose by your very presence. It can only end in a wicked bad way. The life of an outlaw is no life for you; you can trust me on that. Come back with old Blacky to Jackals and stay a week or two with me in Tock House while we forget all about our part in this sorry adventure.'

'I'm sorry, Jared. I've risked everything to have this chance, to be standing here – and I have so very little left to return to back home. I'll make those prigs on the High Table eat their words, I'll bring back an airship full of Camlantean artefacts and fill the corridors of Middlesteel Museum with the expedition's finds as a reminder of their bloody-minded ignorance.'

'I believe you've made the right decision,' said Quest.

Amelia looked at the crown of Camlantis in his hand, the inset crystal gleaming like a devil's egg. She had made the only decision she was able to, but as to the rightness of it, all she could hear was the mocking laughter of an old hag roaming the Cassarabian desert.

'You jiggers,' shouted Bull Kammerlan. 'I find your second-rate shopkeeper's precious crown for him, and this is how you pay me back?'

One of the Catosians dragging him to the cell rabbit-punched him under his armpit. 'You haven't had your payment yet for betraying our master.'

Billy Snow stood by sadly, listening to the beating, his arms weighed down by metal restraints. The officer of the brig glanced up from her desk at her two new tenants. She had empty cells, but it was always easier to concentrate them in a couple of holding pens and keep an eye on what they were up to. She sized the two new lads up and pointed at Bull.

'Put the mutineer in with the lashlite and his insane friend.' She tapped Billy's straightjacket. 'Does this grizzled old fellow really need this?'

'High security at all times,' replied the soldier. 'The First says he can fight in witch-time.'

'Even sightless?' said the brig officer. 'Impressive.' Another damned problem prisoner. She pointed past the cells along the corridor and indicated the stairs down to the armoured hold. 'Lock him up with the Court of the Air's agent, then. They are both of an age, and it will give the old woman someone to complain to other than myself about the disrespect we show our elders.'

Bull moaned.

'The mutineer has cloud sickness,' warned one of the escorts. 'He threw up outside the glider capsule hangar.'

'You would think he'd have better air legs,' laughed a soldier.

'I'm a seadrinker,' snapped Bull. 'U-boats don't move like this, blondey-locks.'

The brig officer pushed him angrily into the entry lock of a cell. 'You make me clean out your cell floor, Jackelian, we'll be seeing if no rations for a week improves your gut's disposition.'

True to the guard's words, Bull's cell contained a lashlite, the winged lizard sitting uncomfortably in a corner while a wide-eyed man rocked and moaned on his knees.

'How do, boys. So which one of you is the lashlite and which one is the madman?'

Down below, the round armoured door shut and Billy Snow inspected his new quarters, his senses curving outwards to test the prison. No bars on the door like the cells he had observed upstairs; instead a single viewing hatch the size of a cheap penny dreadful, except that even the hole was shimmering under the protection of a cursewall. He doubted any of the other cells contained an old woman bent under the weight of a full hex suit, either. They circled each other warily, the old woman breaking the uneasy silence first.

'And who are you?'

'Obviously not someone as dangerous as you.' He clanked his arm chains. 'Or perhaps they only have one full hex suit on board.'

She moved her fingers under the weight of her gauntlet in what might have been taken for a nervous twitch.

Billy smiled. 'I'm not a wolftaker.'

'Then how did you know what I was signing? And more to the point, with those milky dead eyes of yours, how in the Circle's name can you tell I'm even in a hex suit, let alone see what my fingers are doing? I may be buried away inside this armour, but I can still connect to the earthflow and you are no sorcerer – there's not been a twinge of sorcery in this cell since you entered.'

Billy shrugged. 'There are different sorts of magic, damson. Borrowing the powers of the leylines is one, but there are others. There are the natural powers, the powers of science, even the power of learning is a kind of magic, wouldn't you say?'

'Yes,' agreed Damson Beeton. 'I would say that's true enough. I always go with my first instincts when it comes to people, old man, and I have decided to trust you.'

'Call me Billy. Billy Snow.'

Veryann found Abraham Quest in the transaction-engine chamber on the *Leviathan*. He was standing on the gantry, listening to the turning drums of the massive calculating machines below. Some of the initial data from the information gem they had recovered from the lake was revolving on those drums now. Transcribed into Simple – the ancient language of the transaction engines – by the house's cardsharps and engine men. How the mill owner found peace amongst the clacking and the din of such places was something she could never understand.

'The keys to Camlantis are inside the crown's gem?' asked Veryann.

'Oh yes,' said Quest. 'Three to four days left before we arrive, and we shall have the key by the time we get there.'

'It was made difficult to decipher?'

'Naturally,' said Quest. 'But mathematics has not changed over the millennia, even if much else has. And the ancients wanted their legacy to be understood, eventually.'

'By those worthy to follow in their footsteps,' noted Veryann.

'You think we are not?'

'There is an old man in the brig who clearly believes that to be the case,' said Veryann.

'So there is,' sighed Quest. 'Yes, it's about time he and I had a chat.'

'He will tell you nothing,' said Veryann, 'and you should trust not a word that comes out of his mouth.'

'Indeed. But I do owe it to him to try.'

'Speaking of debts,' said Veryann, 'Amelia Harsh has requested access to your second crystal-book.'

'I had hoped she would be distracted by the contents of the crown's gem,' said Quest. 'There is enough data inside its structure to keep her busy for the next thousand years.'

'She suspects your two crystal-books were transcribed by opposing sides in the civil war,' said Veryann, 'and she is enough of a historian to know that there are two sides to every tale of conflict.'

'Give her the second crystal-book, then. But give it to her raw. It took my engines years to reconstruct the material at the end that was struck by information blight – the work will keep her occupied for the next three days at least.'

'Don't underestimate her,' warned the Catosian. 'She is clever and those arms of hers could toss you through a port-hole before we shot her down.'

'When we have done away with hunger and poverty and war we will need a historian to record our age of miracles,' said Quest. 'Even if the hands that hold that pen could snap the spine of a bear.'

Veryann watched the engine boys below moving over the calculating machines on their web of pulleys and guide ropes. 'There is more to the woman than I can fathom.'

'The chattering of the craynarbian witch doctor you told me about?' smiled Quest. 'I believe in the fate we choose to make, not the toss of bones and cogs, or the throw of magic potions into the temple fire.'

'She has the luck of the devil.'

'We're Jackelians,' said Quest. 'We did away with our devils when we cast down our gods.'

The commodore looked around the chamber – an open space surrounded by tethered ballonets, the room shaking with the turning rotors on the other side of the hull. There was a gantry with a machine for opening up the lifting globes and filling them with celgas under pressure – Quest's unique high-lift mix – but it was the noise that attracted the commodore here. Little chance of being overheard. Or noticed.

'You did not want Amelia softbody to be party to our plot?' asked Ironflanks.

'Just yourself and T'ricola,' said the commodore.

'I think we could trust her,' said Ironflanks.

'It's not a matter of trust, old steamer, although I won't pretend that thought hasn't crossed my mind,' explained the commodore. 'Now we're no longer about his mad goose chase, Quest has written the three of us off. But he still wants Amelia working for him. I've seen the way Quest makes sure there's always at least one of his people standing around by the professor, watching her. Making sure we don't change her mind about leaving for home.'

'So,' said T'ricola. 'Billy Snow.'

'Yes. Billy. Bad, mad Billy Snow,' the commodore nodded. 'He's served with me twice before, navigated my boat through fields of mines and sat silent by my side while the God-emperor's bully boys tried to tickle us to the surface with their depth charges. He's shared my salted jerky and saved my life and if Quest knew anything more about seadrinkers than the cost of a cargo run across the Sepia Sea, he'd know we don't leave our own behind.'

'But is he our own?' asked T'ricola, the bony hand of her manipulator arm opening and closing nervously. 'He deep-sixed us back on the surface of the lake.'

'After leading us safely through the greenmesh,' pointed out Ironflanks, his voicebox set low. 'That cut he gave me on the seed ship was the strike of a master swordsman! I could count on one hand the number of steammen knights who could duplicate such a feat. If he had meant to make me deactivate, my thread on the great pattern would surely have been severed by now. He was trying his best not to harm us, even as he fought us to destroy the Camlantean crown.'

'There's a blessed sight more to this affair than Quest has admitted to,' said the commodore. He looked at T'ricola. 'How long have you known Billy?'

'I've crewed with him for years, for as long as anyone. I

didn't even know he carried a sword in that cane of his, let alone a witch-blade.'

'I met a boy like him once,' said the commodore. 'A fey lad with wild blood in his veins and a talent for getting into scrapes. Billy's older, but he always did move about like a cat on my u-boat – like no blind man I have ever seen before or since. Crewing on a seadrinker craft is a mortal clever way to travel around the world undetected, always another sailor in port to vouch for you, no ties to the land to gainsay your stories or your identity.'

'Our merchant friend knows who Billy softbody really is,' said Ironflanks.

'No, I think Quest recognized *what* he is,' added T'ricola.

'Not a wolftaker, though,' said the commodore. 'Not an agent of the wicked Court of the Air. Not if Veryann is telling the truth, which on this matter, at least, I think she is.'

'There are only two people with the answer,' said Ironflanks. 'Our erstwhile employer and Billy softbody himself. Of the two, I believe I would be inclined to trust our old sonar officer far more than the fastblood who has been paying our wages. If Abraham Quest has told a single truth about this expedition since he engaged my services, it has been by accident.'

'Ah, but I have already asked to see my nephew in his cage on the brig,' said the commodore. 'Veryann just laughed at me. I doubt whether we'll be getting visiting hours with our Billy.'

'How then?' asked Ironflanks.

Commodore Black tapped the metal duct beneath their feet. 'An airship is not so different from a u-boat when she's running at this altitude, eh T'ricola? Nothing to breathe outside, only her tanked air to keep us going. They have to breathe down in the brig as well, now, don't they?'

'There may be an intruder detection system running in the vents,' said T'ricola. 'Quest seems the cautious sort.'

The commodore scratched his beard. 'Then we're lucky to have the finest engineer to grace the *Sprite's* decks along with us to throw a spanner in it.'

'I am too big to crawl through such a confined space,' said Ironflanks.

'But you have two grand eyes,' said the commodore, 'like a pair of telescopes bought from Penny Street; and sound baffles so delicate I dare say you could tell me the weight of a stalking sleekclaw from her prowl. You'll do fine standing on watch.'

'It will be dangerous,' said Ironflanks.

'Your people once risked a whole company of steammen knights in Liongeli to recover one of your own. Besides, I want the mortal truth out of Billy Snow.'

'There is an ancient saying,' noted Ironflanks, 'originating, I believe, from you fastbloods. The truth will set you free.'

'No, old steamer,' said the commodore. 'In my experience, the truth will get you sent to the bottom of the ocean with an anchor chain wrapped around your legs to buy your silence. But it's the truth I need, all the same.'

It was also the truth that occupied the mind of Abraham Quest, standing more or less squarely on the spot that the commodore was planning to break his way into. Billy Snow waited on the other side of the viewing port, as unconcerned by the presence of the airship's master as by the existence of the cursewall fizzing between them.

Billy pointed to the motionless, abacus-like screen on the wall. 'You could have used your Rutledge Rotator to talk to me.'

'The one in your cell seems to have stopped working,' said

Quest. 'Even though none of my mechomancers can find a fault with the equipment anywhere on the airship.'

Billy shrugged. 'You can't get the staff, can you?' He raised his arms, free of their shackles. 'They didn't even secure me properly.'

'Actually, normally I can get the staff,' said Quest. 'If you shaved your beard off, Mister Snow, and dyed your hair a shade darker, you would be the very spit of a man who tried to kill me a little over a year ago.'

'Obviously he failed.'

'Obviously,' agreed Quest.

'What happened?'

'After the assassin died, my friends in the Department of Blood at Greenhall ran his sample through their great transaction engine halls. Not only did they find no record of his existence as a Jackelian native, but he had a previously unknown type of blood pumping through his veins.'

'Probably foreign then,' said Billy.

'Not entirely dissimilar to some of our own blood types in Jackals, but unique enough to be classed as an aberration. An aberration of one.'

Billy glanced over to where Damson Beeton sat in the corner of the cell under the weight of her hex suit. She was doing a very good impression of minding her own business. 'Aberrations happen.'

'True enough,' said Quest. 'Mules are born when the race of man interbreeds with craynarbians or graspers.'

'Craynarbians and graspers *are* part of the race of man,' said Billy. 'Just changed by the circumstances of their environment, their bodies whittled to a different pattern by the flow of life.'

'So our learned journals would have it,' said Quest. 'But now it seems my would-be assassin is no longer an aberration

429

of one, but of two. And my medical staff have been sent into an apoplexy because your blood work is not just similar to the dead rogue that tried to murder me last year, it is absolutely *identical* – not even the difference of twins to separate you.'

Billy shrugged. 'Small world. What's the chance of that happening?'

'I have heard rumours such things may be possible in Cassarabia, womb mages turning out copies of the caliph's favourites when their immortality drug has lost its potency on members of his clique.'

Billy inflated his cheeks like a frog. 'I'm a little too fair-skinned to be one of the caliph's children.'

'You may look like one of us,' said Quest. 'But the work-ings of your body are so off the scale, you might as well be a different species – a lashlite or a steamman.'

Billy smiled and wiggled his fingers at the side of the metal straightjacket he had been jammed into. 'I certainly feel like a member of the race of man.'

'Would there by any point in my bringing one of my worldsingers down here for a truth hexing?' asked Quest.

'It would certainly help pass the time.'

'And there are other forms of interrogation. The sort my friend Veryann and her people specialize in.'

'I am sure she is very accomplished,' said Billy. 'But those techniques only work against people who *can't* deactivate their pain receptors at will. As I'm sure you know, if you took one of me alive a year ago.'

'Why?' said Quest. 'Why don't you want me to reach Camlantis?'

'Because I think you know what is up there,' said Billy, 'and even if you don't, I'd probably still try to stop you.'

'You don't think I'm ready?' asked Quest.

Billy nodded. 'You. Jackals. The continent, the whole damn race of man.'

'We need it,' said Quest. 'We need your knowledge.'

'A knife can be the tool that cuts the barley and feeds your family,' said Billy, 'and it can be the tool that you pull across your neighbour's throat before you steal his fields. Trust me, Abraham Quest, none of you are ready.'

'If you don't want anyone to open the door, why leave a key under the mat?' asked Quest.

'Because you don't burn books,' said Billy. 'But equally, you don't give your books to young children to deface. You give your knowledge to them when they're wise enough to respect the gift.'

'And you get to decide when we're old enough?'

'That's what librarians do,' said Billy.

'Then it's a pity you are locked up down here,' said Quest, 'while we're outside, running around the shelves.'

'A grave pity.'

'I'm surprised I haven't seen more of your people,' said Quest.

'There were only seven of us, and as you know, we are only too mortal.'

'A little *more* than that, I think,' said Quest.

'Our anti-aging treatment was only perfected during the last days of Camlantis and there was the civil war and the barbarian incursions to distract us.'

'It can't have been easy. All these years, going on and on, while everyone around you moves along the Circle sooner or later.'

'A rock in the stream while the water passes,' said Billy.

'And you have been fashioned to survive. You are capable of violence.'

'Most of pacifism is social conditioning and meditation,

only a very small part of Camlantean society was based on blood engineering.'

'Still . . .' said Quest.

'I was created to be capable of accessing a part of the brain the race of man have long suppressed – the snake part, the ancient lizard that lurks in all of us; the devil hiding in our soul that urges violence and murder and rape and hate. But unlike your kind, I get to turn it on and off at will. In a little twist of irony, we obtained the blood marker for the genetic switch from one of the greatest psychopaths or our age, the Diesela-Khan. A hair sample obtained by one of our heralds.'

'Just a barbarian warlord,' said Quest. 'You really should have been able to stop him.'

'The Camlantean tools of mass psychological manipulation had one fatal weakness: they worked a lot better when the tribes were unaware of the techniques we were using. The end came very quickly after the Diesela-Khan captured one of our expert passive-defence groups and began running counter-cultural interference through the horde's druids. Our allies and the buffer states collapsed one by one until only we were left.'

'How ironic,' said Quest. 'If I could go back in time and change things, I would. A single airship like this and a couple of companies of redcoats and I could rout the Black-oil Horde.'

'What is gone is gone,' said Billy. 'All things come to an end.'

'Including the age of darkness we've been suffering since the fall of Camlantis?'

'You know the price for ending that . . .'

'I do,' admitted Quest.

'Then you are not fit to possess it.'

Quest paced the corridor. 'At least some of your people had a different idea. Perhaps even the majority of them. One side of a civil war is always branded the rebel side – and I'm guessing your creators were the minority that rose up. You were on the rebel side . . . the *winning* side.'

'Nobody ever truly wins a war, Jackelian,' said Billy. 'There are only degrees of loss, and there was none greater than that of the Camlanteans.'

Quest smiled. 'But *you* got to write the history of the winners, didn't you? I can see traces of your hand all over that. The noble people of Camlantis – the great pacifist race that committed mass suicide so that their legacy would not be corrupted.'

'The story is true enough. In a manner of speaking,' said Billy.

'A very loose manner, I think. I've seen your crystal-books, old man. Your own side's and *theirs*.'

'Bloody things,' swore Billy. 'I've hidden away more of them than I care to remember. Of all the books you had to find, why couldn't it have been the poem-recordings of some self-absorbed child finishing their schooling?'

'One last chance,' said Quest. 'Will you help me decode the key to enter Camlantis?'

'No.'

Quest shrugged and looked down the corridor. It was time for him to go. 'I'll unlock it without you. Your people buried the key deep in encryption, but codes were meant to be cracked.'

'You're a clever man, I can see that.'

'Clever enough for this task.' Quest started to walk away. 'Even though you're blinded, I can see you have Pairdan's eyes.'

'Children were not left to chance in the old days,' said Billy. 'We took a little from all of our parents. Grown in bottles, the way science intended. I believe around thirty percent of my body's pattern was inherited from Pairdan.'

433

'I believe that makes you a bastard,' noted Quest.

'Yes,' said Billy, 'we share that in common. Except that you're a self-made man.'

Quest shook his head in sadness at Billy's decision to hold onto Camlantis's secrets and disappeared.

'You're an interesting fellow,' said Damson Beeton when she was alone again with Billy Snow. 'There's more to you than meets the eye.'

'I don't suppose the Court of the Air has any more agents left on Quest's airship fleet?'

'No,' said the old woman, 'I think he's rolled us all up.'

'Then we're done for,' said Billy. 'We are all royally done for.'

In the transaction-engine rooms on the *Leviathan*, the cardsharp nervously lifted his pile of blank punch cards, dropping them into the inscription position in his typewriter-like machine before brushing the keys for luck. This last instruction set would either validate the previous day's work and move them forward (perhaps even to the end; but don't even dare think that), or knock them right back to the start.

'We're overheating,' called a voice from above. It was one of the grease monkeys, the uplander lad hanging from the gantry lines. 'The drums are running fit to burst.'

'We need to hold the revolutions steady,' said the cardsharp. 'We're close. I can feel it.'

'You've been saying that all afternoon,' complained the grease monkey. 'We're burning up in there.'

'Vent in more cold air from outside,' said the cardsharp. 'Use the next grade of oil. Just keep the drums turning.'

'We're running on special oil right now,' said the grease monkey. 'The transaction engines cannot take it any more.'

It was true. There was a smell of burning beer in the

chamber. The engine men cut the oil with the good stuff from Jackals' drinking houses, swearing it got them better performance from an engine running seriously overclocked.

'Just a little bit longer,' muttered the cardsharp. His fingers flickered over the keyboard, translating the genius maths sent down from the master's quarters upstairs, symbol keys jouncing with a satisfying resistance, the tattoo of holes in the punch card getting ever more complex. Even though this wasn't his program design, even though he was acting as a proxy to the genius of the great Abraham Quest on this project, there was still art in what he was doing. His fingers were on fire. *His* translation of the maths would make the difference between failure and success. The whine from the engines below acted like adrenalin, supplying the urgency, feeding him with the pressure he needed to produce his best work.

One of the chief engine men climbed out of the pit of machines to repeat the grease monkey's concerns, but seeing the cardsharp at work he held his tongue. He was senior. He had some understanding of the art that was going on up here – unlike the young upland turnip swinging from his girdle, dripping oil onto the floor from the cans dangling from his belt.

With a final bash of the keyboard, the punch card lifted out of its cradle, held by an automatic arm. 'There,' spat the cardsharp. 'Inject that into the system.'

One of his runners snatched the card and sprinted away.

'Carefully, lad,' called the senior engine man. 'Gutta-percha tears if you push it in too fast. More haste, less speed.'

The cardsharp looked over the paper imprint that had been left behind on the punch-card writer. It was too late now if there were errors in the code, but he checked his work anyway. He should have had a partner logic-checking his efforts, but there were few in the House of Quest that could follow the master's work. In the cardsharping game, it was often said the difference between the fourth and fifth best coder in the business was that the fifth best could look at the fourth's work and not understand a line of what had been written. You flew lonely when you flew so high.

From the depths of the pit, the transaction engines changed their pitch, the thunder of the rumbling drums absorbing the new instruction set. Few laymen could tell the difference, but to everyone in this chamber it was as if a completely new hymn was being sung down below. The cardsharp tapped his desk nervously, not daring to rise. There were so many possibilities for error. All the raw data from the crown's crystal that composed the key had been laboriously copied and transferred. What effect would too high an error rate in that data have on their attempt to crack it? Nothing good. Nothing productive, that much was certain.

The rumbling grew louder, shouts of alarm sounding as some of the transaction engines overloaded, oily smoke pouring upwards and drums cracking under the stress, grease monkeys converging on the danger spots in a swish of pulley lines.

'Look,' cried one of the engine men. 'The Rutledge Rotator.'

His screen was starting to spin, the abacus-like beads flowing from left to right.

'Who left it on screen output?' shouted the cardsharp. 'We need paper output, paper! This isn't some bloody dockside inventory count we're handling!'

One of them switched the settings just in time, the first of the result cards falling into a collection bin, a backup spool of paper winding around at speed alongside. The cardsharp snatched the result card and sighed in relief. The initial symbols on it were validly formed. This was the first of many cards that would be returned.

'Make sure the blanks aren't sticking together,' ordered the cardsharp. 'And send word to the master. The key codes to open Camlantis have been deciphered. Tell him. Just tell him, the gates are open . . .'

CHAPTER SEVENTEEN

'Billy,' hissed the commodore. 'Billy Snow, are you in there?'

A face appeared on the other side of the viewing slot, its features distorted by the shimmer of the cursewall. 'What are you doing here, Jared Black? Our next cell check is due in ten minutes.'

'I know,' whispered the commodore. 'I've been watching your wicked Catosian maiden come and go from the other side of the ventilation grille, my old frame squeezed between her jail's walls like the meat in a sausage roll.'

T'ricola crept past, taking position at the bottom of the armoured hold's stairs, her ears and the fine hairs on the back of her armoured skull quivering for any sound of the guard's return.

Billy shook his head. 'If they catch you down here . . .'

'Ah, Billy, we've risked a lot to reach you. Creeping like tiny little rats through these infernal shafts, nearly chopped into pieces by rotating fans, squeezing through spaces so small you wouldn't send in a vent girl to risk her neck to clean them, some so iced up we needed chisels to break through, others wired with snares and wicked devices of Quest's invention. But none of them were of any concern for old Blacky and your brave crewmates.'

An elderly female voice sounded behind Billy. 'Who is it?'

'A fool,' answered the sonar man, 'come to get himself killed on my account.'

'Ah, they've given you a lady friend to keep you company,' winked the commodore. 'They are not as bad as they seem, then. As for us, we don't leave our own behind, or we're no better than Quest and his gang of renegade mill hands.'

'You need to go,' insisted Billy. 'Your skill with locks is no match for this hold. It makes our old cage back in the siltempters' jungle kingdom look like the lock on a toy music box.'

'Don't say that, Billy. My genius has never been bested yet, and as clever as Quest is, he knows more about counting-house ledgers than he does of tumblers and cursewalls.'

'Maybe,' said Billy. 'But we're certainly not going to be sprung from here before the next cell check is due.'

'Take a little heart,' said the commodore. 'I'll crack this yet.'

'There are greater things at stake. My fate is settled, but there may yet be hope for the race of man. You need to return to Jackals and come back with help.'

'Who is to fly as high as this monstrous fleet of Quest's?' whispered the commodore. 'The RAN has no airships that can pursue a flotilla at this altitude.'

'I'm not talking about running to Admiralty House,' said Billy. He pointed at the woman sharing his cell. 'Her people. I know you have had dealings with their profession before, black aerospheres that can climb as high as these airships of Quest's.'

'A blessed wolftaker is she?' The commodore stepped back

in alarm. 'Don't ask me to make contact with the Court of the Air, old friend. They'll have my poor suffering bones in a cell half the size of this one and a hundred times more secure within an hour of muttering my first "good day".'

Billy sighed. 'I know all about your royal blood, Jared – or should I say, Duke Solomon Dark. But this is more important. My companion here can give you pass phrases, pass phrases that will overrule any desire the Court may have to toss an aging royalist into their cells. Listen to me. I have a story to tell you. The true story of ancient Camlantis, reduced to five minutes of telling with a spare minute for you to squeeze back into your air vent.'

The commodore listened and the terrible truth dawned on him. He was going to have to contact the wicked dogs of the Court of the Air after all. There was simply too much at stake. Nothing else would do.

Amelia looked up. The assistant from Quest's team had brought back another ream of translated papers. This must be what it was like to be appointed to the High Table, an army of scribes and undergraduates following every twitch of your efforts – doing the donkey work, copying and translating and cross-referencing and looking up facts in dusty volumes it would have taken her days to get permission to view back home. She thanked the boy and noticed he had brought in something else on his coattails – Commodore Black.

'Jared.' She glanced at the carriage clock on the corner of her workbench. 'Is that really the time?'

'Time for us to be going, lass. We're nearly out of Jackals' acres and over the Sepia Sea.'

'So many days have passed already?' She had become so engaged in her work that she would have been hard-pressed to say whether it was currently day or night outside the airship.

Another of Quest's people was admitted by her Catosian sentry, a bunch of cables clutched in the boy's hand as if he had brought flowers for the professor's desk. 'The fault in the crystal-book reader has been located and fixed. It was—'

Amelia waved him away. 'Thank you. I'll be down to the reader room in half an hour.'

'You could still come with us,' said the commodore. 'You could be back on the grand, solid soil of Jackals within the hour.'

There was a sense of urgency seeping through the commodore's words that seemed out of place. Amelia half noticed it, but wrote it off to her tired imagination playing tricks on her. How long had she been working now? Snatching sleep at her desk in hour-long stretches. So much to do, so much to achieve and read and soak into her brain. If only the worldsingers could work their sorcery on her mind as they had on her arms.

'My place is here now, Jared. The real expedition is only just beginning.'

'I've left my beautiful boat behind,' said the commodore. 'Don't be making me leave you behind too.'

'I'll see you again, you old sea dog. Under very altered circumstances. Parliament will pardon Quest when they see what we discover up in Camlantis. Do you think the Guardians will want the secrets of the Camlantean civilization landing on one of the city-states of the Catosian League? Catosia's more advanced than Jackals in many fields of science already. The House will write off Quest's theft of their proving vessels as the erratic prank of a childish genius and offer him a title for his troubles, you wait and see. It was you who once told me that success has many fathers . . .'

'. . . And failure is an orphan,' echoed the commodore. 'My own blessed words coming back to haunt me. All the same, lass, you should be coming with us.'

'I could say the same to you,' said Amelia. 'You travelled with me all the way up the Shedarkshe to peek at the mere ruins of the Camlantean basin – now we're a day or two away from the greatest archaeological discovery of our age, the sundered city itself. Don't you want to see that?'

'I travelled with you for the sake of my boat, lass, and now she's at the bottom of Lake Ataa Naa Nyongmo. And I came to keep you safe, too, but I won't travel any further. You'll make me an outlaw twice over and old Blacky needs his few remaining comforts, not a new life on the run. There's only so many times a worldsinger can re-mould my face before I forget who I am and why I'm blessed running.'

'Then this is goodbye,' said Amelia.

'So it is then. I'll pass your good wishes onto T'ricola and Ironflanks.'

'You be careful, Jared. Ironflanks may claim some experience pushing around a sail rider, but there's a big difference between jumping off a cliff on the Mechancian Spine with a chute of silk above you and piloting down a hot glider capsule.'

Amelia noticed Commodore Black peering over at her assistants; as if he would prefer they were not present at their parting. Odd, Jared had never come over as reserved before. She had seen the submariner skipper walk into a hardcore parliamentarian jinn house and sing long-forgotten royalist songs just to get a rise and think nothing of it.

'Mad old Ironflanks used to be in the Pathfinder Fist,' said the commodore, trying harder than he should have to raise a smile. 'You could drop him out of the airship's fin-bomb bays and he'd just bounce on his landing.'

'And T'ricola has her hard skeleton shell to protect her,' said Amelia. 'But all you'll have to cushion your landing is the weight of Quest's silver coins, so you glide down safe all the same.'

* * *

Veryann watched the last of the commodore's crates of money being loaded into the glider capsule, the silk-lined wings being furled to her side by the sailors. The Catosian soldier wouldn't be staying in the hangar when the three survivors of the expedition launched – the lack of air at this altitude would asphyxiate anyone without an air mask within a minute. Veryann crossed the hangar, pulling her high-altitude coat tighter to ward off the cold in this unheated section of the vessel.

'You need to launch now,' one of the hangar crew was advising the commodore, T'riocla and Ironflanks. 'We're approaching the edge of western Jackals. You'll be floating in Spumehead harbour and praying for a fishing boat to see your lights before you sink if you leave it much longer.'

Commodore Black was staring at Ironflanks climbing inside the capsule to finish off their pre-flight checks, T'ricola following to inspect the engineering. The old u-boat officer turned back to the airship crewman. 'I can see your iron pigeon is no seadrinker vessel. We'll head for the western downs right enough and leave the pleasures of the sea until we're back on solid ground.'

'No more adventures for you, then?' asked Veryann.

'If I had wanted to sail the heavens on one of these aerial battleships I would have taken the RAN's silver shilling, lass, and become a jack cloudie. You'd be as wise to join me.'

'The free company owe Abraham Quest a blood debt.'

'Then I hope you and your fighters have enough blood left to pay it.'

'We never did finish that last game of chess we started,' said Veryann. 'Drawing pieces in the dirt of the cage floor back in Prince Doublemetal's realm. There's a real board or two on the *Leviathan*. Who knows, I might even let you win – and that's not an offer I make often.'

'You've a sharp mind, lass,' said the commodore, 'and the vigour of youth besides, but I would have beaten you in the end.'

'What makes you think that?'

'Because you are a touch too predictable. You follow your warrior's code, but when you make that the heart of you, you give up something in return.'

'I think you have a code,' said Veryann, 'even though you pretend that you do not.'

'No, lass. There's no code for me, anymore. I just let myself be pushed around by the cruel tides of fate and survive as best I can.'

Something was nagging at the Catosian officer. Was it the haste with which the expedition survivors were trying to load the money into their glider capsule? Or was it the stiffness in the commodore's manner – an unease that should have been well sweetened by a glider stuffed full of Jackelian guineas; enough money to outfit a flotilla of new u-boats and more besides. The commodore should have been dancing a jig at the thought of leaving the danger of their high-altitude exploration of the firmament behind.

Veryann followed her instincts. 'Stay a while longer, Jared. You should see your nephew before you go. He may be a filthy oath-breaker, but you should at least say goodbye to him before you leave. It may be your last chance for a very long time. Quest will have him thrown back in Bonegate to finish the rest of his sentence when we return.'

The commodore picked up the last remaining chest of coins, wheezing under its weight. 'Now, if only you had been so reasonable the other day when I asked. As it is, we are running out of the green and pleasant land of Jackals to make a soft landing on. If I say my fare-thee-wells to Bull, poor Ironflanks will be paddling us back to the coast on his back and my treasure will be waiting on the seabed for a fisherman's nets to claim it.'

Veryann nodded as if in sympathy. Quest might not understand the deep loyalty of the crew of a seadrinker boat, but she did. They were not so different from the bonds of a Catosian free company. 'There is that. But we're still holding onto the child of Pairdan in the cells. You can get both your farewells over at once.'

'Two farewells would take longer than one.'

Veryann signalled her sentries forward from the hangar lock. 'Maybe you should say goodbye to them anyway.' A line of soldiers raised their rifles up towards the expedition members. 'While you consider telling me just how it is you know Billy Snow's real name.'

'Uncle silver-beard,' said Bull, glancing up as Commodore Black, Ironflanks and T'ricola were pushed into his cell. 'Misery loves company, eh? The food's better than the slop that came down the feeding tubes in the tanks at Bonegate, but the conversation here isn't up to much.'

'You are this braggart's kinsman?' said Septimoth, ruffling his wings in annoyance. 'This cell isn't half as big as it needs to be to contain two from the same family.'

Commodore Black looked over at the frenzied figure squatting behind the flying lizard, scrawling an intricate line of writing on the cell floor with the smeared remains of their last meal, coughing and shuddering as if in the grip of a fit. 'You've got that right, my lashlite friend.'

Turbulence shook the deck of the *Leviathan's* bridge, which was more crowded than Amelia had ever seen it. Not only were the command crew of the airship in attendance, but there were engineers preparing the mountains of equipment that Quest promised would prove the mechanism to unlock Camlantis – some of the components strangely familiar to Amelia: shades of the tower Coppertracks had been building at Tock House to communicate across the void. Helping supervise the work was the strange Quatérshiftian exile – Robur – whom Quest had assured Amelia possessed a genius to match the mill owner's own.

A gust caught the airship and even with the stat's bulk she tipped to the side, Amelia's hand snaking out to grip a guide rail. The *Leviathan's* crew showed steadier air legs, the sailors in their green-striped shirts barely moving with each shift of the bridge's wooden decking. Not one of them had lost the cap off their head yet, unlike the engineers, sliding and cursing as they made their final adjustments to the transmission mechanism. The question was, the transmission mechanism to what? Outside the sweeping arc of armoured glass that was visible past the steersmen's two wheels, the sky seemed preternaturally clear. Amelia's own airship voyages – previously confined to Jackals' merchant marine and her university's pocket aerostat – had never ventured even a tenth as high as their present altitude. But even with Amelia's limited experience, she doubted that the airstream this high up should be so vicious in an empty, cloudless sky.

'There's nothing here,' she opined to Quest as his airmaster rolled up the sky charts and passed them over to one of his jack cloudies, folding the compass back into the map table. 'What good is your key now? There's no lock for you to fit it into.'

'It's not that sort of key,' said Quest.

'Oh, is that so? Then why here?' asked Amelia. 'We're so high up I can barely see the Sepia Sea underneath us any more.'

'This is where we need to be, Amelia. I have had months to scrutinize the contents of the other crystal-book of the pair my antique dealer turned up for me back in Middlesteel. The second book contains the plan for the sundering of Camlantis – exactly where the rock formations would need to be split by the force of the leylines. How much earthflow energy would need to be concentrated to reverse the gravity of the rock layer under Camlantis, the trajectory, the height the city was to be set adrift at. If you know that, then you know where in the sky to search for the lost city.'

'There's nothing here now.'

'That's what the key inside the crown you brought back is for,' said Quest. 'The city *is* here, just folded away, caught between the cracks in the walls of the universe.' He indicated the glowing crystals protruding from his machinery. 'Stand back and watch.'

'There's one thing that puzzles me,' continued Amelia. 'As best as I can tell, the losing side in the Camlantean civil war seemed to be in the majority. Most of the Camlanteans favoured a direct solution to the Black-oil Horde when it seemed like their civilization would finally fall.'

Quest folded his arms behind his back. 'Actually fighting the barbarians to preserve their civilization. Yes, from what I have seen, I would certainly say that was the case. The Camlanteans were desperate in their closing days.'

'Yet, it was the few that still clung to the tenets of pacifism who attacked Camlantis, denying the city to the horde and murdering their enemies in the civil war. Doesn't that strike you as more than a little perverse? Surely it should have been the faction that favoured violent action that should have been willing to attack their pacifist rivals with the tools of aggression, not the other way around?'

The mound of machines on the bridge began to throb, an uncomfortable sound, just drifting in and out of the range of hearing.

Robur walked over to them, tapping his trousers with a clipboard heavy with schematics. 'You would understand such contradictions better if you had survived a decade in an organized community in the Commonshare, professor. The hand that preaches greater love for your neighbours and the forsaking of all personal gain, that hand is all too ready to turn into the fist that beats your family into submission.'

Robur's presence made Amelia uneasy. There was something about this man, a manic energy that manifested itself like a halo of light around him. It was as if Robur was capable of doing anything, flipping instantly between moods. He might suddenly sprint away, break down crying, or fly into a fit of violence. All it would take would be a gentle push. He was clearly a broken man, his soul torn to pieces in Quatérshift, hanging together by the thinnest of threads. Amelia had a terrible suspicion that thread might be her own dream of utopia. What in the Circle's name did that say about her dream, her obsession? As it was, Robur's attention was presently directed towards keeping Quest's latest creation functional.

Amelia noticed a faint spark in the sky outside answering the throb of light from the machine on the bridge. Each pulse from the mechanism mirrored by a heartbeat in the thin, cold atmosphere outside.

'It works!' cried Robur. 'After all this time . . .'

'We both toiled on this,' said Quest. 'We knew that we would succeed.'

Robur watched the flickering light outside, hypnotized. 'Without the transmetric valves of your devising this would not have been possible.'

'I merely refined the concept on my transaction engines. The basics were published in a Royal Society paper a year or two ago,' said Quest. 'Increase the power. We need to match the transmission frequency precisely, or knowing the key from the crown will prove useless.'

Robur waved his clipboard at the engineers and they adjusted the wheels and levers around the pyramid-shaped contraption. The foreign mechomancer started to mumble something, shifting his weight from foot to foot.

'Is that a prayer?' asked Amelia.

'I prayed to the Sun God morning, noon and night once,' said Robur. 'For my family to be spared. For my friends to survive. For food for them to eat. To taste the air again as a free man. But my prayers were never answered. Now I am like you Jackelians; I have made a religion out of believing in nothing. So in answer to your question, no, I am not praying. I am repeating the sequencing key for the valves.'

'We don't believe in nothing,' said Amelia. 'We believe in each other.'

'I think I would find it easier to believe in the Sun God again.' Robur rushed forward as a hiss of steam erupted from one of the pipes servicing his device, closing the connection while his engineers wrestled a backup duct into operation. Outside, the light was becoming more intense – almost too bright to stare at. Robur stumbled back. He was soaked in steam from the leak and his forehead was covered in sweat. 'I have seen no evidence of the Sun God or the Child of Light in the world. But I have seen Lord Darksun in the hearts and faces of my countrymen. I have seen Furnace-breath Nick striding across the land!'

Amelia was torn between watching the spectacle outside and the scarecrow figure of Robur, shaking like a mumbleweed addict too long without a drag on his pipe. Robur snatched up Amelia's hand and pressed it hard, a look of fanaticism crossing his face. 'We'll cast them out, the demons lurking in our souls. There! There are our tools to remake the world . . .'

Beyond the airship, the light was shifting, becoming planes of dancing energy. She had seen that light before at the bottom of the basin of Lake Ataa Naa Nyongmo. The light had taken them somewhere else, then: might it also be able to transport something back into the heavens above their Earth?

'Signal the other ships,' Quest shouted at the airmaster of the *Leviathan*. 'Have them move back. I don't want their crews needlessly lost if we are wrong about this.'

A wall of light pulled away from them, moving at incredible speed, every mile it fell back revealing an incredible sight: a sight Amelia had dreamed of, a sight she had never thought she would see outside the grainy images of a crystal-book. Tears rolled down Amelia's cheeks. 'You weren't wrong.'

Cheers erupted from the crew, echoes of their ovation rising up in the corridors outside. Faces throughout the giant airship and her sister craft pressed up against freezing cold portholes, for down beneath them hung Camlantis, floating in the air. Proud, beautiful Camlantis, her spindly towers and wide boulevards empty of life, her parks full of fossilized trees, starved of water and light in the folded-away pocket of a sideways universe where she had been banished for so many millennia. The people who had made her had turned to dust, but the organic lines of their city might as well have been preserved in amber. Only the underside of Camlantis showed the devastation that had struck the city, trailing girders hanging out of the sundered rock, severed atmospheric tunnels leading to twin shafts at the bottom of a lake in Liongeli a thousand miles away. There had never been a floatquake so large. Gravity reversed across a single landmass that stretched for miles. If this floating monster collapsed into the Sepia Sea now, the resulting tsunami would sink half the Jackelian downlands.

Quest walked over to Amelia, taking her hand. 'Are you all right, professor? You look faint.'

'I can't believe we've done it.'

'Your dream,' said Quest, 'and mine. We've always known the city was there.'

'Look at the size of it. We can't keep this a secret. Every paddle steamer making a course for Concorzia will be landing in colonial harbours with stories of a new floatquake land hanging in the heavens.'

'I think we'll have the run of the place for a while yet,' said Quest. 'Time enough to explore the ruins.'

It was true. They were beyond the reach of the RAN, beyond the reach of almost everything except the obsession that had driven them both here, that and . . . something else that counted itself master of these empty skies.

'Skrayper!' cried one of the sailors, her head covered with bulky earphones. 'Word from the aft watch on the *Minotaur*. Skrayper sighted at four o'clock.'

'I have it,' confirmed one of the crew, letting go of his arm-mounted telescope. 'Two miles away and heading straight for us.'

The airmaster pulled his cap down tight. 'This high up, it was only a matter of time. Damn my eyes, but I warned you, Mister Quest, those monsters are fiercely territorial.'

Amelia took the abandoned telescope and twisted it down to where the watchman had been pointing it. There. An elongated tube of transparent flesh as large as one of their own colossal airship flotilla, organic gas twinkling inside its body like a thousand star motes in the painfully clear sunlight. Jellyfish-like tentacles dangled from its belly, deceptively thin at this distance. Amelia had read enough tales of skrayper attacks on Jackals' aerial shipping in the penny dreadfuls to know that those arms were covered in wiry toxin-filled hairs that could lash apart the catenary curtain of an airship. Normally the sunlight feeders only came low enough to maul aerostats when the creatures were wounded or dying. But then, Quest's exploration squadron was operating at no normal altitude.

'Sound action stations,' ordered Quest. The undulating scream of a siren broke across the bridge, the sound of air-boots stamping past in the corridor outside. One of Quest's young academy boys – almost too small for his green uniform – came running past, handing a breather mask to Amelia. She copied the other sailors and pulled the strap over her head, letting the leather cup dangle under her chin, the flask-sized oxygen canister tied to lie across her chest. A token, only. If they were holed at this height, the decompression would take care of her long before she needed tanked air to breathe.

'The *Minotaur* will have field of fire first, sir,' the airmaster informed Quest.

'Signal her, then. Make ready on the harpoons and prepare our own too, in case the *Minotaur's* aim proves unsteady.'

'Harpoons?' questioned Amelia. 'We're no slipsharper out of Spumehead hunting for blubber and oil.'

'High altitude flight has its perils,' said Quest, 'and we have not come unprepared. This far above the ground I was antici-pating at least one attack a day until the skraypers recognize this is our territory and learn to respect our limits.'

'And how are you going to teach them that?'

Quest pointed to their sister airship manoeuvring beyond the bridge's viewing platform. The *Minotaur* shuddered as she released two rockets from her belly battery, twin lances pulling away on spouts of fire and heading straight for the glistening shape closing in on the flotilla. Both rockets impaled the skrayper and exploded inside its transparent body, the shimmering sun-feeding gas turning a dull green in the detonation's aftershock. The infection of colour spread throughout the creature's bulk quickly, like dye in water, then the whale of the sky began to slowly rotate, the diaphanous wing-like fins on its flank crumpling and folding up in agony. The skrayper's trajectory changed, arrowing down towards the carpet of cloud cover far below.

'Basic chemistry,' said Quest. 'Altering the composition of the gas that keeps a skrayper aloft and allows it to feed. Now, every time the poor creature tries to draw sustenance from the sunlight, the energy is transformed into a level of voltage that is higher than its body can tolerate. It's burning itself out with every new breath it takes.'

Amelia looked on, not sure whether to feel relief at the end of one of the legendary krakens of the heavens, or pity for such a cruel end. 'You thought of that?'

'Admiralty House has been offering a prize for a weapon capable of driving skraypers off our airships for three centuries,' said Quest. 'One of the members of the Royal Society bet me that I couldn't claim it.'

A bet. He had developed a method of securing Jackelian aerial shipping for a mere wager. Amelia shuddered. Sometimes it was the small things that served as a reminder that this was the man who had tried to buy the nation just because he *could*; who had nearly bankrupted the Jackelian economy and destroyed her life before they had even met. He belonged here in the clouds thinking his wild thoughts, too large for the nations of the ground below to contain. But it was Quest's storm-basin of a mind that had led them here, where no one else could tread. He had found the foundations of Camlantis where no one before would have dreamed looking – at the bottom of a rotting jungle. It was he who had set her on the path to the key to unlock the ethereal ruins of this city, as surely as his pilots had plotted a course in their flotilla of high-lifters – riding at altitudes that nobody would have previously believed feasible.

Quest nodded to a sailor on the helioscope platform and

he began to flash a message to the other airships in their small fleet. In front of them, the *Minotaur* switched course, drifting above the city's towers and seeding it with glider capsules, triangle wings folding out of the iron craft, white silk chute tails popping out to brake their descent. Amelia could hear a bass rattle in the heart of the *Leviathan* and guessed that they were also emptying their rails in the hangar below.

'We're here to explore the city,' Amelia said. 'Not occupy it.'

'You archaeologists do the same thing at your dig sites,' replied Quest. 'You lay out a grid and explore each sector in turn.'

'We use trowels and brushes. Not Catosian free company fighters and your poorhouse academy cadets.'

'They have orders not to break anything,' said Quest. 'I'm an impatient man and they will be our scouts. We already know the rough shape of the city from the outline of Lake Ataa Naa Nyongmo and with the landmarks contained in your crown and our two crystal-books, we should be able to orient ourselves very quickly after we land.'

The *Leviathan* was heading across the metropolis towards the centre of Camlantis where a massive spire-stalk stood, towering high above the surrounding city, a furl of flower-like petals starting to rotate around the building's apex.

'Sweet Circle.' Amelia watched a series of golden lights patterning up the huge tower.

'The crystal-books were true,' said Robur. 'The buildings do feed on the light of the sun. Just like a skrayper.'

'The city has been in hibernation,' said Quest, 'awaiting the return of its people.'

'We're not its people,' said Amelia, 'we're just pilgrims come a-visiting.'

Quest shrugged. 'Well, actually . . .'

Amelia looked restlessly at the merchant lord. 'What is it, Quest? You've been holding out on me again?'

'I told you when we first met that yours was not the only academic heresy I have been funding the investigation of. What do you know of the Maitraya?'

'Theology has never been my strong suit,' said Amelia, 'but isn't that a technique from the book of Circlelaw, an enlightened state of being you enter into after weeks of deep meditation?'

'That's how it is interpreted now by our church,' said Quest. 'But if you follow the scripts back to their ancient roots, it was said to mean *an* enlightened being. Not a state of being, but a very wise teacher. As an archaeologist you must have come across broken totems of the old Jackelian gods out in the counties, fragments from the age before the gods were cast down and the druids chased off?'

'Not my field, but of course I have. I've dug up temple artefacts from Badger-haired Joseph, the White Fox of Pine Hall, Old Mother Corn, Diana Moon-Walker, the Oak Goddess, Stoat-gloves Samuel – I could go on, the druids had deities for every season and lake and mountain in Jackals.'

'All the better for extracting tithes and tribute from their tribes. Two related questions for you, then,' said Quest. 'How do you cast down your gods and how do you destroy a civilization?'

Amelia saw where Quest was going, saw a glimpse of how his ingenious mind worked. Making connections between unrelated disciplines. Joining the dots to draw a picture whose existence no one else had even guessed at, let alone seen. Asking questions so outlandish that he would have been laughed out of every lecture hall in the great universities.

'You can't—'

'You can't destroy a civilization,' said Quest. 'Not truly, not without a *trace*. There were Camlantean embassies in other nations, Camlantean traders travelling abroad, there were the distant wheat plains and plantations worked by the Camlanteans' great machines of agriculture, Camlantean refugees fleeing from the fighting and the Black-oil Horde.'

'Camlantis was removed from the world,' said Amelia. 'It's here, beneath our deck.'

'The city, yes. And its libraries and its accumulated knowledge, the majority of its people too,' said Quest. 'The dust of the bones of millions of people blowing in the wind beneath our feet right now, exiled from the Earth for millennia. But there would have been at least a scattering of Camlanteans left alive down below to remember the glory their people had once held to.'

Amelia asked the question. It was almost rhetorical now, but she needed to hear Quest say the words. 'Where would they have gone?'

'Where indeed,' said Quest. 'They would have concentrated, would they not? Our own experience in the streets of our capital shows that. The steammen living together in Steamside, the craynarbians congregating in Shell Town. Fleeing the victorious Black-oil Horde in the east, I believe the Camlantean survivors fled as far west as they could travel, settling on an island.'

'Isla Verde?' said Amelia. 'Or do you mean Concorzia? There's nothing we've ever found there across the ocean that would suggest—'

'Jackals was an island once,' said Quest, 'before she drifted back to fuse with the continental landmass. Or so say some disreputable geologists your colleagues in the colleges would be hard-pressed to give the time of day to. If they have dated the timeline correctly, it would have been right around the time that the Maitraya appeared and inspired the island's tribes to reject the druids' teaching.'

Amelia watched the central spire of Camlantis drifting towards them through the sweep of armoured glass, the view from the bridge interrupted only by the airship's twin navigation wheels, manned by a sailor apiece. Quest had done it again. Twisted her worldview on its head and shaken it until there was nothing left of the old.

'There's a little of the Camlanteans in all of us now,' said Quest. 'The interbreeding that must have happened in the centuries since between the Maitraya and the tribes of Jackals. But in some, the breeding has run purer than others, the call to the old ways positively humming in their blood . . .'

Amelia steadied herself against a bank of navigation equipment. The blood that had acted as her passport into the strange world beneath Lake Ataa Naa Nyongmo; the blood that had allowed her to claim the crown of Camlantis with its dense information jewel. The same blood that had sung the song of prophecy to a hag of the Cassarabian dunes and a witch doctor in a Liongeli trading post. *Her* blood.

'We're coming home,' whispered Amelia, the city sliding beneath her feet.

The first scouts from their airships' glider launch were already arriving back at the foot of the spire in the heart of Camlantis by the time the *Leviathan* docked underneath its rotating petals. A perilous negotiation of wildly differing standards of engineering ensued– perilous, at least, for the jack cloudies lowering themselves on lines and welding on a docking ring; leaving arcs of mist in the air from their breathing masks as they swung back and forth thousands of feet above the abandoned city. Finally, a tunnel of cantilevered metal segments was manhandled across and riveted in place, joining spire and airship, a jury-rigged bridge between the modern world of Jackals and the ancient domain of Camlantis.

When Amelia stepped across, a sack full of jottings of their best-guess maps of Camlantis over her shoulder, her way had already been crudely marked in red paint. Arrows scrawled on the clean white floors and walls reminiscent of the corridors under Lake Ataa Naa Nyongmo and showing the way through the labyrinth. In this city, though, the spire's doors and lifting rooms seemed to work for everyone, not just her. Was the lack of security a feature of the trusting nature of the Camlanteans, or the functional practicality of a large metropolis? There were no visible signs of the civil war between the two factions of the Camlantean polity. No scorch marks or damage – no evidence of conflict at all, beyond the existence of the dead city itself, rent intact from her old moorings in the world below. But then, how would pacifists fight? Amelia wondered. Badly, was the answer, she suspected. *Totally*, whispered something from deep within her. Camlantis itself was proof of how pacifists fought. A cold, calculated, carefully engineered floatquake. Millions dead within a minute, gasping for air as the land they had called home lifted beyond its reach, before the rebels' dark engines translated the dead city somewhere even colder, somewhere still and folded away from the rest of humanity – far beyond the sight and conscience of their murderers.

The assistants assigned to her field team gasped in awe as they stepped into the lifting room running down the interior of the tower; its walls, ceiling and floor so transparent the structures might as well not have been there. Columns of light ran up the inside of the spire, rainbow bursts exchanged between floating copper spheres the size of houses. Her team chattered to each other, excited by the alien sight, voices muffled behind their air masks.

Amelia was aware she should have been more moved by the display than she was. Why did she feel so little, seeing these wonders? Wasn't this what she had worked all her life for, her father's legacy finally fulfilled beyond any of the dreams he and his daughter had shared when he was alive? Just the *chance* to be standing here. He should have been here with her to share this triumph. Then she might have been able to explain to her team that the pillars of light they stood in awe of were nothing more than raw information, capable of recharging the crystal-books of the city's inhabitants with any fact or finding known to the long memories and ancient storage devices of the Camlanteans. Levels of data so anti-quated they had to be filtered across hundreds of parsing stages before they could be interpreted by modern Camlantean minds and their information systems. She should have been able to explain that when the energy of the sunlight had faded in cold exile, the massive devices before them had frozen the data in a singularity point no larger than a fingernail, a compact string of exotic matter that must have joyously expanded when the life-giving rays of the sun struck the tower again an hour earlier.

They might have looked at Amelia as if she was mad or possessed, but the living echoes of this city were beating in time to her pulse now, and instead of being filled with elation at her dream finally being met by reality, all she could do was curse the cold and pull tighter the large, fur-lined high-altitude coat she had been issued with for exploring Camlantis. Something her father had once said to her came drifting back. *Pity the person who has no dream. And pity the person whose only dream is realized.*

Behind Amelia's head, her father whispered, 'Even an echo must end.'

She whirled around. 'Pappa!'

'Professor?' One of her team looked at her quizzically.

'Did you hear something, did you say something?'

'Just the crackle of the lightning exchange over there. This is it, professor,' said one of the explorers. 'This is what we have come for.'

'Is it?'

'It's magnificent,' said someone behind her. 'Do you think they had a museum down in the city? The things we might learn . . .'

'I believe we will find dozens of them.'

Even the street outside felt no more substantial than the phantom projections she had glimpsed at the bottom of Lake Ataa Naa Nyongmo. The light seemed impossibly bright, painting the eerily empty boulevards and buildings with an intense, pale clarity, feeding the deserted city the power it needed to begin functioning again. In the middle of the street, a strip of road was moving forward, an adjacent strip cycling a little faster while a band beyond them pulsed faster still. Her team gauged its purpose immediately, stepping on the first strip and waving as they were carried down the road.

'A transport system built into the road itself,' laughed a sailor below her breather mask, clearly finding the concept amusing.

Amelia tried to raise a smile at the discovery, but found she couldn't. Above them one of the *Leviathan's* sister ships drifted, not searching for a mooring on their spire but cleared for action, her gun ports turning vigilantly – something told her the airship wasn't on the alert for more skraypers turning up to attack the high-altitude trespassers. Then Amelia realized. Of course. She had heard enough tall tales from the commodore of the wolftakers and how they had hunted the last of the royalist fleet down at Porto Principe. Now the Court of the Air had a rival in the heavens and it would only be a matter of time before they visited the unexpected new arrivals in their sinister black aerospheres, trying to answer the questions that would be burning in their minds. No wonder Quest's mapping of the city had been planned with the precision of an invasion. An impatient man, indeed. Surely the Court wouldn't interfere in a scientific exploration far over the Sepia Sea? But then, there was also the matter of Quest's airships, the first aerial rival to the Jackelian high fleet since the science pirate Newton had terrorized the skies. Would the most cabbalistic of Jackals' secret police forces judge Quest's actions any more kindly than they had mad, bad Newton's? No, they were not the forgiving type.

Amelia's high-altitude coat was still covered in wood shavings from the crate it had been pulled out of half an hour previously. She brushed the packing off her fur, a dusting of it landing on the surface of the flawless pavement. A second after the shavings fell, a slot opened on the side of the rain gutter, discharging a flat discus on wiry legs that scurried over to the mess and consumed it, before sidling back into the darkness. Amelia felt for the lines of the slot on the pavement, but they had disappeared as decisively as the little cleaning creature. No wonder there were no mummified corpses littering the streets and buildings. The victims' dust had been tidied away using the city's dwindling reserves of power, even before the last age of ice had consumed the world during the coldtime. There was something terribly sad about that. This city was alive, but its people were not – and a city without people to occupy it had so very little point.

Walking past an oval booth Amelia triggered a still functioning sensor, a female head and shoulders shimmering into view in front of the stall. 'Kalour Iso? Kalour Isotta?'

They had no verbal record of the Camlantean tongue, but Amelia had mapped the written script of the crystal-books against what she had imagined would be the correct phonetic matches; debated the possibilities with other collectors and Camlanteaphiles in their amateur journals.

Information today. Information now.

Was it a request or an offer? A series of spinning shapes materialized by the side of the face as Amelia stepped closer, and she instinctively reached out to touch one. As she did so, a list of symbols appeared, each shape revealing its own list of sub-options. These she understood: the same script that had been pieced together by the universities in Jackals. Plays. Festivals. Education. Dialogues of council. Dialogues of consensus mind. And at the head of the list a phrase she had never seen before – Update of hostile action. Even in ancient Camlantis, war reporting had taken front page, it seemed. Amelia activated the symbol and the woman's face began speaking at a speed she could barely keep up with, only a sprinkling of the words in her commentary comprehensible. But the images that flashed up spoke clearly enough.

Continued advance. A sea of petrol-belching chariots viewed from above, a dust storm in the wake of a thousand spiked wheels grinding the ground, the picture device zooming in to show figures in leather and fur cavorting on the roofs of their vehicles, waving axes at the source of the images and making rude gestures towards their prisoners – scarcely alive – chained to the prows of their land craft.

Continued atrocities. A massive Camlantean farm machine lying smashed in a field of burning crops, flayed bodies dangling from the crumpled organic hull of the harvester, barely an inch of skin left on the ruined mess that had once been living human beings.

Neighbour-friend's collapse. A sacked city shadowed by a pall of smoke, zooming in to show a column of refugees trudging away, carts piled high with possessions while tired-looking soldiers in odd-looking angular armour used spindly rifles emptied of charges as crutches and walking sticks, grimly shepherding the survivors away from the poisoned wells and broken walls of what had once been their home.

Amelia watched hypnotized as the scenes flickered in front of her, misery after misery, massacre after massacre, until suddenly the report was over and the face announced: 'Timo-Felcidaed Iso' and incongruously moved across to a vista of children in yellow robes solemnly processing down one of Camlantis's boulevards, tossing petals from baskets while older children danced on a series of carnival floats pulled by cat-like creatures. Amelia gawped. Festivals held today. Was this some sort of crude propaganda? Their world was collapsing around them, but they still had the time and inclination to hold flower festivals as the barbarian horde closed in on the gates of their city?

It didn't make sense. These people had either been indulging in the most gigantic act of sticking their heads in the sand the world had ever seen, or they were simply expecting their lives to go on as normal. Neither option seemed likely, not in the slightest.

There was something desperately wrong here, and Amelia didn't need the pulse of whatever percentage of Camlantean blood flowed through her veins to realize that all the history she knew no longer added up.

'Quiet, now,' muttered the commodore. 'This is a delicate matter.'

'It is an outrage,' said Ironflanks as the commodore's left hand held open his chest panel while the plump fingers of the submariner's right hand probed inside the steamman's body. 'A blasphemy against my race.'

The commodore peered inside the dark recesses of Ironflanks' opened chest. 'You said yourself you have siltempter components, and don't those rascals swap parts of their bodies like the urchins along Pipchin Street trade marbles?'

'There is still part of me that is a steamman knight,' protested Ironflanks. 'The Pathfinder Fist do not submit to such indignities.'

'Ah, well that part of you had best stay very still while I see if I can do this.' The commodore glanced irritably across the cell towards where Cornelius Fortune sat, rocking and moaning. 'Be a good fellow now, I need to concentrate. How long is he going to stay like that, calling like a blessed crow that has lost its mate? He'll bring the guards in on us with that hullabaloo.'

'There were times in the organized community in Quatérshift when he would stay in such a state for weeks,' said Septimoth. 'That's why the community committee ordered his arm to be cut off. They thought he was shirking his duties in the camp and the threat of amputation would be enough to make him stop faking illness. As with so much else, they were wrong about that, of course.'

'I know a way to shut him up,' said Bull Kammerlan, bunching his hand menacingly into a fist.

Septimoth flicked a talon towards Bull. 'If you lay a finger on him, I promise you it will be your last act, little monkey.'

'You can't fly away from me in here, lashlite,' spat Bull, 'and—'

'Belay that talk,' ordered the commodore. 'We've got enough problems with an airship full of Quest's soldiers and jack cloudies to contend with. My nephew makes a rough point, old bird, but he does have one. If we're to get out of this cell, we're all going to need to be pulling on the anchor rope at the same time. Your friend isn't going to get very far like that.'

'There is another way,' said Septimoth, looking at Cornelius hunched and whimpering in the corner. 'But it loses its potency if it is used too often, and the one suffering can go mad – visited by the gods of the wind in their dreams.'

'If ever there was a time for your medicine, this would be it,' said the commodore. 'And as for madness . . .' he nodded towards the shivering form of their cellmate.

Septimoth sighed in agreement, pulling out his bone flute and raising it to his beak. He sat himself opposite Cornelius and began to play a low, haunting melody, so gentle that it barely registered on the ears at all. Everyone in the cell had to stretch their hearing to focus on the melody, losing themselves inside the tune as they spread their senses to catch it.

Bull began to make a disparaging remark, but T'ricola hushed him with a whisper. 'I've seen a lashlite play a half-crazed exo-beast to sleep with one of their pipes. Keep quiet for once.'

'This is no ordinary song,' said Ironflanks in awe. 'There are Loas being called. I can feel the power of it echoing within my boiler-heart.'

Around their feet a gentle wind began to circulate, warm to the skin, blowing at their trousers, flowing with the cadence of the unearthly tune leaving Septimoth's flute. It rustled the feathers along the lashlite's folded wings and swirled around Cornelius, his keening growing lower as the swish of air surged stronger. Wrapping itself around Cornelius like a cloak, the air seemed to solidify, pulling at his clothes and levitating him an inch off the ground. He stopped moaning and with a sudden inrush of air the wind filled his mouth with its power, disappearing inside the man. Cornelius's chest expanded as his lungs bulged with the unexpected blessing of the lashlite gods of the wind and he slumped back to the floor, gasping as if having just survived drowning.

Septimoth lowered the bone flute, leaving his alien tune still whispering in the minds of the other prisoners even though his pipe had fallen silent. 'How do you fare?'

Cornelius blinked and looked around the cell at the faces staring at him. 'We are still on Quest's airship?'

'If the guards' chatter is to be believed, we have landed on Camlantis,' said Septimoth. 'But you are correct. Our position as prisoners here is unaltered. They dragged you out to see Abraham Quest . . .'

'Yes, I remember that. He wanted me to save the world.'

'There's a coincidence,' remarked the commodore. 'For I was going to ask you the very same thing. You with your strange rubber face, you're just the fellow to do it.'

Cornelius pulled himself to his feet. 'The world doesn't need saving: it needs punishing. And this isn't my face. Quest still has it.'

The commodore resumed his probing within Ironflanks' innards. 'Well, let's be saving ourselves first. We can debate about what to do with our mortal freedom after we are well out of here. Now, there's the fellow . . .' he removed a skein of crystalline cable, a thin wafer of dark silicate etched with delicate golden metal attached to the other end. 'If only my darling Molly were here by my side, her with her fierce quick affinity for the life metal. She would be able to do this far faster than a weak old fool who has allowed himself to be tricked into this terrible adventure. Betrayed by his greed for Quest's pennies and his deep, pure love for the *Sprite of the Lake*.'

Cornelius noticed the wall behind where the commodore was fiddling: the panel to the transaction engine lock had been levered off. 'You can break the lock on the door?'

'I forced the panel open. He's been trying to crack the combination for most of the day,' said Bull. 'And we're still here.'

'You've got not a whit of appreciation for the art behind this, nephew of mine,' complained the commodore. 'If you had, you wouldn't have been languishing in the tanks at Bonegate Prison waiting like an idiot for your sentimental old uncle to come and rescue you from parliament's bully boys. You could have swum up to the surface and tickled their clumsy gates open for yourself. This lock is no humble stand-alone affair, the transaction engine sitting behind that panel is a slave to the great monsters Quest has steaming away in the heart of his flagship. It draws on all the power and quickness of his main transaction-engine chamber. Fuelled by their potency, this abominable lock is almost a living thing, its mathematics able to roll and change to counter every drop of cunning I can squeeze out of my poor, tired mind.'

'Then we're finished,' said Cornelius.

'Not yet,' said the commodore. 'When you can't win at the game, it's time to play a new one. Ironflanks, step closer to the lock. T'ricola, I'll ask you to hold the cable straight while I work, hold it as still and as gently as if it were a ruptured gas line back on your engineering deck. You may blow me a little tune if you like, Septimoth. A tune for luck and to steady my old fingers while I try to avoid setting off the hundred alarms and tripwires Quest has paid to be installed behind that panel.'

'The music of the race of man is too simple,' said Septimoth. 'Your notes possess no power and having forsaken your ancient gods, you Jackelians no longer play in worship of them, as is proper.'

'That's a pity, then. A nice shanty, that's what I could do with. Are you sure you don't know My U-boat, She's No

467

Sinker? No matter, no matter.' Sweat trickled down the commodore's forehead as he worked the wafer from Ironflanks' body deep inside the transaction engine, then spent half an hour fiddling and cursing Quest's mechanism and all the cunning of the merchant lord's transaction-engine chamber. At last he nodded and reached inside Ironflanks' chest, changing the configuration of a cluster of crystals and completing his travails.

'You should have been born a steamman,' said Ironflanks, in reluctant admiration of the commodore's work. 'Have you done what I think?'

'If you think your short term memory board is now running as a facsimile of the main transaction-engine system for the entire brig, then you are thinking right,' said the commodore. 'Just don't move and dislodge the cable, is all I am asking. While Quest's transaction-engine chamber is talking to you, believing you are the lock, I shall be having my own conversation with the little engine inside here. Let us see how clever this lock is now it's all on its own, with only a single drum turning inside it to outwit the great Jared Black. If I do this right, I can spring our cell door and Billy Snow's at the same time.'

'You must be joking,' spat Bull. 'That blind codger tried to kill us back at the lake.'

'I like him already,' said Septimoth.

'He's a Camlantean,' said Commodore Black. 'This is his city and I need his wily arts put to good use working in my service.'

'Time for a promenade around the city square, then,' said Cornelius.

'Ah, if only I had a small drink to steady my nerves,' wheezed the commodore as he worked away inside the panel, matching the encryption routines left running inside against his self-proclaimed genius. 'A thick ruby-red claret of the sort that used to come from Quatérshift when the Sun King still held sway across the border. Or a tot of jinn, even though a war hero of my respectability should only allow himself to be seen drinking on Beer Street rather than Jinn Lane. Yes, even a rare tot of jinn would do just fine to steel my mind for a miserable second or two against the perils of this dark, dangerous affair.'

With an almost frustrated whine, the transaction engine behind the panel finally gave up its fight with the commodore. The thick steel door of their cell slid open. 'There it is,' announced the commodore with satisfaction. 'I have matched my wits against the toys of the cleverest man in Jackals, and, just as I promised you, it is Abraham Quest who has been found wanting, not Jared Black.'

Nobody was listening. Tasting freedom, the other prisoners piled out of the cell, Septimoth's wings unfurling to stretch and fill the space of the brig's corridor – but, as Ironflanks broke his connection with the cell's lock, the transaction engine behind the panel started shuddering. The drum began spinning wildly inside the lock's mechanism, filling the cell the steamman had just vacated with a vexed screech. Billy Snow stumbled out of his own high-security cell, his head just visible bobbing at the foot of the stairs leading up to the brig's upper level. As the commodore exited their compartment, last to leave, the heavy steel door suddenly jammed shut behind him, causing him to stumble back.

'That was a blessed close thing—' the rest of the commodore's words were cut off as Cornelius dived at him, both of them rolling backwards as a heavy bulkhead slammed down from a slot in the ceiling, only avoiding slicing the submariner in half by a couple of inches. Commodore Black stared in horror at the bulkhead. He and the face-changing lunatic were sealed off from the others.

Cornelius banged on the steel. 'Septimoth, can you hear me?'

'We are trapped,' came the muffled reply. 'Doors have come down on both sides of us.'

Cornelius looked frantically at the commodore. 'Can you?'

'He can't,' announced a voice behind them. Billy Snow walked forward and traced a hand down the steel barrier, as if he was feeling the mechanisms built into the bulkhead. 'The brig has gone into lockdown. The guards will be coming down here in strength to secure the place long before any of us can crack these open.'

Cornelius banged on the wall in frustration. 'Where's Damson Beeton?'

'Still in our cell. Her hex suit shocked her into unconsciousness when she tried to step over the threshold. The suit must need a counter ward to allow her to leave. Quest is damned clever, belts and braces on all his systems. Now she's sealed back inside again.'

'We can get her out. I'll get you out, too,' Cornelius called. 'Septimoth, can you hear me, I'll get you out?'

'We'll sell our freedom dearly when they come for us,' came the tinny reply from Ironflanks. They could almost see him raising his four arms in defiance.

Billy laid a hand on Cornelius's shoulder. 'Sorry, but there's no time for this. We only have minutes left at large at most. And Camlantis is outside, waiting for us. Jared, did you manage to get through to the Court of the Air before you were detained?'

'No,' said the commodore, miserably. 'We didn't even succeed in leaving Quest's terrible floating flagship.'

'Then we have work to do.' Billy pointed down the stairs to the high-security level. 'You've already been through the air vents once before and deactivated the snares I can sense hidden in there . . .'

470

'Is that it, then?' muttered the commodore. 'We're to be crawling around Quest's rotten airship like rats in a trap, hunted by thousands of his wicked sailors and fierce fighting women. The three of us pitted against his rogue's navy? What sort of hope is that?'

'All the hope we have,' said Billy Snow. 'And unfortunately, right now, all the hope the world below has too.'

Quest stood in the shadow of the *Minotaur*, the airship having made the landing that was traditional when no Jackelian docking rail and hangar were available. Mooring rockets had been fired downwards into the dirt of what had once been a park – a ruin now, after cold millennia in exile from the warmth and nurture of mother Earth – sailors with drill clamps slung around their backs abseiling down lines to fix the anchorage. Heavy equipment was being winched down from the airship's hangar, uni-tracked metal boxes with stubby cannons riveted into existence by engineers, carriages belching into life as compact steam engines were fed with bricks of coal from the House of Quest's own mines. Their mobile fortress was partially erected on the high ground of the park's slope, a defensible base of operations while the scouts reported in from every corner of the city: many with wondrous tales of awakening buildings and living machines, a few with reports of destruction left by the ancient floatquake, and a sad handful not at all – their glider capsules having failed to negotiate a safe landing among the spires and towers of Camlantis.

Robur stood bent over a camp table, twin trails of mist rising from his breather unit as he examined the scouts' reports. 'We have found no central source of power yet for the activity we are witnessing. No main generation station.'

'Nor will you, Jules,' said Quest. 'The power is distributed evenly, part of the fabric of every building and street in Camlantis.'

'You are so sure?'

'It is the way I would do it if I had the necessary level of engineering available to me,' said Quest. 'A single point of energy generation is vulnerable to failure, to catastrophe, to the unexpected. These were a people who built to last.'

'They should have lasted,' said Robur. 'How different would the world be today if their society had not fallen. Quatérshift and Jackals would be provinces of a peaceful federation of nations living in harmony and enjoying the fruits of a super-science so advanced we might seem as demigods. An existence that would make the wild imaginings of the authors of celestial fiction look like the art of aborigines.'

'And the Circle willing, we shall have that world again,' said Quest. 'Or rather our children will. We just need to find it, before the meddlers from the Court of the Air turn up to see if what has been returned to the world will endanger the stillborn vision of their sainted Isambard Kirkhill.'

'They will come?'

'They always do. We can be certain of their pursuit – even if we were not holding a handful of the Court's agents prisoner. Their telescopes can point across as easily as they point down.' Quest indicated his mobile fortress and the material being unloaded. 'But I have a few military innovations waiting for them that they won't find deployed by the new pattern army down in Jackals.'

Robur accepted a roll of fresh reports from one of their scouts. 'We shall find it, yes, we shall.'

'Leave the location of the tomb to our scouts,' said Quest. 'That's what they have been trained and briefed for. You have other more pressing matters to attend to. The second stage of our scheme; the reason why I went to so much effort to free you from your captors in the Commonshare . . .'

'I shall keep up my end of things. I have my equipment and test subjects already loaded onto your armoured carriages,' said Robur, his eyelids blinking nervously. 'They are just waiting for the tomb to be sited. With all your resources behind me, achieving my vision was only a matter of persistence and application.'

'I think you overestimate the worth of my Jackelian shillings. You could just as easily have completed your work for the Commonshare.'

'I would have done so for the Sun King,' said Robur, 'but for the revolutionary scum that stole his throne? They were more interested in completing Timlar Preston's designs for his supercannon and vicious toys like these—' the mechomancer pointed to the iron carriages being assembled.

'For every idea, there is a time,' said Quest. He stared up at the spire where the *Leviathan* lay docked. 'This is your time, Jules. And mine. The dream that is Camlantis is about to be reawakened and your vision shall come to fruition alongside it.'

'We would need a hundred years of uninterrupted peace to even begin to understand the knowledge contained in this city.'

'A hundred?' said Quest. 'Why ask for so little? I shall give you a thousand.'

From the south came the unoiled squeal of a six-wheeled velocipede, its back wheels turning on a fan belt, propelling a vehicle little more than an open frame with an iron umbrella to shield its two occupants. One of which was Veryann, the Catosian officer leaping out as she drew up in front of Quest. 'We have a situation.'

Quest adjusted his breather unit. 'Has the *Leviathan* sighted the Court's aerospheres so soon?'

'This is more a disaster of our own making,' said Veryann. 'The cell level on the *Leviathan* has gone into lockdown.'

'A breakout? I thought the cursewalls my sorcerers had laid around the high security hold would contain a five-flower worldsinger?'

'They would have,' said the officer, 'but they were facing the wrong way. The breakout came from the standard security cells. I don't have all the details yet; half the guards up there are dead, but it looks like three of our prisoners managed to get beyond the cell deck before it was sealed down tight – Cornelius Fortune, Commodore Black, and worst of all, the thing that calls itself Billy Snow. All the other prisoners were caught by the lockdown and are back in custody.'

Robur had gone albino pale. 'Furnace-breath Nick! Furnace-breath Nick is out to pay me back for having played him false!'

Veryann looked with disgust at the quaking mechomancer. 'He is merely a man in a carnival mask.'

'I agree,' said Quest. 'Fortune and that fat fool of a submariner are of little account. It is the child of Pairdan we need to worry about – this is his city. He may well know where the tomb is, and he absolutely must not be allowed to reach it before we do.'

'You don't understand,' moaned Robur. 'Furnace-breath Nick is walking this land with the darkness inside his heart. I have seen him. He is real, he is real. Don't be fooled by that man-suit he wears.'

Quest grimaced. 'Pull yourself together, Jules. Besides, I know exactly what Furnace-breath Nick is going to do.'

Robur looked horrified at the unholy perception of the mill owner. 'You do?'

'Yes. He's going to come here to try to kill me.' Quest's

hand lashed out, striking Veryann's nose, unleashing a fountain of blood and disarming her with a nerve-strike to her wrist. 'Although, if he had ever seen Veryann train with practice swords, he would have known she was left-handed.'

The two figures joined in a blur of limbs, the Veryann impersonator kicking out, trying to shatter Quest's knee and bring him low enough to step forward and snap his neck, but Quest caught the boot and turned it high, pushing back to overturn his assassin. Another kick swept out to try to bring Quest to the floor, but he leapt over it, both legs frogging up to his chin. Then Quest flipped back. Behind them, Catosian soldiers from the airship ran over with their rifles drawn, but the free company fighters were hesitating, both figures too close to one another to risk a shot. Robur was quivering behind the camp table, oblivious to the fact that Furnace-breath Nick had come to kill the organ grinder, not the monkey.

The Veryann doppelgänger had a boot dagger out, moving in for a professional cut – low into the stomach and up, aiming to spill the contents of Quest's gut with a single stroke. A flurry of blows, rapidly exchanged, Quest blocking each knife flick with the heel of his hand. The mill owner possessed the luxury of long months of training, with the money to hire the greatest sword masters and pugilists of Jackals' duelling halls and the intellect to integrate their skills into a scientific fighting system that had been merged with the Catosian free company's own austere regime of war. This was the first time Quest's combat method had been matched against the dirty fighting style of the Jackelian underworld – a nameless system filtered through the rookeries, jinn houses and lean-tos of the slum areas of Middlesteel, as if it were the sewage that ran underneath the capital. A system not perfected on the polished wooden floors of duelling halls, but that survived and prospered with the blood of its practioners – mutating and evolving along with corpses left face-down in the puddles of Driselwell and Sling Street. Abraham Quest had risen from the gutter. Now the gutter had returned to strike back at him.

Quest left a small opening in his defence and Furnace-breath Nick lunged in to push his blade into the mill owner's heart, realizing too late that it was a trap – Quest's hands crossing and capturing his assassin's wrist, turning the bone at an angle the body was never meant to withstand. Quest stepped back, twisting his would-be killer's arm to his side, keeping him pinned to the ground with a pressure-hold as his soldiers rushed up and seized the assassin. Sophistication had triumphed over savagery. As the female soldiers pulled Furnace-breath Nick away he snarled and struggled like a wild animal. The city had never witnessed such a display of animal passions, not even during the horrifying advance of the Black-oil Horde.

'Keep him away from me!' begged Robur. 'He's come for me.'

'Every heaven must have its devils capering around the walls of paradise, it seems,' said Quest.

One of the Catosians raised her rifle to the assassin's head and slid the safety catch off her gun's clockwork hammer mechanism. Quest shook his head. 'Not yet. There's time enough to cast down our demons. You should have stuck to terrorizing Commonshare committeemen on the other side of the border, Cornelius Fortune. You've interfered in my plans once too often – but I shall permit you a small glimpse through the gates of paradise before I expel you.' He turned to one of the airship crew. 'Signal the *Leviathan*. Find out if he was telling the truth about exactly who escaped from the cells. Then find the real Veryann and have her send a company to protect Amelia Harsh's group.'

Robur appeared to be calming down, now that his tormentor

was being bound in chains. 'You think that the child of Pairdan will try to harm the professor?'

'Amelia is the closest thing our expedition has to a true-breed Camlantean. With the stakes being what they are now, murdering her would be a logical step to help ensure we don't breach the systems that will be protecting the tomb.'

'You're as dead as this city, Quest,' shouted Cornelius Fortune, his face disturbingly half-melted between his natural features and those of the Catosian officer he had been impersonating. 'We're not meant to be here and the city will kill you, even if I don't.'

'I wouldn't place too much faith in whatever Billy Snow told you,' said Quest. He pointed down the barren slope, towards Camlantis beyond. 'His rebels murdered millions here to achieve their ends, but they couldn't murder the idea of a perfect society. Once something has been imagined, it cannot simply be unimagined, it can only be hidden away.'

'I'll see you dead,' yelled Cornelius as he was dragged away by the soldiers. 'You and your utopia, both.'

'You first, then,' laughed Robur, finding the courage to step out from behind the table. His body had become a bag of nerves in the presence of the assassin. 'You first, you filthy demon of darkness.'

CHAPTER EIGHTEEN

Amelia was inspecting a series of artefacts under glass, the cabinets in the centre of a hall illuminated by sun globes that had risen to hover on columns of compressed air as they entered the museum. Her party were making notes and sketching each of the finds, ignoring the sound of the whining from the walls; the revived building's systems struggling to cope with the cold of their altitude. They had not tried breaking open any more of the cabinets, not after forcing the first one had cracked its objects, turning them to dust and cold rubble with the sudden inrush of air into vacuum. Whatever method had been used for preserving these ancient artefacts, it wasn't compatible with the Jackelians' current brutish methods of archaeology. But how ancient were they, that was the question? The Camlanteans seemed to have reconstructed a prehistory that was as far removed from their own age as their ancient civilization was distant from modern Jackals. Artefacts ranged from the simple – a shard of pottery handsomely painted with miniature swans on a lake – to the indecipherable: a yellow egg that looked as if it was moulded in hardened gutta-percha covered in buttons with a clean panel at

478

its centre. It was a pity that the golden rods lined with voicebox grilles next to each case had not survived the eons-long exile of Camlantis. What commentary would these rods have spoken if they had functioned? What forgotten histories could they have revealed?

Amelia was examining a case displaying a piece of granite embedded with fossilized cogs and gears when Billy Snow struck from the shadows, a shard of broken glass in his hand in place of his confiscated witch-blade. She ducked down and reacted on instinct, using her arms to add momentum to his flying kick, tossing him over a case to land sprawled across the floor. As fast as she was, she was too slow to avoid a pass of the shard ripping open the muscles on her forearm. Her terrified team of young academics had scattered like an explosion of squawking chickens. Unlike them, Billy didn't have a breathing mask; somehow the old man was managing to thrive on the thin, cold air, back on his feet again, his arms moving in a slow dance-like style of combat, a cobra trying to hypnotize a mouse.

Behind her, she heard the barks of more new arrivals to the museum. Orders to clear the way. The first of the Catosians' shots exploded into Billy's chest, barely slowing him down as he ran towards Amelia. He was running against the force of a storm, the crack of glass shells behind Amelia building to a crescendo. She could hear the soldiers shouting and yelling at each other, shocked at how little effect their rifle volley was having on the escaped prisoner. Still Billy Snow came, shuddering and jerking against the hail of fire. It was as if he was trying to prove the old maxim of the Jackelian redcoat regiments: the false boast that it took a man's weight in lead to kill him. Amelia crouched, mesmerized, as the blood-covered shell that was Billy Snow finally collapsed in front of her.

'Why Billy, why?'

'Get back from him,' shouted Veryann. 'He may be feigning.'

Feigning, her right foot. The old sonar man had taken a man's load of lead and there wasn't enough of him left to crawl another inch.

'Why, Billy?' Amelia repeated.

'Because – you can – never – find – Camlantis,' coughed Billy. 'You have – to – build – it.'

She ignored the warnings and bellows of the Catosians and knelt down to hold him. His hand reached up weakly, taking Amelia's arm, kissing the skin where he had wounded her. Then the old man rested his head back and moved no more.

'You damn fool,' swore Veryann, poking Billy's corpse with her boot, keeping a pistol trained between the blind eyes on his grizzled skull. 'He came to kill you.'

'He was one of them, wasn't he? One of the people of Camlantis.'

'He was a weapon, professor,' said Veryann. 'As much a sword as that living witch-blade of his. And I would hazard a guess that he and his rebels caused more deaths in this city than every battle-match fought by every free company in the Catosian League combined.'

Cold air from outside spilled into the hall as the museum's glass doors opened. 'We've found it!' shouted an airship sailor. 'Come quick, we've found it!'

'What's he talking about?' demanded Amelia.

'The reason Billy Snow wanted you dead. A challenge worthy of your talents at last,' said Veryann. 'Come. It is time we finished this.'

In the cold of the monitorarium, surveillant twenty-four pressed the pedal by her foot to rotate her seat away from her great cannon of a telescope, turning towards the monitor on the gantry. As if a personal appeal face-to-face would have more effect than the angry exchange of words they had just had over her speaking tube.

'I'm telling you, there's a new landmass above the Sepia Sea, well outside the location of any mapped or known floatquake atoll.'

'And I'm telling you that I have logged it for the day watch to follow up,' came the monitor's answer over her phones. 'We have sweep orders for three missing airships and half the counties of the uplands still left to examine.'

The surveillant swore under her breath. As if the missing airships would be heading south for Cassarabia. What need did Abraham Quest have for the caliph's gold, when he had just thrown away a mountain of his own money by absconding with the property of the navy?

'Orders are orders,' said the monitor. 'Leave the creative thinking to our analysts. Report and view, view and report. Save your amateur geography for someone who doesn't need to have a sheaf of sweep reports filled in by daybreak.'

Surveillant twenty-four reluctantly placed her face back into her rubber viewing hood, the transaction engine clicking and filtering the view, turning down to the mountains and lochs of the south – searching for incongruities that might indicate camouflage nets large enough to cover an airship.

Which was a pity, because if she had increased the magnification where her scope had previously been angled, she might have seen the lonely figure sitting on top of a Camlantean spire with a stolen helioscope, cursing every one of his unlucky stars and counting down how many hours of air remained in his mortal tank as he flashed his urgent message out.

A message loaded with pass phrases that would immediately have been recognized by any agent of the Court of the Air.

* * *

Amelia looked at the train of armoured vehicles drawn up outside the building, belching boiler smoke, trailing their own tanks of air to help feed their furnaces. It was more than the vehicles' pollution of the city that offended Amelia's sight; the single-storey building in front of her looked wrong too. It had been constructed along different lines to the rest of the city. Not open, but closed. No windows. No doors. A tomb, it reminded her of a tomb. And where normally her curiosity would cry for such as this to be levered open to disgorge its ancient secrets, her only instinct here was to run away, as far and as fast as possible.

'What is this place?' Amelia looked at Veryann and Quest.

'This is your heritage,' said Veryann.

Quest nodded. 'The resting place of the Camlanteans' greatest secrets.'

'Isn't there enough information for you in the city's main spire?' asked Amelia. 'If we can find the mechanism for extracting it down to our crystal-books, the whole of Jackelian academia will be teaching nothing but ancient Camlantean for the next few centuries in their efforts to translate this place's treasures.'

Quest tapped the walls of the tomb. 'And this is where they stored the greatest of their learning. Mined to ensure it could never fall into the hands of the Black-oil Horde.'

'Mined?' Amelia looked at the brooding presence of the low-slung construct. 'Are you mad? If the tomb is wired into their system of power and it is detonated, we could lose the entire damn city.'

Quest pressed on. 'We've come so far, risked so much.'

'You're risking the lives of the expedition, the whole bloody city!'

'Not with your blood,' said Quest. 'The dream of this place is in my soul, but it's part of your inheritance, your very flesh.

One last secret to unlock, Amelia. If you can't succeed in getting in with the blessing of whatever sentinels the Camlanteans have left looking after the city, you have my word we won't try to force our way in. We'll content ourselves with the parts of the city that were left off the latch.'

Taking off her thick wool gloves, Amelia placed her palm on the wall, the tomb's surface so cold it was almost an ache. She could feel the hidden lines of a portal, just awaiting the command to open. The building was as alive as the rest of the city, more so perhaps, deep wells of power buried within to keep this last store safe, no matter what carnage the Black-oil Horde committed. Warmth flowed out from her hand, her arms vibrating, as numb as if they had gone to sleep.

With the hiss of a murderous serpent, the security door rolled back, an outrush of warm air carried from the interior. The glow of the streets and surrounding spires disappeared, boulevard by boulevard, the tomb sucking up energy from the surrounding area, draining power into itself with a deep breath. There was a moment's confusion as the expedition members activated their gas spikes, lighting the scene.

Amelia entered through the portal, two beams of light flickering down the length of her body, dying away as they reached her boots. 'Keep back. I don't think this is safe for you yet.'

Quest's airship sailors and expedition members needed little urging.

A raised podium – a white circle – pulsed with light inside, beckoning her closer.

Quest watched from just outside the tomb. 'Is that similar to the transportation devices you said you came across in Liongeli?'

'No,' said Amelia. 'I think it is a keyhole. Unfortunately, I think I am the key.'

She made to step onto the circle, nearly there, when she doubled up in pain.

<Don't do it!>

'What is it?' cried Quest, seeing Amelia collapse in pain.

'My mind, he's inside my mind.'

<Don't do it.>

The cut on her arm. The last kiss. The blood bubbling up from his mouth.

'Who's inside your mind?' demanded Quest.

'Billy Snow!'

Her voice spoke, but not with her words. <Pairdan, Jackelian, I am Pairdan.>

'Get out of me!' Amelia yelled.

<First, you leave this place.>

Amelia tried to step onto the circle in front of her, but her legs were frozen, contradictory orders raging across her body. The tomb growled in anger. It had sensed something wrong. Billy Snow was no part of its creators' scheme. The civil war, the Circle-damned Camlantean civil war. Power was building up. Preparing to be released in a single murderous burst if this was an intrusion attempt by the enemy.

'You'll kill us all,' cried Amelia.

<Yes.>

She made one last effort, kicking and thrashing like a mad woman towards the circular platform. Her brain was burning, the headache to end all headaches. As she reached the platform the light pierced her, lifting her off her feet and rotating her around – giving her a crazy view of the other expedition members spinning outside the portal. She was washed with a sensation like water, cold water flowing across her every cell. Testing. Probing. The building made its judgment. *Compatible*. She fell to the floor, paralysed, whether by Billy Snow's possession or as a result of being drained of every iota of energy by the tomb she was uncertain.

Behind her a second portal hissed open, a moving walkway down in the depths below beginning to run. Darkness was overwhelming her, the room starting to fade.

Quest knelt down beside her, talking to her, but not talking to *her*. 'You realize, I trust, that it was the blood copy of you that tried to kill me last year that helped make all this possible, child of Pairdan?'

<Damn you.> Amelia's lips were moving, but not by her command.

'We could hardly have combed the great engine rooms at Greenhall for a compatible blood-marker like Amelia's unless we had a little Camlantean blood to begin with, could we?'

Then, came the blackness.

Amelia woke up, unsure of where she was, uncertain even who she was. She tried to move but her arms were manacled behind her back, the wound on her forearm burning with the restricted flow of her blood. Camlantis. She was still in Camlantis.

'My arms – why are my arms tied?'

One of her assistants came around the corner, followed by two Catosian soldiers, their high-altitude jackets shrugged off in the warmth of the tomb. 'My apologies, professor. Abraham Quest said you were possessed.'

Now she remembered. 'I can't feel anything inside me now. Untie me, kid.'

Veryann appeared behind her soldier. 'I don't think so. I warned you back in the museum not to touch Billy Snow. Now you have been betrayed by your Jackelian compassion.'

'I'm fine! Take these damn manacles off me.'

Veryann shook her head. 'Ingenious, don't you think?

Wounded. Dying. But you can still infect your enemy. Turn your enemy's weapons against their own side using one of their bodies.'

'Right now, I find it difficult to appreciate his cunning.'

Veryann pulled Amelia to her feet. 'Then perhaps, instead, you can appreciate how little I presently trust your intentions.'

Amelia was shoved out into a corridor, its roof held up by glass columns. There were dark shapes swimming inside the columns, darting about a crimson liquid. Like heated wax in oil, the clouds changed shape, reaching out to touch the glass, then recoiling, the surface burning them. Their movement was slow, sinuous, almost sensual. Where had she seen such things before?

'What are they?'

'Prototypes,' said Veryann.

'For what?'

In answer the Catosian waved a hand in front of a triangle etched onto the wall and the enclosure vanished, revealing a hall filled with machines – the organic systems of the Camlanteans interspersed with the crude machinery of Jackelian engineering, leaking oil and steam across the clean surfaces. Quest's retainers swarmed over their equipment, Robur at hand, along with someone else she recognized: Bull Kammerlan. The slaver was spitting invectives at the soldiers manhandling him. Next to him was another figure, also chained. The other prisoner's features were hideous, melting and reforming between different faces – one of which she briefly recognized as Commodore Black's. He was a shape switcher! What was this madhouse?

'Quest,' called Amelia. 'You lying son of a bitch, there's no crystal-books down here, no information store.'

The mill owner turned from his work and walked towards her, his arms open in supplication. 'Professor, up at last. No storage for facts, perhaps, but storage of a different nature.' He pointed to the face-changer. 'Plenty of room for my friends, down here, as well. This is Cornelius Fortune. He pushed me out of the way of a bullet once, a reaction he must be regretting now.' Hearing the mockery, Fortune tried to struggle free of his chains but he was too well secured. 'Walk with me, Amelia, you are entitled to see all the wonders of the tomb you have opened up for us.'

Quest led Amelia – still followed by her escort – to a gantry rail and motioned for her to peer over. A chasm vanished into the darkness of the rock below, the space surrounded by level after level of crystal coffins honeycombed into the sides of the pit.

She looked up. 'What is this place? There must be millions of coffins down there. We can't be on Camlantis anymore, that pit is far deeper than the bedrock under the city in the air.'

'Amazing, isn't it?' said Quest. 'The Camlanteans could do things with the fabric of our world; stretch it like the garters of a jinn-house serving girl. No, we're still in the tomb you opened – it's just bigger on the inside than the outside. I was hoping the passenger inside your mind might be able to tell us some more about the forces involved in achieving such a feat.'

'I'm fine now, I told your soldiers.'

<Warn her,> said her voice. Amelia groaned. The spectre of Billy Snow was still inside her, squatting within her mind like an unwanted toad in a garden.

'That's better,' said Quest. 'No need to be shy, Billy Snow, or may I address you as a child of Pairdan?'

Amelia cursed her forehead – the throbbing had started all over again. <Let her see your *paradise*.>

'There are as many coffins down in that pit as there were

once citizens in the city,' said Quest. He indicated a storage area behind them, shelved with hundreds of crowns – the same style of crown that she had seen worn by the Daggish Emperor, the same style as the crown under Lake Ataa Naa Nyongmo. Except that these coronets didn't contain an egg-like crystal-book: instead they were mounted with a circle of tiny gems joined by copper wires.

'Enough crowns to make you King of Jackals, if you had a throne to go along with it,' said Amelia. 'What are you planning, you devious jigger? You knew that this place was down here . . .'

Quest picked a crown off the rack and slipped it over his mane of golden hair. 'Can you tell the difference?'

'It makes your ego look even bigger than it normally is.'

Quest smiled. 'Perhaps, but when I wear this, it also hides my soul. The fire of my id is cloaked as if I did not exist, as if I was never born. Which is precisely what it was designed to do. The coffins down there perform much the same function, with the added benefit you can sleep in them and they will feed you and keep you alive. You could sleep for centuries down here, protected, hidden away from the world.'

Amelia shook her manacles in frustration. 'You want to hide from the airships parliament will send after you? There are cheaper ways to buy them off than mounting an expedition like this.'

'Now don't be facetious. You and the uninvited passenger inside your head have woken up just in time for our tests, Amelia. After all these years, we need to make sure the Camlanteans' measures to save the world are still fit for purpose.'

<You're not saving the world, you're stoking the furnaces of hell, you fool.>

'The majority of your people didn't think so, old man.

There was no coffin for you and your blood-father's followers down there, was there? You are Pairdan's child all right, for all the artificial nature of your nativity. You and your rebels preferred entropy and the victory of the Black-oil Horde.'

<We preferred history and the natural course of things.>

'Then you've had your wish,' said Quest. 'For too many thousands of years you've had your own way. But I choose to shape our destiny, shape it to an improved pattern.'

He waved to one of his engineers and the wall at the end of the chamber became transparent, revealing a series of rooms, each separated from the others like cages in an underground zoo. In the first of the rooms was an old lady Amelia did not recognize until the uninvited passenger in her mind supplied her name. <*Damson Beeton. An agent of the Court of the Air.*>

A series of metal boxes lay in an adjacent cell – hex suit-like coffins, only the prisoners' heads visible. More agents of the Court; the unfortunates who had been given the job of infiltrating the House of Quest. Inside the next cell, T'ricola paced about. Then there was an empty room, followed by a cell holding Ironflanks.

Amelia struggled desperately in the grip of her escort. 'T'ricola, Ironflanks, what are you doing here? You should be safely back in Jackals!'

'And your colleagues would be,' said Quest, 'if they hadn't so foolishly decided to betray my trust. That's something I have learnt from my Catosians, the value of total loyalty. There's something comforting in their binary philosophy, don't you think? You, *them*. Friend, *enemy*. Loyal, *traitor*.' He turned to one of his engineers, pointing to the cell filled with hex-suited coffins. 'Let's start with that one.' He tapped on the transparent partition holding Damson Beeton. 'I told you I would find something useful to do with your friends from the Court of the Air, damson. They made very poor bookends.'

Quest's staff moved about the controls on the Camlantean machinery. A slot appeared at the bottom of the agents' cell, a black liquid starting to puddle out. The fluid fingered across the floor, moving under the coffins, then it began to bubble and froth, a dark mist forming above the floor. It spiralled upwards, higher, rearing above the heads of the trapped agents whose shouts were muffled by the viewing wall. The vapour swayed from face to face, having difficulty choosing with so many trapped in the room.

'The craynarbian woman next,' said Quest.

On his order, a similar puddle formed in the corner of T'ricola's cell, the u-boat engineer backing into a corner at the sight of the liquid. The fluid moved as if it were alive, licking across the floor with slow, curious intent.

'Now the steamman.'

Ironflanks dipped down to try to block the small slot forming, but to no effect; the inky substance began entering his cell too. The steamman's voicebox trembled. 'You soft-body lunatic, what is this foul oil?'

In all three rooms the liquid had started to froth and boil now, angry, furious, becoming a vapour. Quest nodded in approval. 'This is the final instalment of my payment to you, scout. For taking my coin and repaying me with treachery.'

As he spoke, the mist fell down upon the occupants of the holding cells, the captured agents of the Court of the Air twisting in their hex suits as the mist devoured them. T'ricola banged madly against the glass, her exo-shell boiling in the haze, her body burning away – her flesh transforming, becoming mist, adding to the vapour's volume.

Amelia kicked fiercely at her guards, but they punched her down, then forced her face towards her friends' death throes, making her watch the lesson. In the first two cells there was nothing left, every drop of living matter absorbed by the ebony vapour; but in the third, Ironflanks stood untouched, the black gas curling around his metal feet, as flaccid and as harmless as a marsh mist.

Quest looked at Amelia, heaving a sigh at the sight of the intact steamman. 'Of course, you knew that was going to happen.'

'I—' Amelia was struck dumb in horror, but the unwelcome passenger in her mind answered for her. <The steamman's race came after our time.>

'Not quite true,' said Quest. 'I am sure King Steam was wandering the nations of the world, a lost lonely soul, when your city was alive, much as you yourself must have done for so many centuries.' The mill owner turned to Cornelius Fortune. 'Well, we have confirmed that the Camlantean mist does not function on steammen, just as we know it certainly does work on those who have mastered the worldsinger arts as well as offshoots of the race of man, like the craynarbians. But what do you think about something rarer and altogether more alien, something like a lashlite?'

Pushed into the chamber by a mob of airship sailors, a lashlite arrived, forced along by long metal poles capped with wire loops, the proud lizard's wings bound by straightjacket-like belts.

'No,' cried Cornelius, his face freezing on his true features as he realized what was about to be done. 'Septimoth. NO!'

Damson Beeton banged on the glass of her cell, smashing the chest piece of her hex suit against the partition; but the glass was made of something as near indestructible as made no difference.

'Toss him inside the empty cell,' ordered Quest. He looked over at Cornelius Fortune. 'I offered you a place in my service, once, Compte de Spéeler. Unless I'm mistaken, your reply appeared to be a trail of my people left dead in the *Leviathan's* brig and your dagger thrust towards my heart. Let me show you what a poor decision that was, for both you and your flying pet.'

Septimoth pulled towards his friend, seven of the airship sailors struggling to hold him in place, their wires cutting into him. 'I always knew that you damn hairless apes would finish the job you began on my flight in the mountains of Quatérshift.'

'Sadly prescient,' said Quest, 'even without the use of your third eye.'

Septimoth's gloved hand managed to get enough purchase to fumble free his bone pipe and toss it towards Cornelius. 'My mother's spine. Honour it. And if you have the opportunity, honour mine, old friend.'

'I'll get you out of this,' shouted Cornelius. 'I got you out of the camp in Quatérshift, I can get you out of this.'

Quest scooped the bone pipe up off the floor, tucking it behind the struggling prisoner's belt. 'I suggest you use it to play a death dirge for the both of you.'

Septimoth gazed at Damson Beeton as he was dragged past her cell. 'Remember, damson, nothing for the enemy. Nothing. You know what to do.'

The old woman pressed her armoured hand against the transparent surface, her tear-filled eyes just visible beneath the bulk of her hex suit. 'No sustenance for the enemy. I remember, old bird.'

Septimoth was shoved into the cell next door to Ironflanks, and at last free of the airship sailors' wire snares, he began tearing off his bindings, unfurling his wings and gnawing at the gloves constricting his talons. He had almost completely freed himself when the black liquid began to enter his cell, transforming into a mist in front of him, as if the vapour was trying to form itself into a shadow-copy of the winged lizard.

Then the mist darted in, striking the lashlite on the bony feathers of his chest. Septimoth fell into the mist, clawing at it, trying to disperse the cloud. For a moment it was as if the glass of the viewing gallery had been painted black, obscuring their view of the combat, but when the darkness cleared, the winged beast lay on the floor, his arms flung out and his body torn with a thousand cuts. Unlike the agents of the Court and T'ricola, and in a cruel mockery of the lashlite religion, Septimoth's mangled corpse had been abandoned on the floor rather than disintegrated by the cloud. Vapour chased around the cell in wild circles. It had tasted a soul and its flesh and it was eager for more.

'Not quite as tidy an end as the mist gives to the race of man,' said Quest, 'but then, I would expect that. Sentience is the key, is it not.'

Amelia realized Quest was talking to the uninvited passenger inside her skull, but she could hardly hear the mill owner for the screams of insane rage being hurled towards him by Cornelius Fortune.

Quest walked over, muffling the prisoner's cursing mouth with a breathing regulator, then produced a strange demonic-looking mask and slid that over the prisoner's air supply. 'Time for that expulsion from heaven we talked about. Take the great Furnace-breath Nick to the edge of the city and throw him over the side. And take his flying pet's corpse back to the *Leviathan* for dissection; if there is something about lash-lite physiology that makes it unattractive for complete absorption by the mist, I need to know what it is.'

In front of them, Cornelius Fortune started laughing, a terrible unearthly sound. It was almost as if he had grown larger now he was wearing the mask. 'You can't kill me now. Nothing can. You poor deluded fool, I can't die.'

Quest seemed amused by this. 'I believe it is time to put

493

that theory to the test. Goodbye, Compte de Spééler. We won't be meeting again.'

Damson Beeton banged on the window of her cell as her erstwhile employer was dragged away to be thrown to his death and Quest wagged a finger at her. 'Patience, damson. I already knew that the mist works on your kind. And if more of your friends from the Court of the Air come visiting Camlantis, I may yet be needing you alive, to carry them word of what will happen should they try to interfere.'

With most of the prisoners murdered a tomblike silence descended on the chamber.

'Interfere with what?' shouted Amelia. 'Is this your Camlantean paradise? An exotic execution chamber floating in the sky?'

'Ah well, at least one of you inside that pretty head understands,' said Quest. 'As I was saying before I was so rudely interrupted, the key is sentience. Your people designed very well, child of Pairdan. The Camlantean mist only seeks out that which can reason. A drover taking his geese to market would be slain in an instant by the mist, though his flock would be left behind unharmed. But then, what kind of world would it be without birdsong?'

<Where is your sentience, Quest? Where is your ability to think?>

'Here,' said Quest, unfurling a roll of charts and calculations down the floor of the chamber. 'The maths your people did so many years ago; and the numbers I found in your crystal-book have not altered a jot since I updated them with the figures for our world as she lies now.'

<There are things that are beyond calculation.>

'I disagree. Here are the estimated number of deaths that occur each year on our continent from war, here the number that die from starvation and malnutrition, here the numbers from sickness, here the mortality figures from poverty.'

Amelia's hand rose of its own will to indicate the field of black that covered half the chart. <And those?>

'The death of every living, thinking being outside this chamber,' said Quest. 'But you meant that to be rhetorical.' His hand jabbed down on the line climbing beyond the field of black. 'Here's the replacement level of population generated by a society modelled on the Camlantean pattern.'

Amelia felt sick to her stomach. How do pacifists fight? *Totally.* The replacement population supplied from here, by people held on ice like eels on a fishmonger's slab.

'Break-even within three hundred years,' said Quest. 'Everything after is a numerical gain. No more poverty, war . . . misery.'

Amelia spoke with her own voice now, but she was talking for both of them. 'You can't build a new Camlantis on the foundations of mass murder.'

'Don't tell me what to do!' Quest yelled at her. 'I tried to work by the rules, but you just kept on changing them.'

<She's right.>

'You hypocrite,' barked Quest. 'You and your Camlantean rebels played by the numbers of your own calculations. A couple of million dead in this city to save how many more millions in the world outside? But preserve those lives for what kind of existence? For watching my sister cry herself to sleep every night in an alleyway because she didn't have enough food to eat, starving while the gaslights of packed restaurants burned on the road opposite? For watching my older brother die of waterman's sickness because the only water we had to drink was from the gutter? You saved us for this? You immortal halfwit. You could have erased the Black-oil Horde, you could have erased everything and started again with *this* as the seed. We could have enjoyed two thousand years of prosperity and peace, we could be living in the Camlantean age right *now* and have known nothing else for millennia.'

<You can't build paradise on a sea of blood. My people were wrong then, as you are wrong now. No one ever asked the rest of the world if they minded dying to make way for a greater Camlantean Commonwealth.>

'I can forgive you for killing all your brothers and sisters in Camlantis. They were your kin to murder. But I can't forgive you for all the generations of us that followed, scrabbling in the dirt and the mud of the misery you left us as your inheritance.'

'There are other ways to change things,' said Amelia.

'You don't think I haven't bloody tried?' Quest shouted back. 'I could have rebuilt Jackals from the ground up on the principles of modern science and spread our democracy across the continent, used the RAN to overturn the killers sitting in the Commonshare, chased that fat fool of a caliph off into the desert. Jackals was mine. I owned everything and everyone in the land, but the old owners childishly decided they wouldn't honour my deeds to the property.'

<The world is changed by the one and one.>

'Oh *really*, is it? Do you think my model manufactories with their sanitary plumbing, free suppers and open lending libraries actually made any difference? Or my poorhouses and academies? I funded the Levellers to power and even they were wading in parliament's sewage, trying to pass the smallest reforms. Every one of my efforts to create the perfect society was a drop of clean water in a stagnant millpond. It's time to drain all the filthy waters and start afresh.'

'No,' pleaded Amelia.

Quest looked over at Jules Robur and pointed at Ironflanks. 'But we're not clearing our acreages to allow the steammen to inherit the Earth. *We* will survive inside this chamber. The coffins below are built to shield those who sleep inside their confines, while my people moving around the tomb will be protected from the mist by their crowns. A year inside the tomb will be long enough to allow the mist of Camlantis to exterminate the nations of the surface, but I have no intention of waking up to find a second horde – this time one composed of angry steammen – ready to storm my paradise.'

Robur murmured into a speaking trumpet. 'Introduce test subject twelve.'

A door opened in Ironflanks' cell, a tracked steamman crunching across the threshold. Amelia could see that there was something wrong with the new addition, the steamman's arms jerking in spastic movements, his head juddering while his vision plate danced with a peculiar pattern rather than pulsing with the calm, steady light of the life metal. Ironflanks sensed the wrongness too, backing away into the corner of his cell, but the newcomer tracked towards the scout, an iron hand rising up as if in greeting. A modem screech began to issue from the new arrival's voicebox. Amelia was no expert on the machine language of the steammen, but she had heard enough of their hymns to the Steamo Loas to recognize that this was not one of them.

Ironflanks stumbled back, trying to cover his sound baffles and drown out the siren song but, he could not. Swaying, Ironflanks began to lose control of his body, his four arms shaking, his metal legs jerking in the same obscene, involuntary dance as the other steamman. The scout tried to say something, but his mind was no longer capable of teasing his thoughts into vocalizations through his voicebox. He turned pleadingly towards the window where Amelia was watching and his turn became an uncontrolled dervish spin. Where was Ironflanks' softbody friend? He tried to focus on her, on the figures outside the room, but there were only random shapes floating through his vision. Ironflanks' telescope eyes began to flex out, his head lolling to the side as he stumbled around the room.

'Ironflanks,' cried Amelia. *'Ironflanks.'*

The two steammen started to circle each other inside the cell in an idiot's waltz, poking each other with their manipulator arms.

'You are wasting your breath, professor. Your scout now lacks the higher mental functions necessary to understand you,' sneered Robur. 'My ingenious little steamman disease is spread at the sonic level – it doesn't even require a joining of cables between steammen to spread. A few infected specimens pushed up the stairs to Mechancia and within a week, the mountains of the Steamman Free State will be inhabited by nothing but oil-drooling imbeciles.'

'You jigger!' Amelia struggled in the grip of the guards. 'You filthy shiftie jigger.'

Robur just smiled at her threats. 'The Sun King had grown tired of the steammen knights defeating his regiments. He desired something to distract the people of the metal from the length of their border with Quatérshift. Then the revolution got in the way of our project. Ironically, it was a lot easier to complete my work on the disease in a multiracial society such as Jackals, with its ready supply of steammen components and bodies.'

Quest addressed the passenger lurking inside Amelia's mind. 'It was the steammen grave robberies that first made you suspicious, wasn't it?'

<You shouldn't have stolen such ancient parts.>

'But it was ancient parts that I needed,' said Robur. 'Ancient components have their encryption patterns broken, their unravelled designs circulating as common currency among mechomancers. King Steam makes sure he advances each new generation of his people, always trying to frustrate the work of my noble trade. I needed to dig very deep into their filthy race's nucleus to design such a potent steamman plague.'

'Turnaround is fair play,' added Quest. 'I have seen enough of my cardsharps infected with transaction-engine sickness to realize that my colleague's unfinished project had considerable merit.'

'You're the sickness, Quest,' spat Amelia. 'You and your pet shiftie.'

'We are not monsters,' protested Robur. 'Do you not understand that I and my Jackelian friend have imagined countless times the terror the innocents below will feel as the Camlantean death mist seeps through their lodgings and starts to pull them to pieces? I see little else these days, but their myriad, murdered faces as I drift to sleep. But the body of the race of man is riddled with cancer and we must cut it out if we are to survive. You would understand better if you had seen what we did to each other in the organized communities of my nation. Such things cannot be allowed to continue. We must change.'

'I'll stop you!' bellowed Amelia. 'You're not going to do this.'

'Then you have made your choice,' sighed Quest. 'There is no room in our new world for division and opposition, professor. You of all people should know that if Camlantean society is to be reborn it will require harmony on the part of its citizens. But there is still one thing left to test . . .' He took off his Camlantean crown and gave it to one of his airship sailors. 'Put the crown and Professor Harsh in one of the cells, then throw him—' he pointed at Bull Kammerlan,'—in after her. I am fairly confident the Camlanteans' crowns still function after all these centuries, but I think a demonstration of their operation would be prudent first.'

'You're nothing but a pathetic little shopkeeper,' Bull yelled and struggled as they dragged him after Amelia. 'You're not fit to run a sewer works, let alone a new world.'

'You don't approve of my calculations either?' said Quest. 'Let me give you a new sum, then, something that even a lowlife royalist like you should be able to understand. One crown and two souls that need cloaking. You do the maths.'

Amelia was shoved, struggling, into the cell, Bull Kammerlan thrown onto the floor beside her and the room sealed.

'One crown, dimples,' said Bull, 'and two of us. That sum isn't going to change.'

'I opened this tomb for him,' groaned Amelia. 'I've murdered everyone in Jackals with my obsession for Camlantis. You take the damn crown and survive.'

A slot in the wall began to open where it joined the floor.

Bull shook his head. 'From where I'm standing, there are two of you on your side of the room.'

<If I was by myself, my belief system would require me to give you the crown.>

'But you're not by yourself, are you?' said Bull. 'You always were a queer one, Billy Snow, with your strange tales and your taste for damn vegetables, but I never knew the half of it.'

The black liquid started to puddle across the floor, the very sweat of hell.

Amelia kicked the crown towards Bull. 'I don't want it.'

The vapour was forming around their feet. At close quarters Amelia could see it was a soot-storm of a billion dark flecks. Tiny living machines – Billy revealed their construction within Amelia's mind – designed to take apart that which was sentient one cell at a time, to breed, to spread, to absorb, until anything more intelligent than a Jackelian rat-pit terrier was scrubbed from the face of the world.

Bull picked up the crown. 'My family were stewards of our

land once, until Quest's kind decided it would be better run by counting-house clerks.'

The cloud was starting to rise, becoming two mocking silhouettes, as if both the prisoners' shadows had grown detached and insane.

Bull proffered the crown to Amelia. 'And haven't they done well with it?'

'I opened the tomb.'

'Then between you and that mad old coot riding around your skull, you've got what you need to close it.'

Bull tossed the crown towards Amelia as the cloud formed into a lance and hissed viper-like towards his chest. 'You be sure and tell that fat oaf of an uncle of mine how I died.'

<One must live.>

Her hands struck out of their own will, seizing the cloaking crown and jamming it over her mane of hair.

The mist wrapped itself around the slaver, concealing him, followed by a macabre fizzing sound, like bacon on the griddle. It grew darker and denser, absorbing the new matter, swirling around in a frenzy. When the mist dispersed the slaver had vanished. A conjurer's trick. No blood, no bones, not a trace that he had ever existed. Bull Kammerlan had died without even a cry leaving his lips. Hovering in front of Amelia, shapes formed and flowed within the inky motes. There had been someone else here. Someone the mist was required to feed on. But now there was nothing. It circled the room for a couple of minutes. Then it retreated, confused, towards the floor, reforming into a liquid that flowed repellently out of her cell. The slot sealed shut.

Bull was gone. T'ricola dead, Ironflanks left a helpless cripple, the face-shifting madman and his lashlite pet murdered. Just one left alive, Amelia and the ancient Camlantean ghost echoing around her skull.

Amelia sunk to her knees. 'What now?'

<Now Quest will activate the ignition process in the nanofactury buried below,> whispered the voice in her mind, showing her an image of the death mist's huge breeding tanks. *<And he will remake the world. After he has first slaughtered it.>*

CHAPTER NINETEEN

From the safety of his tower roof, the commodore pulled out a telescope from his bag of purloined supplies and extended the brass tube, training it on the street below. It was obvious where the tomb Billy Snow had warned them about sat; you just had to follow the trail of carriages and material being moved across the city, ant-like columns of vehicles leaving the airships on the ground.

He focused on the group of figures moving to the edge of Camlantis. It was nearly dawn now, the waters of the Sepia Sea just visible beneath the gaps in the cloud, a mirror of crushed diamonds glittering far below.

'Ah, no,' Commodore Black cursed beneath his oxygen regulator.

It was the face-changing lunatic Cornelius Fortune, being dragged along by a guard of airship sailors. And if Fortune was no longer at liberty, then it could only mean that devil Abraham Quest was still alive. The trail of fresh vehicles shuttling out from the airships surely meant that Billy Snow must have failed in his attempt to prevent the expedition accessing the tomb too.

Two of the three escapees finished. So it was all down to

him again, then? Would the world give him no blessed rest? Hadn't it had enough of him perched on the edge of this floating mausoleum, signalling the Court of the Air to no avail? Their wicked eyes had had little trouble noticing him when brave old Blacky had worn the name of Solomon Dark and harried parliament's shipping with his royalist freebooters. Now, the one time in his life he actually needed the Court's people to come calling with their dark ships and their cunning weapons, they were all asleep on their watch deck.

He shook his head sadly and pressed his eye to the telescope. With a brief struggle the airship sailors unlocked the chains binding the prisoner then tossed the figure off the edge of the city – *walking the air*, as the jack cloudies called it when they executed a sailor sentenced to death in the sky.

Jared Black got a brief glimpse of a Furnace-breath Nick mask flapping on the madman's head, caught behind his neck on its ties, the winds playing with the tumbling body like a cat clawing a mouse. Cornelius Fortune had freed a bone-white pipe from his belt as he tumbled down, growing smaller and smaller, and the commodore heard a faint whistling as the fierce cross winds blew a funeral ditty through the pipe for him on his fall. Smaller and smaller, then the carpet of clouds swallowed the dwindling dot.

Commodore Black tugged a flask of the airship sailors' rum rations out of his stolen sack. Blackstrap, they called it. As thick as treacle and filthy cheap stuff, but beggars could not be choosers. He took a swig and raised a toast to the last survivor – well, the last but one – of their brief intrepid jailbreak from the *Leviathan*.

'You got the best of that one, you daft daring loon, leaving poor old Blacky to face these devils alone. Always me alone, always alone to save us all, damn my stars.'

* * *

The staff in the Court of the Air's monitorarium huddled together in an unauthorized conference on the gantry. Rarely had the handover between the day watch and the night watch in the massive spherical chamber become so heated.

'Floatquake lands tend towards the static.'

'But they can follow the leylines, we've seen that happen.'

'There's no sky mass of such a magnitude even recorded.'

'It could be a fresh floatquake . . .'

'Then where's the devastation on the ground? And there are buildings on this one.'

A hornet-like buzzing came from the bell near the speaker wire and monitor ten broke away from the exchange to look over the gantry, the slowly rotating scopes and their riders below like a carnival carousel embedded within an inverted planetarium.

Monitor ten picked up his speaking trumpet and phones. 'What is it?'

The surveillant's voice came back tinny over the wire. 'Skraypers and lashlites.'

'You've interrupted me for a lashlite hunt? I logged a dozen flights out hunting in the clouds yesterday. We have missing airships and a new sky mass to consider.'

'No,' said the surveillant, waving up from the scope below. 'The sky is full of skraypers. *Full* of them. And the lash-lites . . .'

'The lashlites? How many in the flight, man?'

'All of them!'

Around the monitors' platform every bell started buzzing as the watchful eyes of the Court of the Air began calling up in panic at the inexplicable sight. The monitors scattered to their posts, runners from the higher levels of the aerostat city bursting from the sphere's lifting rooms as the chamber signalled for backup.

Monitor ten caught a brief glimpse of the numbers on the report being tallied and torn off to be ferried away by the runners.

'Skraypers and lashlites. Oh my.'

Amelia watched the last section of the sausage-shaped pocket airship being inflated above her. They were putting it together in the centre of one of the city's squares. A semi-rigid, just large enough to lift its three cabins – one for Amelia at the very back of the craft, a rear observation post without even a gantry across to the other two cabins, one for the pilot room, and directly connected behind the crew's bridge, a hold full of infected spastic steammen, fizzing and shaking at each other as they blundered about the storage space. The old lady from the testing rooms was being manacled to the bench alongside Amelia, the mouth slot of her hex suit just large enough to accommodate the tubes of her breathing mask.

Abraham Quest came over, his head circled by the same cloaking crown that had saved Amelia from the death mist, and stood on the steps of the rear cabin. 'You've made your choice, professor. All this way to find Camlantis, only to reject it. Such a waste. I shall dream of Camlantis for you, for when I awaken, I will find it reality.'

'You don't have to do this.'

'I am afraid I do.' Quest pointed to three sailors wearing cloaking crowns, climbing up the steps to the airship. They entered through the storage hold and locked the pilot room door on the infected idiot steammen. Unlike Amelia's window-less observation cabin, the forward pilot room was sealed with glass. Quest's crew would travel in relative comfort while the two prisoners shivered on the seats of their exposed berth. 'They have orders to release you on the soil of Jackals before travelling on to the Steamman Free State. You and the old lady can enjoy the countryside for the few days it will take the Camlantean mist to propagate and hunt you down. I don't suppose the last days in Jackals will be pleasant, but you will have the solace of knowing that whatever panicked savagery you witness will be the race of man's last.'

'Someone will live down below,' spat Damson Beeton. 'Someone will survive and come back to pay you and your murdering followers back for what you've done.'

Quest shook his head sadly. 'If it comforts you to think so, damson. But no, in two days' time the only Jackelians left alive will be the ones in our little kingdom beyond the waves. In three days the last peasant in the pampas of Kikkosico will be dying. Within two weeks there will be nobody left alive in Concorzia or Thar. By the middle of the year the last u-boat of the Spumehead trade fleet will be desperately surfacing for its final taste of air and any polar barbarians remaining alive will be falling in their snow-covered longhalls. I am sorry, damson, but Isambard Kirkhill's bankrupt vision is about to be retired, and everything else that is left—' his hand swept across the city, '—will be Camlantis. A world of sanity, peace and reason – forever more.'

<Please,> begged Billy Snow's spectre.

'Too late for that,' said Quest. 'We're brewing up nicely downstairs. An hour for the mist to reach critical mass, another hour to bed down the first generation of our new Camlanteans in their cloaking coffins . . .'

Again. <Please.>

'Your revolution has run its course, child of Pairdan. Your city is about to live again.' Quest beckoned Veryann over. 'See that our guests are sent off on their way.' He mounted a velocipede and was driven away towards the tomb.

Veryann secured Amelia to a seat next to the agent of the Court of the Air.

'How does his plan sit with you?' asked Amelia.

'It is the plan of my liege-lord,' said Veryann.

'That doesn't sound like much of an endorsement.'

'It has a cruel logic,' said Veryann. 'That which is fit, prevails. That which is not, perishes. It is the way of life and the code of our free company.'

'The code of the Catosian city-states,' said Amelia. 'How much of Catosia will be left after the Camlantean death mist drifts across your lands and people?'

'We will be left,' said Veryann. She looked out. The hull was nearly ready now, the linesmen fitting in support struts to strengthen the airship's catenary curtain. 'And we are no longer counted as true Catosians by our people. We were banished.'

'Banished for losing one of the codified little tournament wars your cities hold to settle disputes,' said Amelia. 'Hold far out on the plains, so that the cities are not damaged and the innocents in them are not hurt by hostilities. That is your warrior's way, isn't it?'

'He is our liege-lord,' repeated Veryann. She got down from the rear cabin and pushed the collapsible steps up into the pocket airship's floor.

The expansion engines on the side of the pilot cabin coughed into life, rotors spinning up, the airship starting to rise above Veryann's golden hair. Amelia shook her head in sadness and looked down at the officer. 'Enjoy Camlantis.'

'Goodbye, professor.'

Before the pocket airship could depart, one of the sailors standing by an anchor rope twisted his mooring stake back down into the ground, kicking his colleague off balance, a second boot lashing out to smash the linesman into stillness. The renegade lifted a cutlass out of his belt. 'Let's save our goodbyes for later, lass.'

Amelia's heart leapt. Commodore Black!

Veryann slipped out her Catosian sabre, her eyes glancing up at the pocket airship listing at an angle against the anchor as it tried to break free of its mooring. 'You should have stayed hiding in the apartments of this ruin, Jared.'

'Don't be dying for that rich madman you call master,' pleaded the commodore.

She warily circled the paunchy submariner. 'I don't intend to.'

A line of soldiers running towards the two fighters from the other side of the square suddenly scattered, shouting in alarm. The heavens above Camlantis were dark with hundreds of skraypers. Steering-cables trailed up to their lashlite masters, the organic zeppelins tamed by skin hooks. Thousands more of the winged lizards rode the currents of the upper atmosphere in intricate formations, slowly drifting chevron V's, pointed hexagons, arrow-braided columns – the talons of Stormlick and the other fierce gods of the winds.

'It never rains but it pours,' said the commodore. 'They must have heard you're holding their fine-feathered friend Septimoth in a cage.'

'Then they've come a long way for his corpse. They can have his lashlite bones back for a harp,' spat Veryann, slashing the single line holding the pocket airship to the dirt. No longer bound to the ground, the stat rose away from the square, arrowing off low to avoid the beating wings of the lashlite battalions above them.

'Head for Mechancia,' Veryann yelled up towards the pilot cabin. 'Deliver those steammen to the Free State at any cost.'

'Tell the lashlites to bring us down!' Amelia cried down to the commodore on the ground. 'We're a steamman plague ship, we're—' then the craft was pulling away into the sky, the rest of her words muffled by her air mask and the cross-winds blowing over the city.

Amelia was gone, the pocket airship diving between the spires to evade a passing skrayper, destined for Jackals and the Steamman Free State. Death and plague for both lands following close in their wake.

Commodore Black turned a sabre cut and pulled his cutlass back as Veryann tried to catch the edge of the sword and rotate the blade out of his hand. 'This is a very different board for our little game of chess, lass.'

The air above them was afire as the *Minotaur* launched a series of aerial harpoons at the skrayper formations, but there weren't nearly enough of the weapons in the exploration fleet to slow down the mass of creatures. One of the lead skraypers made it through the volley unscathed and brought its tentacles down across the middle sphere of the airship, ripping her hull and spilling a flock of ballonets into the air. The high-lift globes rose up like a line of air bubbles shooting for the surface of a lake.

Veryann's form angled sideways and her blade cut ahead and forward, her right boot stamping down with each flourish. Commodore Black wheezed as he parried the attack.

Veryann struck again with renewed vigour. 'Yes, but you're twenty years and as many pounds ahead of me on this board.'

It was true. Her shine-swollen muscles made her a tigress, a living weapon of muscle, trained and honed for a singular purpose: war and its victory. An airship sailor reloading his rifle to their side spun around behind Veryann as a plummeting lashlite lance found its mark in his chest.

Commodore Black mustered his strength and ignored the ache in his arms, giving her a taste of her own medicine, but she was so much faster than him, meeting each blow with a clang of steel and pushing him away every time with an intricate counter lunge.

He was soon back on the purely defensive, the vapour from his regulator soaking his forehead. 'You've a sophisticated style about you, lass. As befits a Catosian maiden.'

She feinted left then cut up, severing one of the tubes from his mask, the rubber cable hissing half his precious air reserves away into the thin atmosphere. 'Yield now, before your heart gives out.'

'Ah, you've already broken that, girl.'

Their swords sparked in the centre of the ancient Camlantean square, the clashing of steel lost behind the rumble of one of Quest's tracked carriages as it cut a corner, its stubby cannon emptying a shell towards the lashlite formations spiralling above.

'Yield, and I can hide you away in one of our spare sleeping capsules.'

'Your blessed new world would be a sight too tame, clean and quiet for old Blacky,' wheezed the commodore, the mask hanging off his face. 'A sight too quiet for a Catosian fighter, too.'

She closed in for the kill. 'Then it's time for a different kind of sleep, old man.'

CHAPTER TWENTY

A melia jerked against her wrist ties, but the leather loop was too firmly stretched between her hands and the chains on the wall. She tried yelling and whistling for the lashlites, but failed to attract their attention over all the carnage in the sky. Two of the Jackelian airships were still in the air – the *Minotaur* just barely, broadsides from her cannons being answered by diving skraypers controlled by seemingly suicidal riders. The *Leviathan* was still tethered to the central spire and her three interlinked globes were crawling with lashlites tearing and breaking through her hull, like ants swarming over a picnic left on the grass.

Rifle and cannon smoke drifted over the city. Flights of the winged lizards dived down, striking with unerring accuracy from their gliding formations, leaving hails of lances falling behind them, any lashlite warrior who survived the answering volley fire from the ground pulling up to rejoin the sky-borne armada. Camlantis had known centuries of peace locked to the Earth and centuries more in her cold banishment; it had never seen an explosion of violence of this magnitude. No quarter was asked for. No quarter was given. Wounded

Catosian mercenaries inching bloodily across the white pavement were left still and pin-cushioned by swooping keen-eyed lashlite braves. Lashlites unlucky enough to be downed alive were mobbed by Quest's academy soldiers and airship sailors, their wings torn by bayonets, skulls crushed in a frenzied flurry of rifle butts.

Amelia yelled out again to the lashlites, her voice cracking with the effort.

'We're too far away, dearie,' said Damson Beeton. 'And lashlites are too proud to hunt a fleeing pocket airship. The god Stormlick fills the wings of those who hunt worthy prey, and that does not include chasing cowards who flee a fight.'

Amelia struggled vainly. 'The people of the winds have got to stop Quest.'

<They are too late,> said the voice in her skull. *<The chamber you saw in that tomb was designed to withstand all the ingenuity my rebel grouping within the Camlantean polity could throw at it. The House of Quest can seal their people inside and release the death mist at their leisure after it has been produced in sufficient quantities to guarantee the extermination of the world. Lashlite lances will not break their way in.>*

'There has to be a way to get inside it.'

<There may be an alternative. But to get to it we need to be free and back down on the streets of the city again. Which of your hands do you value the most?>

'What?'

<Left or right?>

'I'm right-handed.'

<Left it is. Grit your teeth. Your screams will draw the attention of the crew.>

They did. One of the sailors put down the sounding scope he was using to guide the pocket airship between the Camlantean spires and turned around.

'Have we been boarded?' demanded the bosun, his peaked cap swapped for one of the soul-cloaking crowns.

'It's that bloody university woman,' replied the sailor, staring out of the porthole. 'Yelling like she's being rogered by a pike.'

'Go back and see what she's about,' ordered the bosun. 'Unless she behaves, I'll put her off early—' he made a tipping motion with his hand, '—and give her a little wash in the sea without the bother of a landing.'

Unhooking one of the pistols from the gun rack on the wall, the sailor slipped a glass charge into the weapon's breech, then unlocked the door to the storage cabin. Black oil washed the floor of the next compartment, thirteen imbecile steammen juddering about and spitting system fluids over the cargo hold, their voiceboxes humming in the nonsense tongue of a low-order language. Thirteen of the damn infected things. Unlucky for them and the future of the Steamman Free State both.

A tri-wheeled creature of the metal slipped up in front of the sailor, its dome of a head rotating before it pissed a stream of dark oil up at the airship sailor's striped shirt.

'Oh, you dirty little bugger,' cursed the sailor.

One of the jack cloudies stuck his head through the pilot room door and laughed at the sight of his colleague. Humiliated, the fouled sailor kicked the idiot thing over with an angry lash of his boot, then squeezed around the steel box in the floor where the clockwork of the rudder guidance system was clacking away in response to the helmsman's touch. Making enough of a noise that the sailor didn't hear the strange whining from the steamman lying in the corner. Not that he would have recognized the sound if he had heard it. There wasn't a mechomancer in the world – let alone an airship sailor – who would have recognized the noise of siltempter components resetting to zero in a final attempt to clear away the putrid steamman infection; for no mechomancer had ever been to the Liongeli jungle and made it back alive from the realm of Prince Doublemetal. And the annoyed skyman was many things, but he was no mechomancer.

The sailor opened the stern door of the storage hold and stepped out onto the rear gantry, calling across to the observation cabin behind. 'Shut your cake-hole, woman. If you make one of us use the jenny line to come across to you, you'll have cause to scream.'

But Amelia only yelled louder still as the thing that had burrowed deep into her mind continued to work its way down her bloodstream to her bound wrists, converting the salts in her left hand's sweat glands into acid. Burning liquid bubbled from Amelia's now blackened skin until at last the bonds snapped.

<Rub your wrist over the damson's hand ties now,> commanded the voice inside her skull.

She did as she was ordered and screamed as the cold metal of the agent's manacles came into contact with her skin.

'I'm bloody warning you for the last time,' the sailor shouted.

<That's it, professor. I'm converting the chemicals in your blood into a healing hyper-accelerant now. The pain's mostly in your mind.>

In the opposite cabin the sailor lifted his pistol and drew a bead on the bobbing woman opposite.

<You should have enough acid left in your hand to rub onto the box on the belt of the damson's hex suit. That's the mechanism to unlock her armour.>

'Get ready to duck,' said Damson Beeton, bending her head as far as the hex suit would permit to look across at the sailor. 'I will tell you when.'

The sailor's finger was closing around the trigger when Ironflanks' four arms wrapped themselves around his chest.

And *compressed*. It was the sailor's turn to scream, struggling as the scout turned him about and pushed him into the gaggle of infected steammen, the imbeciles pawing his snapped ribs with metal manipulators and whistling in childish awe at his shuddering conversion into a broken bag of meat and bones. With a crack, the pistol in the dying sailor's hand detonated into the steering box, the springs and cogs of the clockwork mechanism flailing as uselessly as the suddenly non-responsive rudder control turning in the pilot's hands. The pocket stat pitched down; her externally-mounted expansion engines swivelling at angles that Quest's airship works would never have envisaged, the dome of her pilot cabin shattering along with the mirrored glass of one of the Camlantean spires. Pushing forward, the pocket airship rammed herself deeper into the Camlantean structure, the rise and fall of her expansion engines fading as her propellers broke themselves trying to walk across the floor.

One of the remaining crewmen lay impaled on a shard of glass, but the bosun was still alive. He stumbled out of the wreckage into the tower, lifting up a brace of bell-barrelled pistols as he turned back towards his wrecked ship. Ironflanks appeared at the door of the cabin, an angel of vengeance covered in the oil of his kind and the blood of his softbody enemies. Ironflanks' voicebox trembled with fury and the bosun recoiled back, his heart exploded by an arrow of sonic energy directed by the steamman like a punched nail. The commanding officer of the small craft slapped down, as dead as his airship.

Amelia slowly pulled herself out of the crumpled rear of the vessel, followed by Damson Beeton, her hex suit left abandoned in pieces on the observation cabin's floor. Shattered glass was moving across the floor, flowing back up the wall to rebuild the broken window – regrowing itself around the foreign element that had attempted to pollute the integrity of the spire. The sound of the winds and the fighting outside was cut off as the window repaired itself.

'Ironflanks, you are alive. But I saw you—'

'I am reborn, Amelia softbody, but you may not like what I have become. A *savage*. A siltempter boiler heart driven by the wreckage of a steamman mind.' Removing the cover from the airship's broken expansion engine, Ironflanks balanced a pistol shell from the cabin outside the gas-mixing chamber.

Damson Beeton recognized what the scout was doing. She picked up the dead bosun's brace of pistols and tucked them in her pinny, then pulled Amelia to the side. 'Back we go, dear, let's take cover.'

Inside the storage hold, the vision plate of one of the infected steammen pressed itself against the porthole.

'Ironflanks,' Amelia called, 'your people are still inside there. You got better – there may be a cure!'

'This is the cure,' said Ironflanks, moving back as the blow-barrel gas ignited, the engine bursting apart and covering the pocket airship in flames. With the oil already inside the storage hold, the end was mercifully quick for the plague victims. Nodules appeared in the ceiling above, attempting to put out the fire, but the spire's water supply had long since evaporated.

The thing inside Amelia's head had become oddly silent.

'Billy? You said there was another way to stop Quest and—'

<*I am decaying. This was only meant to be a battlefield copy of my essence, a combat transfer, an underhand trick to spread confusion among the foe. The synapses in your prefrontal cortex are rewriting your mind's pathways back to their natural condition. You are forgetting me.*>

'You said there was a way to stop Quest releasing your mist . . .'

<An oblique way,> Billy used her voice for the benefit of the others. <The dark engine my faction concealed inside Camlantis to banish the city into the no-space realm after we blew her into the sky may still have enough power left inside its energy sinks to repeat the exercise. If so, we can send the city away again, trap Quest and our disassembler weapon in a place where his terrible solution – my people's solution – will wither in absolute isolation.>

'*May* still have enough power?'

<We must go, my time left with you here is short.>

Amelia fingered the skin on her burning left hand. Part ruined, the remains of it felt like a lump of numb meat. She sprinted away, followed by Ironflanks and the elderly agent of the Court of the Air.

Quest watched the disciplined lines of his academy cadets filing down into the chasm, suspension capsules hissing open to swallow each young man and woman in turn, then filling with the strange yellow gel that would allow them to sleep for years, their bodies nourished, and – more importantly – their souls cloaked from the ravages of the cleansing mist. Young, malleable minds that had known nothing but loyalty to the House of Quest. Rescued from the cruel streets of the capital and the other industrial towns, then fed, clothed, taught, nurtured, *honed* into the best they could be. Philosopher kings. The first generation of Camlanteans to seed an empty world.

Briefly, Quest felt a twinge of grief that there hadn't been someone like him to save his own siblings from their early deaths in the crowded, dirty tenements of Middlesteel. He sighed. He always felt so normal, so average. But the rational part of his mind realized that a person such as himself was born only once in a thousand generations. Well, the universe had borne him into her grace as a watchmaker, so it was beholden on him to fix the broken clock that was their world. Honour the vow that he made over the dirt of his brother and sisters' paupers' graves after the last of them had moved along the Circle for their new lives, leaving him all alone.

'No more poverty,' he whispered. 'No more needless suffering.'

His engineers busied themselves about the chamber, cloaking crowns fixed around their scalps, the sounds of battle filtering down the moving stairs along with the crates of supplies still being portered inside the tomb. There were enough Catosian fighters and airship crew to hold off the lashlites for the final half hour he needed. Then the dirty lizards' lifeless corpses would be raining out of the sky as the black mist climbed to embrace their aerial regiments.

Nobody would miss *them* in his brave new world.

Robur stood up, the melted components of the steammen still white hot in the ruins of the pocket airship. The soldiers of the Catosian company escorting the mechomancer stood silently behind him, wisely holding their tongues and their judgment on this debacle.

He hadn't needed the sailors' garbled reports of a murderous steamman running about at large in the streets with a couple of murderous women by its side to tell him of his mission's failure – the ruptured heart of the airship bosun spoke volumes for which of his thirteen test subjects had shrugged off his virus. Was Ironflanks' survival due to some esoteric technique of the knights steammen, like their ability to fight with sound? Abraham Quest was not a forgiving man and word of this disaster was sure to filter back to him, imperilling Robur's seat in the perfect new world they had planned together.

Robur looked up at the commander who stood at least a

head higher than the top of his own thinning skull. 'You have a tracker capable of following them?'

She saluted. 'There is a worldsinger cowering in the *Leviathan*, a soul-sniffer. He can follow the trail of their essence like a bloodhound if we motivate him properly.'

'Send for him.'

He was not stymied yet. This was a setback, not a complete failure. What had been imagined by the mighty mind of the great Robur could not simply be unimagined, and there were plenty more steammen he could kidnap and infect with the work of his genius. He just needed to perfect the technique. Yes, the dissection of a certain steamman scout running around outside would be the first step to a far more potent form of his virus of the metal.

Robur beckoned for his mechomancer's tools, watching while his assistants placed his oak cases in front of him. Behind Robur, the Catosian commander looked on with professional interest as he removed a series of blades and rotating teeth belts, attaching them to a hilt with a high-tension clockwork drive. The Catosian city-states had so little experience fighting the people of the Steamman Free State. But he would show these unnaturally muscled beauties how it was done.

'What is that?' asked the officer, unable to contain her curiosity any longer.

'A hull-opener,' said Robur. 'A steamman hull-opener.'

CHAPTER TWENTY-ONE

Three of the House of Quest's armoured vehicles steamed backwards, their single tracks bouncing over the boule-vards, the short stubby cannons on their prows at maximum elevation, tossing shells upwards. Reversing through the stream of fleeing sailors, they were followed by the tenta-cles of a skrayper, gel-swollen trunks of flesh lined with spines swaying and slaying as they went. But even the reins inserted above the skrayper's sensitive ridge of optical cells could not urge the monster to squeeze any lower between the spires, so its lashlite handlers had to be content with trailing its twitching tentacles along the pavement, whipping across lines of Catosians as the soldiers emptied their rifles. A few of them were left flailing, impaled on the wiry flesh as if they were so many insects on Dr Billickin's patent flypaper.

One of the tentacles curled out, guided by the heat-sensing flesh inside the limb and, wrapping itself around the hot barrel of a vehicle's cannon, battered two tanks off the road before raising the vehicle – treads spinning useless in the air – into its monstrous maw filled with whale-like teeth. The skrayper fed on sunlight, but it had to get its trace minerals from some-where. A cannon gunner attempted to climb out of a side hatch but only succeeded in falling into the gullet early, passing straight through the teeth and into the jelly-like absorption gel. The armoured carriage followed him, rotating slowly through the stomach liquids as the last of its energy expended itself through the track. A shiver ran down the skin of the skrayper. Oh, this was good. Far richer in irons than the massive schools of helium globules that drifted through the strato-sphere. After this day of feeding it would be able to drift lazily through the heavens for months, just filling itself with the glorious white light.

At the end of the boulevard the *Minotaur* crashed through the buildings of Camlantis, one of its three massive aero-spheres severed and making its own last flight into the heavens, the remaining two hull units blanketed by the bodies of as many skraypers as could latch onto the airship, squeezing the life out of this strange new entrant into their realm. It took every iota of the lashlite riders' talents to keep the creatures focused on ripping apart the *Minotaur* and not flailing their tentacles at each other. This was not breeding season and without the pain the lashlites were able to cause with their riding wires, the sky would have been filled with a mass of furious, sparring skraypers.

On the ground, a line of Catosian soldiers ran towards the collapsing airship only to be driven back by the ferocity of the lashlite assault. Fifty flights of aerial warriors were circling overhead, each squadron of the flight taking a turn to peel off from the formation and fill the air above the downed aero-stat with a storm of lances – whistling down to strike the hundreds of crewmen trying to climb out of the torn walls of their airship.

'Withdraw!' barked a Catosian centurion, recognizing the

grim reality of their situation. 'Find a spire and mark your targets from the tower windows.'

A bugler took up her command and sounded the retreat, poignant echoes of it bouncing off the shining skyline of Camlantis. They kept their line, each woman in lockstep as they fell back, sliding glass charges into their rifles and maintaining a volley of fire up at the diving lizards, closing ranks where lances thudded through their number. The enemy seemed almost fanatical about retrieving the corpses of their lifeless warriors; but unlike the lashlites, the free company fighters had no compulsions about abandoning the bloody carcasses of their fallen behind them.

Waving her pistol, the centurion fell back through an archway into an arcade of what might once have been shops. Striding out of a lifting room at the centre of the arcade came Veryann.

'First!'

'What is your disposition, centurion?'

'Casualties are running at half our strength and the only aerial support left effective now is the *Leviathan*, but those winged jiggers have jammed her mooring lock on the spire. She's stuck fast and running thick with lizards. Boarding parties are being repelled on every deck.'

'And your orders?' asked Veryann.

'Stand and hold, First.'

Veryann reached out to steady her officer. 'We are Catosians. That is what we do. We stand and we hold.'

'One of the airship people told me they thought they saw you blade-to-blade with that fat u-boat skipper.'

'Ah, yes,' said Veryann. 'The commodore. That peacock always did like to boast about his prodigious talent at the game of tickle-my-sabre.'

'The actuality fell short?'

'He was proficient enough in sword-work for someone who has never drilled as free company. But I don't think the outcome was ever in doubt.'

The centurion pointed outside the arcade, her troops taking positions around the entrance. 'We received word from a runner a few minutes ago. Abraham Quest has asked for your presence at the tomb to command its final defence.'

'So, it has come to that, then?' sighed Veryann.

The officer saluted. 'We shall hold the lashlites off to our last.'

'Carry home victory,' said Veryann, using the traditional Catosian farewell, 'or carry my body home on my shield.'

The officer watched her head for the tomb. It was only after Veryann had left that the soldier realized what had been nagging at the back of her mind while they had been talking. Veryann had been clutching her left arm to her gut, as if it had been wounded. Or as if she hadn't wanted anyone else to get a good look at it.

While the sewers of Camlantis had the advantage of having been free of night soil for many thousands of years, it appeared there were disadvantages too – the eerie hissing of something in the pipes above them following Amelia, Damson Beeton and Ironflanks as they travelled down the tunnels.

'You buried your dark engine down here?' said Amelia. 'You were hoping the smell would hold off your rivals in the civil war?'

<More than a bad smell, professor,> answered Billy Snow using Amelia's voice. <There were difficulties with the integrity of the systems down here, even in my time. It was never a problem when the people of Camlantis were alive. When the recycling and sewer devices bred corrupt and began running contrary to their instructions, they would be replaced by a

superior generation who would eliminate the old until they too needed upgrading. But there has been nobody to control the sanitation equipment for a very long time. The ages move to a different tock and tick in the no-space realm where Camlantis was banished, but even so, the systems in the sewers have been feral for many centuries.>

'The same as Middlesteel,' said Damson Beeton. 'Nobody wants to venture down into the lower levels of the city.'

<Yes, but not all of the Camlantean undercity was ripped into the sky by our floatquake,> said Billy. <You see around you the distant ancestors of the Daggish and they are coming out of hibernation. Trickle-down power from the towers above is awakening their systems. We must hurry.>

'I sense movement in the tunnels behind us,' said Ironflanks. 'Many small things moving.'

They broke into a run, Amelia letting Billy's lurking presence in her mind guide her. 'You managed to assemble your dark engine down here before.'

<Quite a few of my bodies died doing it, and the children of Pairdan were heavily armed with specialist weaponry to disrupt and subvert the systems of the sewer creatures.>

'Sadly, I noticed your witch-blade locked up back on the *Leviathan*,' said Ironflanks.

<My earlier copies were armed with a little more than that,> Billy told the steamman. <The witch-blade is a primitive weapon in comparison, intended to survive the ages in a low-maintenance environment.>

The hissing in the pipes above them grew louder.

'I like primitive, ducky,' said Damson Beeton, looking up towards whatever was scraping after them overhead, matching their speed exactly. 'I can always use primitive.'

A plug in the floor of the tunnel ahead suddenly levered open. Two matt-black bodies emerged, glistening above spider-like feet, scorpion tails dangling with tunnel-scouring disks that had mutated into rotating razors.

Amelia heeded the advice given silently in her skull by the Camlantean and swivelled around to make for a side-tunnel, only to see a pack of pallid worms the size of tree trunks sliding out, forked tongues greedily tasting the air. The worms were hunting together with the bugs in front of them. Just like the damn Daggish hive.

'There,' pointed Damson Beeton. A series of footholds in the wall led up to a narrow walkway on a second level of the tunnel. Amelia scurried up, following the old lady's ankles, Ironflanks climbing after her backwards using his two manipulator arms while his pair of war arms swung their weight into one of the massive worms rearing up after them.

They sprinted along the walkway, the mutants below marking their flight, hissing and drumming their limbs on the floor. Calling for more of their kind to come and consume the filth that had invaded their realm. Amelia found a service door and slapped her hand on the keypad, whispering a frantic meditation to the Circle that it would prove as functional as the sewer cleaners trying to scour the three of them away. There was a faint buzzing as the lock mechanism recognized her blood, but then the door smashed open from the other side, the worldsinger who had been pushing on it tumbling forward, off the walkway and into the claws of the monsters below, leaving the three of them standing nose to nose with a stunned line of Catosian soldiers and Robur.

The roar of a mighty steamman hull-opener firing into life cut short the split second of shock on both sides, leaving the three of them a fleeting panicked moment to try to close the door against the rush of soldiers.

*   *   *

'There it is,' cried one of the seers of the crimson feather, indicating the tomb below.

It had taken the lashlite flight longer than it should have to follow the broken leylines of the rendered land back to their source, so long had they lain dead after being ripped from the living grasp of mother Earth. But the Camlanteans had understood the secrets of earthflow only too well and, as expected, the terrible instrument of their final desperate solution lay at the centre of a web of them.

By the seer's side, the war chief waved his baton down towards the building and a dozen flights of warriors hanging above him tilted their wings, diving onto the smoking rifles of the ground-hugging monkeys surrounding the tomb. As they dived, the roof of the tomb slowly began extruding a ring of white horns, a grille of dark holes opening along each of the horns' length.

'Too late,' moaned the seer.

'What are those things?' asked the war chief.

'That which has been foreseen in the Stalker Cave,' said the seer. 'The terrible chimneys of the dark wind which will scour our people from the nests of the world.'

'I cannot hold them here forever,' said Ironflanks, his voicebox trembling on full power.

It was a desperate contest of strength – the door wedged on one side by the knight steamman; his stacks burning red hot, as on the other side an entire company of Catosians pushed at the portal. Life metal versus the bull-women of the city-states.

Damson Beeton dropped to her knees, punching a fist through the armour of one the beetle things trying to pull itself up the wall's handholds. Down below there was a feeding frenzy as the creatures chopped apart the corpse of the worldsinger who had tracked them down into the feral Camlantean maintenance levels.

<I am fading,> said Billy Snow, using Amelia's throat. He had to shout to be heard over the screeching din of the hull-opener coming from behind the half-closed door. <There is very little of my pattern left now. I am trying to preserve the knowledge of the dark engine's location and the security protocols necessary to activate the engine's ignition sequence.>

'Go,' called Damson Beeton. 'Go. We shall keep them here.'

Amelia hesitated. Damson Beeton switched into witch-time, her arms and fists chopping down almost too fast to see at the horde of creatures trying to mount the walkway. There were few who got to observe an agent of the Court of the Air's fighting tricks and lived to tell the tale. And unfortunately, it didn't look like Amelia was going to be one of them.

'Any time soon would be good, dearie,' called the old woman.

Amelia fled along the narrow second-storey gantry – her escape feeling like betrayal even though it might be survival for the world. There was no time for farewells.

That would come soon enough, soon enough for all of them.

CHAPTER TWENTY-TWO

The Court of the Air's black sphere hung above the city, high enough that the army of lashlite warriors and their captured skraypers were sweeping through the heavens at a healthy distance below. The sphere was drifting over the sundered land, the Special Observer Corps with their portable scopes seeking to provide an adequate reconnaissance before feeding their findings back to the Court. The models of Jackelian society that turned on the vast drums of the Court's transaction engines needed masses of accurate data to hold the nation true to the course laid down by the late, great Isambard Kirkhill.

'There's some good news,' said the SOC surveillant from his bucket seat. 'Our three missing airships are down there.'

Their mission commander wound his seat down from the pilot dome. 'What's the bad news, old stick?'

'Well, I have to say, that would be just about everything else.'

A hatch opened and a head poked out from the heliograph operations room. 'Analyst level back home have identified the style of architecture, but they pretty much had to go to the

529

fiction shelf to do it.' He passed up a stretch of tape that had been flashed across to the mission commander.

'You've got to be bloody joking me,' said the wolftaker reading the message. One Harold Stave. He looked down on the spires of Camlantis. 'There's a bit of classical history repeating down there, lads. But is it for the good or for the worse, that's the question?'

And there was a more fundamental question that greater minds than his would be puzzling over, too. The three missing airships, property of the most glorious House of Guardians, made this their problem. Their location, far out over the Sepia Sea and well beyond the writ of Jackals, made it someone else's.

Which viewpoint was going to prove stronger?

CHAPTER TWENTY-THREE

At one end of the sewer chamber stood a row of sentient tree-trunks – something approximating faces in the bark gurning and leering at Amelia – their branch-like limbs wavering towards her in silent agony. They put her in mind of Tree-head Joe and the Daggish, bringing back memories of Bull Kammerlan's offhand comments concerning the ruler of the greenmesh. For a rogue and a rascal with the scruples of a Gallowhill alley cat, the hole left by the u-boat privateer's death ran deeper than it should have.

<*These creatures digested night soil,*> said Billy Snow. His voice in her skull was growing fainter every minute now, the echoes more distant. <*Filtering waste into different elements that could be transformed by our machinery into useful substances.*>

'Keep your strength,' said Amelia.

<*I need to talk. Each second that passes without an active thought from me allows your neural pathways to re-establish themselves, eroding my presence. I am decaying at an exponential rate now.*>

There! By the far wall. The dark engine she had seen in Billy's memories, a large polygon of jet-black material, sucking down whatever small vestige of energy was still available through the glow tubes in the ceiling above. The device sat there, at least as tall as she was, distorting space itself. Tiny currents of matter rippled around the polygon. Looking at the abominable thing was like trying to stare through a wall of water. Twin horns curved out of the top of the dark engine, tapering to needle-sharp points. They were the horns of a demon.

Behind Amelia the line of filtration trees appeared to undulate in fear as she approached it. Had the trees somehow gleaned the dark engine's purpose? Did they ascribe their millennia-long banishment and hibernation – their long dark night – to this terrible device?

'What do I need to do?'

<Place your palm on the central panel on the surface of the engine. I am going to attempt to interface with it through your body.>

She laid her good hand – her right palm – on the dark object and it seemed to suck her in with a tug like gravity; then her skin started to tickle, the tickle becoming a flare of agonizing heat. 'You could have bloody warned me . . .'

<Connecting. Blood pattern recognized.>

'. . . I would have used my left hand, the acid-ridden stump of it you've left me.'

<Living cells better to maintain the – connection. Keep – hand – pressed. Maintain connection.>

Lights appeared on the side of the polygon. Red sigils. An information language similar to Simple, but evolved by a couple of thousand years. What the enginemen and cardsharps of Jackals would give to see this. What she would give to trade places with them.

<The energy sink has decayed,> said Billy. *<There isn't enough power left for a second stable translation.>*

'Then we're jiggered,' said Amelia.

The world was dead. She was dead.

<*There's not enough power for a* stable *translation of Camlantis. There is enough left for a* cruder *manoeuvre into a spin-state.*>

'Just fire up the boiler on this damn thing.' It was taking every inch of Amelia's willpower to keep her palm pressed against the engine. 'Throw us as far from Jackals as you can.'

<*My faction's consensus was to preserve Camlantis for those who were to follow us.*>

'Good for your people!' screamed Amelia. 'If they want to book an airship berth up here they can come and vote us down. You fling Camlantis back into the bloody void.'

<*Fling us where?*>

'Exile! Banishment!'

<*I can't remember,*> said Billy Snow. <*I can see again. With your eyes. Who are you?*>

'BILLY!'

<*Who is Billy?*>

At last, one of the creatures that had been following the Jackelians through the sewer pipes had revealed itself, deeming the time right to claim its prey in the confusion. Damson Beeton rolled to the side, throwing the winged insect to the left. It was mosquito-fast: even fighting it in witch-time it clawed at her face with cantilevered mandibles, the agent barely turning her head in time to see its rotating teeth slip past her cheek. She danced around the thing, waiting for it to try and take her throat out with its mandibles, then, as it lashed forward, she smashed its compound eye with a fist. It twisted to bring her into the field of vision of its remaining eye, just where she had been expecting it to go – she blinded the last eye with a second crack of her hand. Kicking the thrashing thing back into the swarm of insect machines won the damson a couple of seconds as its comrades devoured the wounded creature.

Ahead of her, Ironflanks was dealing with more rotating teeth, these ones belonging to Robur's hull-opener – the Quatérshiftian swinging his weapon furiously and with little care for where it landed, the whine of high-tension clockwork intermingling with the dull thud and slap of its blades accidentally cleaving the flesh off Catosian soldiers. The knight steamman fought to pull apart the mechomancer, using the door he had torn off its hinges as a shield.

There was a grudge to be settled here. Not just between Ironflanks and the mechomancer – one of the filthy softbodies who made a trade out of turning deceased steammen out of their graves before the rites of the Steamo Loas could be followed. Not just between Ironflanks and a Quatérshiftian; the perfidious neighbours of the Steamman Free State who – come monarchy or Commonshare – were always ready to throw their armies across the border in attempts to seize the alpine meadows and high peaks they believed were theirs by right. This, *this* was the plague creator who had schemed to utterly empty the halls of the mountain kingdom of steammen, leaving Ironflanks' people rusting corpses too mindless even to feed fresh coke into their boilers. Carbine balls glanced off Ironflanks' makeshift shield, while behind him a sea of mutated maintenance-level creatures advanced on both sides, the reports of the mercenaries' weapons echoing off the enclosed space. For the first time in an age, Ironflanks invoked the battle cry of the Steamo Loas, the steam from his stacks spearing out in the forms of his ancestors, Legba of the Valves and Sogbo-Pipes.

Behind him, Damson Beeton backed into the side tunnel, nearly slipping on all the blood. She used the enclosed space of the maintenance tube to channel and slow the charge of undercity vermin. In front of her, two Catosians slipped past Ironflanks' shield – a corner of it being chewed off by the hull-opener – and tried to bayonet the steamman's telescope eyes. He sent one sprawling back with an upper-cut from his heavy war arm, caving in the knee bone of the other soldier and stealing her fur-lined cap with a deft snatch of a manipulator arm as she collapsed.

'Oh, that's handsome.' He settled the hat on his metal skull and pulled down the earmuffs while blocking the thrust of another bayonet.

'I'll take your boiler heart for my collection,' shouted Robur, a scream of metal sounding above the mêlée as his hull-opener cut another hole in Ironflanks' improvised shield. 'Your steamman cogs and crystals will allow me to perfect the destruction of your kind.'

'First you must show the heart necessary to take it,' roared Ironflanks, 'and you will find me both more and less than a steamman now. I am a siltempter!'

Robur cut down, holding the whirling collection of steel teeth and rotating blades with both hands – shattering through Ironflanks' shield and severing three of the steamman's manipulator-arm fingers, oil pumping out of the severed metal.

'Well, you bleed like a steamman,' laughed Robur, 'and I'll dissect the rest of your secrets on my mechomancer's slab.'

A pair of Catosians slipped past the savage duel – to be clear of the wild cuts of Robur's blade and to murder the agent of the Court of the Air guarding the steamman's rear. Damson Beeton stepped back and freed two belt daggers from the corpses of their fallen comrades, the insects feasting on their bodies snapping at her hands. Their three-pronged blades fair danced in the agent's palms, rotating with an artist's flourish. The Catosians came in silently and professionally, no wasted moves, from two angles simultaneously to make it harder for her to parry. Damson Beeton caught the bayonet of the first one's carbine and kicked out at the tunnel, running along its roof fast enough to take her over the heads of her opponents. Now the two Catosians were the ones facing a wall full of slavering fury coming down the tunnel and Damson Beeton abandoned them to their fate at the jaws of the artificial insects as she rolled under the whirling blades of the hull-opener being thrown about by the shiftie. More Catosians were reloading their carbines on the other side and if they had been expecting a seventy-year-old to dive into their ranks with twin blades slicing through their thick high-altitude coats, they did not show it.

Robur's brutal hull-opener battered down and down, the wounded steamman finally collapsing to his knees, a swarm of metal fragments from his shield showering his head. Robur kicked the broken remains of the door out of Ironflanks' hands. 'There we are, my sweet. Let's see what's inside you that enabled you to resist my plague . . .'

The mechomancer raised his hull-opener, ready to drive it straight down through the fur-capped skull of the kneeling steamman. Ironflanks swivelled his voicebox up, towards the rattling pipe above, emitting a screech that severed the duct's bracket stays. The battle cry spilled a mosquito-like pair of wings onto Robur's head – a twin of the wicked thing that had struck at Damson Beeton earlier – the creature sinking two fangs into the shiftie's neck. Robur's body went rigid, struck by poison and instant paralysis.

'That was the steamman part of me,' said Ironflanks. He rose up from his knees and head-butted the machine insect burrowing into Robur, sending it tumbling away. Ironflanks lifted Robur up and wrapped him with all four arms in a fierce bear hug, squeezing until the mechomancer's ribs broke, a crackle of splintering bone rustling down the man's chest. 'And that's the siltempter part of me.'

What was left of Robur dropped to the floor. Ironflanks picked up the two-handed hull-opener, its multiple teeth rotating to a halt now the trigger was no longer being clutched. He smashed the buckler of the weapon on his chest and let out a victory roar that filled the tunnel with the hooting of thunder lizards and the whine of sleekclaws.

The music of the Liongeli jungle had come to the ruins of Camlantis.

Abraham Quest glanced up from his console, counting the seconds down to the start of his new world. There was so little time left now. The end of poverty. The end of war. The end of famine. That the start of this age of glory meant the end of everything else, well, that was such a small and fleeting price to pay.

Veryann came down into the control chamber and was issued with a cloaking crown by the sentries on the door. She looked perfect. An amazon queen to complement his coronation as the creator of a perfect new society.

'How goes it up there?' asked Quest.

'Fierce work,' said Veryann. 'But the free company is holding, just. Are we close to releasing the Camlantean mist now?'

Quest pointed to the thousands of green glowing coffins in the chasm below. Their people, sleeping, protected and cloaked from the mist. All that had gone before would be a bad dream. They would wake up to paradise. 'Soon. Everything we need is with us here. You have done well, Veryann. Of all the things we had planned for – pursuit by the RAN, intervention by the Court of the Air – to think that our plans were nearly upset by a handful of lance-wielding tribesmen from Jackals' own mountain nests. Savages, nothing but savages.'

'History likes to repeat itself,' said Veryann. 'The Black-oil Horde . . .'

A siren sounded from the chasm below, a long string of icons in red appearing on the console in front of Quest. Critical mass had been reached in the underground mills producing the black mist. He only had to enter the ignition code that had been teased from the crystal-book discovered in Jackals. It was time for the end and the beginning of the world.

'Yes, we have come full circle.' Quest's hand slid back the firing panel. 'And now it is time to heal the world of all sickness.'

<I remember the sea,> said Billy Snow. <Or was it a river, with a u-boat?>

'Remember *this*!' shouted Amelia, her palm pressed down on the dark engine, her life force being drained from her by the second. 'Camlantis. Remember Camlantis.'

Behind Amelia the limbs of the twisted trees walling the chamber undulated towards her. Imploring her Camlantean blood to release the sewage of her kind for them to filter. Imploring her for purpose.

<Yes, Camlantis. It has been so long.>

'Make it even longer, Billy. Activate this engine of yours and send Camlantis back to the long night.'

<An engine. Is this thing an engine?>

Damn him. Amelia glanced desperately around the chamber. How many thousand years had Billy Snow haunted the Earth as guardian of the Camlantean civilization's secrets only to choose now to fade into oblivion? Centuries as a living weapon. Yes, of course, a *weapon*. A weapon that could be transferred upon the failure of its host. She raised her acid-wrecked hand and plunged it down on one of the dark engine's horns, impaling her swollen palm on the razor-edged thing. It was like bursting a balloon.

'Time to move on, Billy,' Amelia yelled through gritted teeth. 'This thing has got the equivalent of a transaction engine turning in there, I can sense it. Combat transfer, Billy.'

Waves of pain flared through the acid-ridden ruin of a hand, slicks of her blood pouring down the spike and feeding the horn. She nearly passed out with the agony, black spots dancing around her eyes. The engine's horns battered her with waves of gravity, gripping her with nausea, making her body part of its antennae, joining her crucified hand to the skin of the universe, drinking the energy and soul from her body, and her blood – the blood that was still fizzing with whatever was left of the ghost of Billy Snow.

Amelia had to fight to keep her remaining good hand pressed to the central panel of the dark engine, shivering until the icons flickering there started to blur and reform in front of her eyes, changing into Jackelian common script.

LOAD51. Charging spin-sinks now. Singularity leakage is no longer being contained.

'Billy, are you safely inside that thing?'

LOAD12. Confirmed. Download to the engine-mind is completed. All degraded portions of my combat pattern are running in damage simulation. Not much time left for either of us, now.

Amelia wrenched her hand off the dark engine's horn, trying not to scream as the lump of flesh was hauled free. 'Is there enough power left inside your dark engine for a second expulsion of the city?'

The answer flowed across the dark engine's central panel: REBUILD-PERS8. Confirmed, there is sufficient power, but the no-space translation will definitely not be stable this time. You must go.

'In the name of the Circle go where, Billy? We're scraping the stars on a couple of miles' worth of broken floatquake land high above the Sepia Sea.'

The dark engine was shaking the walls of reality; she could feel the power of the dreadful thing, rewriting the equations of the universe around them, dimensions that were never meant to coexist remade and squeezed into their own world.

PERS8-REBUILD-SUCCESS. Go as far as possible, professor. If it comes to it, you must jump. If that isn't possible, find a charged pistol and use it on yourself. The alternative – staying here after the city's translation – will not be pleasant.

On the dark engine's central panel the sigils had become numbers, counting down. Counting down fast.

CHAPTER TWENTY-FOUR

The sincere faces of Abraham Quest's engineers – their heads weighed down by cloaking crowns – had gathered in reverent silence to watch the moment they were to inherit the Earth.

'This will be a day you speak of for many years to come,' cried Veryann.

'Indeed it will,' said Quest. He looked at the assembly, nodding at his followers in proud approval, then entered the first digits of the firing code on the black mist's release panel. 'The day of the death of every imperfection that has marred the race of man since its inception.'

'Your death!' said Veryann, plunging her dagger into the mill owner's chest.

Quest stumbled back from the console, looking in disbelief at the dagger protruding from his breast.

Veryann's face melted away to be replaced by the features of Cornelius Fortune. 'I remembered to use my left hand this time.'

'You – you—'

Cornelius removed a glass sphere from underneath the folds

of his fur-lined high-altitude coat, pressing it into the blood-stained hands of the mill owner. Quest stared dumbly at the little clockwork head whirring around on top of the grenade, two hemispheres of explosive liquid separated by a thin crystal membrane. The others in the room broke the silence and the shocking unreality of the moment with a collective howl of fury, rushing towards the killer who would murder their beloved master. With his spare hand Cornelius pulled out a demon mask and slipped it over his skull, filling the chamber with the terrible laughter of Furnace-breath Nick. He flopped behind the shelter of the console as the grenade blast sent the mob of attacking engineers and Catosians flying back towards the black mist's testing rooms.

Only Furnace-breath Nick stood up from behind the smoking ruins of the console, fire and sparks shrouding his figure as he shrugged off his airship coat. Abraham Quest was still alive – barely – and was crawling towards the balcony overlooking the sleepers' coffins, leaving a snail's trail of gore in his wake, when he heard the eerie whistle-song.

Furnace-breath Nick sauntered in front of him, playing a bone-white pipe. 'I'm not as good a musician as Septimoth was, but sink me, his mother's spine always did carry a first-rate tune.'

Good enough to have summoned the queen's people and the seers of the crimson feather as they travelled up towards Camlantis. Good enough to have sent a flight of lashlites diving after Furnace-breath Nick's plummeting body, catching him and depositing him back on one of the city's spires.

Quest pulled himself to the edge of the chasm, the yellow light of thousands of gel-filled capsules illuminating the agony on his face. 'My – children – my – people.'

'They'll sleep longer than a year,' said Furnace-breath Nick, 'and I don't know what they'll wake up to, but whatever they find, it isn't going to be Camlantis.'

'Please,' begged Quest, 'you can still – change things – enter the code.'

'Oh, but I am changing things,' laughed Furnace-breath Nick. The demon-masked figure looked back at the ignition console. It was a smouldering ruin, as wrecked as Abraham Quest's dreams of utopia. There would be no black mist replicating across the face of the world. No resetting of the world to zero. No philosopher-kings ruling a sanitary realm of superscience. It was the mill owner's vision of a serene, clean, society of plenty that lay burning in that fire.

Quest raised an arm, pleading. 'Fool – you are condemning our future to – stay – this violent, impoverished hell.'

'Yes, but isn't that what a devil does?'

'Please – think what – you are – doing – please, you are a man – more than a mask . . .'

Furnace-breath Nick raised two of his fingers in the ancient Jackelian affront – the insulting, inverted position of the lion's teeth – then walked over to the moving stairs to the surface. He left Quest's dying, broken form to gaze upon the last of the Camlanteans. Sleeping now, for time without end. The future was rude, crude and raw. Alive. The future was Jackelian.

The eyepiece in his Furnace-breath Nick mask automatically adjusted to the wild energies outside. In the shadow of the tomb, the ground was shaking, splintering howls echoing from the towers and spires of the forgotten land, while above him the sky was pulsing with light. These planes of radiance were not the ordered forces that had summoned Camlantis back from her exile, but instead an angry storm of nameless colours that swarmed around each other, whirlwinds of energy spiralling down, decapitating spires and walking destruction across the city, sucking whole districts into a netherworld they would never return from.

'*Oh, what larks,*' whispered his mask. '*Camlantis is growing on me. A pity about Abraham's bright shiny new world, but you wouldn't have liked it, no, not our cup of caffeel at all.*'

'Shut up,' ordered Furnace-breath Nick. 'And enjoy the view.'

In the atmosphere above, the lashlites were swarming away from the dying zone while the ground cracked beneath them. Over the sounds of the collapsing city, the hypnotic rise and fall of expansion engines filled the air. It was the *Leviathan*. Some of the sailors had blown the nose dome of their airship off with improvised explosives and the tattered, torn explorer of the heavens was limping away on her remaining two engines. The airship's hull was clear of lashlites now, but her torn catenary curtain spilled ballonets into the air from a dozen gashes along her starboard. The *Leviathan* was leaking lift even as she fled, fatally shattered.

Furnace-breath Nick opened his arms in greeting and danced an absurd jig outside the tomb, vast clouds of dust from the destroyed buildings enveloping him.

Now this, *this* was more bloody like it.

Amelia only just managed to pull herself out of the hatch and onto the trembling pavement before the ladder-lined service tunnel crumpled into itself. A geyser of rubble exploded out of the hole. Ironflanks was nearly flung off his clunking feet, still holding the torn-off manhole cover, the smooth round shape forming and reforming in his hand, trying to close a seal it was no longer attached to.

Damson Beeton steadied the steamman and shielded her face against the sunlight of the upper city – harsh and intense after the flickering world of the maintenance levels. She closed her eyes and extended her agent's witching perception to feel the ground. 'I sense no release of the black mist yet.'

Amelia pointed to the distant, dark shape of the departing *Leviathan*. 'Then that's our only luck . . .' The *Leviathan* was limping along with her forward sphere nosing down, the back of the airship still under full lift. 'There goes our ride out of here.'

Ironflanks waved the hideously large hull-opener, trying to attract the attention of the fleeing regiments of lashlites above, but they and their captured skrayper steeds had realized the wound in the heavens was closing up. Few lashlites were staring down now at the floatquake land crumbling away beneath them. The battle was over, only escape and the selfish matter of survival concerned any still left alive here.

A spire at the end of their street stood surrounded by twirling fingers of the dimensional storm, creaking until it was ripped whole from the ground, vanishing into the hungry micro-vortex. For the second time that day Ironflanks invoked the spirits of his ancestors, as if he expected Zaka of the Cylinders to appear and convert his buckled and injured body into a vapour of stack smoke capable of surviving the final fall of Camlantis. Amelia pushed the storm-driven hair out of her eyes. Her dream was dying here, dying around her, an entire life's work and purpose. Perhaps it was fitting her bones should end up on whatever cold, eternal orbit Billy Snow's dark engine was casting Camlantis into. The three survivors reeled around as the clacking sound of an armoured carriage's tracks carried across the corner of their road. Narrowly missing one of the collapsing towers and cutting through the rising cloud of wreckage, the iron vehicle was skidding all over the boule-vard, towing something ungainly behind it that was swinging to and fro in the storm's gusts. Seeming to notice them, the carriage righted its wavering passage and crunched towards the three survivors, the stubby cannon turrets on either side of the vehicle jouncing, dark and lethal.

Damson Beeton sighed and unshouldered the carbine she had liberated from one of the Catosian corpses. There was a single charge inside her rifle, one bullet against six tonnes of iron-riveted beast. 'Circle on a stick, you've got to be kidding me.'

The carriage made a sickening slapping noise as it ran over dozens of corpses, human and lashlite, that littered the boulevard. But instead of running them down, the carriage grumbled to a stop. A moment's silence, then the door wheel on the side of the left-flank turret started to spin; the door groaned open, the large frame of the commodore squeezing through. 'Ahoy the street. You're a fine sight to see out here, scurrying around like rats in a terrier pit while this monstrous ancient place tries to bury us all.'

'Ahoy yourself, you old fraud,' said Amelia. 'Where in the Circle's name have you been skiving off to while we've been fighting for our lives against Quest and his bludgers?'

'Giving a little fencing instruction, professor,' said the commodore. He pointed at the rear of his armoured carriage where a glider capsule with furled wings was fixed by chains to the vehicle. 'Before testing my mettle on the *Leviathan* and her ground camp to liberate this contraption. It was a rare narrow thing, too. It took all my cunning and bravery to fight and deceive my way through to the airship's hangar, beating off lashlites who took my borrowed sailor's shirt for the real thing and matching my cutlass with all the jack cloudies who did not.'

Ironflanks pointed out towards the disintegrating cityscape. 'But Jared softbody, there must be dozens of glider capsules left abandoned in Camlantis by the airships' scouts?'

'Ah, but this one has a special cargo worthy of a little sweat and blade work,' said the commodore, patting the iron hull of his glider. 'The fee that was promised to me. With a little extra thrown in from the House of Quest's vaults, just to alleviate the financial burden and the pain of my heartbreak in losing my fine beautiful boat on Quest's wicked errand, you understand.'

Down the boulevard another magnificent white tower collapsed like a falling tree, its foundations simply ripped out from underneath it.

'That damn fee is unneeded ballast for the Sepia Sea,' snarled Amelia.

'Don't be angry with me, lass. I needed some meagre pittance to show for this fools' outing of ours, to help my conscience in resting easy at night,' wheedled the commodore. 'Ironflanks, check the sails and chutes on my little bird. You and your fighting order's gliding tricks are about to be put to our service. I'll navigate this iron bathtub to the edge of Camlantis and then—'

'—The edge of Camlantis is coming to *us*,' cried Damson Beeton.

They could barely hear the agent's bellowed warning, but the sight in front of their eyes was siren enough. At the far end of the city, the dimensional storm conjured by the dark engine had coalesced into a single raw sheet of chaos, sucking ancient buildings into its maw, each section of the city sliding away in turn, accompanied by the death squeal of matter being translated across a terrible void. All four of the friends frantically abandoned the street for the cramped confines of their glider capsule, Amelia last in and struggling to close the hatch one-handed while the storm bore relentlessly down on the craft. Then came the pop of warm thick air being pumped into the cabin. Ironflanks threw himself into the pilot bucket – far too small to comfortably accommodate him – their hull shaking as fierce winds rattled the craft, bits of rubble bouncing off the viewing dome in front of them.

With an almighty crack the ground sheered away from their sight and the glider plunged down through a hail of wreckage that had, seconds before, been their street. Amelia clawed for a handhold on the rapidly rotating capsule cabin. She crashed painfully against the crystal nose-dome of the glider, Ironflanks trying to push her body away from his view of the tumbling sky. They were beneath the floatquake land now, below the sundered ground and inside a blizzard of debris. Thousands of winged warriors were swarming out from under the shadow of Camlantis. Amelia blinked in disbelief at the pair of lash-lites carrying away a figure from the race of man. Their talons were hooked into the demon-masked gentleman like a pair of owls carrying off a Jackelian field mouse, while to his side a flight of four lashlites bore away the torn remains of one of their own kind in a burial shroud. Wasn't he the lunatic from the tomb?

Amelia's glider capsule whistled past the figure and his lash-lite carriers – missing them by no more than a foot – and she swore old demon-face met her eyes for a second through the cockpit glass as she hurtled by, nodding to her and raising a bone-white pipe to the leering lips of his mask in salute.

It was turning out to be a queer old day.

CHAPTER TWENTY-FIVE

The redcoat of the Second Parliamentary Foot knelt down on the hill and laid out his rifle on the grass – a cheap Brown Bess milled in a Middlesteel manufactory and topped by a whetstone-sharp bayonet – before resting his tired back against the wreckage of the airship. He reached inside his pocket for his pipe and extracted a small wax paper-wrapped parcel of mumbleweed from his coat. Striking a light that could be seen at night while on sentry duty was normally a flogging offence, but their sergeant was of the same opinion as the rest of the company: standing guard on the wreckage of an aerostat to deter looters was not proper work for the men and women of the Second. Not when there were shifties to guard against in the east and desert raiders moving about again in the south, all of whom would benefit from the proud sharp cutlery slotted on the end of the Second's rifles.

There had been a bit of excitement earlier in the day when the engineers from the cannon works had arrived on the isolated downs and found one of Quest's armoured carriages nearly intact in the debris. But that was as exciting as this duty was going to get – without the warmth of a proper barracks fire to shield against the cold Jackelian autumn nights, or the distractions of a town's drinking houses nearby. He sighed contentedly as the first puff of mumbleweed warmed his chest and hardly noticed the hand that reached out from behind him and massaged his neck, felling him onto the wet grass instantly.

A figure stepped out of the ruined airship; his blind eyes turning across the moonlit downlands to see if any of the other sentries had noticed their comrade was sleeping. A second man dressed in monk-like robes emerged from between the steel ribs of the *Leviathan's* ruins, nearly identical in every way to the first intruder, except that his back was weighed down by a sack stuffed full of crystal-books, not to mention a rather buckled crown with an information gem glittering in its centre. With the right tools, the plunder would crack and be exposed to information blight, ending up as useless curios on the mantelpiece of a Jackelian cottage.

The first intruder pointed towards the distant south and his twin nodded, jerking his thumb towards the east and his own journey. Theirs was a lonely calling. Meetings between their kind were rare. With so few of them left now, having even two in the same location was an appalling risk.

'Where are you travelling to next?'

'Back to the wild north. I'm presently serving as a shaman for a tribe of polar barbarians.'

'Ah, you live an enviously simple life. I came over by clipper from Thar as a trader, but I suppose I shall have to stay by the coast in Jackals now and make sure that nothing too dangerous is recovered from the old days. It's been a long time since I needed to be a fisherman. The knowing of it will come back, and I won't be sorry if I never have to pick up a merchant's ledger again. I'll confer with you in a hundred years or so.'

His compatriot leant on his cane, listening peacefully to the break of the sea on the rocks on the opposite slope of the downs. It was a beautiful sound. The kind of sound you could lose yourself in. The crash of eternity on cold coves, a reminder that the land was here before them and would be so long after they, as nearly immortal as they were, had gone. But no time to dawdle. They were close to the port towns here; there was always the danger that someone in this county might mistakenly identify either, or both of them, as Billy Snow.

The first one rubbed his scarred blind eyes, so empty of one sight and full of another, and answered. 'The next century, then, brother.'

By the time the Second Foot's sergeant found his careless corporal asleep on sentry duty, the two children of Pairdan were long gone.

There was a frothing in the warm waters as the pearl diver cleared the surface. She blinked the itching salt water from her eyes then swam back to her boat. Her sister sat on one of the hulls of the catamaran, cleaning the bronze diving helmet that belonged to the strange foreigner who had paid the two of them for a week of their time. The foreigner wasn't used to the heat off the shallow Catosian coastline, sweating like a pig at the slightest exertion; wearing clothes that seemed too thick and hot, just like all the stupid Jackelians that visited their land.

'It is where you said it would be,' the pearl diver called. She did not ask what the glider craft – obviously fallen from one of the bloated aerial vessels that the city-states had forbidden to overfly their lands – was doing sunk in Catosian waters. She and her sister were being rewarded for this work to such a degree that their discretion was taken as granted.

'Of course it's down there, lass,' said the Jackelian. He

glanced across at the other Catosian. 'Now help me squeeze into my sea-skin and I'll show you how an old u-boat hand dives for his pearls.'

The woman passed him the antique helmet, crowned with a brass moulding of an octopus, watching her sister climb up onto the deck.

Still dripping, the diver looked with disapproval at the lumbering Jackelian sea gear. Was that really the best their clumsy mills could manage? None of the elegance or mini-aturization that her own people were capable of crafting. 'Coral has already started growing over the wreck of the glider. Opening the hatch down below will be difficult.'

'Ah, the coral loves the warmth. Your proximity to the Fire Sea keeps everything growing and a-bubbling at a fair old rate of knots.'

The Jackelian picked up a towel and wiped the sweat off his brow. Was that a tear she caught sight of rolling down his fat cheek? She saw the stranger had noticed she'd become aware of whatever unvoiced sentimental musings were swim-ming around his mind.

'You put old Blacky in mind of someone, is all.'

The pearl diver did not ask. And he did not tell. It was not the time for the tale of a woman who had saved her nation and all its inhabitants by falling on a rusty cutlass, letting in a thrust that she could have so easily parried. There should have been a blessed great statue raised to her in every city square in Catosia, but they did not raise monuments to warriors who had betrayed their sworn liege-lord – even by so subtle a degree as throwing a duel.

Checking the foreigner's neck seal after he had shouldered the helmet, the pearl diver raised a thumb to her sister. 'What is inside that wreck down there, old fellow?'

'Ah, a paltry few pennies,' smiled the Jackelian from inside his helmet, 'to help keep a poor seadrinker in his dotage. That's not too much to ask, is it? A modest pension to provide a full pantry and a little jinn to warm my lonely nights?'

As usual after an ambush, the siltempters stood in a crude circle, pushing and shoving each other above the corpses of the dead craynarbians while Lowbolts rifled through the cart of pelts and furs, searching for the choicest, rarest pieces to incorporate into his monarch's cloak now he had declared himself the Grand Duke of Liongeli.

Lowbolts' stacks steamed in the excitement of the raid on the craynarbian trading party, and he waved his hulking war-arms at any of the other steamman-like creatures that strayed too close to his plunder. He was the strongest, the most brutal. This was his *right*.

From somewhere deep within the canopy came a cry from a voicebox that shook the creepers and caused an explosion of fear among every jungle dweller within earshot. It wasn't a sound Lowbolts had heard for many weeks now, not since he had stripped the last siltempter reckless enough to call a challenge against him down to the fool's components, the new ruler giving the loser's parts out as gifts to his courtiers at a feast.

'Who *dares*?'

Swinging into the clearing on a vine, the impudent stranger dropped just outside of the line of slain craynarbians, his powerful legs landing him with the dexterity of an ape.

'I dare,' said the newcomer. 'I have heard that you have declared yourself Grand Duke of the siltempters, Lowbolts, and there is only room in this land of ours for a single Lord of Liongeli.'

Lowbolts released a spear of steam from his stacks in angry derision. 'Lord! I see no lord. I see dead metal walking. Have you actually sought me out to call the right to challenge, you four-armed freak?'

'We have.'

Lowbolts swivelled his head unit to look for encouragement among his followers, who clutched their airguns and hooted monkey-like noises of support back at him. '*We*? I see only a lone, foolish mongrel, defective after too many seasons of rain without resealing.'

'We!' said Ironflanks, unshouldering the largest jigging hull-opener any siltempter had ever seen – had even imagined *possible* – casting aside its thunder lizard-skin scabbard and triggering the blades into a fearful, whining rotation.

Amelia gazed out of the window down into the quad. Still the same manicured lawn, the students in their black gowns, following the sound of the steam whistles to their seminars. Nothing had changed here, nothing except herself, herself and the absence of a Catosian woman on the lawn with an intriguing clue for a disgraced academic to decipher. Maybe history really did repeat itself. Cycle after cycle. Age after age.

'Professor.'

Amelia turned to see Sherlock Quirke pouring her a nice warm cup of caffeel. 'I'm sorry, professor, my mind was wandering. You were saying . . .'

'You can see the position of the High Table, the potential embarrassment.'

Amelia smiled. 'Oh, yes.'

The Sepia Sea was bobbing with the rubble and bric-a-brac of an entire civilization that had never officially entered the history texts – whatever wreckage hadn't been sucked into eternity by Billy Snow's dark engine. Yes. She could certainly see the potential for embarrassment.

'Why, I got this myself from one of the undergraduates

back from Hundred Locks. Sixpence from a fishing stall on the docks above the great shield wall.' He lifted the white Camlantean cup and poured some milk into it, then turned it over to spill the liquid onto his desk. He showed her the inside of the cup, left perfectly clean, not a stain or a trickle of milk remaining. 'Frictionless surface, do you see? The Circle knows how their people did that.'

'What, you mean a caffeel cup that doesn't officially exist?' said Amelia. 'Or the frictionless surface?'

Quirke politely ignored her teasing. 'I am certain there will be a revision authorized soon. A significant but *discreetly* handled revision of the texts. And should the blushes of the High Table be spared in the penny sheets and the journals, I feel certain that resources to document and archive all this new material will not be stinting; especially not for the person who found Camlantis in the first place.'

Amelia stood up. 'Thank you for the drink, professor. You can tell the High Table three things. First, I'll think about their offer. Second, I don't come cheap – engagement in the world of private capital has opened my eyes to that old adage about knowing the price of everything and the value of nothing, and third . . .'

Quirke opened the door for his colleague. 'Third, professor?'

'Tell them that I didn't find Camlantis. Tell them that you can never find it. You can only build it.'

Lord Meldrew patted his waistcoat. As if he were feeling the tweed to see how much room there was left in his stomach for the meat he was being helped to at the table. Damson Beeton nodded approvingly at her hired evening staff serving on the other side of the table, the spread sparkling with candlelight, their finest silver laden with food.

'But Dolorous Isle has had a tenant for many years, damson,' continued the elderly lord, looking at the guests newly arrived by boat and being ushered into the hall by crimson-coated retainers. 'And this is the first soirée he has thrown for his neighbours since he moved in?'

'We found ourselves with a surfeit of food in the pantry that needed getting through before it went off, my lord.'

Lord Meldrew chortled. 'Oh that's a good one, that's sharp indeed, damson.'

'More roast potatoes with your meat, my lord? I spiced them up with a little concoction of my own devising.'

'Capital,' said the ruddy-faced nobleman. 'I don't suppose I could entice you into my service, damson? It's only the next island across. You could teach my old cooky a thing or two about how to relish the humble spud over at m'pile.'

'I fear not, Lord M,' said the housekeeper. 'The truth is, I'm secretly watching the crook that owns this place for a covert department of the Jackelian state.'

'Really!' Lord Meldrew's face glowed like a steamman's stack as he rolled with laughter. 'Oh, capital. That's rich; but then your employer looks like a queer one, a fellow who appreciates a good ribbing now and then. That was him playing a flute in the orchard and ignoring all his guests as we walked up to the house, wasn't it?'

'The very same, sir. I'll chase him into the mansion later on.'

'And I shall chase some more of your roast down m'gullet while we wait upon his presence. Charcoaled and chewy, just the way I like it. It's quite gamey, actually.'

Damson Beeton carved another slice of Septimoth off the table's spit. 'Yes, he was a tough old bird, sir.'

Nothing for the enemy. *Nothing.*